BRIDE W...

Amy Lynch is a... ...ion and writing is her passion. She loves to write humorous romantic fiction, but not always with fairy tale endings! Amy has been working in the charity sector for twelve years. She is married to Eoin and is the mother of two young children. When she is not writing, Amy can be found juggling school lunches and two Shetland pony-sized rescue dogs.

Bride without a Groom is her debut novel.

Bride without a Groom

AMY LYNCH

A V O N

A division of HarperCollins*Publishers*
www.harpercollins.co.uk

AVON

A division of HarperCollins*Publishers*
1 London Bridge Street,
London SE1 9GF

w.harpercollins.co.uk

erback Original 2015

2

ght © Amy Lynch 2015

Amy Lynch asserts the moral right to
be identified as the author of this work

A catalogue record for this book is
available from the British Library

ISBN-13: 9780008152277

Set in Minion by Born Group using Atomik ePublisher from Easypress

Printed and bound in Great Britain by
Clays Ltd, St Ives plc

MIX
Paper from
responsible sources
FSC **FSC® C007454**
www.fsc.org

For Eoin. Sorry about all the burnt dinners, darling.
As you can see, I've been a little busy...

Prologue

This is it. I can feel it. Four years of waiting for my beloved Barry to pop the question. Four years of hinting. Four years of dreaming and praying and wishing. Tonight's the night.

He has chosen the perfect evening for it. You've got to give the man credit where credit is due. I mean, surprising me with an engagement ring on my thirtieth birthday in Jacques restaurant? It's elegant class. I couldn't have scripted it better.

I spied the velvet box last week, accidentally stumbling upon it when I was innocently vacuuming under the mattress. I'd already gone through his wardrobe and chest of drawers with a feather duster and rummaged through his bedside locker with a wet cloth. OK, OK, you've got me. I don't dust. I don't vacuum. I don't wipe sticky things clean with wet cloths. Yuk! I admit it, I was snooping. But can you blame me? The suspense was killing me.

Fumbling with the box, so close to opening it, I heard the key in the door. Rumbled! Sneaking back later, he'd moved it. Next thing you know, he's booked a table at the most pretentious restaurant in town. All deliciously suspicious behaviour.

The night is upon us. I have taken glam to a whole new level, even shelling out for a new posh frock, a designer one. The works! My tan is flawless, not pasty, not orange, just perfectly in the middle. My lipstick and shellac nails are a deep vixen red. It's the kind of

1

colour that says 'Yes, I'll marry you, my darling. And I'll rip you apart in bed later.'

Barry is driving so that I can have a drink when we get there. Super sweet! He probably wants to keep a clear head. You know, for the proposal and all. I close my eyes. I love Barry so much I could explode.

'Now, I just got you something small for your birthday. Give it to you later.'

He plays a good game, I'll give him that. He's throwing me off the scent.

Yeah, right! Something small, is it? I love the whole fake out. So devious of him!

'Of course,' I wink at him. He doesn't wink back. 'Sure, the best things come in small packages, eh?' I wink again.

He glances sideways with a confused look on his face.

'Yeah, I suppose so.'

Oh, this is great! Bless him. He really thinks he has me fooled! Of course, to spare his manhood, I will naturally act all, like, shock horror when he produces the bling ring. The poor man is probably sweating buckets. It must be so much pressure to ask someone to marry you!

He is concentrating hard on the road, probably practising his romantic speech. Perhaps he is considering whether he should go down on bended knee or not. Maybe he's worried he'll cry when I say yes. I send him a telepathic message.

Bended knee, yes! Declaration of love, yes! Tears, no!

The man needs his dignity, after all.

'You're quiet,' he breaks my fantasy.

I'm thinking about my supersized reaction and visualising the smattering of applause from the waiters.

'Just thinking how lucky I am. You know – being whisked out for my birthday, and all. Special night, eh?'

'Absolutely. You only turn thirty once, right?'

Don't remind me. At least I will have reached the goal I set when I was twelve to be engaged by the time I am thirty. I have no intention of failing. I will have scraped to the finish line by the elastic of my knickers. If he pops the question before midnight, I will be on target.

Barry opens the car door for me. He's always such a gent! The waiter shows us to our table. I am grinning so much that I have a pain in my jaw. It doesn't matter. I want to mentally record the whole evening.

'This is magical. Don't you think it's magical?'

'Yeah, sure.'

'Champagne?' I suggest to Barry as the waiter approaches with our menus.

'Eh… Sure, order whatever you like. I'll have a Coke.'

Sweet! He's dedicated to remaining sober and clear headed so that he doesn't muddle his words. He's probably overwrought with emotion at this very moment.

'Jesus, I'm bloody starving,' Barry is looking around for his starter.

I will have to edit out his impatience when I regale our freckle-faced-pig-tailed grand kiddies with tales of the storybook evening. 'Tell me again, Granny, about the night Granddad proposed,' the little ones will plead as I sip my G&T.

The dessert is coming now. I can feel the anticipation building. It's either anticipation or heartburn due to the copious amount of Bollinger I am knocking back. The jury is still out. It's nothing a ridiculously large rock on my ring finger and a bumper packet of Rennie's can't cure.

Barry reaches subconsciously for the pocket of his sports jacket and taps lightly. I hold my breath. He is checking that the lush velvet box is still safely nestled, waiting to dazzle me.

Still, I play the game. We are making small talk. We are weaving and bobbing. What holiday do I think we should go on next year? How is work going? Is that a new dress? Where am I off to with the girls tomorrow night?

The waiter arrives with banoffee and profiteroles.

'Bon appétit.' The waiter beams at us. He gives a quick glance at my cleavage and then smiles into my face.

OH…MY…GOD! The waiter knows! The whole restaurant is probably in on it. It is all one big conspiracy. Do Mum and Dad know? Did Barry ask Dad for my delicate hand in marriage? Did my BFFs help him with the arrangements?

The banoffee is heaven sent but I can't stomach it. Still, I make a pretty good attempt so as not to be rude. I don't want Barry to be suspicious.

'So. I almost forgot,' Barry clears his throat and puts his fork down. *This is it.*

'Yes!' I cry, startling the couple at the next table.

'Eh, so…yeah. Happy birthday, Rebecca.'

Barry reaches into his breast pocket. Here it is. I watch in slow motion. I can't take the suspense any longer. It is killing me. I nearly shout at him to hurry the flip up, but I catch myself in time.

'Oh, what's this?' I force my eyebrows back down.

'Open it and see. Just a small little something. I saw you admiring it a while ago in the jeweller's window.'

Holy Flipping Divine. I try a deep breath. The banoffee is performing somersaults. The box looks too big for a ring, now that I examine it a second time. It must be a whopper. He must have blown a packet on it.

Slowly, tantalisingly, I tease open the box. I am savouring the moment of joy. Tears are pricking my lids in preparation. As the velvet lid opens ajar, I get a flash of diamond. There, in all its glory is a… surely not. What the?!

'It's a …' I swallow.

There is an uncomfortable lump in my throat. Perhaps the dessert is coming back up for its final revenge. I reach for my champagne flute but it is empty. I reach for the bottle, which is also empty.

'A…' I can hardly pronounce the word, a dirty word, a vulgar word. 'Bracelet…'

'Yes, it's the diamond tennis bracelet. I saw you admiring it in the window of Weir's in Dundrum town centre. That's the one you were pointing to, yeah?'

I try to speak but can't. All I can do is nod mutely. Inside, I am screaming.

'Yes, that's the one alright.' I scrounge a smile.

He's right. It's the one I pointed to. However, it was *after* I'd pointed to the engagement rings. It was a greedy afterthought, following much drooling at the diamond and platinum pretties to the left.

'Do you like it?' Barry looks hurt. I'd better say something. I'd better fix this. I'm ruining the evening.

'Thank you,' my voice is small. 'So much. I love it.'

The waiter doesn't even glance in our direction. There is no mariachi band hiding behind the curtains to serenade the newly engaged couple. There are no fellow diners clapping and smiling. The dream is over. Soon, it will be midnight and my golden carriage will turn back into a pumpkin. My dress will turn into rags. The waiters will turn into mice.

A twelve-year-old Rebecca is shaking her head; the mission will be marked harshly with an ink stamp.

DEADLINE PASSED.

Barry is oblivious. 'Cheque, please.'

I tell him I'm tired, bit of a headache, too much champers perhaps. We drive home in silence.

One

What will the girls think? I'm a wreck; we're talking tears and snot, here. Scrambling through my overstuffed Chloé handbag, in between soggy tissues, my wallet and a hairbrush, I retrieve a make-up bag and study myself in a compact mirror. Once I wipe away the panda eyes and smooth my sleek blonde hair, I'm passable. A dash of daring red lippie finishes the patch-up job. *You can do this!*

The taxi pulls up at the Ice bar, and I thrust a tenner at the driver. He mutters something, but doesn't even have the decency to ogle my legs as I get out. I'm scuttling towards the door to escape the drizzle which threatens to frizz my hair. This is not easy in an overpriced pair of Manolo Blahniks, as they are of six-inch-heel proportions, and are already killing me. Still, they make me feel like I might pass for my late twenties, so I decide that it will be worth it. Beauty is pain!

A few stiff drinks will be just the ticket. *Yes, Barry and I have had the mother ship of arguments. No, last night's birthday dinner didn't exactly go to plan. But deadlines are extended all the time. It will all work out.*

I'm ready to make an entrance.

The girls have already arrived, and are sitting in a booth with the drinks lined up. They spot me instantly and are on their feet to greet me.

'OMG! Rebecca, you look so thin!' Emer squeals in approval as we air kiss.

'Becks! You skinny malink.' Pam kisses me twice on each cheek. I think the month in France at the family chalet has gone to her head.

I'm sucking in my tummy.

'No! Are you serious? I've bloody ballooned. Thanks, though.'

Quick aside: I'd squeezed myself into something very tight and black before the taxi had honked. FYI, the ensemble was over a one-size-too-small pair of Spanx that I had purchased (with huge shame) in Marks & Spencer's. Judging by my gal pals, it has sucked me in at all the right places and created a slimming illusion. Honestly, it is a kind of black magic – worth every penny. Breathing is so over-rated, anyway.

Since I've now passed the big Three-Oh threshold, I'll need to be on major frump alert.

'Happy birthday,' Emer and Pam chorus as I slide in beside them.

Pam passes me a Brown Thomas gift bag, and I air kiss her again. It's probably a darling lipstick from the Chanel counter. Pam slides a birthday card over to me, with a badge that reads 'I'm 30, buy me a drink!', and there is a spa gift voucher inside.

'Thanks, girls,' I give a watery smile. 'Let's hope this evening is better than last night.'

The girls exchange uneasy looks. I'd texted them both this afternoon in a right state, so they know that something is up. Hopefully, they can utter words of wisdom in between cocktails.

'What happened, pet?' Emer asks.

Dressed in a jersey wrap dress and expensive jewellery, Emer oozes effortless class. She smacks of old money. You know, there's not much of that about these days. Such a pity. Her blonde hair is shoulder length and sensible.

Pam, on the other hand, is dressed in a black shapeless dress, and her auburn hair is scraped into a large clip. I can tell that she's hungover from the night before by the way she's knocking back her Malibu and Coke. Her eye make-up is smudged.

'Well,' I sigh dramatically for effect.

The girls lean in closer. I'm the centre of attention, and loving every minute.

'I think I'll start with a Sex on the Beach. For old time's sake.'

'Forget the drinks!' says Pam. 'Tell us!'

'What's up?' Emer rests her chin on her left hand, and I notice her dazzler. At three carats, it's hard to miss. You can probably see it from space. I'm practically blind looking at it, but can't avert my gaze. The bitchy school girl in me shouts how gauche it is, but I know that if I had a granny I'd sell her for one just like it. Emer orders us a Strawberry Daiquiri, a Mojito and an Appletini. I'm ready to divulge the sordid details.

'It's all gone tits up, girls. Barry took me out to dinner last night for my birthday and gave me this.'

I produce my limp wrist with the bracelet dangling, and study their faces for a reaction.

'Oh, wow. It's gorgeous.' Emer strokes the diamonds.

'Yeah. I suppose. Kind of hoping for something else though, you know?' I point to my bare left ring finger.

'Ah, Rebecca, don't worry. Give him time.'

Emer is right, of course she is, but I can't help it, I'm devastated.

'Anyway, this morning before work we had a massive row.'

'Jesus, another one?'

Pam can be a tad cheeky. I decide to take the high road. Much less traffic.

'He says he's not ready to get married just yet.'

'Selfish eejit,' Pam declares.

'He stormed off to work and I haven't seen him since. He hasn't called to check on me or anything. I think it's over. I had to ring in sick to work, I was in such a state.'

'He'll be back,' soothes Emer. 'Let him cool off.'

I'm fluttering my fingertips at my eyes, as if I can shoo the tears back in. One lands with a plop on the table. I feel all wobbly. Perhaps it's the emotional trauma of it all. I didn't sleep a wink the night before. Now, I know it's hard to believe, but if I don't get my full ten hours a night, I'm a complete diva! Besides, according to Tyra Banks, the best thing you can have in your make-up bag is a good night's sleep.

'You poor thing,' Emer continues.

That's more like it.

'Thanks. And you know, all I said to set the war off this time was "What are your thoughts on wedding lists?" It's a simple enough question, yeah? I mean, am I not allowed to make conversation over breakfast? Are people these days meant to resort to censorship? This isn't communist Russia, last time I checked!'

'Good riddance to him. Like I always say,' Pam is slurring already, 'another man is just around the next cocktail!'

Pam raises her glass and loses half of the contents of her Malibu and Coke. Emer elbows her in the ribs and gives her a warning look.

'Ah, give him a chance.' Emer touches her pearl earring with a French-manicured finger.

Pam is the devil on my shoulder and Emer is the angel. They're kind of a package deal, you know? It's like buying the lasagne sauce and getting the free dish. We all met in the late nineties in Trinity College Dublin (or Trinners, as we fondly refer to it). This was, of course, back in the days before we discovered mobile phones and fake tans. Frankly, I don't know how we survived before either. Emer completed an honours business and marketing degree and graduated first in her year. In sharp contrast, Pam had started an arts degree like myself, but never quite limped to the finish line. A trip to India got in the way. She went to find herself, but I think she's still looking.

Emer has it all. While I slip slowly into insanity in a dead-end job, she's a successful marketing director with a finance firm in the city centre. I'm still not sure exactly what that entails, although she's explained it to me a few times, but I know it involves a lot of hiring and firing of incompetent assistants and wearing tailored suits. While I drive a beaten-up Volkswagen Golf with windscreen

9

wipers that don't move (not ideal in this climate), her latest bonus allows her to drive a convertible Mercedes. And most infuriatingly, while I can't seem to get Barry to commit, she and husband David are DINKS – Double Income No Kids. They enjoy luxury breaks and the latest gadgets. It's ever so slightly sickening, really. If I wasn't simply mad about her (oh, and if Barry and I didn't holiday in her Majorcan villa), she would likely be someone I would despise.

Pam, on the other hand, is not so lucky. This is especially true in love. Between you and me, she is like a Jedward performance when it comes to the romance department. Quite the cringe fest! She bounces from one poisonous relationship to the next. Married men, sleazy men, men who don't call the next day – she has experienced them all. Twice. The worst part is that she gives them so many chances, and then Emer and I have to tell her to *cop the flip on.* Still, it doesn't seem to dampen her enthusiasm. Bless her.

'Anyway.'

I give a blow-by-blow account of the row of the century that we'd had this morning. They nod sympathetically in all the right spots as I rehash every unpleasant detail. By now, they're no strangers to the dilemma at hand: *Barry will not commit.* We've thrashed out the issue and analysed the details many times.

'I mean, Barry hasn't taken me on a romantic spa mini break in practically *weeks*!' I whine, trying to force out another tear. 'This back won't massage itself. I'm so tense!'

The girls nod dutifully.

'He's busy with work,' Emer reasons.

'He's selfish!' Pam cries.

'And another thing,' I rage. 'Barry is definitely commitment phobic. According to Dr Phil's *Relationship Recovery,* you have to invest in your emotional currency!'

I've got the full collection of Dr Phil's enlightening books, and I've memorised certain quotes from them. You can borrow one if you like. Also, I don't mean to brag, but I took an entire lecture in psychology once. I'd accidentally stumbled into the wrong lecture hall in the arts block, and was too hungover to leave. A surprising amount of useful information must have sunk in.

Pam erupts into hysterical laughter and then burps. Not very lady-like if you ask me. I'm starting to suspect that she's not taking this at all seriously. Undeterred, I go on, full throttle. I start at the top of the list of Barry's flaws and work my way down. Like Pam's flatulence, this stuff is better out than in.

'Oh, and he outright refused to attend a wedding fair with me last week. Something about his grandfather's removal? Shoddy excuse!'

Emer's jaw drops. Her eyebrows would be raised if the Botox wasn't so potent. My tummy churns with the guilt of slagging Barry off, but sometimes I just need to vent to the girls.

'Look, he doesn't deserve you,' Pam manages to get a word in.

'Damn right!' I thump my fist on the table in agreement and slosh half of a Piña Colada on Pam's shoes. She doesn't seem to notice. The three of us make our way through the cocktail list and the ex-boyfriend list. We murder both.

I smile. To my delight, another tray of the overpriced multi-coloured drinks arrives. Before I can weakly protest, Emer whips out her platinum card. Pam points to a nearby table. A group of lads are smiling over. One says something to the other, and they howl with laughter. Pam says they're cute and they probably fancy us, so she wants to join them, but I'm afraid of losing my audience. Besides, I haven't even gotten to the part about Barry's refusal to sample wedding cake yet.

'Anyway,' Emer lovingly diverts the conversational traffic back in my direction. 'Did you go to look at engagement rings that time? You said that he was going to take you ring shopping?'

A deep burgundy hue creeps up my neck, and the stomach churn returns. The ever so shameful truth is that, *technically*, he did not promise anything of the kind. *Technically*, I led him blindly by the arm to Weir & Sons the last time we went to Dundrum town centre. I'd accidentally on purpose taken a wrong turn, falsely luring him to the centre with a sneaky suggestion that he take a look in Tommy

Hilfiger for a new polo shirt. His old one was decidedly shabby, I had convinced him. I couldn't give a flying flip about his polo shirts, but the tactic worked. He allowed me to stand and point at the window in the direction of engagement rings. The chocolate cake I'd fed him moments before from Butler's made him sluggish and docile. He's easier to manage that way. Sadly, as you may have guessed, it was the tennis bracelet that caught his eye.

'Absolutely,' I lie. 'He can't say he doesn't know what kind of ring I want. I mean, I bloody pointed to the exact one. Remember? It's the two-carat, Edwardian-style, oval-cut solitaire diamond ring with pavé detail? It's set in platinum and rose gold? Just like the one Tom Cruise gave to Katie Holmes on top of the Eiffel Tower?'

They know. I've only mentioned it, like, a bazillion times. I do have exquisite taste.

'Also, I left him a magazine clipping of it in his lunchbox one day, along with a little love note…'

They laugh, and I don't correct them. Perhaps it's best if they think I'm joking.

I decide that I've done nothing wrong. Let them snigger. There is absolutely no point in taking a chance and ending up with a hideous article to be worn 'till death do us part'. The shame would, quite frankly, be too much to bear. Let's be honest – the first question you'll be asked upon announcing your impending wedding is about the bling, and there's just no getting around it. Research shows that an oh-so-subtle hint dropped here and there in the right places is merely a gentle way of leading a clueless chap towards the right ring. My plan is to feign surprise when he chooses correctly, and then brag to my girlfriends that he knows me so well. Flawless plan, yes?

My ring-size and preference are just information I've passed along to Barry a few dozen times. As I said, I picture diamonds, platinum and perhaps a princess cut. Sometimes I worry that Barry doesn't have these words in his male vocabulary. Besides, returning an ill-fitting or generally revolting ring to the store and thus ruining my engagement buzz hardly seems like what a bride to be dreams of. What's more, Barry has a distinct lack of creative flair. I'm purely thinking of him – saving him from himself, you might say. This is far too important a job for Barry to mess up!

'So, where do you think he went?' Pam's gaze is fixed on the hotties across the bar. She is really half-assing my birthday night out; she should be putting her whole ass into it!

'Who knows!' I reply. I'm trying to adopt a tough attitude, but I'm not convinced I can pull it off. 'Probably his mother's. Honestly, though, I can't face calling her. I mean, don't get me wrong, Margaret likes me, and she's lovely. But she's going to take his side.'

It's best not to tell the girls about the wedding singer I went along to see last week, and I'm interrupted before I can launch into my thoughts on wedding scrapbooks. (Surely everybody does this? Weddings need themes!) A stocky man in a black shirt is standing over Emer. Highly annoying.

'Just a packet of dry roasted peanuts,' I wave my hand. I wish that he would go away before the subject is changed and I don't get to hear their opinions on church music.

'Eh, no…' The man is still standing there. What does he bloody want?

'Fine. Salted, then,' I roll my eyes.

'Would you like a drink?'

Rudely, he's not even asking me, the birthday girl. He's focussed on Emer, as in the non-birthday girl!

I can't help but notice how the top button on his crisp black shirt bulges ever so slightly. It's probably because his muscles are so ridiculous. Honestly, who does that? Come to think of it, his arms are quite chunky too. You know, if you're into that sort of thing.

Before I can protest, he and his staggeringly handsome friends have joined our table and Pam's laughter has reached hysteria. Emer is, as always, demure. Pam is flirting up a storm. I decide to join in. Besides, there's a strong chance that they'll be coughing up for the next round of drinkies and mine's going to be a large one.

13

Ciaran sits next to me. His enthusiasm to impress me reminds me of Milly, our beloved poodle when I was growing up. I admit to myself that he's quite a hunk, but that might be just the Kir Royale talking. And yes, he's paying.

He's a tad young for me, but yum nonetheless in a Colin Farrell kind of way. He has a Dublin accent, but it's not strong enough to make me think that he's going to try and steal my purse.

If it wasn't for the excessive tanning on his rippling biceps, he might be my type. Ciaran tells me that he and his mates all work together at Go Gym, and that one of them has recently appeared on the car-crash TV show *Tallaght-fornia*. It's all so working class. I'm really slumming it now!

'Really, Ciaran? Tell me more over another drink. I'll have a Cosmo.'

I notice that Pam's skirt hemline has definitely gone up a couple of inches. She's so shameless! She drains the last of her Screaming Orgasm, and insists that her new admirer order another one for her personally. We all titter around the table.

'So. And are you with anyone?' Ciaran's blue eyes penetrate mine.

I stop. Am I with anyone? Good bloody question! We've got the joint mortgage but no wedding ring. We also have our beloved fur baby cat. That has to mean something, doesn't it? I mumble about needing the loo, and shuffle off to the ladies. In the mirror, I see a hot fluster has spread across my face. It's a boost to my recently battered ego.

It's one o'clock in the morning, and Pam has just spotted one of her ex-flings sitting across from us. The mood has gone decidedly downhill. She gives him the evils across the bar, and Emer and I stop her from lunging over there to tell him what's what. We make a sharp exit onto the street, leaving the lads behind.

'They were cute,' says a sozzled Pam.

'I suppose,' I admit.

We stagger on, making plans for the rest of the night. Pam is demanding garlic fries and is slumped against a wall. She gurgles something about Leeson Street and the late wine licence. She tries in vain to tie her shoelace but slips and falls on the pavement. I laugh so hard that a bit of wee comes out. Then I laugh at that.

Emer has hailed a taxi. Says she's had enough and wants to go home to David. Pam and I choose Leggs nightclub as the next venue. I hope we don't get dancefloor-related whiplash again. With so much booze on board, we can get a little carried away.

'Seriously though, Rebecca.' Emer's recently knocked back gin and tonic has taken full effect. 'Are you alright, pet?'

'Never better.' The churn in my stomach tells me that that's a lie.

Two

Barry stalks down the driveway and revs his Jaguar into full throttle.

Who the hell does Rebecca think she is? Pampered princess!

As soon as he turns the key in the ignition, he fires off a quick text message so that she knows he's on his way.

She'll understand. She'll listen. She always has time for me.

The car crunches down the driveway. Barry steps on the accelerator, unable to get away fast enough. Soon, the house is a mere speck in his rear-view mirror. He tunes his powerful stereo to 80s FM full blast and veers his sports saloon onto the Stillorgan dual carriageway. There's very little traffic since it's a Friday morning. He reaches the solicitor's firm on Clyde Road in minutes.

'Hey, Bar,' Shelley looks up from her desk.

'Hey, Shell.'

'Got your text. What happened this time?'

Barry notices two brown paper bags from Maxi's Deli – his favourite.

'Thought you might be hungry,' Shelley scoops her long brown hair behind her ears and pushes her glasses up to the top of her nose. She tears open the wrappers to reveal two breakfast bagels. One has extra mayo and a layer of crispy bacon, just how he likes it. They tuck in with gusto.

'Suppose we'd better prepare for this conference, then,' Barry sighs.

'Forget that for a minute. What was the fight about *this time*?'

Barry rubs his temples.

'OK. So, remember I said I was taking her out for a slap-up dinner last night for her birthday? Fecking Jacques of all places. Got her this bracelet she wanted. Cost a packet, too. I'm thinking... nice one, Barry. Some major brownie points coming my way. Right?'

'Right.'

'Nope. We drive home without a word. She's got some bloody huff on about something. I thought she'd be happy. This morning she's back to hinting about getting married. She's like a broken record.'

'Barry, honestly. She doesn't deserve you. She's totally obsessed with getting married.'

Irritation surfaces. He has felt this before with Shelley. It's OK for him to let off a little steam, but he doesn't want to hear anyone else saying a bad word against Rebecca. The gentleman in him wants to jump to Rebecca's defence.

'We're just not on the same page right now, that's all.'

'She's like Bridezilla. Dragging you to wedding fairs and band rehearsals. Ordering bridal magazines like they're going out of print. Talking about cake tasting. Unbelievable!'

Barry feels guilt prick his conscience. He shouldn't have told Shelley so much over the last few months. But he needed someone to vent to.

'No. No, I mean... I love her to bits. Maybe I should just propose.'

Shelley closes her eyes. Is that a flicker of jealousy he sees? He puts the thought straight out of his mind. Surely Shelley doesn't think of him that way. They are just friends. Aren't they?

'No. Bad idea. Listen, Barry. Some women want to marry just for the sake of it. Some girls I know? It's all about the big day. You need a break away from each other. Don't even call her. Don't go home tonight.'

'Really? You think?'

'Definitely.'

Shelley stands to throw the wrappers in the bin and Barry notices how her tight jeans cling to her pert bum. He shoos the thought away.

At six o'clock, Barry switches off his PC, and Shelley comes to his office.

'Tough day?'

'Yeah. I'm swamped.'

Barry places a buff folder containing the documents for the conference next week under his arm.

'I can read all this on the flight on Saturday. Gonna call it a day. Have a good weekend, Shell.'

Shelley closes the office door and stands close to Barry. She leans in closer. Before he can move away, her lips are wet and her tongue is in his mouth.

Three

When I wake up, Barry is not beside me. His side of the bed is smooth and empty. My head pounds as I lift it from the pillow; my mouth is like sandpaper. I've accidentally knocked over the dregs of a bottle of wine I took to bed the night before, like a child brings his blankie. I reach for the alarm clock to shut up its incessant ticking. Why must the world move on when I have been abandoned?

As rubbish moments in my life go, this is the worst. It even tops the time I was subjected to a four-hour drive to Kerry with Barry's five-year-old twin nephews. Barry's brother was meeting us in Killarney and the Chuckle Twins had tagged along for the entire car ride on our way from Dublin to a plush country hotel. I mean they're cute kids, but they had blatantly gate-crashed our romantic getaway. Just stop for a minute and imagine about four hours of the little darlings mashing crisps into the grey leather upholstery whilst demanding the Wiggles Greatest hits (believe me, they aren't that great) on a loop. For a full week I had that 'Hot Potato' song going around and around in my head. When I have kids one day (you know, when I'm old and saggy) I'll ban children's music!

There's an annoyingly upbeat ringtone piercing my skull. When I find the offending article in my coat pocket, I see 'Pam' on the caller ID.

'I think I'm going to die,' I answer.

'Just checking you're still alive, birthday girl.' I can actually hear her smirking.

'I wish I wasn't. What happened?'

'I swear to God, I've absolutely no idea.'

I fumble in my bedside locker for a pain pill and wash it down with the dregs of the wine, praying that I'll be able to keep it down for long enough to feel human again.

'Any word from Barry?'

'Not a sniff. What am I going to do?? I mean, if he has no intention of this relationship going anywhere, like marriage and kids, then don't waste my bloody time!'

'Yeah,' Pam agrees. 'But the kids part? Nah. They are sticky, whiny things.'

'Well…'

I pout. Who will want me now? I'm on the wrong side of thirty and single. I used to laugh at people like me. I'm a cliché on top of a cliché, wrapped in a pathetic lonely desperate blanket of despair. OK, enough amateur dramatics. Let's just say that I'm destined never to be loved again and leave it at that.

'Honestly though, Pam. I miss him. It's so quiet here without him. I used to curse his snoring, duvet hogging, drooling and heavy breathing. The sharp toe-nails on his hairy hobbit toes scratch me, and the other night I threatened to banish him to the spare bed if he didn't put a sock in it. I should be grateful to be living in a fart-free zone. He's no Jon Bon Jovi, that's for sure. But Jesus, I'd give anything to have him here. The big lump!'

'God, you have it bad. Forget him.'

'I can't, Pam, I love him.'

I had tossed and turned all night and by my calculations had only managed to get about seven hours' sleep. How is anyone expected to act rationally and reasonably on that kind of rest? I read about sleep deprivation in a magazine once in a doctor's office, and it frightened the life out of me.

The stress might lead me to depression or to drive my car off a steep cliff. This is the rubble that Barry has reduced me to. Now, thanks to him, I'll be forced to drink caffeine all day. This is in direct conflict with my previous ambitions to detoxify using Gillian McKeith's strict regime.

'Perhaps you don't have a hangover. Perhaps you're suffering from a common celebrity complaint.'

'Oh?' Now she has my attention. I feel like maybe I was a celebrity in a past life. Or someone regal. Possibly both.

'You know, like, emotional exhaustion? Jennifer Anniston apparently was treated for it after the whole Brad Pitt/Angelina Jolie thing.'

I toy with the idea. Perhaps I'll have to check myself in for some rest, relaxation and intensive counselling at whatever the Dublin version of Betty Ford is. Naturally, I shall use Barry's credit card to cover said expenses – the whole damn thing is of course his entire fault!

'Nah. Probably just a hangover. We had a truck load of cocktails, Pam.'

'True. Anyway, I've got to go. Meeting Doug for brunch!'

Before I can half heartedly ask 'Who?' she is gone.

'My life is ruined! I'll be like Miss Havisham sitting here, waiting for Barry to come back.' I reach out to Jess, our long-haired white cat. He's been my loyal companion since Barry and I rescued him from the animal shelter I volunteer at, and he's quite a good listener. He's curled up at my feet and unresponsive. He wears a pink studded collar with a little jingly bell. Sometimes I think that Jess is a dead ringer for that snooty cat on those cat food adverts. You know, except he is morbidly obese. I poke him where his ribs should be, but just feel fur-covered blubber. He doesn't move. Perhaps he is dead. No, he's still breathing, but offering me no comfort.

This birthday weekend is a big fat disaster. I climb back under the cool cotton duvet, which is slightly damp from last night's wine spillage. I'll try to get back to sleep and shut the world out with my pink glitter eye shades. I've nothing to get up for now, anyway. It's not like I have exciting plans, thanks to my feeble excuse of a boyfriend. The worst damn part is that it is Saturday – a whole depressing weekend of loneliness and despair stretches out in front of me. That's just *typical* of inconsiderate bloody Barry.

By eleven o'clock, my need for deep fried food is taking over my need for wallowing. I throw back the duvet and sigh.

'Waffles will help me get through this rocky patch,' I tell Jess, 'and plenty of them.'

Walking down the stairs requires far more effort than I'd expected. I dip the waffles into the deep fat fryer.

'And another thing…' I address the empty kitchen as I reach for the ketchup '…Slimmers' Club can take their membership this week and shove it where the sun don't shine.'

The last thing I need on top of my crippling grief is to be named and shamed on a weighing scales like a common whale. That patronising Debbie can keep her 'never mind' smiles this week. I've had enough humiliation for one weekend, thank you very much!

Back in bed, I reach for the chocolate marshmallow cookies that I keep buried deep inside my bedside locker, and slovenly roll over to reach for my iPad and proclaim my total and utter devastation to the entire globe via Twitter. The only downside is that you have to limit your whinging to one hundred and forty characters.

Barry doesn't get the whole *Twitter thing*. He calls it TWITer, with an annoying overemphasis on the twit part. Once, he told me that only wannabe, Z-list celebrities like Jordan are on it, and all they talk about is what they had for breakfast. It's so much more, I had argued. Sometimes they tweet about lunch and dinner too. Barry is hilarious. He doesn't even have a Facebook account. I mean, that's simply outrageous!

Personally, I love Twitter. I can pretend that Oprah and I are friends. One of these days, she'll re-tweet something deep and meaningful I've commented about her pet dogs and we'll no doubt strike up a lifelong friendship. She just doesn't know it yet. She's probably just busy out with her friend Gayle and hasn't followed me back. It isn't personal. Any time now, Gok Wan will reply to one of my fashion insights about wearing the right bra size. Or Alan Carr will use one of my hilarious anecdotes in his stand-up routine. I can just feel it!

Somewhere between unconscious and awake, I visualise Barry. He enters the room, discovering me in a pool of blood. Scratch that, it's red wine. I'm clutching a photo of him in one hand, and a Cadbury's Flake in the other in our tastefully decorated home. Discarded on the floor, he finds a chocolate-smeared letter. 'Goodbye, cruel world,' are my last words. I'm strewn dramatically over a green velvet chaise longue. That reminds me, I should buy one for such an occasion. They have an adorable little one in Harvey Nichols that might be in the sale by now.

'Don't die on me now, damn it!' Guilt is streaked across Barry's unshaven face. 'I need you. Kiss me, you fool!' A solitary tear runs down his plump cheek. He thumps the wall and vows never to love again. He can never forgive himself for leaving me, the love of his life!

A large celebrity crowd gathers around the coffin. Brad Pitt is there. He's simply inconsolable and tells that Angelina Jolie to sling her hook. 'Death by broken heart' is written on my headstone.

Jess opens one yellow eye and glares in my direction, as if to say 'Yeah, death-by-chocolate, more like.'

As I answer a call from Emer, I fish under the bed for my pink fluffy slippers and make my way down the stairs again and into the sitting room. Since it's now officially the afternoon, it's socially acceptable to have a little drinkie poo. I mix the cool white wine with a splash of lemonade – after all, I'm not a total lush!

'Now listen, darling,' Emer instructs in her polished Southside accent. Emer can be very bossy. 'It's going to be alright. Just give the poor man time. Get out of those onesie pyjamas, get off the couch and step away from the cakes.'

How does she know?

I'm standing at the fridge, deciding between the macaroon and the carrot cake. It's a no brainer: both. The blood rushes to my face as I see the message on the fridge door. It is pinned with a magnetic bride and groom and reads:

VW, 2PM, Saturday.

Sweet Jesus! I'd written the message in code so as not to alert Barry. Every self-respecting girl knows that VW stands for Vera Wang. I'll keep the bridal boutique appointment. You know, in case Barry changes his mind about the whole engagement thing. Fingers crossed! I mean, wedding dresses must be ordered months in advance and altered a dozen times. If Barry comes to his senses and pops the question, I can hardly choose an off-the-rack gown. I shudder at the thought. Even Katie Price wouldn't stoop that low.

I race into the shower, dress and speed off in the direction of the city. Driving while hungover is never a good idea.

'Rebecca! Welcome,' Marianna greets me. 'Want to try it on again? Just to be sure?'

This is my eighth visit to the shop. I've pored over the whole strapless/sleeveless debate, but now I know that this is The One. Marianna fetches it for me and laces me up at the back. In the full-length mirror, I imagine myself swishing down the aisle. I'm in love. How can one describe perfection? It's a plush cream off-the-shoulder number with lace overlay and Swarovski crystals. On the big day, it will be teamed with Manolo Blahniks of dangerously high-heeled proportions and miracle-working sucky-in pants.

'Beautiful,' breathes Marianna.

She's right, the dress is beautiful. I, however, need to seriously whip myself into shape if I'll ever be able to lace it up. No-one wants to see the bride's knickers flapping at the back! I thank her, but I have to admit, I think she's being kind.

Now, not only do Vera's have the most amazing (note: pronounce 'ah-maaaay-zing!') frocks to try on, but they also serve champagne while you are doing so. I've conveniently forgotten that I've got to drive myself home afterwards.

'Cheers,' Marianna hands me a flute, breaking my fantasy of throwing the bouquet. 'So! What date is the wedding, again?'

Uh-oh! What did I tell her the last time? Oh, what a tangled web I've weaved.

'Well, it's… you see it's… July,' I pluck a month from the sky.

'Right. And did your engagement ring come back from the jewellers yet? Such a shame the first one was stolen …in that drive-by armed robbery…'

'Such a shame. Yes…'

'And your maid of honour. Has she recovered from her coma?'

'It's touch and go…'

'Sure. Well, would you like to secure the deposit today? I wouldn't want someone to beat you to it.'

Perhaps I'm imagining things, but this week the mood has changed. OK, she's on commission. I get it. She has got to close the deal. I've hummed and hawed over dozens of dresses and quaffed many a glass of bubbly. Today I only get a half glass. Marianna is being pushy. One must be one hundred percent sure before committing. Forget the groom, this is the biggest decision of a girl's life!

'Yes. Absolutely. I'll just move some money about.'

I mumble something about a Swiss bank account, and strip off with a vague promise. Now, I'll be honest. Between you and me, the frock ain't cheap. When I say it's to die for, I'm not exaggerating. In fact, I may have to sell my left kidney on the black market to some shady types in order to come up with the deposit. However, it'll be totally worth it. Sure, you only need one kidney to survive. That's why God gave me a spare.

On second thoughts, I'll wait until Barry has finally popped the question before paying any deposit. Then I can bat my eyelids and ask him sweetly. It's better if I'm in possession of all my essential organs on the big day.

How strange, I seem to have wandered into the wedding gift department. Quite spooky, really. Maybe it's an omen. I've decided to register some little pretties. I won't go mad, just get a head start. It'll be one less thing for Barry to have to worry about. Sure, I can cancel them if Barry and I don't kiss and make up. I point and click the scanner on some stylish Waterford crystal vases and exquisite Newbridge silverware photo frames. Barry probably doesn't even know what a butter dish is for. He would eat straight from the tub if I let him, the silly billy!

I leave with a churning in my stomach. *What the hell am I doing?*

I'm home and exhausted. There's still no word from Barry. The hangover pills are wearing off, so I take some more. I nestle onto the sofa to watch back-to-back episodes of *Don't Tell the Bride*.

Donna from Swindon (overweight, pale, plain Jane) is marrying Garry from Manchester (unemployed, bald and tattooed) in dismal circumstances.

'It's so unfair,' I tell Jess who has not moved an inch all day.

The groom completely messes it up, which thrills me beyond belief. The bride's dream of an elegant castle wedding with fine silver service dining has gone out the window, since the budget is blown on the stag do. The bride's unusually orange face registers horror when she discovers the cream puff wedding dress and sees the sausage roll reception at the local community sports hall. The devastation cannot be hidden under a false smile. There are fisticuffs on the dancefloor as the best man lunges at the photographer.

Their misery lifts my spirits. It's just the tonic I need. I block out the memories of my fight yesterday morning with Barry by watching recorded episodes of *Ricki Lake* and *Neighbours*. This is the type of thing that Barry refuses to watch and labels as 'tosh'. Fat Americans are reunited with old flames, and skinny Australian characters in the soap squabble over petty problems. Everyone has found true love except for me.

'Damn people with their damn perfect lives,' I spit, spraying crisps on the cream carpet.

The key is in the door. It's Barry. Hiding the crisp packets under the cushions, I wipe the crumbs off my face.

'Hi.' Barry looks worn out.

'Hi.'

'We need to talk.'

Crap!

'I went to Mum's after work. Needed some space. We can't keep having the same fight over and over. I'm sick of it.'

'I know. It's just that, well, we've been together for four years now. Don't you want to get married? Be a proper little family? You, me and Jess? Don't you think we should take it to the next level?'

'Look, Becks. I do. I'm just not ready yet. You keep pushing me and pushing me…'

'I'm so sorry.' My voice is small.

This is all my fault. Our relationship was like a glorious golden soufflé rising from a hot oven, but I came along with my wedding talk and stabbed it with a sharp knife until it was nothing but a sunken soggy mess.

'I know.' Barry has his head in his hands. He looks up and I notice the dark circles around his eyes.

'I'll try to stop…'

Our conversation is cut short. There's someone at the door. The bell rings again and Barry stands.

'Whoever it is,' I bark, 'tell them to kindly shove off!'

'Father Maguire!' Barry cannot hide his surprise. The conversation at the front door is muffled, and I'm ear-wigging like my life depends on it.

'Won't you please come in?'

Oh no!

The miniature priest is standing in our living room. I'm feeling decidedly queasy.

'Ah, Rebecca. Thank you for your email last week. I was just passing, so I thought I'd pop in quickly. Hope it's not a bad time? How's your mother?'

'I… She…Of course, please have a seat.' I scooch Jess from the couch and he hisses at me.

I'm staring at the priest blankly and Barry is making a puzzled face behind him. The penny drops.

My email! Last week!

'Thank you,' the priest receives the tea that Barry has brought in on a tray.

'Biscuit?' Barry offers.

'Yes, please. Well, now. First of all, congratulations.'

Sweet mothering divine Jesus H Christ our Lord and Saviour.

I pray that the ground will open up and swallow me. God declines my request. I have lied. To an actual priest! I've told porkies right into his sweet innocent Catholic face. I'll surely burn for all eternity. Barry's eyebrows are raised and his eyes are piercing mine, but I stay silent.

'So. You were requesting dates for the church.' Father Maguire flicks through his black pocket diary.

'Well, I...we...' I'm unable to form the words.

'Aha. Yes. You're in luck. Now, it's usually booked well in advance. Especially the Saturdays. But we do have a cancellation for February. What date were you thinking?'

I've never seen that particular shade of purple on Barry's face before. The power of speech has eluded me. I've been caught red handed, it seems. Lock me up and throw away the key.

'Pencil us in for June,' Barry's face is like thunder.

'Right. So, there's Saturday the twentieth? Two o'clock?' his pencil hovers over the date.

'Fine.' Barry refuses to look at me.

'OK, then...' the priest is unable to understand. He has missed the punch line of the sick joke.

'Please excuse me, Father. I'm off on a business trip this evening, so I need to get packing. Thanks for stopping by.'

Barry shakes his hand and leaves the room without glancing in my direction.

'Eh, more tea?' There is a tremor in my voice and the teapot lid is rattling.

'Thank you, Rebecca, but no.'

Father Maguire is on his feet and moving in the direction of the front door.

'Must be off. I'm on my way to see another parishioner. Just recovering from a stroke, poor dear. God bless. I'll be in touch.'

My hands are glued over my mouth and nose as Barry returns to the room.

'Listen, I can explain...'

Barry doesn't interrupt me.

'Honestly, he must be getting senile or something. I just, like, ages ago, emailed him to see how busy the church is. Just an informal enquiry.'

Barry remains silent.

'Good catch on the whole business trip, ha-ha. That lit a fire under the old geezer, eh?'

'Rebecca, I *am* going away tonight. The conference? Jesus, does anything I say actually register?'

'Oh, yes!' I pretend.

'The flight leaves at nine, I've got to get packing and leave for the airport at six.'

'Airport. Right.' I scramble.

I'm sure that he has told me. He has no doubt been banging on about it for weeks despite my distinct lack of interest. Approximately half of Barry's boring work banter goes in one ear and out the other. It's so dreary that I cannot focus. My brain is like a sieve – it filters out the tiresome and retains all information pertaining to celebrities, fashion or weddings. He really should know this by now.

'To Berlin!' I say.

'Bangkok. I'll be back next Saturday.' His face is still deadpan.

'Yes. I knew it started with a B. Ha-ha.'

Barry is shoving shirts and suits into a suitcase and I'm sitting on the side of the bed. I'm still trying to read him. Important questions are running through my mind.

Am I forgiven? Who will put out the bins while he is gone? Will he bring me back a gift? If so, what kind?

Barry is usually only this quiet during football matches. Thankfully, I don't let him hold the remote control very often.

29

'There is some post for you on the kitchen counter. Will I get you something to eat before you have to go?'

I am upbeat and aiming for considerate, but he's so quiet.

'A snack would be nice.'

Great! The silent treatment is over. Barry can never resist a bit of grub.

At the dining table, Barry tucks into his home-made burgers while opening his post. Well, when I say home-made, I mean Supervalu made them. They're fully defrosted and cooked all the way through this time. Another bout of food poisoning is highly unlikely. I feel like I would make an excellent wife. I open a bottle of wine.

'Look, there's something I should tell you. It's about yesterday at the office…' Barry has put his knife and fork down, so it must be important.

'Yes, love?'

He glances at the credit card statement on the table and squints.

'What the…?' Barry is on his feet with the papers in his hands.

'What's wrong? Are they still frozen in the middle again? I'll sue that crowd in Supervalu.'

'What? No! Fifteen hundred euro has been charged to…' He runs his finger along the statement. '…Honeymoons Direct?!'

Oh. My. God. I'm sick, but I can't blame the burgers this time. I didn't think the deposit would come through so fast. They promised me it wouldn't be charged this month. Cold sweat has broken out over the old sweat. It's basically a new layer of sweat.

'I'll call the bank. See has our card been tampered with.'

'No, don't,' I pull his arm. 'It's not a mistake.' My voice is a whisper.

I fear that each fistful of Pringles I'm shoving into my mouth and washing down with Pinot Grigio will come back in reverse.

'OK. Funny story. So, I saw a special offer to this five-star resort in the Maldives. All inclusive for two weeks. A bargain.'

'And?'

'And… surprise!'

Barry is looking at me as if we have never met. Perhaps he's considering alerting a shrink to have me psychiatrically assessed.

'Look, Barry, who says a trip to the Maldives has to be a honeymoon? The fact that you get to stay in the bridal suite and order champagne for breakfast is just a bonus, for God's sake. I thought you'd love it!'

'Fifteen hundred euro,' he repeats slowly.

Barry can be a stick in the mud. He knows I have expensive taste. He knows that I break out in a rash if hotels use cheap washing powder and that I have strict requirements when it comes to catering. He's overreacting. Cracks are appearing in the fantasy that I've been nurturing all week. I allow myself one last peek at the exclusive tropical island before Barry smashes it with a sledgehammer.

There is white sand between my manicured toes and the turquoise water laps. My new wedding ring is sparkling in the sunshine next to my engagement ring. Wills and Kate sit next to us over a candlelit supper and we swap stories of how we met. Dressed in a designer bikini, I'm the skinniest I've ever been. This is thanks to the, like, gazillion calories I've burnt off with the honeymoon nookie. Later, we enjoy the warm breeze while Fernando serves us more ice for our drinkies and fans us with a palm leaf.

'Yes. But according to the brochure...' I try to find where I put the damn thing. It's probably hidden with all of the other wedding-related contraband. It's with the massive scrapbook and back issues of *Confetti* magazine.

'A personal chef will whip up anything you fancy.'

I know the nosh will pique his interest.

'And they have these dreamy four poster beds? And they scatter flower petals on the sheets. Oh, and they make these, like, little towels shaped like baby elephants!'

Barry tries to get a word in edgeways, but I don't allow him. I haven't come to the hard sell, yet.

'So anyway, they have these wicked Piña Coladas with sparklers in them. Pierce Brosnan got married there, I saw the pics in *OK!* magazine.

'But,' interrupts Barry.

'But what?'

'But... We're not engaged, Rebecca.'

Rub it in, why don't you?

There goes my dream honeymoon. I wave goodbye to the luxury spa and award-winning golf club.

'I just got carried away…'

'You've been doing a lot of that, lately. Like I said, Rebecca. It's too much pressure.'

'I'm sorry.'

'Look, I need to get going. The conference will give me time to think. You know? A bit of space from each other.'

'*Space?* Space?' I realise that I'm shouting, but I can't stop. I reach for another bottle of wine.

'We can talk when I'm back. I just… I just don't know about us any more.'

His words are a dagger in my heart. In response, I throw a cushion at his head. I hear the reassuring tinkle as the wine hits the glass. Barry drags the suitcase to the car and speeds off.

'God. I've really done it this time, Jess.'

Hopefully, the neighbours haven't heard me through the cardboard-like walls. I sneak out and pretend to move the wheelie bin. Bernie next door is twitching at the curtains. She'll have plenty to gossip about with the other stay at home mammies. Little Katie and Shane have torn themselves away from *SpongeBob SquarePants* (or whatever other pre-school drivel they're glued to) and join their gawping mother at the window.

I slam the door shut. We should have gone for the detached house. Then we could have had blazing rows in peace. Barry had said that we couldn't afford a detached house on this side of Dublin. He can be a real wet blanket like that. Everybody knows that Leopardstown is, like, the Marbella of Dublin. He was just being a meanie with the cash.

I tune into *Corrie* for a bit of distraction. Tracy's having a blow-up with Gail Platt. My life is starting to look even messier than hers. Before I know it, I'll have the protruding neck veins to go with the bad haircut!

Four

Barry opens the second button on his polo shirt as the plane takes off. Maybe Shelley was right all along. Maybe Rebecca just wants the big day. I mean, contacting a priest? Putting a deposit on a honeymoon? Madness!

Shelley is seated to his left and an unbearable nine hours stretch out in front of him. The kiss at the office was a mistake. The sooner he lets her know the better. He tells himself that it was just a kiss. Nothing else happened. It was a close call, but he had managed to pull away before things went too far.

Still, he recalls, it was quite hot. He never thought of Shelley like this before. She's his pal, his go-to person at work. He'd better straighten this out before it gets weird and awkward.

'Listen, Shelley…'

She looks so good dressed in casual jeans and a low cut T-shirt. It makes a pleasant change from the business suit. She's wearing her contact lenses, and he notices that her eyes are an unusual shade of green. He pulls himself back to the task at hand. Focus!

'About yesterday…'

Have her lips always been this pouty? They curl into a smirk. 'Yes?'

'Well, the thing is… I mean, I'm with Rebecca, so…'

'Did you tell her?'

'Well, not exactly. I tried, but…'

This is proving trickier than he had anticipated. A flash crosses his mind. He had squeezed her bum in those tight jeans as they kissed in the office. Were her hands in his hair or were they around his neck?

'I was about to tell her, but we got into another…'

Shelley raises one eyebrow, and Barry chooses his words carefully. The last time he vented to Shelley about Rebecca, they ended up practically on top of each other. It's best to be clear.

'…discussion. It doesn't matter. Anyway. Still friends?'

'Sure.'

Christ, this is painful. Shelley puts on her headphones and selects an in-flight movie. Barry does the same and orders another beer and pretzels. This is going to be a long trip. The seatbelt light has been on since the turbulence over Singapore. The pilot makes an announcement instructing all passengers to return to their seats. Shelley is still asleep and he is in no rush to wake her. Things between them are still strained. She's breathing softly – unlike Rebecca, who snores like a fog horn.

A frazzled woman at the top of the aisle is struggling to keep her three-year-old son under control, much to the annoyance of the highly bronzed air hostess and fellow passengers. The child screeches in defiance and Shelley stirs.

'Honestly,' Barry mutters. 'Why anyone would drag a small chid halfway across the world is beyond me.'

The child's mother smoothes her frizzy hair in an attempt to tidy herself. Like her unruly child, however, her hair fails to cooperate, leaving her exasperated. She offers the child chocolate buttons if he will just return to his seat and he reluctantly agrees. Relief spreads through the aeroplane.

'Great. That's just what the kid needs – more sugar!'

'Hey, what's eating you, Bar?' Shelley rubs her eyes.

'Nothing.'

The flushed air hostess scowls. Her midriff bulges in the turquoise polyester Trans Air uniform and she clutches her seat. The plane dips and bumps.

'Hey, the joys of travelling economy class, eh?' Shelley smiles.

'You'd think that they'd have coughed up for a business-class ticket, seeing as how we are hauling our asses all the way to Thailand for this conference.'

'True. But just think,' there is a boyish grin on Barry's face. 'Nigel is just through those curtains. He's probably flicking through a copy of the *Financial Times* and talking absolute rubbish.'

'Hey, yeah. I bet you he's swilling expensive champagne and deciding between the salmon or fillet steak. No doubt he's ogling the air hostesses.'

Shelley makes a face and they both laugh. Barry can't remember the last time he and Rebecca laughed like this. Everything is so serious lately. At least Shelley knows how to have a good time.

'Yeah. Thank God we don't have to endure that pompous windbag for nine long hours, eh?' That last beer is making him a little light headed.

'So. Go on, Barry. Tell us what the fight was about this time.'

Barry hesitates. 'The usual.'

His stomach lurches as the plane circles over Bangkok. If he hadn't given Rebecca such a hard time, she'd have helped him pack his luggage like she always does. She wouldn't have let him forget his travel sickness medication, that's for sure. She always remembers the little things. On the other side of the aircraft, the young boy rests angelically in his mother's arms. She runs her fingers through his dishevelled blond hair.

Shelley follows his gaze. 'Didn't you tell me once that Rebecca doesn't want kids?'

'No! I mean…she does, just not yet.'

'Yeah. She thinks they'll ruin her figure, you said?'

'No. She was only joking. She likes kids, she's just not ready.'

'And she's still a broken record about getting married. It must be doing your head in.'

Barry holds back. He doesn't want to reveal to Shelley about the priest and the honeymoon booking. The plane makes its final descent. The last time he'd flown long haul, Rebecca had insisted that he take the window seat to help with his travel anxiety, and let him squeeze her hand even though it must have hurt. She had packed his sleeping pills and an air cushion for his old shoulder injury sustained back at university.

'She sounds like a drama queen.'

Shelley's words hang in the air. The aircraft hits the runway with a slight bounce. Barry is queasy, he knows he shouldn't have had that last drink. He doesn't reply. Instead, he stretches his long stiff legs under the seat in front. His toes search for his missing shoes.

Yes, thinks Barry. *But she is my drama queen.*

Five

Barry's last words before he left echo on a continuous loop.

I just don't know about us any more.

It's time to face the harsh reality. I'm a bride without a groom. I've been planning a bloody wedding before Barry has even popped the question! Now he's well and truly fed up.

'What's the harm in being organised?' I ask an unconscious Jess. 'Just in case.'

There are endless decisions to make about flowers, cakes and cars. When the guy plucks up the courage to finally ask me to marry him, I want to be ready. According to Barry, I live a champagne lifestyle on a lemonade budget. He says I can't manage money. It's such tosh. I mean, I got a C in maths. It would have been an A, except I was upset that year, what with Dad refusing to buy me a car and all. Little does he know, I've been planning out the finances for our entire wedding. I have a spreadsheet and everything, labelled 'Work stuff' so that he will not stumble upon it on our laptop. I've kindly worked out what the whole thing will cost him.

Over the years, I've planned every glorious glistening detail. I've fantasised about the cake Kim Kardashian and Kanye West chose. It had five tiers and was a six-foot-tall black and white chocolate and vanilla masterpiece. I've pictured myself married in Manolos, parading about in some stylish and elegant wedding venue (preferably something that was featured in *Hello!* magazine). I've entertained romantic daydreams of being presented with a glittering rock by Barry-on-bended-knee.

But four years have come and gone. We're no closer to tying the knot. Barry is twenty thousand feet in the air and having serious doubts about us. He's crushing my dreams of a fairytale ending. What a kill joy.

I can stand the empty house no longer, and Jess is proving to be a pretty poor conversationalist. I dial Karen's number. I've been meaning to get in touch for ages.

'Scuba slut!' she answers the call in an ear splitting shriek. 'Happy birthday!'

Karen and I are old college buddies. Time spent with her immediately pulls me back in time to sculling pints of Scrumpy Jack cider until I passed out in the Buttery Bar, Trinity College. Or 'The Scuttery', as we called it. We skipped more lectures than you've watched *Corrie* episodes. Married with three kids under three, Karen's life has changed dramatically while mine remains stagnant.

'Dive babe!' I reply. 'Been ages!'

The nicknames are a long story. Basically, we joined all kinds of clubs in college in order to meet dishy men. Our most successful endeavour was the Scuba Leisure Undergraduates Team – or SLUT for short. We met hunks in wet suits, shared air tubes and held hands under the water whilst pretending to drown. It was kind of like damsel in distress meets *Titanic*. Anyway, our plan was going swimmingly (get it?) and we were snogging our way through the club like good-oh, when we realised the fatal flaw in our scheme: neither of us likes getting our hair wet. Also, the wet suit adds at least ten pounds and does not flatter from behind. We moved on to something in-doorsy and male-dominated – Judo. It involved being pinned down on mats by cute guys and we were deliberately awful at it.

'Great to hear from you.' Karen talks like the clappers and I try to squeeze in a syllable.

'I've been meaning to call, but the kids are hanging out of me non-stop. Driving me nuts. Hashtag crazy mama!'

Oh, I forgot to tell you. Karen talks in hashtags. No, really. It gets old pretty quickly. As a stay at home mum, Twitter is her only social outlet some days.

'Barry and I had a whopper fight,' I interrupt.

'Ah, no!'

'Will we meet up some time? For a real catch-up.'

'Yeah! What about tonight! Let's get hammered! Hashtag old school! FRANK!' she bellows. 'FRANK! FRAAAANK! I'm going out.'

'Oh. OK, then. Are you sure that's OK for tonight? Won't Frank mind?'

'Nah. Believe me, it's my turn to get out. Haven't done this in forever. FRANK! FRAAANK! Can you get the kids in the BAAAAATH! FRAAAAANK.'

There is a ringing in my left ear.

I've suggested a local Chinese restaurant that hosts karaoke sessions on a Saturday night. It's been christened 'Curryoke' by yours truly. Am I not so clever? Anyway, I find that at your lowest point, eating a few prawn crackers with the girls and belting out a couple of good old 1980s power ballads is the perfect night out. Never fails.

Karen meets me within the hour. She's only too thrilled to escape her domestic drudgery and teething toddlers for the evening. We hug hello at the restaurant.

'You look amazing,' I smile at Karen.

Sickeningly, her twins are only babies and her daughter is nearly three, yet she is skinnier than me. It's not fair. I vow to fatten her up by ordering something deep fried.

'What? Sure the kids have me run ragged.'

'Ah, no. Really?'

'Yeah. Sure, Anna still doesn't sleep through the night!'

'Ah, but sure kids are like pancakes. The first one is always a throwaway.'

Karen howls with laughter. I've no idea why.

'Hilarious. Fecking Frank is working, like, all the time. I think he's avoiding us. I don't get *any* sleep. Oh, and this is the only thing that didn't have baby vomit or snot on it!' She points to her sequined top. 'Hashtag ewwwww!'

We are escorted to our tables and hand our heavy coats to the waiter. I'm wearing a new black dress and was thrilled to have an excuse to take the tags off. It's very forgiving around the stomach area, which is handy because I plan on going to town with the spring rolls.

'All OK at home?' I enquire. 'Do you need to call and check?'

'Nah. I swear to God,' whispers Karen, as if in confession. 'Let fecking Frank get them to bed for a change.'

We study the menu briefly and order a bottle of house white. Karen is giddy to be out of the house and away from 24/7 mammying. Soon the meal for two arrives. It is an embarrassingly large array of skewered chicken satay, baby ribs, spicy kung pao beef, egg fried rice, chips and noodles.

Karen continues her monologue. She reveals the nightmare of sleep deprivation and admits to suffering from migraines since the twins were born. I feel a fleeting pang of guilt that I still have not come to visit the babies who are now three months old. Then I remember that the babies had colic, so no wonder I've been avoiding them like the plague. It's a wonder that poor Karen is still sane with three pesky kids rubbing off the cream walls, with their boundless energy and unreasonable demands.

'I think I'd need a lie down in a dark room after just one day of that,' I admit.

Karen isn't like my other married friends. She doesn't rattle on about clever potty training, or what ingenious things her brood can do until you want to stab yourself in the eye with a chicken skewer. She bitches about competitive mums and reveals what a pain in the ass it is to have to deal with nappy rash (if you'll pardon the pun). She scoffs at others who tell you how angelic their little demons are. She tells it like it is.

'I've instructed fecking Frank to only call me in an absolute emergency. And that does not include calling to ask me where the bloody Calpol is!'

'Good luck to him!' I raise my glass.

We order a second bottle, as both of us seem quite thirsty.

'Yeah, sure the last time myself and fecking Frank were out together on a date, I'd never heard of the term negative equity! Honestly, and all we talk about is whose turn it is to change the nappies!'

Barry and I are starting to look like the Waltons in comparison. I top up the glasses and go over the whole Barry saga again in detail. It's a refresher course in case she missed any bits over the phone.

'I love him but…He just won't commit!' I leave out the bit about my dress fittings and cake tastings.

'He will. Just give him more time. Honestly, he'll come crawling back from the trip and thank his lucky stars he has such a ride like you. Hashtag hot stuff!'

'Ah. Thanks.'

I don't think I can take another hashtag. I never thought I'd reach hashtag saturation point, but here I am.

The next bottle of wine tastes even better than the last and the banana fritters arrive. Across the restaurant, we spy a couple on a date. They're holding hands across the table. We titter. Their peace and quiet is about to be shattered gloriously. The waiters clear the top table and a large screen descends. Realisation dawns on the happy couple, as the word 'Karaoke' displays on the screen.

'You've had your dinner,' I raise my glass to Karen. 'Now, here's the show!'

I snatch a microphone and laminated song book from a passing waitress and clear my throat. Let the games begin! There's no need to consult the book, that's for amateurs. I don't mean to brag, but you have my permission to describe me as a karaoke master if you like. If they ever start giving out black belts for karaoke, I'll be the first in line. I scrawl my choice on a scrap of paper and thrust it into the hand of our waiter. As Dr Phil says, 'This ain't my first rodeo.'

Karen scribbles her selection and returns her attention to the cocktail menu. She orders two Cosmos and claims that they are for Dutch courage. The big moment is upon us. The opening lines of 'Don't You Want Me Baby' by The Human League appear on the screen.

'You were working as a waitress in a cocktail bar,' warbles Karen, 'when I met you.'

The staff exchange uneasy looks and diners shift in their seats. The happy couple have hastily paid their bill and are reaching for their coats. I grab the microphone from Karen for the chorus.

'Don't you want me, Barry? Don't you want me, woah!'

Karen can't sing any more because she is doubled over with laughter. She drains the last of her Cosmo and orders a Martini in an attempt to recapture our lost youth. I'm hogging the microphone for a passionate rendition of the Beyoncé classic 'Single Ladies'.

'If you like it then you shoulda put a ring on it.'

Despite the fact that I'm pointing to my bare left ring finger during the heartfelt performance, the microphone is taken from me at the end. There's a minor scuffle.

'Uh-oh. Hashtag awkward!'

'Shush, Karen.'

We endure a tuneless rendition of Robbie Williams' 'Angels' from the next table. They're murdering it, so we talk loudly over it. Some people are so tone deaf! I've retrieved the microphone, and treat my enchanted audience to a touching duet from 'Dirty Dancing'. I play the part of Patrick Swayze aka Johnny Castle (quite convincingly, I think) and Karen plays the role of Jennifer Grey aka Baby. Not everyone finds it as hilarious as I do when I repeat 'Johnny!' into the microphone and Karen launches herself on top of me. She is, of course, attempting the iconic 'lift' from the film.

However, we're not as graceful as we thought we'd be. This is due to:

a) our staggeringly high blood alcohol levels, and
b) our lack of an idyllic lake setting.

Sadly, I'm unable to catch Karen, and we both end up under the table. The microphone has been passed along to the next table and I suspect that I may in fact have carpet burn on my bum.

The restaurant is empty now, and the lyrics to 'All By Myself' line up. I decide to give it a bash. It's a bitter and tearful performance. Karen lines up a shot of Sambuca to keep us on our toes. She can no longer pronounce the word 'hashtag'. Thank Christ. The waitress keeps yawning. It's such an insult to my art form. Another waitress is stacking chairs and one is polishing the glasses. I suppose that's what you do at three in the morning.

'Rack 'em up,' garbles Karen incoherently. She's pointing vaguely to the cocktail menu, and in desperate need of subtitles at this point – even I cannot understand her.

'Yeah! Surprise us!'

We've sampled the full array of beverages, and are unsure of what to order next.

'Yeah!' I address the youngest waiter. 'Use your initiative!'

By the way, 'initiative' is an impossible word to get my tongue around.

The screen is blank and the power has been cut from our microphones. I'm tapping ferociously.

'So many songs are left unsung. We're only getting started! Hey! You there! You don't know who you're dealing with here, buster! I was Gretel Von Trapp in the 1992 school production of *The Sound of Music*. I had to say "I have a sore finger". It was critically acclaimed!'

The staff are oblivious to my pleas, and I seem to have spilled my last drink. Since I don't remember all of the words to 'My Favourite Things' or 'Doe a Deer, a Female Deer', I drop the subject. Pity, really. Still, this little setback doesn't dampen our enthusiasm. With tears rolling down my face, I launch into 'I Wanna Know What Love Is'. This is easily the best Foreigner hit. Who needs a backing track when you've a belter pair of lungs and a belly full of heart ache?

The bill, along with two black coffees, is placed on our table. A miniature mint decorates the saucer. Karen is playing air guitar against the backdrop of a Chinese pan pipe version of 'Lady in Red'.

It's absolutely genius; if only I'd thought of it first. Our long-suffering waiter stands beside us with the pin pad, and we blatantly ignore him. How dare he stifle my creativity? He is raining all over my parade!

'Would you like a taxi, ladies?' a little Chinese man offers kindly.

'How absolutely *dare* you?' I snigger.

Karen and I make admissions of undying eternal love to each other. Then we have a Mrs-Doyle-style row over who will pay the bill.

'Put your money away,' shouts Karen. 'Your money's no good here.'

I produce Barry's credit card and punch in the pin number with glee.

'Barry's treat. Serves him right for not marrying me! Ha-ha!'

Karen has to help me up off the floor because I've just realised that I'm possibly the funniest person in the world. Really, I should write this stuff down. I might even win the Perrier Comedy Award some day.

We wave to the staff and promise to return soon. Ling Ling the waitress and I are now soul mates. I'll send her a Christmas card. I never knew that we were kindred spirits. Karen links my arm as we make our way unsteadily onto the cobblestone pavement, and then bundle into a waiting taxi. It's with great determination that I finally turn the key in the door. There's much curtain twitching from that cow next door. I can feel a hangover starting already. This is possibly not a good sign. The house is so still. So silent! I pan around the downstairs – the flat-screen TV, the cream leather couch, and the Shaker-style kitchen. I climb the stairs.

Alone in our king-sized bed, I sob into my duvet, my mascara staining the Egyptian cotton pillow cases.

I would have made a beautiful bride!

Six

I've woken up with that awful feeling where you can't remember the wheres and whats of the night before. You know the one. I'm scrambling for the details in a cold sweat. It's a mixture of dread, guilt and fear all rolled up in a bow with a generous dollop of nausea on the side. A vague dream lingers.

I stand at the top of the aisle in a cream lace dress. Barry is looking dapper and family and friends fill the church pews. Suddenly, Debbie from Slimmers' Club is pointing her finger at me. I say 'Who invited you, you skinny cow?' And now I'm naked. Buck naked! I take the cream rose bouquet to hide the cellulite on my bottom. Father Maguire is cackling. I'm running and there is a rabbit chasing me.

The only explanation is that there must have been tequila in at least one of the drinks last night, which is a fatal error and may have accounted for my terrifying nightmare. Tequila and I are no longer friends. We are sworn enemies since our run-in back in 2001 I don't want to talk about it.

My head has a heartbeat of its own and a fuzzy image starts to tune in. I clutch the duvet. It's time to work through the checklist and assess any harm done.

Check 1: Male company in the bed? Negative. Only a feather boa and a crushed photo of Barry accompany me.

Check 2: Underwear? Affirmative. Smalls have not been lost slash stolen.

Check 3: Embarrassing conversations? Affirmative. Scan shows traces of whimpering and crying.

Check 4: Embarrassing actions? Affirmative. Scan detects that I skidded on an Abrakebabra wrapper on the street. In addition, scan shows image of me asking the taxi to stop as my kung pao beef gave an encore performance. Scan does not recall making it to the toilet on time.

I brace myself for the final check.

Check 5: Inappropriate use of mobile phone: Negative. Sent box is nil for picture texts of rude bits. Phone log is nil for calls to Barry, Barry's mother or Barry's office. Phone records show that the only number dialled was for 'Soon Fatt' Chinese restaurant in search of the best curry chips this side of the Liffey. Said curry chips are lying squashed in the bed beside me, I must have rolled over them in my sleep. It's OK, they still taste good.

The moral of Check 5 is: don't drink and dial. The use of a mobile phone when combined with a recent fight with your boyfriend is a poisonous combination. I'm relieved. What willpower. What success. What a bender!

I glance at my phone again. Not even a measly text from Barry to see if I'm still breathing, for goodness' sake! Perhaps I'll call him to see that he landed safely. Then again, it's best to wait until the painkillers have kicked in.

I swallow the pills with a grimace. What if we don't make up? What if Barry ends this? My stomach heaves and I reach for the bin. A text appears from my younger brother Ian.

hey sis. Heard you had a blazer with Baz.

Little shit, I think. I hastily text back.

It's Barry, not Baz you Neanderthal!

He knows it winds me up no end when people shorten Barry's name. So common! I reach for my much treasured *OK!* magazine on the bedside locker. There's an intriguing article about HRH (His Royal Hotness) Prince Michael and his recent flirting with some model or other. He's quite dishy for a royal. I'm just saying.

I answer my phone before checking who's calling – a classic mistake. It's Mum. News of our big blow-out, it seems, has slipped back to family HQ.

'Come around for a talk, darling,' simpers Mum. 'You can tell me all about it.'

'Don't want to.'

I've reverted back to a pouty thirteen year old with an attitude problem and raging hormones.

'I've been baking,' she chirps.

'Fine!'

Blast Mum and her bribes. In the shower, I have to lean on the tiles for support. I struggle to turn the shower head on and then give up, opting for deodorant and some dry shampoo instead, it's far less demanding. I drag myself into a pair of old jeans and a well washed jumper. Perhaps I'm actually dying from a hangover. I could be the first in the world to actually die from excessive Chinese food and cocktails, I'll be in the *Guinness Book of World Records*. Sweet. A pair of giant Beckham-style sunglasses eases the glaring November sunlight as I fumble with the keys to my Volkswagen Golf. Indicating and switching lanes requires more brain cells than I now have at my disposal, and I need to keep the windows down at all times for fear of vomiting into my lap. Sadly, the mechanism on the electric windows has gone, so this is a manual job now. Also, the windscreen wipers still don't work and annoyingly it's raining. *Again!*

I squint. A truck blasts its horn as it passes me. It's not *my* fault I can't see where the continuous white lines on the road are! My last pay cheque went on a darling pair of diamond earrings, so I will try and get to the garage next month. So worth it, though. See how they sparkle?

I arrive at Mum and Dad's and try my best not to violently puke in the flower beds and poison Mum's gladioli. I'd never hear the end of it; she's highly strung like that. One year I showed up for Christmas dinner with the mother ship of all hangovers, and she still talks about 'the year I ruined Christmas' like I'm the Grinch or something. Believe me, forcing yourself to eat reheated Marks & Spencer's turkey roll when your body has gone into shock due to alcohol poisoning is not pretty. I did this to keep my mother happy, since she kept reminding me of how she had 'slaved over a hot stove'. Sure, I think I was being rather selfless, actually.

In my defence, Barry and I had been at his work Christmas Eve bash the night before. The mulled wine reception preceded the free bar, so you do the maths. It would have been rude not to take full advantage. I was nervous as hell. Let's just say that the night ended in robot dancing, ripped tights and tripping down the main stairs of the Shelbourne Hotel.

Mum greets me at the door in her apron and slippers, arms outstretched. Her adorable little poodle, Boy George, scampers up to greet me. Dad is on the landing pretending to polish, but blatantly ear-wigging. He has been given instructions to steer clear. I slump at the kitchen table, my head in my hands. I get dizzy if I move too quickly.

'Let's have it.' Mum sits across from me.

'What?' I tickle Boy George on the tummy.

Mum raises her eyebrows. She's pouring the tea and layering thick butter onto the scones. This will be the perfect cure if I can keep it down. Mum took early retirement last year and Ian has finally flown the nest. Like any Irish mammy with time on her hands now, she bakes.

'Hello, Fairy,' Dad kisses me on the forehead.

He has called me that since I was six and had a monstrous appetite for fairy buns. It was rather unusual for a child of that age, he would tell all of my boyfriends who visited over the years, to have such an unstoppable appetite for baked goods. He would then reveal the anecdote involving a plump six-year-old version of me and a note from the teacher saying that I'd pinched a fairy cake from another child's lunchbox to the cringing boyfriend-of-the-month. The theft was never proven, and I deny it vehemently.

'Hi Dad,' I give a watery smile.

'Gerry,' Mum hisses. 'Rebecca and I need to talk.'

Dad scuttles off behind the door, pretending to dust. He rearranges ornaments and whistles the theme tune to *Blind Date*.

'So, what happened, darling?' Mum cuts straight to the chase.

I roll my eyes. Mum has made it clear over the years that she doesn't approve of Barry and I living together in sin. She's even keener than I am on the idea of us getting married, and only dying to announce a wedding to her Bridge Club biddies. This relationship is her last shot at grandchildren. That's assuming Ian is firing blanks or too immature to have a kid.

Last Easter, she brought up the subject of my biological clock after a few too many sherries. She wanted to know when she would be buying a new hat. Dad tried to change the subject and was promptly shushed. I threatened to become a lesbian if she didn't put a cork in it. She stalked out, and Barry nearly choked on his trifle. He comes from a more refined home. No wonder he ran away from me. It's definitely my family's fault.

'Look, it's nothing really. We just had a bit of a barney.'

Mum pours more tea.

'He says I'm going on about getting married too much.'

'...And are you?'

'Well. A smidge,' I confess. 'Last week, he overheard me on the phone to Links of London ordering bridesmaids' gifts. Hit the roof. It's too bad, they were fab. And he thinks that booking the honeymoon was taking things too far. He copped the deposit on the credit card statement yesterday.'

'Oh dear.'

'He saw me flicking through *Confetti* magazine last week and said I shouldn't have asked the girls to be bridesmaids yet. Jumping the gun, he said.'

'And what did you say?' Mum looks worried.

'I said, sure you can pick whoever the hell you want as groomsman. Just make sure he looks good in a tuxedo and doesn't ruin the pictures. No-one likes bulging buttons on a waistcoat.'

Mum is not laughing.

'Anyway, Mum, he says that's not the point. He says I'm too pushy. Now he's fecked off to flipping China or somewhere on some conference or other. Says he needs time to think about our relationship.' I use the sarcastic bending of fingertips to show how silly he is being.

'It's not looking good for us.'

I feel a tear prickling my eyes.

Mum takes me in her arms. I'm too hungover to fight the tears, and they trickle down to my chin. She says nothing, and I inhale the scent of her familiar perfume.

'It's so unfair,' I cry.

'Just try and give him a break, darling. You don't want to push him away. He'll do it when he's ready.'

Dad appears at the table and Mum pours him some tea.

'There you are now, Gerry,' she slides a buttered scone in his direction.

We discuss everything from *Coronation Street* to the muppets running the country, but sidestep the topic of Barry and my shambles of a relationship.

'Did you spend your birthday vouchers yet, Fairy?'

'Not yet, Dad.'

'Will you join us for dinner, darling? We're having beef?'

I recall the sharp exit stage left of last night's curry beef and shake my head.

'And fairy cakes for dessert!' Dad smiles. 'And Ian will be here soon.'

I'm reaching for my handbag. Facing my little brother as he surfaces from his student hovel in Rathmines is best avoided.

'Call that man of yours and sort it all out,' Mum calls after me at the hall door.

As I turn to open the gate, a taxi pulls up.

'Have you got ten euro, Dad?' Ian greets us.

'Can you not catch a fecking bus?' Dad mumbles and reluctantly hands over the cash.

'Alright, sis,' Ian shuffles past me. He is dragging a large black bag which I assume to be his washing. He hands it to Mum. 'Happy birthday.'

'Thanks. Mum still cleaning your skid mark jocks for you, then?' I smile.

'Eh, yeah,' Ian replies weakly.

He shoots a glance at Mum. Clearly, he has been told not to wind me up today. I must really be in a bad way.

Seven

I've managed to make it to the downstairs toilet before the tea and scones come up in full force, and then I collapse on the couch. I'm torturing myself with the idea that Barry will phone any minute now and say it's all off. The poor creature has had time to think and he's had enough. You couldn't be surprised. I've been a royal pain. He'll say he's fallen in love with some Vietnamese lady boy or what not. He'll say he was pushed into the arms of some oriental jezebel, and that he wants his jewellery back. And who can blame the poor guy? I mean, yes, he loves me, but he thinks I'm some sort of mental patient.

'We will have to sell the house,' I confide in Jess. He is a good listener, but he will really have to do something about his breath – it's like a tuna fish died or something. 'And after all of my admirable interior design efforts, too! You'd best scope the neighbourhood for another couch to sleep on, old friend.'

The cat doesn't come across as overly concerned. I don't think he is quite grasping the seriousness of the situation.

'People will have to come and view the property and snoop in the hot press and make insultingly low offers. They will look down their noses at my failed gardening attempts and then traipse muddy footprints over my pristine cream rug. The wretches!'

The geriatric cat is choking on a hairball. Perhaps he is worried on a more subconscious level, after all. Maybe he's imagining that he'll end up in the retired cats' home being bullied by some bigger more masculine cats. My poor little Jessikins. Jess is a bit of a wimp I don't think he could stand up for himself. He has trouble just standing, period. Besides, he doesn't have many teeth.

When I open a family-sized bag of Kettle Chips, I let the nightmare possibilities wash over me.

'And then I'll be bankrupt!'

Jess doesn't budge. I'm starting to think he's not even listening. Normally, I let Barry worry about bills, the mortgage and other such tedious things. I give my token financial contribution every month, and spend whatever is left over. Barry balances the books. I don't pay attention to credit card bills and glaze over when he talks about home insurance. I don't watch the news and I don't read newspapers. It's all recession doom and gloom. I just switch to 80s FM when the headlines come on the radio. My annual subscription to *OK!*, *Hello!* and *Cosmopolitan* magazines hardly counts as keeping up with current affairs in the media. I'd much prefer a bit of celebrity hot gossip.

Besides, Barry earns an awful lot more than I do. He's a solicitor and I'm an executive assistant. Although, I don't mean to brag but I *do* have sole responsibility for stationery ordering and I'm fully in charge of planning the office Christmas party.

And another thing, I swallow my worries along with a lavish amount of sour cream dip on my crisps, I'm carrying a light store debit card debt. Nothing to worry about, just a couple of thousand.

I pull on my pink floral wellington boots and pink tracksuit. Sunday afternoons are the highlight of my week, and I'm not going to let my hangover or argument with Barry ruin that. After a twenty-minute drive, I park my car at the DSPCA animal shelter.

'Hey, Becks,' Tammie greets me with a hug.

'Hey, Tams. How's Marmalade?'

I've fallen in love with the orange cat that was brought in last week. Once I've patched things up with Barry, I'll start working on him to agree to a flatmate for Jess.

'Marmalade's a mama! She had six kits after you left last Sunday.'

'No way!'

Tammie and I muck out the horse stables and drag the heavy bags of dry dog food towards the dog section. The barking is deafening.

'Five new residents since last week,' Tammie points to a trembling terrier, who is huddled behind the chicken wire. 'We're calling him Bailey. He was in pretty bad shape.'

'Poor chap. Where's Major?'

I've been harbouring quite the soft spot for the old English sheepdog that has been here for a month now.

'Oh I totally forgot to tell you! A young couple came on Monday, filled in the papers and took him home.'

Tammie and I have been volunteering together for six months now, and I don't even know her last name. All we talk about is animals. It's like taking a holiday from the real world for a couple of hours.

One day, when Barry and I are married, I'll jack in my job and volunteer here full time. If I didn't have to worry about money, I could be here every day, matching little fur babies with adoptive mummies and daddies, and not just Sundays. I'm pretty pants at my day job, and being polite in an office all day is exhausting. At the shelter, I get to do something important, something I'm good at.

To be honest, I'm quite happy for Barry to play the whole breadwinner role! I'd have no problem trading my grey work suit for my pink floral boots. Barry would benefit too, because I wouldn't be so worn out from the office. I could even throw the odd dinner party to impress his important corporate types. I'd play the enchanting hostess, presenting a perfectly plump turkey from an immaculate kitchen while Barry pours the sherry and entertains the CEO. I'd laugh at his little jokes. Sure, Samantha from *Bewitched* makes it look easy!

All I need are a few cookery lessons. How hard can it be? Oh, and a full-time nanny if we have little ones. Now, I won't go as far as the old pipe and slippers routine. I'm not a Labrador at the end of the day, for goodness' sake.

Back home, I tell Jess the good news about Marmalade. The throbbing in my temples is back, so I open a bottle of white wine.

Hair of the dog is the only thing left to try.

'Jesus, Jess. If Barry and I don't make up, we could become homeless!'

I'm imagining my bleak future without Barry. *My personal hygiene has taken a sharp decline and I've shaved my head like Britney Spears after her split with Kevin Federline. I'm forced to shop in Argos and Iceland, and have a cunning disguise so that I can mooch around Lidl for bargains without being spotted. I have no choice but to cash my gold at some seedy pawn-style establishment, and have to hock my large collection of shoes on eBay to scrape some measly euros together. I haggle with grubby types at car boot sales over my Dolce & Gabbanas. I'm living in a sordid trailer park rubbing shoulders with 'The Great Unwashed'. My teeth have fallen out, and I've been invited to appear on* The Jeremy Kyle Show.

'Good God!'

I shudder as I pour another glass of wine and consider moving back to Mum and Dad's gaff if our relationship horribly crashes and burns. It'll be a pride-swallowing moment, and I'll have to resume a child–parent relationship with two people whose intentions are admittedly good but incredibly annoying. On the plus side, the grub is great. There will be lashings of tea and sympathy on tap from the old dears, with Sky Movies hooked up to the flat-screen telly and all the mod cons at my fingertips. Their legendary Sunday dinners with a heavy slathering of gravy will be good enough to make me forget my troubles. My version of events will always be morally superior to those of the 'Man-of-whom-we-do-not-speak'.

I realise that the only alternative is that a friend allows me to sleep in their box room amongst their sad collection of dusty books and flowery wallpaper. Most of my friends are loved up, so I will end up as the gooseberry from hell clutching my earplugs as they frolic in the night through frighteningly thin walls.

'Welcome to hell, Jess.'

Jess yawns. He is so emotionally unavailable.

We'll have to sort our collection of CDs into cardboard boxes. Barry can keep his greedy paws off my *Dirty Dancing* soundtrack.

The gloves are off, now – that's a limited edition collector's item, signed by Patrick Swayze himself (God rest his handsome soul). He hardly ever listens to it. Charitably, I decide that he can have Depeche Mode's *Greatest Hits* back. I only faked an interest in that one when he produced it one Christmas in lieu of my specific request for Duran Duran. He may also keep the *Karaoke Christmas*. His mother bought that one. Bit of a Christmas turkey.

Will dinner parties become unbearable if our friends take sides in our vicious dispute? Will we be bitter rivals who can't be in the same room, just like Michael Douglas and Kathleen Turner in *The War of the Roses*? Surely, they will all side with me, the victim in all of this. But will they stay in touch? Will they send Christmas cards? Will I be excluded from smug happy couple events?

Will we haggle over furniture and whose Tesco club card points are whose? The custody battle for our possessions will be like Dustin Hoffman and Meryl Streep fighting over their child in *Kramer vs. Kramer*. Of course, Meryl is way too old to play me if this all ends up in court and is splashed all over the media and then turned into a million dollar budget movie. Perhaps Reese Witherspoon would be a more appropriate casting.

I'm consuming my own weight in chocolate, flicking channels and tormenting myself with images of what lies ahead. Later, I wake up on the couch with a crick in my neck and a chocolate biscuit mashed into the cream cushion.

Emer calls to discuss the latest Jodie Marsh scandal, which is splashed all over the tabloids.

'Frankly,' she confides, 'I saw it coming a mile off.'

'Mmm.' I can't bring myself to muster even a mild gossip.

'So, still no word from him, then?'

'Not a sniff.'

'Hang in there. He'll call. Let him get settled in after the long journey.'

Time for a shower, I decide as I catch a whiff of myself. I'm not down and out just yet.

Eight

The Mandarin Oriental Hotel Bangkok is pretty damn plush. According to the website, it boasts five stars, so it's bound to have a well stocked mini bar at the very least. Barry holds his leather holdall on his knee as the taxi speeds through the capital city.

The heat is so oppressive, sharing a taxi is like sharing a sauna with Shelley and Nigel. Neither of them are saying much, and Nigel is not the freshest after the flight. It's hard to determine whether the BO is strongest from Nigel or the chatty driver. The heady scent of Nigel's business-class brandy mingles with Shelley's sickly sweet perfume. Shelley hasn't spoken a word since the flight. He wonders if this is from exhaustion or whether things between them have become uncomfortable. He feels a headache start to peck at his temples with a chisel.

They enter the cool air conditioned lobby and a small elderly man in a heavy uniform takes their luggage, while another hands them welcome drinks. Barry's drink is pink with a swizzle stick. He doesn't care if it is the gayest drink he has ever clapped eyes on. He doesn't care if it's the middle of the night; he just hopes there is alcohol in it.

The elderly man is sprightlier than he looks and manages to handle the entire luggage at once. The buttons on his heavy crested jacket go all the way up to his neck. Barry wonders how he sticks the heat.

Barry had been expecting penny-pinching Nigel to shack himself and Shelley up in some red-light district, flea-bitten hostel with heroin-addicted lady boys, breakfast not included, but he's pleasantly surprised.

'Get some rest,' Shelley breaks her silence.

Barry nods and inserts his key card into the doorframe of the bedroom next to hers. He throws his jeans on the bathroom floor. In his boxers, he lies on the king-sized bed with a vodka tonic and the smallest tube of Pringles he has ever seen. *At eight dollars a pop, Nigel better be coughing up for the snacks*, he thinks.

He flicks on the TV. For once, he's allowed to operate the remote control. His lids feel as though they are made of concrete. He only plans on closing his eyes for a second, but a dream tunes in straight away.

Barry is standing at the top of the aisle, dressed in a top hat and tails. The church organ plays the Phantom of the Opera. *The guests crowd the pews, dressed in black. He cannot see their faces. A figure moves towards him, dressed in a white meringue. She has a white lace garter and reveals a slender leg. He pulls back the veil. It is Shelley.*

A knock on the door wakes him.

'Hey, Barry!' hisses Shelley. 'You still up?'

'Hi!' Barry leaps off the bed.

'Quick!' she giggles.

Through the peephole, he can see that she is dressed in a white hotel robe. In her hands are three vodka bottles and a packet of macadamia nuts.

'Oh my God, Shelley, you nutter! Get in quickly before anyone sees you. Just a sec!'

Barry searches for his robe. He can't answer the door in his jocks. He squirts some deodorant on his armpits and fumbles with the lock.

'Hey, classic! You're in the robe too! Legend. Have you checked out the bathroom? It's amazing! Here.' She thrusts the booze into his hands and enters the room.

Barry is reminded of the boy scouts jamboree camp in Liverpool back in 1991, when he was twelve. He feels the same excitement now. He feels like he has snuck from the boys' tent to the girls' tent to meet Jenny and play Spin the Bottle.

'So! According to Nigel's new PA, Jessica, he's covering all expenses for this trip. Let's make the most of it. Cheers!'

Shelley has downed a bottle of the mini vodka straight without any mixer.

'Come on in, then!'

They sit on the floor and empty the contents of the mini bar. Sitting at the table feels too formal and sitting on the bed feels too close.

'Check out the little mini Snickers. So cute! Oh and they have rum!'

Barry smirks. Shelley is so charming. It's amazing that he has never noticed this before.

Shelley releases her long brown hair from its tight ponytail and lets the hair cascade onto her shoulders. She folds her glasses and places them in the pocket of her dressing gown. She is wearing a lot more make-up than usual.

It's three o'clock in the morning local time, which makes it about nine o'clock back in Dublin. Barry knows that Rebecca will be back from the shelter by now and already in a fleece onesie and glued to an episode of *TOWIE*, and he's tempted to call.

It's as if Shelley reads his mind. 'No. No way. You are not to call Rebecca. Promise? Let her sweat it out. It can wait till tomorrow.'

Barry sends a brief text instead while Shelley is busy at the mini bar.

'Hey! Awesome!' Shelley fishes out something from the back of the mini bar. As she reaches over, her dressing gown flaps open ever so slightly at the front. He can see her blue silk slip underneath.

'They have Singha!'

'They have what?'

'Singha! Thai beer. Nice one.'

Shelley retrieves two and finds a bottle opener. Barry tries to keep his gaze on her eyes, but they slide back to her chest. That robe looks loosely tied, it wouldn't take much to open.

'Well, OK. When in… eh… Bangkok,' Barry cheers.

Shelley throws her head back and laughs. Rebecca never seems to find him funny. They have been fighting a lot lately, but with Shelley, he feels like an award-winning comedian.

The beer is cool and they clink bottles.

'Cheers!'

Shelley is serious, now. She takes a swig of the beer but her penetrating eyes don't leave his. She bites her lower lip and pouts.

'So. No hard feelings, then?' Barry studies her face nervously. 'Still friends?'

'Friends,' Shelley smirks. 'Good friends.'

Shelley reaches her right hand inside Barry's robe and rubs the hot palm of her hand down his stomach and then along the waistband of his boxers. His erection is throbbing. He's reminded of the first time he pitched a tent, that summer in 1991 with Jenny.

Shelley spills her beer and Barry automatically reaches for it. He thinks of the cream couch, cream carpet, cream walls – cream bloody life back in Dublin. He pulls back his outstretched hand and watches it glug glug onto the hotel carpet. Let someone else worry about it for a change.

Shelley's arms are around his neck and she sits on his lap. Their faces are dangerously close together. Barry's mouth opens to protest, but in one smooth move, Shelley's white robe heaps onto the floor. She rubs herself against the bulge in his underwear, and slips her tongue into his mouth. Her hands paw through his hair.

In the background, a phone is ringing. But Barry's bedside locker is a million miles from the floor. Shelley shoots a warning glance at Barry.

'Don't answer it.'

The trance is broken and Barry snaps back to reality. It's as if a hypnotist has clicked his fingers in front of his face – except instead of Barry finding himself on stage pretending to be a chicken, he finds himself playing tonsil hockey with a scantily clad woman. Barry recoils. *This is wrong!*

'Shelley, no. Don't.'

Barry stands, leaving Shelley on the floor, reaching for her robe.

'I'm sorry, Shelley. I'm with Rebecca. I think you should go now.'

Nine

The TV is really rubbish for a Sunday night, and my muscles are aching from all of the shovelling at the shelter. I try to half heartedly flick through some celebrity hot gossip magazines. Even *OK!* can't hold my attention for long. There's this really juicy feature on the Kardashians, but I just can't be bothered. My mind drifts to Barry as I reach for some more wine from the fridge. His text is unusually cryptic. I read it over and over again, analysing every punctuation mark or lack thereof.

Hello.

What does he mean by this, exactly? Is he being purposefully formal? Is this merely a greeting?

I've landed safely.

What am I, his mother? I didn't ask if his plane had plunged into the Atlantic, or whatever ocean there is near Japan. I just want to know if he's still in a big fat snot over the whole honeymoon misunderstanding.

The hotel is nice.

I'm not a travel agent. I didn't ask what the hotel is like.

Call you tomorrow.

This is the worst line yet. Why didn't he call me today when he landed? Leaving me to hang until tomorrow is torture. There's no clue as to whether he is missing me or hating me. There's no hint as to what kind of present he'll buy me from his trip. There are no kisses at the end! No smiley faces! Not even a measly LOL!

It's best to decide to swallow my pride and follow Mum's advice. She says that I should just call him and apologise, even if he is a non-committing selfish toad. I may have added in that last part. Emer and Mum must be in cahoots, because she is also nagging me every five minutes to give poor Barry a break. I've given in and dialled his number. There's a funny ringtone but no answer.

'Hello, you have reached Barry Costello, of Hodges Myrtell and O'Brien Solicitors. Please leave your name and a detailed message after the tone. Thank you.'

I hang up hurriedly, as I'm now sobbing at such a high pitch that only dogs can understand me. *Why did he not answer me?* I'm sure there is some, like, time difference shenanigans going on over there in Cambodia or whatever third world country he's in, but this is preposterous. Barry is the reliable kind. That's one of the things I love about him. He calls me every lunch break without fail. Surely he's missing me too by now?

There's a celebrity special edition of *Come Dine with Me* that has just started. I watch between blowing snot into a tissue and shoving barbeque nuts into my mouth. A tangerine coloured WAG rifles through the knickers drawer of a failed 80s pop star, whilst verbally berating her fondue.

Pam's name appears on my mobile, and I answer it as I've nothing better to do.

'Emer says he hasn't called yet? Honestly, Becks! Dump him! Get there first before he dumps you!'

I explain about the time difference in Bombay, and fill her in on the text message to get her honest opinion – it's bleak and I regret asking.

'Crap. Maybe we're headed for Splits-Ville. Breaking up with Barry will be a bit like grieving,' I ponder aloud.

One of my gal pals once told me during a zealous drinking session in Temple Bar that breaking up with *her Kevin* was a bit like grieving. At the time, I thought she was being dramatic and attention-seeking, shamelessly trying to steer the conversation away from my 'what to wear to my ex-boyfriend's wedding' saga, which was clearly a far more pressing matter at the time. Perhaps, I realise as I drain my glass, she had a point. This must be what Oprah means by an 'Aha!' moment.

I'd worn a ravishing red off the shoulder number to the wedding, by the way. Just in case you were wondering. I'm not one to let the lack of an invitation stop me from attending. Tiernan, my ex, must have thought I was the one who got away. I'd say he was cursing himself for breaking up with a hottie like me. Yes, he smiled for the camera that day, but really he was hiding the pain. Asking me to leave was just for show. He was checking me out in between posing for wedding snaps and speeches. His bride was decidedly plain, I'm not being cruel.

'I dunno…' Pam says.

'Seriously, though. A break-up is like the five stages of grieving. I think they covered that in our psychology, but I must have out been sick that day.'

'Or hungover,' Pam sniggers.

'True.'

Please note if you have not already done so, that I'm not some thicko. I'm an educated, accomplished woman who scraped a pass at a top university. My four years at Trinners were a fulfilling time that led to many introductions to eligible men. I juggled ten hours of lectures a week plus a full dating schedule. I'm washing the sour cream and onion crisps down with another gulp of wine, and recalling the theory. It goes a little something like this:

Phase 1: Denial

> OK, things have gone belly up with Barry. He thinks I'm a priest-stalking, honeymoon-booking, *Confetti*-magazine-reading psycho. Fine! But maybe there is still hope that he will come home and forgive me and all will be rosy again. You know – like Ross and Rachel?

Phase 2: Anger

> Barry boarded a plane to the other side of the world, despite the fact that we are at a critical relationship crossroad. I've a

fire of rage that burns deep in the pit of my stomach. Either that, or the wine is cheapo plonk from Aldi.

Phase 3: Bargaining

I'd give anything to have Barry back. Anything, I tell you! Except for my shoe collection. They're like my children, and will go to the grave with me.

Phase 4: Depression

I love the bones of Barry. Anyone with a pulse can see that I'm depressed – even a New York retail therapy trip couldn't cure me. I've got a red blotchy face and bitter tears that ruin my new mascara. Soon, I'll be hitting my GP for Valium and will have the Samaritans on speed dial.

Phase 5: Acceptance

The only thing that I can accept right now is that I drove Barry mental, and it's all my fault.

'God, Pam. This is the pits.'

I gently move Jess off the couch so that I can stretch my legs. He makes a swipe for me but thankfully I had him de-clawed last year.

'If he comes back from the conference and dumps me, I'll have to change my status on Facebook from "In a relationship" to…'

'Single…' Pam finishes my sentence solemnly. 'Do it now. Go on. Log on.'

I realise I must do everything in my power to prevent this catastrophe.

'There are more phases, Pam. Like Phase 6? Consuming the daily calories of a sumo wrestler.'

'Defo!'

Pam has had enough break-ups to earn a PhD in misery. For once, she's an expert on something.

'When Wayne dumped me, I became a bottomless pit. Honestly, I had more chins than a Chinese phone directory.'

'Yeah, I remember.'

She was a bit of a fattie after that train wreck.

This weekend, I've fallen victim, through no fault of my own, to the lure of junk food. But I ask you. Who among us doesn't cram Jammy Dodgers into their lonely mouths when the going gets tough? Let she who is without sin cast the first stone. The truth is that custard creams have a soothing quality.

'What about Phase 7?' suggests Pam.

If only she'd applied herself this well at Trinners, she'd have an impressive arts degree like me.

'Starvation.'

She's right. This post-break-up stage afflicts celebrities all the time. They become child-sized versions of their former selves, unable to lift their forks to consume their usual prune juice and lettuce diet. The drama turns them into lollipop people.

'Mary-Kate or Ashley is exhibit A. And when Posh became even more of a skeleton during the whole Rebecca Loos episode!' Pam is over-excited now.

Unfortunately, I've yet to experience the starvation stage. Perhaps it'll come, I think optimistically, reaching for the cheddar cheese Kettle Chips.

'Phase 8. Drinking like Charlie Sheen,' giggles Pam.

'Well, we did that on Friday night, eh?'

I'm cringing. If Pam could see the large glass of wine in my trembling hand she might suspect that I'm some booze-soaked lush like Britney, although she's far more messed up than me. At least I haven't shaved my hair. Anyway, I've had no choice but to replace the dream that was so harshly snatched from me with copious amounts of alcohol and carbohydrates. It's out of my hands.

'Oh, Phase 9. A woman scorned. Imagine if you slashed his tyres! Or if you ripped up all of his suits! Or sold his Jag on eBay! That would be hilarious!'

Luckily for Barry, I love him too much to do that. Besides, he hasn't dumped me yet. There is still a sliver of hope.

'We should write to that professor guy, say that we've created a whole, like, new theory.'

I laugh at her ridiculous suggestion. Then again, maybe we'll get some sort of honorary doctorate like celebrities do. You know, for our humanitarian effort? Or a Nobel Peace Prize. Possibly both. I close my eyes. I'm dressed in a pink Chanel trouser suit. 'Dr Rebecca Browne, PhD, MBE,' the Queen knights me, just like Sir Elton John!

Pam is talking about her recent date. I'm trying to focus on what she's saying. Really, I am. I catch the words 'blind date' and 'never again'. Then there's something about trying to escape from a moving car, but she's very dramatic so you should take what she says with a vat of salt. By the end of her monologue, she has turned full circle and is considering giving the creep a second chance.

'Maybe Barry will give me a second chance. Maybe I should lay off the whole wedding pressure,' I craftily steer her back to the most important topic of the day.

'Look. The relationship is dead in the water, Becks. Maybe you should trawl the water for some new fish?'

I don't find Pam in the least bit philosophical. She knows I don't like fish, they're too fishy. Also, I'm not great on boats.

'Come speed dating with me tonight! You'll love it!'

'Oh, I don't know, Pam. I mean, Barry's no Johnny Depp, but he's attractive in an overweight Richard Gere kind of way. I couldn't bear to break up with him.'

Pam says that she won't take no for an answer and that she's on her way over with the speed-dating tickets right now.

'I can't be single, Jess,' I deliberate as the cat purrs softly on my lap. He's a good listener and doesn't interrupt, but hasn't got much to offer in the way of guidance. 'It isn't my destiny!'

I don't know how Pam handles all of those speed dates and blind dates, and then picks herself up when it all goes horribly wrong. I mean, imagine! The stench of aftershave and sweat and desperation. Trying to summarise my entire life story into the allocated three minutes before the bell rings. Impossible!

And just think how cringey online dating would be! I don't even know the language. GSH and WLTM? Not a clue! And I'd have to do up one of those mortifying profiles and everything. Pam told me that they expect snazzy pictures and quippy descriptions. 'If you like Piña Coladas and getting caught in the rain' is a bit cheesy, although I do enjoy a good cocktail, it must be said.

Then of course there's the Lonely Hearts columns. Look, if I absolutely *had to*, my advert would look like this.

WANTED: *6'5 hunk, uncanny resemblance to Patrick Swayze. Available for wedding fairs and cake tasting. Good Sense of Humour, ridiculously wealthy, enjoys Dirty Dancing (the movie and the actual dancing), chocolate and shopping. Contact me for endless celebrity gossip and copious amounts of wine.*

Of course, the more likely outcome is that I'd end up with a five-foot, cash-strapped hobbit from Cork, who has never even *heard* of Patrick Swayze!

Lord, if Barry pulls the plug and our relationship circles the drain, please don't let me be single forever. I'm already rocking the cat lady look. Also, don't let me fall for a jailbird if I meet someone online. Prisons have computers now. I heard about someone who was on death row once, writing mushy emails to some poor unsuspecting creature, broadband courtesy of Arizona State Prison. These criminal inmate types are not all stylish and charming like Leonardo DiCaprio when he cheekily defrauds everyone dressed as a hunky airline pilot in Catch Me If You Can. *Some even have brutish ways and tattoos. As you know, I'm not a snob, but I do have to think of my reputation! Amen.*

PS, one of the Ten Commandments is, um, forgive your neighbour. So, Barry should really be calling me by now and saying that all is forgiven. Just saying! You're the boss, you could make that happen.

I pour another drink that contains more rum than Coke, and wonder if Barry is thinking of me right now. How can Pam even suggest speed dating when my heart is pining for Barry? There's still a glimmer of hope. And besides, I just want Barry. Good old Barry.

Ten

Pam must be absolutely bonkers if she thinks I'm going speed dating with her tonight. I'm tired, and I've got my entire Sunday night mapped out. You see, the second season of *Orange Is the New Black* has just launched on Netflix, and I hear there's some great snogging action in the prison shower scenes. I couldn't possibly miss that. Besides, Barry might ring, and I'd miss the call.

Jess looks at me like the sad pathetic creature that I am, and then turns away from me to lick himself.

'Oh, for goodness' sake, Jess! OK, I'll go. Happy now?'

I'm telling you, my darling kitty is like a reincarnation of Gandhi himself. With just one look, he can communicate such profound wisdom.

I've ripped the tags off a new black slinky dress. The Spanx and Wonderbra are digging into me, but that's not what's bothering me. The main wardrobe dilemma I'm having is that I can't seem to get the right kind of cleavage. You see, there's a science to it:

Minimum cleavage is suitable for a job interview. You want them to notice your lovely face, and the horn-rimmed glasses you impulse-purchased in Claire's Accessories for five quid that definitely make you look smarter, right? You don't want them to be distracted by 'The Twins'.

Medium cleavage is a good choice for first dates, blind dates and speed dates. You want to communicate that yes, you are hot and probably out of their league. However, you are a smart, sensitive woman who wants to a) be taken seriously, b) be introduced to their mother and c) become their blushing bride one day. Side note: medium cleavage is also suitable for funerals. People need cheering up for goodness' sake.

Maximum cleavage is excellent for third dates, upon which time, the chap in question might even get to see those beauties up close. Important appendix: make sure that you hide the chicken fillet padding before you strip off, so that you're not accused of fraud. Maximum cleavage is also good for weddings, christenings, bar mitzvahs and other celebrations where your chin-tipping, eye-popping lovelies are on display.

With medium cleavage attained, I peep out through the bedroom net curtains. Pam has abandoned her 1999 Toyota Starlet on the road outside my house, the back wheels partially blocking my wretched neighbour's driveway, and she teeters towards my front door in a pair of peach peeptoe stilettos. I cannot believe that Pam has talked me into this silly charade. Who ever would have thought that I would be parading myself about at some seedy pub function room, looking for love?

Within ten minutes, we're halfway through a bottle of Tesco Finest Chardonnay, and Pam has upskilled me in the speed-dating department. There's a lot to know. Luckily, Pam has been around the block a few times, and knows the potholes.

'Will you relax, Becky!' Pam tops up her glass. 'I know you're still hoping that Barry will call. But, sure, what's the harm in keeping your options open?'

'I suppose.'

'Sure, it'll be a laugh!'

The taxi has arrived, so we drain the last of the wine.

'OK, but Pam? Remember the safety words, right?'

'Right.'

Pam and I have craftily devised safety words, which will be used to alert the other in the case of being trapped in conversation by any

70

stamp-collecting, still-living-at-home-with-elderly-parents, I've-got-a-tattoo-of-Cheryl-Cole-on-my-bum kind of weirdos. I mean, a girl has to protect herself. Now, how exactly we can manage to subtly insert the words 'banana' and 'cucumber' into conversation is not entirely clear as of yet, but I'm sure we can just improvise. Pam has sworn blind, and on various grannies' graves, that she will come running to my rescue if I use my safety word in a hysterical fashion. This is also to be accompanied by hand flapping to show the seriousness of the situation, and not a false alarm. I have also negotiated the right to bail out on her, and collapse into the nearest taxi, if it all becomes too much. Seems fair.

The taxi pulls up outside The Hot Spot in Temple Bar. Rain bounces off the cobblestones.

'Right, here we are. Out you pop,' Pam nudges me out of the taxi.

'Cant. Won't,' I pout like a spoiled three year old. 'Scared.'

'Will you get out, Becky!' Pam thrusts a tenner at the driver. 'The tickets cost a bomb. Not that I mind, they were for charity. But still. Go!'

'What was the charity?'

'Huh? Oh, I don't know. Sick dogs. Something like that. Anyway, the first drink is free…' she sing-songs. 'Come on!'

I'm snookered. Pam knows I'm a sucker for poor, sweet, defence-less dogs, especially sick ones.

'Huh. Fine.'

Once we've passed our tickets to the bouncer, Pam orders a couple of stiff drinks, while I sneak to the loo to check that my lipstick is still on straight.

'Here. Get that down you,' Pam passes me a large gin and tonic, which I sip straight away.

'Ta. Cheers.'

'So,' Pam smirks. 'Who do you like? What about him?' she tips her head in the direction of a man in his thirties in a charcoal suit.

'Yeah, a bit of alright,' I smile. 'My Barry has a suit just like that. He wears it with the cornflower blue tie I bought him last year. It really brings out his eyes, you know?'

'And that one, Becky?' Pam points at a Jamie Dornan lookalike who is leaning against the bar with a grin.

'Nah. He's too slim for me. I like them with a bit of meat on their bones. Like my Barry.'

'Actually, hands off,' Pam continues. 'I bags him. Saw him first.'

'Let's get another,' I suggest, shaking my empty glass. There's a sick swirl in my stomach that a vodka and blackcurrant might drown out.

Nearby, a microphone is tapped lightly, and conversation in the pub dims to a low hum. Pam and I turn our heads in the direction of a small stage.

'Ladies and gentlemen,' a slim woman with cropped black hair taps the microphone again. She looks vaguely familiar, but I shake the idea away.

'If I could just have your attention for one moment, please? Welcome! I'm Grace, your hostess for the evening. Ladies, please take your seats, as we are about to start. You'll find your name tags on the table here in front of me. There are dating cards on each table, just place a tick next to anyone you'd like to meet again. Gents, when the bell rings, please move in a clockwise direction to the next table. You'll have three minutes before you hear the bell again, and then you'll need to move to the next table. Good luck!'

I feel faint. And before you say it, no, it's not from the Chardonnay, gin and vodka mixture in an otherwise empty stomach. The bell rings.

'Good luck, sexy!' Pam flits past and then sits at the table next to me. She's such a pal, she has just deposited a Malibu and Coke into my shaking hand.

'Hi, I'm Dan,' a tall, blond, tanned man with a blue Hollister T-shirt reaches out his hand to shake mine.

'Rebecca. Hi.'

If we had babies, they'd be so blond. Like miniature Scandinavian Ken and Barbie dolls. They could model clothes in catalogues. Just saying. I bet you that Dan's a surfer.

'So! What do you do for fun? I'm a surfer, myself.'

Told you!

'Wow, that's gr—'

'Yeah, just back from Sligo. Some ripper waves, you know? Awesome. Nothing like Oz, though. I spent a year there, thinking of going back there again.'

I cannot get a word in edgeways, managing to only squeeze in 'Yeah, see you later' between the bell ringing and the next chap sitting down.

'Hi. My name's Brian.'

The man in the charcoal suit who I'd spotted earlier is now beaming at me, white teeth sparkling all in a neat row. He's even better looking up close.

'Rebecca. Hi. So…' This is starting to feel like a job interview. 'What do you do, Brian?'

Yes, I know, unoriginal. But when you're on the spot, it's hard to know what to ask a total stranger, especially when he's staggeringly handsome. Give me a chance!

'I'm a solicitor. And yourself, Rachel?'

'It's Rebecca…'

'I'm a solicitor', my mind plays on a loop as my heart pangs. A solicitor. Just like Barry. A sneaky thought takes shape. This man could be a stand-in, you know? A little switcher-oo. He could be like an understudy in a play. People might not even notice! Sure, I could call him 'Barry' as a pet name. He'd grow to love it. The wedding plans could still go ahead, just with one minor substitution. I could still keep the 'B&R' monogrammed bath towels I have ordered. He could be Barry version 2.0. Not quite the original model, I'll grant you, but a toothier, sexier upgrade.

'I work for a PR firm, Brian. Sloan Publicity?'

'Oh? You might know my brother, he works in PR too?'

Why is it that everyone who lives in Ireland likes to play the 'six degrees of separation' game? Just because I went to the same school with someone doesn't mean that I know your cousin. OK, I probably do, but that's beside the point.

'Our surname is Ramsbottom?' Brian continues.

73

'Oh.' I try hard not to snigger, really and truly I do. But you must understand that Malibu makes me decidedly giddy. It's like dosing an orang-utan with laughing gas.

Mrs Rebecca Jane Ramsbottom. Dear Lord! The deal is off. I couldn't possibly marry someone with that kind of surname. My friends laugh at me enough as it is. I'll have to call the Actors Casting Agency, and tell them that I no longer require their boyfriend substituting services. Anyway, he might have straighter, whiter teeth than Barry, and he might fill that suit very nicely indeed, but I think I prefer the original, crooked-toothed Barry. Don't ask me to explain it.

In the distance, the bell rings, and my shoulders drop in relief. My next date shuffles over to my table. Now, I'm sorry to be cruel, but he's like 'The Creature from the Black Lagoon', and that's putting it mildly.

'Hi. I'm Rebecca,' I offer my hand, and he shakes it like a cold, limp fish.

I'm not exaggerating, but all I can understand is 'Hello'. His rural accent is so thick, he needs subtitles. There's only so much nodding and smiling you can do in the space of three minutes. By the time the bell rings, I've managed to extract the words 'cows' and 'Tipperary' so I'm guessing that he's some kind of cattle farmer. The mud-smeared boots and enough dirt under his fingernails to grow a crop of potatoes are also clues. He kisses my hand when I extend it at the end of our three long minutes together, and I wipe my hand on the back of my dress as he leaves.

We've stopped for a halfway break, so good old Pam has ordered me a tequila slammer, and a pint of Guinness. That should help things along nicely. As I sit at the bar, I picture myself balanced on a stool next to Cilla Black in a special edition of the TV show *Blind Date*. 'Say hello to *our Becky*, all the way from Dublin,' the permed Liverpudlian grins as the audience cheers. 'Our Becky enjoys wine, OAP makeovers and planning weddings. And now, here's *our Graham* with a quick reminder.'

Graham sums it up during the theme tune. 'Well, Cilla, behind screen number one is Dan. He likes surfing, but you'll have to … *wave*… goodbye to a two-way conversation with this one!'

The audience claps with glee.

'Behind screen number two is Brian. He's a solicitor, but it'd be a …*crime*… to take that surname!'

The audience howls with laughter. I'd forgotten how witty 'our Graham' could be.

'Behind screen number three, it's Farmer Fred. Fred has a cattle farm. But will Becky be …*moo-ved*… by him?'

Cilla is beaming at me, and wants to know which one I choose. She wishes me a 'Lorra lorra luck, chuck.' I try to explain that none of them measure up to Barry.

'Becky? Is that you?' A deep voice breaks the daydream. Cilla and Graham return to the 1980s where they belong.

'Tristan! Hi!' I exclaim in a high pitch.

My brain is screaming various profanities, pressing the 'abort mission' button, and desperately scrambling for an escape pod. It still remembers the drama Tristan caused when he broke my heart back in 2002 at university, and it's trying to do damage control. Last year, the brain issued a stern warning to the heart to stop following Tristan's status updates on Facebook. The heart then coolly informed the brain that it couldn't, as it needed to torment itself with Tristan's posts containing photos of that cow he'd married from the Rowing Club, and their three strapping boys dressed in matching rugby shirts.

'So, Becky… Long time no see. How are you?'

I realise that I'm blinking a lot, but I'm unable to stop. There's no-one at the controls any more.

'Fine. Great. Amazing,' I stutter. 'So, what are you doing here? I thought you were…married?'

'Yes, I am. To Grace over there. See?' He waves over at his stunning wife, who wiggles her slim fingers back at him. 'She's the hostess for the night. We're co-directors of the charity that tonight is in aid of. Furry Friends Dog Shelter? I just spotted you, there, thought I'd say hi. Is the speed dating going well so far?'

'It's…'

'Enjoying the night?'

'Eh… it's…'

'So, how's life treating you, Becky? Are you single now?'

'Oh, no!' I force a laugh. 'No, me? Single? Hardly!' I laugh and wave the ridiculous idea away. 'No, I'm married to Barry. Yeah, life's great, Tristan. Just …great.'

I don't need a mirror to know that a puce hue has crept up from my neck to my forehead.

'That's great, but why…?' he motions towards all of the single-tons in the room.

'No, I'm just here for Pam, you know?' I lean in for the next bit, like it's confidential. 'Poor Pam. She's so …*single*,' I make a face to show him what a good pal I am. 'And I like to support charity, of course. Sick dogs and that.'

Tristan nods his head slowly, eyebrows raised, and an excruci-ating silence follows. I swivel on the bar stool to catch Pam's eye, but she's engrossed in conversation with Brian, too busy drowning in his dazzling smile to notice my distress flare.

'Banana!' I cough loudly into my fist.

'Pardon?' Tristan stares.

'Not you, Tristan. Banana!'

Pam's oblivious. Her flirting with Brian has hit what we like to refer to as Stage Five, now. This stage includes arm touching, throwing your head back while laughing, and pushing your boobs together with your elbows. It's an art, really. Not everyone can master it like we can.

'Cucumber! Gherkin!' I shout. 'Assorted fruits and bloody vegetables!'

Thankfully, that gets Pam's attention. Unfortunately, it also gets the attention of the entire bar. Tristan says he has to go and check on things.

'Sorry, Pam,' I blurt out. 'But I've had enough, love.'

Pam scribbles her number for Brian on the back of a beer mat, and we stagger across the cobblestones.

'Oh my God,' Pam laughs. 'I think you scared Tristan. Serves him right for dumping you, though.'

Pam and I decide that there's never been a better time, albeit standing in the drizzling rain at midnight on a crowded street, to have a heart to heart. It's totes emosh.

'I just *love* you to bits, Pam.'

'No, Becks, I love *you*!'

There's a hen party over from London that look like they've had even more to drink than we have. They're looking for The Temple Bar Inn, and they have tickets to see 'The Dream Boys', which is a male stripper show I've been dying to see. After showing them the way, the bride invites us to join them. At least, I think she's the bride. She has a disco bopper on her head made out of little plastic willies, and she's wearing an L plate.

I've spent my last tenner on the ticket to get in, so I'll have to use Barry's credit card to pay for the drinks. Oh, and it'd be rude not to buy one for all of the hens, too. 'Champagne for everyone!' I slap my hand on the bar.

I'll probably get an invite to the wedding for this. It'll be hilarious when Barry sees champagne from a strip club on his Visa statement. I'm sure we'll laugh about it when we kiss and make up.

'Girls Just Wanna Have Fun' is blasting from the speakers as we take our seats. The curtain retreats, and five burly dancers in business suits and bowler hats take to the stage, parading about with umbrellas to 'It's Raining Men'. Slowly, tantalisingly, their jackets come off, and drop to the floor. Pam and I manage to out-screech the hen party. Next, the dancers kick their shoes off. Since we are pretty close to the stage, one of the shoes hits Pam on the head. It's tricky to tell if she has suffered a concussion or not; her speech was slurred before we got here.

'Come on!' roars one of the bridesmaids. 'Get your kit off!'

One button at a time, the dancers remove their shirts, revealing their toned chests. There's enough oil on their bodies to fry chips. Next, with one swift motion, the Velcro in their trouser legs detaches, and we ogle their muscular thighs. All that they are wearing now are the hats and pants, and they weave through the audience, allowing the women to place five-euro notes in their leopard print G-strings and touch their greased bodies.

The hen party are on their feet, now, cheering. A mahogany coloured brute of a stripper stops at our table. Hopefully the poor man has earplugs, because our screams would perforate an eardrum. He bumps and grinds against the bride, his wrists behind his head as he dances. It looks like he has a small black poodle trapped in those skimpy, tight, PVC, lime green pants of his. He grabs the bride's hand to lead her onto the stage. Jammy cow! The mortified girl refuses to go, so I valiantly volunteer to take her place. It's just how I roll.

Pam shrieks in shock horror as the dancer takes a can of whipped cream and coats his chest in the sticky stuff. He then puts a cherry on top, and I'm instructed to lick it all off, so I take one for the team. Pam and the hen party are howling with laughter and trying to hold each other up. Next, the dancer slowly peels a banana. We all know what's coming next. He places the banana at his crotch and I take a bite.

Lucky me, I've been invited backstage. I've taken Pam with me as my bodyguard, not that she's much use by now. Picture the dormouse *in Alice in Wonderland* with his head flopping into the teacups, and you're in the right ball park. Now, when I say backstage, it's not as glamorous as it sounds. It's really just the dancers' dressing room, with a selection of liquor bottles. Not that I'm complaining, mind you.

The banana-peeling, cream-in-a-can spraying, mahogany-tanned man is called Ramone. You've got to roll your Rs, and splay your hands Flamenco-style when you say it, to get the drama of his name. He came here from Chile to work his way through college. He says that he wants to become a vet one day, and nurse sick animals back to health. How adorable.

'Yeah, yeah,' Pam slurs. 'Take your top off and get us another drink.' Then she falls asleep again.

By two o'clock, Pam is unconscious in the arms of a dancer I've christened Fabio (because of his rippling muscles and long wavy blond hair), and I'm fading fast. The boys aren't as much fun with their clothes on, so Pam and I ditch them for the takeaway next door. The whiff of the vinegar on the chips revives Pam momentarily, like smelling salts in the olden days. She mumbles something. Now, I'm not quite fluent in Pam-ese, but I think she wants a battered sausage. She has lost the ability to chew and swallow, so I finish her grub and pour her into a taxi.

The motion of the moving car has upset poor Pammy's tummy. I'm feeling a little queasy also. That battered sausage must have been off. I've rolled down the window to get a bit of fresh air, but this makes Pam feel worse, and she starts retching. I distract the taxi driver with confusing directions, so that he won't notice that Pam is splattering the upholstery. Well, what do you expect me to do? You know how much taxi drivers charge for spoilage!

'Wake up, Pam. We're home.'

Somehow, I've managed to insert the key into the moving door. Pam is like a sack of potatoes, and I can't manage to get her up the stairs. Gravity can be so cruel sometimes. She won't mind if I plonk her on the couch, and throw a blanket over her. Once she sobers up, she can drive back to her flat.

I've decided that *right now*, at three o'clock in the morning, is a super time to call Barry. You know, just to confirm that I'm missing him shamelessly, in case he was in any doubt. I slur into the handset when I hear his voicemail message.

Who knows if I pressed the hang up button before or after the sobbing, but it doesn't really matter. My tights don't want to come off, but I lie down on my bed anyway. As soon as the room stops spinning, I'm out cold.

Eleven

Barry opens his eyes. The digital clock reads 08.45, but the room is still dark. For a split second, he thinks he's in Dublin, but when he reaches for the other side of the bed and finds it empty, he realises that he's in the hotel. The blackout blinds shield him from the glaring Thai sun.

Last night!

An image of Shelley's robe slipping to the floor flits across Barry's mind. He thinks about the heat of her hand on his skin. She had put herself on a plate for him. The truth is, for a split second, he'd wanted Shelley. God, how he had wanted her. No point in denying it to himself.

Barry reaches for his mobile. If Rebecca's phone call had not interrupted his antics with Shelley last night, he would have done the unthinkable. He feels sick. It's a combination of too much hard liquor mixed with beer the night before, and the realisation of how close he came to sleeping with Shelley.

He breathes deeply to calm himself and to keep the nausea at bay. There's an all-female jury perched on an imaginary bench. They are staring at him, waiting for him to defend his despicable actions. The courtroom is silent.

'Your honour,' Barry prepares his silent deliberation. 'Respected members of the jury. Let's get this into perspective here, shall we?

There's a difference between wanting to cheat on someone and actually cheating on them, am I correct? Let the record show that the defendant pulled away from the alleged affair at the critical moment and declined her advances.'

The jury are nodding their heads. The defendant has no prior record. He has been a loving boyfriend to date with no prior convictions. He was intoxicated and therefore not in his right mind. He is not culpable.

'Not guilty!' the judge acquits him, slamming the gavel on the bench. Barry smiles but his stomach churns. He has gotten away on a technicality but feels guilty as hell.

'Been there before, old chap,' the judge reveals to Barry over a Scotch in his chambers after the crowd have dispersed. 'Jolly close call, eh?'

Barry sits up in bed and smiles as he remembers when he and Rebecca first met in the July of 2010. Back then, he was only a junior at the firm and was dealing with the most annoying, petty cases – neighbours' disputes over crooked hedges and measly compensations from the council for clumsy old ladies who tripped on the cracks in the pavement. 'The Dregs', that's what they used to call them. It was all boring paperwork and very little court action. Still, he was assured that if he stuck with it, he would work his way up the ladder.

'Hey. Got a great one for ya,' Shelley had appeared behind his office door that day. 'Barbie from Malibu is in reception to see you.'

'Who? Ah, Shelley. Take this one for me, will you?'

'Not a chance. I'm slammed with wills and probates. Exciting stuff. Enjoy!'

That's what Shelley had called Rebecca that day – Barbie. Slim, blonde and dressed head to toe in pink, she fit the bill.

'Please, won't you come in,' Barry had instructed her.

He could hear Shelley making a fake phone call to a Ken regarding a property in Malibu in the background. She had sniggered as he closed the door. Rebecca remained, hovering at his desk.

'Please. Sit down.'

'Well, that's just it. I can't.'

Barry looked at her sweet face for the first time. Underneath the acrylic nails, false eyelashes and the florescent pink Juicy Couture tracksuit, he spotted something. He was mesmerised by her. There was something almost childlike about her that made him fall for her on the spot. He had hidden a grin behind his fist.

'OK. So! What can I help you with?'

'Well. I was at this spa. You, know, for some tanning? Anyway, turns out the place is an absolute death trap!'

'OK.' Barry noticed how she twisted her blonde hair nervously.

'I fell asleep for, like, a micro second on this sun bed. It's one of those outdated lie-down ones. Anyway, next thing I know, I wake up and the thing is still on. They're meant to turn off by themselves. Then I got dressed and had a look in the mirror. My ass was on fire. Now it looks like a Texas Flamed Barbeque Beef steak. There are grill marks!'

Barry had tried to cover up his sniggers with a cough. Shelley will die when she hears this one.

'It was agony. So, my friend Sorca said I should, you know, sue the bastards.'

'OK. And have you been to the doctor?'

'Yes.'

Rebecca shuffled through her handbag. It was also pink. She emptied the contents of the bag on his sprawling desk – pink lipstick, pink wallet, pink phone, pink camera and pink diary.

'Aha. Here.'

She thrust some documents at Barry.

'Pictorial evidence. Taken by the GP. Now! I have extensive legal knowledge, Mr Costello.'

'Oh?'

He tried not to sound too surprised, but he couldn't help it. She didn't exactly look like a legal secretary or even an intern.

'Absolutely. I am prepared to stand up in court.'

You can't exactly sit, Barry had smirked.

'Just pass me a bible and I'll swear on it that I've been horribly maimed.'

'That won't be necessary, Ms Browne.'

Barry had shuffled some papers, avoiding her deep blue eyes. There was a well of disappointment in them.

'That's *Miss* Browne. Call me Rebecca.'

She used her elbows to push up her voluptuous breasts as she smiled. The zipper on her tracksuit top was an inch lower than necessary. It was about as subtle as those eyelash extensions. Barry noticed that she carried a slight bit of excess weight – puppy fat, you might call it. He liked it, a bit of meat on the bones, as they say. It gave her curves in all the right places.

'OK. Rebecca.'

'Tell them about the *res ipsa loquitur.*'

'Pardon?'

'*Res ipsa loquitur.* You know, a rebuttable presumption or inference that the defendant was negligent, which arises upon proof that the instrumentality or condition causing injury was in the defendant's exclusive control and that the accident was one that ordinarily does not occur in the absence of negligence!'

Barry was gobsmacked. Where had this glitter-encrusted Barbie doll plucked that one from? He realised in that moment that, despite appearances, she was smart.

'I have the entire box set of *Law and Order,*' Rebecca had offered as an explanation. 'Tell them I object. Tell them I will tell the truth, the whole truth, and nothing but the truth. Tell them I want to sue them for millions. For loss of future earnings. My future in modelling is well and truly fecked now. I mean, I was in *Just Seventeen* magazine when I was thirteen. Tell them there's no *way* I'll ever be on a catwalk with this *disfigurement*. I'll never have a career in acting. Or pole dancing. I'll no longer suit office work, which requires sitting for long periods.'

'I don't think that would be the right path to pursue at this current time. However, I could write a strongly worded letter.'

'Oh, OK. But really rattle their cage.'

And then she was off. Only the mixture of her hairspray and peach perfume lingered in the air. Some of the pink sequins from her tracksuit had left a trail between his desk and the door, like a blonder ditsier version of *Hansel and Gretel*. Barry went straight through the documents in search of the photos. She was right, her bum was well scorched.

'Sweet Jesus,' Shelley's head was back again behind his door.

Barry shoved the photos into a drawer.

'So. What's wrong with Barbie? Let me guess, Ken dumped her and she wants the Malibu beach house? Did Cindy steal one of her My Little Ponies?'

He had plastered a false smile. 'Something like that. But actually she was kind of… sweet.'

'Right. Coffee?'

Barry didn't want coffee. He wanted to see Rebecca again.

He had thought about her all week after that first meeting. The way her brow furrowed when she spoke. Her smile. He had looked her up online and found both her Facebook page and her profile on LinkedIn. Since he didn't have a Facebook account himself, all he could access was her profile picture. She was draped in a pink feather boa, sipping a pink cocktail through a ridiculous pink willie straw. He hoped that this was a hen night snap.

On LinkedIn, she had described herself as a 'Disco Diva'. Under special skills, she had listed 'shopping'. Under hobbies and interests, she had simply stated 'Patrick Swayze'. Her qualifications listed an arts degree and a certificate in acrylic nails.

The next week, she had shown up at the office.

'I just happened to be in the neighbourhood,' she had said. 'Thought I'd check on how it's going.'

Barry had suddenly become aware of his creased suit and wished he hadn't chosen such a loud tie.

Later in the week, he had telephoned her to enquire about her health. She was still on sick leave, she had informed him. She had told the office that she was recovering from life-threatening third-degree burns and that a possible skin graft might be needed. It was touch and go, she had told them. She would let them know if she survived to the weekend. Barry had smirked. He was picturing himself rubbing cream into her behind, which was probably back to its full glory by now.

By Friday evening, Shelley had convinced him to join her for an after-work drink in Mulligan's on Clyde Road. He really wasn't in the mood as he was pretty wrecked, but she had really insisted. By six o'clock, he was glad that he had acquiesced. In walked Rebecca with her entourage. Two pink ladies flanked her on either side, shopping bags in tow.

'What a coincidence!' she had exclaimed.

Shelley's face was like thunder. What was that about? She could be so unfriendly sometimes.

'Hey, Rebecca!'

'My gal pals and I were in the area running some errands, so…' She had thrust the BT2 bags in his direction as proof.

'That's great,' he had stumbled. 'Would you…?' he had motioned towards a vacant bar stool.

'Oh thanks!' Rebecca had beamed. 'I'd absolutely murder a G and T! Sorca and Michaela only drink champagne.'

'…Of course…'

They had become inseparable after that. Expensive dinners, weekends away and movies on Barry's couch followed. Of course, she only wanted to rent films with the word 'wedding' in the title. Soon, it was breakfasts in bed and talk of moving in together. He had even tagged along to the animal shelter on a couple of Sundays, and seen her light up when she was walking and feeding the dogs.

About a month or two into the relationship, Barry's snotty letter had paid off. The spa wanted to settle.

'Serves them right,' she had said, as they walked Benji the bulldog one overcast Sunday evening on the grounds of the shelter. 'They were probably afraid that I would go the press and splash pictures of my charcoaled behind all over the tabloids. As if I'd stoop that low!'

When the cheque came in the post a few months later, it was a mini victory. By then, Barry and Rebecca were already living together in his flat in Ranelagh with an elderly cat they had taken from the shelter.

The digital clock in the Bangkok hotel room now reads 09:00, and Barry knows that he must force himself into the shower and down to the lobby for the conference. He knows what he must do. He'll give Shelley a wide berth for the rest of the trip. He'll resist temptation.

Twelve

I wake at nine in the morning with a pulsating head, and a vague recollection of the voice message on Barry's phone. I try to swallow, but a dead skunk seems to have taken up residence inside my mouth. It's just as well then, that I know just what to do. Hacking into someone's phone and wiping a message is child's play. Think of it as Stalking 101, if you will.

When I draw the living room curtains, Pam shields her eyes from the glaring light like a vampire. I pass her a glass of water and two ibuprofen. She's temping in an office in Sandyford starting half an hour ago, and needs to find her car keys.

Barry has still not called. I'll make a half-hearted attempt to tackle the laundry mountain. The contents are now spilling from the wicker basket and trying to escape down the stairs. I might as well try and do something positive, I think, trying hard to scrape together enough energy to get going. The house is slipping into a tip-like state. Distracting myself with menial tasks might help.

Barry usually does the lion's share (OK, *all*) of the laundry, so I begin the chore by cursing him for leaving me with the unappealing task. He hasn't really trusted me with his work shirts since the unfortunate laundry incident of 2012, when I accidentally put a pair of red hotpants in the wash along with the whites. Various items of his came out a marshmallow pink.

'Mum used to do my laundry before we started living together, so it's her fault for not warning me! Anyway, don't overreact,' I had debated. 'Pink shirts are highly trendy. You should be grateful I'm such a fashion visionary.'

Barry's trust in my ironing skills is even less. Frankly, this suits me fine. Once, I'd left a distinct scorch mark on his ThunderCats T-shirt, and he had gone a tad ape. I'd sworn that I hadn't done it on purpose; it was simply a tragic accident. However, he had remained suspicious as he knew that I detested this juvenile garment and had once tried to donate it to Oxfam.

As I dig through the laundry basket, I spot one of his loud ties, and hunch over to get a sniff of his angelic aftershave, and a tear rolls down my face. This is officially a new low. I throw the soiled garments back into the basket with a hefty shove.

Surely this spat with Barry is merely a small pothole on our road to happiness. We're a team. I first realised this during a game of Trivial Pursuit at Mum's house during our first Christmas together. Mum's TV was on the fritz and I was fuming. I'd thrown a bit of a hissy fit, as I was missing *The Royle Family* Christmas special.

Mum, after one sherry too many, had decided to climb the Stira into the recently converted attic in order to retrieve Ian's old board games. How she completed the task in those high heels and Christmas apron, I will never know.

'Even as a child,' I announced to the room, 'I did *not* like board games. I have absolutely no intention of starting now.'

Barry was licking up, and saying how much he would love to play. With nothing better to do (it was either that or read a copy of the *RTE Guide Christmas Special*, featuring Gay Byrne *again*), I grumpily agreed to play. My arms were still folded across my chest in a display of defiance.

There were three teams in total: Mum and Dad, Barry and me, and Ian and Cindi. Please bear with me in relation to Cindi, it's a long story. Where to start? She's the on-again/off-again girlfriend of my brother Ian. Her name must be spelled with an 'i' at the end, or else she gets very upset. I know this, because I blatantly refuse to spell it as such, and stick a 'y' on the end, as God intended. She studies philosophy and is highly annoying. Also, she's one of those vegetarian types, and refuses to eat Christmas turkey. Ridiculous, I know!

About ten minutes into the game, I was getting rather into it. My competitive streak had started to take things up a notch, and I was screaming out the answers after Barry had whispered them to me. You see, I was the *communications* side of the team and he was the brains. I was engrossed, shouting at the top of my lungs and high-fiving Barry in a *Beverley Hills 90210* kind of way. Also, the white wine that I'd been knocking back in boredom had kicked in by then.

Anyway, the point that I'm trying to make is that, although Barry and I could not be more different, we were a great team. For those of you deprived children out there who have never played the game, let me sum it up – the object of Trivial Pursuit is to move around the board while correctly answering trivia questions. You roll the dice and take turns to collect the pie-piece-type thingies.

Barry promptly answered all of the geek questions such as History (yellow wedge), Geography (blue wedge), Arts and Literature (brown wedge), Science and Nature (green wedge) and Sports and Leisure (orange wedge). Naturally, these pieces of the pie relate to all of the really dull topics. Barry was a total teacher's pet in school, and got a bazillion points in his Leaving Cert, so it's no surprise that he got every question right. Also, he watches a lot of Sky Sports and the History Channel. Needless to say, Dad was most impressed.

Unsurprisingly, Ian was being a total brat and blatantly cheating on his new iPhone.

'Didn't you *study* geography in college?' Cindi asked me several times with a sweet smile. Barry kept pipping me to the post with the blue questions, and she was loving every second. I swear, the geography answers were at the tip of my tongue.

'Well, yes,' I had replied with a hot flush. 'But I was sick the day the professor covered that mountain range!'

Later, I swear that I'd heard her say 'University Challenged' to Ian and snigger, when I announced that the capital of Peru was Mozambique. It took all my self-composure and Zen-like breathing techniques not to pop her in her smug face. She was probably just in a snot because there was no philosophy pie square thing. Also, between you and me, she only attends Tallaght IT which isn't even a proper university, anyway. I call it 'TIT' for short, and that really winds her up nicely.

By now, winning had become my raison d'être. I became increasingly irate as we headed towards the hexagonal hub and into the final lap. If I had a graph, I would show you that as X rose (X equates to the aggression between Cindi and me), then Y fell (Y equates to the amount we cared about making a show of ourselves in our desperate attempts to beat each other).

Anyway, back to how Barry and I discovered we were a super team. OK, everybody knows that you cannot win the game without the pink square piece of pie thing. That's the entertainment category. Luckily for Barry, the pink square was my speciality. It was my chance to shine. I have extensive knowledge of celebrity culture, and as the game unfolded my years of research in this field started to pay off.

I could tell that Barry was astounded by my knowledge of Marilyn Monroe movies. He was amazed that I knew exactly what year Madonna's 'Like a Virgin' hit was released. Thanks to me and my pink-pie-piece attaining ways, we won the game. Barry and I exchanged a glance that I'll never forget. It was one of those moments where I knew I loved him and wanted to be with him forever. We were a team, and that was that.

'Well done!' clapped Mum as we revelled in our victory.

Later that Christmas night, the TV had eventually been restored to its full glory. We snuggled up on the couch to watch a classic episode of *Only Fools and Horses* and broke out another tin of Quality Street. It was just as well actually, as Cindi and I were at boiling point and the telly was a good buffer. Barry had his arm around me, and all was well with the world.

The memory feels like a lifetime ago. We don't seem like much of a team now.

'For God's sake, my life is over,' I complain to Jess in the kitchen.

I pour a large bowl of Coco Pops and think about what my life would be like if I were single. How could I face them at work, with my pathetic solo appearance at the Christmas party? Speaking of Christmas, what would that be like at home with Mum knowing that her daughter had now in fact a fat flipping chance of ever meeting anyone now that she was not getting any younger or thinner?!

I picture myself traipsing through Marks & Spencer's 'Meals for one' section, scowling at happy couples and their gurgling babies whilst accidentally on purpose knocking my trolley into their heels as I pass. I imagine myself tut-tutting at the loved-up teenagers in the back row of the cinema, as I sit with my single-size serving of popcorn, giving them filthy looks. I visualise flicking through the 'Solo club' holiday brochures.

I have a churning in my stomach, probably the mother-in-law of all hangovers brewing. It's ten o'clock already, and there's absolutely no chance that I'm going to work today.

'Screw it,' I tell Jess and go back to bed.

I reach into my bedside locker for a heavy duty painkiller to stop the marching band that is clumping its way through my delicate head. As I check my phone again for missed calls, my suspicions are confirmed: Barry doesn't even care if I am dead or alive.

The doorbell rings. Jesus effing Christ, I can't face anyone. Not even the postman. An overly enthusiastic Jehovah Witness could push me over the edge. Make them go away!

The persistent knocking on the door continues.

'*Barry*?'

My hopes rise for a second. Surely he would use his keys.

'Ian?'

Nah. It's nowhere near lunchtime. There's no way that slovenly ape would be conscious and dressed at such an hour. He's more likely to be lecture dodging in his smelly flat in Rathmines, or passed out on someone's sofa following a heavy night on the Dutch Gold. Also, he doesn't care enough to visit.

'Mum.'

The unrelenting nagging at the door is too annoying to be anyone else. I can hear her fumbling for keys. A quick glance in the mirror reveals my worst fears: I'm hideous. There's nothing quite so depressing as your own mother seeing you look pathetic. You know that the bed head, dressing gown and puffy eyes are going to make her look at you with that pitiful smile, and make her think *What a mess.*

I open the door and squint at the searing November morning sunlight. Mum is standing in the doorway. At five foot two, she's only a squinchy thing, but is carrying a hefty box of groceries.

'Jesus,' I whine. 'What time is it? What…'

'Here, darling. Give us a hand with this stuff, will you? I doubt you've eaten properly. So, did you sort things out with Barry, then? Not by the looks of you.'

I reluctantly stand aside to let the groceries in.

'Thanks,' I mumble under my breath as she surveys the sitting room. She eyes up the dirty glasses, chocolate wrappers and empty bottles of wine. A small gasp escapes her lips.

'The place is a mess, Rebecca. And you look pale…'

'Nice to see you too!'

I roll my eyes like a belligerent teenager.

'And thin.'

'Thanks.'

'That's not what I meant. I see you didn't go to work, then?'

'Hardly!'

I've never really appreciated up until this very moment in time just how undeniably annoying this woman truly is.

'Hmm. Still wallowing, then, I see. Now, your father and I have been talking…'

'Oh, God…'

'Well it's a difficult time for you, I suppose, and you know how you get uptight…'

She clicks on the kettle and starts clearing away some of the debris.

'Barry still hasn't called...' My lower lip trembles.

'You'll sort it out. Don't be worrying. Now, would you like to see Dr Logan?' Mum gets straight to the point of her visit. This is followed by an icy silence. I notice that she's putting far too much sugar into my tea.

'These will help you to ...' she chooses her words carefully '... chill.'

Mum has been picking up on Ian's lingo again. Next thing you know, she'll be saying things like 'totes' and 'amaze-balls'. I smirk as a small brown plastic bottle with a typed white label is thrust into my hand.

'Take one with your tea, darling.'

Mum scurries into her Nissan Micra and reverses out of the driveway. I watch her drive away at a student driver pace. When I unclench my fist and peer at the white label on the plastic bottle, I make out the word 'Valium'.

'Oh, this is shameful,' I grin. 'My own mother thinks I need medicating! Next she'll be carting me away to a high dependence unit!'

I swallow two pills straight away with the sweet tea.

'Might as well give them a whirl.'

Poor Mum has put up with me and my moods all of these years. I feel sorry for her. The most challenging time must have been the teenage hormone-fuelled Goth years, when I blatantly *refused* to wear any other colour but black – even pyjamas. My hair colour and lipstick were also black (wearing dark purple was also acceptable once I was a more established Goth and had earned my stripes).

I used to listen to maudlin music by The Cure alone in my bedroom, painted my room – you've guessed it – black, and hung posters of Robert Smith. Generally, I was a pain in the ass to live with. Mum had said nothing. She had even tolerated the phase where I only dated drummers called Mark. That's a long story, but let's just say it often involved Mum lying awake until four o'clock in the morning waiting for the sound of my key fumbling in the door.

Other than that, I was a doll. I wonder what on earth my mother has anti-anxiety pills for. What does she possibly have to be anxious about? Her life is a bed of roses compared to the stresses and pressures of my life. She doesn't even work any more. She has no demanding boss asking for annoying reports and quizzing her about missing stationery, unexplained sick leave and tardiness. Could baking bloody buns all day make you in need of prescription pills? The pills must be because of having Ian for a son.

I'm picturing Mum with Dr Logan, who had prescribed them for her. He's a real pal because he prescribes anything you ask for, and writes you a sickie cert to excuse you from work while he's at it. I'll take full advantage of his generous nature and call him if I can't face my boss Harry for the rest of the week. I'll squeeze out a few tears and say that my boss is bullying me and that my boyfriend is a pig. 'Oh stress,' he'll say. 'Terrible thing. Take the rest of the week off.'

The dishwasher is full, and I can't bring myself to tackle the dishes that have built up. It is still an unreasonable hour. I'm not in the mood to empty the bins which are crammed full of glass bottles and chocolate wrappers. Besides, that is technically Barry's job, and I shouldn't be expected to do his share of the housework. God, I miss him.

It might be my imagination, but the pills are starting to kick in nicely. I feel a bit cool and groovy. A heavy thud in the hall startles me. The postman has just delivered the post, and whistles as he hops over the fence into next door's garden. I pad over in my slippers, mismatched socks and dressing gown ensemble and freeze as I recognise the contents on the hall floor.

There, in all its glory, is my monthly subscription to *Confetti*. This, my beloved wedding magazine, is like a knife through my heart, and I sob with heavy tears. To add salt to the wounds, it's an extra special edition with a large pull-out feature on top wedding venues that I have been looking forward to for months!

Feeling dizzy, I lie down on the couch. Perhaps taking two of those pills was too much? Or maybe I should have another one to steady me? At a time like this, a girl needs Michael Bolton's greatest hits. I reach over to the stereo and pop in a CD. 'How Can We Be Lovers' blasts out. Michael understands me, he feels my pain. It's probably because he's had much experience in the heartbreak department.

Thirteen

Barry feels his hangover kick in as soon as he painfully opens his eyes. His mind reaches for the details of last night, but hits a blank. All he knows for sure is that he had too much to drink, and that he will pay the price dearly. His head thumps as he turns it to the left. There's a neat little shape breathing softly, curled to face the wall. A single sheet clings to her slim frame. She's wearing a silk camisole. Barry sits up in the bed and puts his hands over his mouth.

No!

He's wide awake now and frantic. Shelley stirs beside him but thankfully remains asleep. It buys him some time to figure out what the hell has just happened. Reluctantly, he allows the highlight reel to show the incriminating acts of the night before. The pieces start to take shape. There was whiskey with the clients, he can barely remember that. There was a nightclub, a seedy, sleazy nightclub somewhere in Bangkok. He was dancing. Everyone knows that Barry doesn't dance. There were Blue Elephant cocktails. They are probably called that because they contain enough blue liquor to knock out said elephant. There was a taxi, there was a mini bar. There was Shelley, on top of him on the bed.

Oh, God!

On the floor of the hotel room, Barry can make out empty packets and discarded glass bottles from the mini bar. The fridge

96

door is wide open and the contents have been cleared. There's a sinister dark patch on the carpet next to a spilled bottle of beer. Like his cheating, no amount of scrubbing will get the stain out now.

Barry thinks about Rebecca. *Yes, she has been a major pain in the ass of late, and yes she has gone completely insane with wedding fever. But she doesn't deserve this. She deserves so much better. She's at home right now, probably fretting over our relationship, shoving chocolates into her mouth and watching soap operas, unaware of what is unfolding here behind her back.*

Barry can hear sirens on the street below. Bangkok is hot and sticky, it's only the air conditioning in the hotel that creates an illusion of comfort. Some of Barry's friends were envious when he told them of his impending trip to Thailand for the conference. They had been to Bangkok and Phuket backpacking in their twenties, and had wild stories to tell. They had possibly copied and pasted some scenes from *The Beach* and had grand visions of themselves, like Leonardo DiCaprio, prancing around paradise in a drug-fuelled haze.

Well, so far, Barry is not impressed. Frankly, he doesn't know what all the fuss is about. The exotic spice markets and luxurious white sand beaches might as well be a million miles away. Apart from last night, he hadn't left the hotel. He's like a captured bird in a golden cage. All of the eating, sleeping and client schmoozing takes place under the same roof. Although it's a five-star international business hotel, he might as well be in a prison.

The hotel has an Olympic-sized heated swimming pool and an award-winning state-of-the-art gym. He read about it in the brochure. However, Barry has neither the time nor the will to investigate either. The hotel also boasts modern art deco design and ground-breaking sculptures, but Barry hasn't the energy to notice this.

The conference had started yesterday. Clearly Sunday was not a day of rest here. Fat chance! He's exhausted, there has been no opportunity to acclimatise and adjust to the time difference. No opportunity to get over the jet lag.

Hours of smiling, nodding and general ass licking with Asian businessmen has left him wiped out. So far, the days here are long – business breakfasts at dawn bleed into working lunches that are followed by lengthy small talk over dinner. Finally, cognac and cigars are expected in the lounge.

Barry slips out of bed and into the bathroom. His reflection in the mirror is grim, dark circles framing bloodshot eyes. He's in his late thirties now, and no Don Juan. What he did was wrong. So very wrong. He has to sort this mess out.

Barry glances over at Shelley. Why has he allowed this to happen? What the hell was he thinking? He tries to understand how he could do such a thing to Rebecca. He has been drinking too much. Shelley kept reminding him of all the things Rebecca has done. She had told him that when she saw Rebecca at last year's work Christmas party she bent everyone's ear about getting married. She had said that Nigel thinks she's a bimbo. She had said that Rebecca doesn't care about him and is only after the big day. It's all lies. It's all fucking lies.

The deluxe hotel suite is beautifully furnished and has ample room. There is 24-hour room service and satellite TV. Barry can enjoy none of this. He's riddled with guilt. This thing with Shelley is getting way out of hand. He's a snake in the grass. Barry hasn't even called Rebecca yet and he's worried he will never hear the end of it. He needs a second to think, to work this all out. It's time to end this fiasco.

Shelley rolls over.

'Hey. Good morning, sunshine,' she purrs.

'Morning,' Barry mumbles, unable to meet her eyes.

Shelley is out of the shower and humming while she applies her make-up. She applies it thick and Barry sees that without it she is pale. Barry dresses as fast as he can and while Shelley is in the bathroom, eager to get away from her.

'Better get down for the breakfast meeting,' he hurries Shelley out the door.

Barry can't put his finger on it. There's something very annoying about Shelley. Was her voice always like nails on a chalkboard? Was her perfume always so sickeningly sweet? Was her eyeliner always so sloppily applied?

Fourteen

Paranoia creeps in as I blow snot into a ragged tissue and place it back into my grubby fleece dressing gown pocket. What if Barry doesn't come home to me? What if he meets someone else?

I've a sudden, overwhelming craving for ice-cream. Luckily, I keep some lush Magnum XXL dark chocolate lovelies stashed at the bottom of the freezer, so I polish one off. Just as well, the Valium mustn't be taken on an empty stomach. Besides, ice-cream for brunch is a middle finger to Debbie. Herself and the Slimmers' Club can well and truly go jump off a bridge today.

Would Barry really leave me for someone else? I don't recall any suspicious phone calls, excessive aftershave wearing, or any inkling of a seedy affair. The truth is that mostly it's hard to get Barry off the couch. Between his day job and all the chores and DIY I have him do around the house, he would hardly have the energy for an affair. I mean, sometimes he has difficulty removing himself from the sitting room fast enough to catch the microwave popcorn before it burns. Every evening at six he reports home, like a faithful Labrador at dinner time. He does his chores, removes his shoes and tie, and then sprawls horizontally on the La-Z-Boy recliner like a washed up walrus.

With a wave of nausea, I suddenly realise that I've failed to explain my absence from work. By now, my boss will surely be wondering where I am. I swallow another couple of Valium – you know, in case the others have worn off – and dial the work number.

'Good afternoon, Sloan Publicity! Suzie speaking!'

Suzie's freakishly cheerful tone is unmistakeable. It's not normal for a woman in her forties to sound like Elmo from *Sesame Street*. I also take issue with her overly jolly nature, it's suspicious. We weren't all up at dawn attending a Pilates class!

'Good morning. It's Rebecca.'

I'm scrambling for an excuse to explain my absence. I've used the dental appointment/period pains/dead uncle already this month, so I need to think quickly. I opt for the miserable truth.

'Rebecca, hi! Isn't it a gorgeous day out there! So fresh and crisp.'

What the hell is she so bloody chirpy about? If she were a budgie of mine, I'd leave a dark cloth over her cage to stop her from cheep cheeping all day long. Then I'd leave the cage door and a large window open accidentally on purpose. You can practically hear the exclamation mark at the end of her sentences.

'I had a fight with my boyfriend,' I say.

I throw in a snuffle for good effect, as I can produce crocodile tears on demand. As I said, it's a gift from God that I use at will.

'Oh, no. I was wondering what happened to you. Thought maybe you'd lost track of time again.'

'Time?'

I'm on the verge of hysteria, like an acrobat walking the thin line. There's a shake in my voice, but I'm unable to control it.

'As if at a time like this…' I wipe my wet nose in my fleece dressing gown '…I would be *aware of time.*'

An uncomfortable pause on the phone follows.

'Time,' I explain, 'stopped when Barry boarded a plane for Taiwan after we had a huge row, and now I haven't even heard from him.'

'Right. So, not coming in, then?'

I rub my temple. Does this woman have the intellect of a pre-schooler as well as the voice? Too bloody right I'm not coming in. My dream wedding might not be going ahead, and I've no reason to go on. I might drink myself into a desperate oblivion, so excuse me if I can't face stationery orders this morning!

'Tell Harry I'm sick.'

I speak feebly and manage a pathetic and strategically placed cough for good measure. Suzie reluctantly agrees. If our company had a 'mental health' day I'd have taken one. Sadly, they don't, which is heartless in my opinion. Harry had called it a 'silly American thing'. In fact, if the company had an 'I've-got-a-deposit-on-a-honeymoon-and-may-never-get-to-go-on-it, so-I-can't-face-you-people' day, I'd have taken one of those as well.

Harry is not the most sensitive of souls. My mother once told me 'If you can't say anything nice about someone, then don't say anything at all' and, of course, I'm not one to say nasty things. Let's just say that the man is a total troll, and I'll say no more about it.

I tell myself not to worry; I'll deal with Harry *mañana*. I have enough to deal with, what with Barry's desertion and possibly not loving me any more (to be confirmed at a later date, possibly with a lie detector test and the expert help of Jeremy Kyle). There has still been no call from Barry, and his mobile is switched off. I know this because, to my shame, I tried it several times this morning. I've become persistent, like Sky News: on the hour every hour. Each time I build up the courage to dial, I get his voicemail.

I have a desperate urge to speak to Judy. If it wasn't for her presence in the office, going to work every day would be a total nightmare. Suzie transfers the call to Judy, and 'Flying Without Wings' by Westlife is the hold music. I'm choking back the tears big time, especially at the Shane Filan part that goes 'Well for me it's waking up beside you, to watch the sunrise on your face'. Along with the singing, I've got the dramatic hand gestures and eye squeezing. Do you know the song? Of course you do. It's a classic.

'Rebecca?' Judy whispers into the receiver. 'Are you OK? Suzie filled me in. Said you had a fight with Barry. God!'

That wretched receptionist! In the space of two sodding minutes, Suzie has spread the gossip like wildfire. No doubt the entire office knows my personal details now, thanks to Susie blabbermouth.

Judy gets the full low-down, and listens to every word. It's just as well, really, I've coached her through some pretty messy break-ups during our time working together. It's definitely her turn to play counsellor. Judy joined the company from a temping agency over a year ago, and has just never left. I think the agency kind of forgot about her. We're inseparable, Judy and I, she just *gets me*. She's my confidante, my bitching partner, my go-to girl. She's also my ass coverer. If anyone calls for me at, say, four o'clock on a Thursday when I'm having my roots done and a quick blow-dry, she answers my phone with a brisk 'She's in the loo.' Harry suspects that I suffer with a rare bowel disorder or something, and is far too mortified to quiz me on it.

Judy's sick leave record is even worse than mine. I'm lucky to have caught her in attendance, working on a Monday is against her religion. Naturally, I often return the favour if she is monstrously hungover, for example.

Judy's desk is next to mine, which means we can carry on like giggling naughty school children. My constant sniggering and twittering with Judy tends to be at the top of the agenda at many performance review meetings with Harry, no matter how hard I try to convince him that we're strictly talking about work. Harry says he fails to see what we find so 'absolutely hilarious' about invoices.

Judy and I had set up Instant Messaging on our computers, so even when we weren't talking to each other out loud, we were tapping away on our keyboards and guffawing. This way, we could look ultra busy, feverishly typing away while keeping the other abreast of important celebrity breaking news or sending smart ass messages such as: '*Get a load of his tie – YUK! LOL!*' Harry, like a frustrated school principal, once tried to separate our work desks. Judy had taken it up with the Human Resources department (i.e. Brendan, who fancies her rotten), and the matter was dropped. After that, our chatting continued uninterrupted. It had been a mini triumph, and a chance to stick it to the man.

'So what happened, babes?'

'Well, after the massive row, he went off to, like, Calcutta or somewhere on a conference and we haven't spoken since. Says he needs space from me,' I sob as Judy listens intently.

'Absolutely. Uh huh. Yes, right away. Certainly, I'll email that to you.'

Judy parrots the familiar script briskly. This is our well rehearsed code for 'Harry is breathing down my neck', so we hang up.

In the living room, the cat is under my feet and I trip over him. Come to think of it, he has been meowing in my face all morning.

'What's wrong, Mr Jess?'

A thunderbolt hits me. The poor moggy hasn't been fed in a day. I've been so self-absorbed and selfish that I'd forgotten. Now, on top of my flaky boyfriend, my cat will probably desert me too! I spoon some tuna fish stuff into a dish.

'There. It's just you and me now, Jess.'

The chunky feline wolfs the lot in two seconds flat, nearly asphyxiating on it, and waddles off towards the couch without as much as a backwards glance.

'Eh, you're welcome!'

I decide to stick with pyjamas as the Dress Code Du Jour. What's the point of clothes? I've heard nothing from Pam, apart from another text reminding me to forget about Barry and move on. She has apparently hit it off with Brian from speed dating. Trust her to meet someone new and abandon me in my hour of need!

Emer has called twice; the general gist of our lengthy conversations was that Barry needs more time, and that I've got to stop pushing him. Mum has checked on me on her way to and from various parish commitments. Earlier, she delivered a care package with delicious Marks & Spencer's grub, and hoovered around me as I lay in my own crisp packet and Kleenex sodden filth.

The only thing that raises the faintest of smiles is reading my *Celebrity Chat* magazine and catching up on the latest relationship catastrophe of Kerry Katona. She always has a way of making me feel superior. Eventually, I can't cry any more. Even Dr Phil's TV special on reuniting broken families, usually a sob fest, has no effect. An episode of *Animal Hospital* featuring Millie the abandoned cat from Grimsby doesn't even produce a whimper. Can you imagine? The poor thing was starving! Some people can be so selfish! The well of tears has officially run dry.

Fifteen

By Tuesday morning, I'm forced to temporarily discard my grubby fleece pyjamas for a desperate Tesco run. Like old Mother Hubbard, the lack of essentials in my bare cupboards leaves me with no choice but to venture forth into the harsh world. The only things that I can scratch up for breakfast are some stale jelly sweets I found in my make-up drawer. I'm all out of staples such as crisps and alcohol, and have even eaten through the frozen food stash, so there's no way of avoiding a much needed trolley dash.

Praying that no-one will spot me, I've thrown on a grey (once black) well washed velour (Juicy Couture knock-off) hooded tracksuit. Upon inspection, I see that it has faded in the rump. I scrape my greasy hair into a bun and take one of Barry's old NYPD baseball caps to complete the tragic look.

I'm hoping that the distinct lack of make-up and use of massive sunglasses will cunningly disguise me. A glimpse of my reflection in the hall mirror as I grab my car keys tells me that I'm like one of those shockingly awful women that you see in the 'Celebrities exposed without their make-up' features in the tabloids. Except this time, it isn't the world laughing at poor sad Pam Anderson sans airbrushing, this is the world laughing at poor sad Rebecca Browne.

My car takes up two parking spaces in the Tesco car park. Frankly, I can't be bothered to correct it. I've skipped the salad aisle and made a beeline for the junk aisle. As I load up my favourites, I feel a sense of calm sweep over me. Cheese puffs, microwave popcorn, frozen waffles, white wine, shortbread cookies, ice-cream, rum and nachos fill my trolley. God knows I deserve it all, thank you very much!

For calorie balance purposes, I've added a six-pack of Diet Coke to the trolley. There's also some tomato salsa, you know, for one of my five a day. Soon, I'll be safely back in my dark cave devouring these beauties, and it'll be just in time to catch an *EastEnders* bust-up between Bianca and Rickaaaay.

'Hello there.'

A smug voice directly behind startles me. Cringing, I turn and silently beg that nobody has recognised me. Perhaps I've been mistaken for a degenerate, or a cast member of *EastEnders*.

'Bernie.'

I grit my teeth in an effort at a false smile, whilst repeating a mantra over and over in my mind: *You absolute cow, you absolute cow, you absolute cow*. My gossiping next-door neighbour has been no doubt privy to the intimate details of our recent arguing, thanks to the cardboard-like quality of the walls. She's the last person I want to meet.

'How *are* you?'

Her head is tipped to the side in mock sympathy. '…and *poor Barry*?'

Poor Barry, indeed! Like a fish, I open my mouth, but nothing comes out. I scramble for something witty to say, something cutting to really shut her up. Something scrappy that I can regale my girlfriends with over a cocktail.

'Gosh, what's that dreadful *smell*?'

Bernie sniffs, oblivious to the havoc that her two demon children are causing as they knock over a cereal display.

'The onions must have gone off,' she continues, smiling.

We're nowhere near the vegetable aisle, and I feel myself perspiring profusely.

'I…' I attempt, clearing my throat '…not feeling well…'

My voice trails off and Bernie nods as she stares directly at the contents of my trolley and then squints her eyes. The Bored Housewife Club will be thrilled with this nugget of gossip.

'Barry is away on business, uh, Japan.'

I steer my trolley in the opposite direction, and plan an escape route, but my exit is blocked by the kids.

'Mammy, what's *this*?' Katie whines.

Shane then kicks me in the shin for no apparent reason, and with no parental correction, I might add. We'll no doubt watch some poor unfortunate victim identify the brat in a police line-up on *Crime Line* in a few years.

As I turn to see what Katie has fished out of my trolley, I think momentarily that I'm going to faint. I've got to steady myself on the ketchup aisle. She waves a large bottle of Captain Morgan rum in front of her smirking mother. Captain Morgan clutches his queasy stomach as the ponytailed girl continues to shake the bottle up and down. Enough is enough. I snatch the bottle of rum from the unruly child and place it into her mother's hands.

'Here,' I utter in a superior manner, whilst looking her children up and down. 'I think you need this more than I do.'

Her face is aghast, which gives me great satisfaction. With that, I turn on my heel (or rather, scruffy runners) and make my way to the check-out in a hurry before she has a chance to respond.

Having to queue for an intolerable amount of time on a Tuesday morning in your local supermarket is simply not acceptable. I'm shuffling impatiently and mentally drafting a strongly worded memo to the store manager.

Dear Jason/Wayne/Brad/Brittney/Tiffany (circle as appropriate),

It's OK for mummies (the likes of Bernie from next door and her delinquent youths) and unemployed people (with nothing better to do than waste time before watching Jeremy

Kyle) *to queue. Their unimportant purchases of cornflakes,*
teabags and toilet bleach are of no importance.

However, please note that some of us have jobs and a
busy life to consider. Some of us have relationships that are
hanging in the balance, with shredded nerves and deposits
on five-star honeymoons!

I urge you to introduce a separate check-out for gainfully
employed tax payers.

Yours scathingly,
Rebecca Browne

I've scanned the area for a suggestion box, but can't spot one.
There's only one self-service check-out, and a staff member is
helping a man with an 'unexpected item in the bagging area'. I've
no choice but to join a long queue. An elderly lady fumbles with
copper coins, separating them from lint and buttons. A mother
of three snot-nosed mono-brow tots scrambles for coupons for
money off nappies whilst trying to bribe her unruly tribe with a
six-pack of Monster Munch. I'm about to explode.

Finally, I'm next in line to unload my groceries onto the conveyor
belt. I close my eyes. Soon, I'll return to the comfort of the telly and
a freshly stocked fridge. I'll close the curtains to keep the world and
its annoying inhabitants out. Perhaps I may even have a lie down
after my blood-boiling run-in with fifty shades of blabbermouth.
I'll pour myself a stiff one as soon as I'm through the front door.

The peroxide check-out girl with dark roots has the absolute
nerve to point out that she is unable to sell me alcohol. At first, I
think that perhaps I'm so young looking that I'll have to rummage
around in my purse and produce some sort of ID to show that I'm
old enough to buy booze. The unwashed greasy hair and tracksuit
hoodie combo is making me look like a student. I'm rocking the
slum dog look. Feeling rather flattered, I rifle through lipstick and
ragged tissues in order to find my wallet and find the appropriate
documentation.

'Sorry. It's been a while since I was asked...'

'I can't sell you alcohol at this time of the *morning*,' the girl deadpans, and in far too high a decibel if you ask me. Clearly, she has no discretion.

The proverbial penny drops, and I clutch at my diamanté watch. At twenty past ten in the morning, it's probably a social taboo, not to mention illegal, to attempt to purchase enough alcohol to:

a) drown yourself in a large bathtub of rum
b) party like it's 1999.

At first, all I can manage is 'Oh...' while I gather my thoughts and take in the scene around me. The queue has grown, and many eyes burn into me. It's as if the whole supermarket is watching me, judging me. The crowd shares a unanimous thought:

Look at the state of her. Her boyfriend left her and she hasn't washed her hair in bloody days. She pulled a sickie from work and is shopping like her parents are away for the weekend.

'This is ridiculous! What an absolute farce.'

I'm back on my high horse, now. It feels good. 'This is discrimination!'

Discrimination against what, I'm not entirely sure. As my cheeks blaze, I insist on speaking to the manager this very *instant*. Unsurprisingly, the manager (called Jason, apparently – told you so) is 'on his lunch'. At this hour of the morning, that's a highly unlikely story. I'm picturing a spotty youth cliché with polyester black trousers and a name badge on an ill-fitting polyester white shirt that his mammy has ironed for him.

I decide to take the matter up with check-out girl directly. In a hushed voice, I lean forward in an attempt at privacy and explain, as calmly as I can in my current mental state, that I don't plan on drinking it until lunchtime *anyway*. I flash my best smile to appeal to her human nature.

It would appear that she is devoid of human nature. Undeterred, and in a louder voice, she again reminds me of the law. It's as if I'm a hardened criminal like the ones I see on *Brookside* repeats, trying to score some crack or whatever it is that they call hard drugs these days, and bury a relative under the patio while I'm at it. She's treating me like some ruffian badgering her for spare change whilst clutching my wine in a paper bag on a bridge in the inner city. How horrid.

Perhaps my current attire and grubby demeanour confuses her. Perhaps she doesn't realise that I'm a well respected executive (OK, executive assistant) with a college education (OK, an arts degree) who is simply having a bad day, and needs to restock the fridge whilst nursing a broken heart. It's an understandable mistake.

The snooty teenager on the till then points a chipped black nail-polished finger at a sign above the check-out. I can feel my throat become swollen and sore, tears threatening to appear at any moment. The hordes behind me shuffle and sigh with crossed arms. Well, they'll just have to wait. I throw the shoppers a dagger look.

Deadpan Deirdre (I'm going to suggest changing her name tag once I locate the suggestion box) doesn't understand. No-one does.

'Listen, Deirdre. My boyfriend shagged off to Beijing. I can't be expected to be conscious of the law regarding sale of alcohol. Quite frankly, it's a miracle that I'm conscious at all!'

She reaches for a button under the till, and calls urgently for her supervisor, whose lunch must have suddenly come to a premature end. She may have been tragically born without a personality, but she sure can turn on the dramatics when she wants to.

I leave the supermarket in tears, the junk food in a carrier bag which drags at my heel. Bernie, smirking at the back of the queue, has mentally recorded the whole debacle. No doubt, the whole affair will be replayed frame by frame, along with my alleged harassment of her beloved offspring in the aisles, to her slackjawed Stay-At-Home-Mammy club members over tea and Jaffa Cakes. They'll brand me an alcoholic diva with questionable hygiene standards, and look down their noses at me from now on.

My hands shake, as I load the groceries into the boot and turn the key in the ignition. Metallica blasts from my car stereo. I'm in a foul mood now and can't wait to crawl back into my cave, so I put my foot down on the accelerator and crank up the volume.

Bernie's car has been parked right beside mine. My passenger door clunks as it hits off her driver's door, and I take her wing mirror clean off when I reverse. Not, like, on purpose or anything.

My phone lights up with an incoming call from Pam, and I juggle the steering wheel to answer it. Did I ever tell you that I am an expert multi-tasker? I can also navigate a roundabout whilst playing air guitar to Status Quo.

Pam launches into the intimate details of her hot new romance, and I try to tell her about my pig of a day. I'm starting to see the funny side of the Tesco debacle. By now, Bernie will have discovered her wing mirror, like road kill on the ground.

Our good old chinwag is then rudely interrupted by blue flashing lights, so I pull over. As I peep over my sunglasses, I notice the smeared black mascara panda eyes. I turn the volume down on the stereo to a tolerable level and roll down the window.

'Do you *mind*?' I ask. 'I'm in the middle of a very important phone call!'

The tall slim man in a navy Garda vest and hat doesn't seem to care about my important phone call. He seems more interested in some Road Traffic Act 2006 or other, and is really banging on about it for some reason. In between yawning, I catch the words 'dangerous driving' and 'failure to comply'. Ludicrous!

'Look. If this is about the wing mirror, I can explain.'

'What wing mirror?'

'Nothing.' I'm an expert at talking, but I know when to shut up.

The big meanie then goes on to insult my driving by saying that I have violated the law by speeding, and that this is a punishable offence. To add salt to the wounds, he also points out the fact that I'm not wearing a seatbelt, and that I'm not meant to be talking on the phone whilst driving. He's really nit picking, now; he must have it in for me. He says that he has a good mind to escort me to the Garda station right this very minute.

'This whole thing is getting way out of hand,' I butt in.

The Garda continues with his list of offences.

'What speed were you doing?' the nasty bully demands in a very serious tone. This must be police brutality, he didn't even say please!

'*Speed?*'

I'm all of a fluster and tut in frustration. This guy is seriously starting to tick me off.

'How am I supposed to know that?'

I roll my eyes. I mean, I can't be expected to check my lipstick in the mirror, hold a full conversation with a gal pal *and* look at the speedometer. I'm not Wonder Woman, for goodness' sake.

Admittedly, I do tend to be a touch Speedy Gonzalez behind the wheel. At least that's what Mum calls it, but she has never driven faster than fifty kilometres per hour, so it's a biased opinion and therefore rubbish. Hopefully, without a speed camera, the officer has nothing on me. He can't prove a thing.

It's best not to confide in him that I'm suffering from a broken heart and that I worry that I may never get to wear my Vera Wang original. He's not giving off very understanding vibes. The sad fact of the matter is that I've no excuses to explain my behaviour. There's no pregnant lady in the throes of labour in the back seat, or blood-smeared toddler screaming in a car seat with half a finger hanging off on our way to the A&E department. I'm not even late for a hair appointment!

Tears prove ineffective, and my pleas of having a bad day fall on deaf ears. I've no choice but to admit defeat.

'I know my rights.'

There's a slight tremble in my voice. I could be in a lot of trouble, here, but the light at the end of the tunnel is that if this goes to court, I have just the right outfit!

With any luck, he'll breathalyse me. Thanks to the supermarket, this is one test I know I'm bound to win. I could rub it in his smug face when the little light alco-test thingy reads zero. Then again, there's been enough alcohol in my bloodstream these last few days to knock out a horse, so it'd be best not to suggest it.

The poker-faced man asks for my driver's licence, which is buried in my purse. It's hiding amongst so much rubble that it takes a bit of effort to find. I'm searching frantically through tampons and several shades of lipsticks, and the Garda's face is like Simon Cowell during a cringey audition.

'Tah dah!'

I thrust the document into his outstretched hand. The Garda looks from my face to the driver's licence and then back again. In front of him, I'm like a junkie coming back from the dole office in a tracksuit and unwashed hair, probably smelling like an armpit at closing time in Club 92. In the licence photograph, I'm coiffed, manicured and posed. My white teeth glisten and my make-up is flawless. You see, I have my photos airbrushed by a pal who works in the *Irish Daily Sun* newspaper – no point in taking chances on a snapshot that is to be used for formal identification. I don't want to be stuck with a dodgy mug shot for the next ten years.

'I don't usually look like this,' I explain. Perhaps my toothy grin is starting to make him uncomfortable.

'Fine,' he scribbles something on an official-looking pad, and then hands the licence back to me. 'You know what? You should take the bus.'

'Bus?'

What on earth is this man talking about? I scrunch up my face at the thought.

'Bus?' I repeat. 'As in, like, public transport?'

This is some sort of attempt at a little jokey-poo, surely. I laugh uncomfortably, relieved to see that the police officer at least has a sense of humour.

'Ah, no,' I beam. 'No, I'm sure it's a lot of *fun* and all that, but I drive.'

'Is that what you'd call it?'

The Garda's face is unreadable, so I just grin.

After a stern telling-off about endangering the lives of others as well as myself, I'm allowed to drive away. Just before I go, he

114

mentions that I'll receive some sort of paperwork or other in the post. I let God have it.

Ah, God!

Now I'm going to be crucified with even more penalty points. Can you not cut me a bit of slack? Honestly, if you've shortlisted me for martyrdom, you'd better let me know. I'll have to declare the extra flipping points to some haughty telesales insurance rep down the phone, much to my total mortification. Barry will hit the roof when the insurance quote comes through. The row will be flipping biblical. You'll have to help me hide it from him. It's the least you can do!

Then the sad realisation sweeps over me like a thundering wave. Barry is thousands of miles away in, like, China or somewhere. I couldn't even locate him on a map. We have far bigger problems than penalty points.

I tiptoe up the driveway. Thankfully, there's no sign of any neighbours. Just to be safe, I'll have to remain indoors for the rest of my life. It's easy, really. I can just ask Harry if I can work from home and order my clothes, takeaways and cat food online.

Upon my teary entrance through the front door, a flash of genius hits me. It's like a drop of water in a drought-stricken Sub Saharan Africa. Barry, in his highly organised state and a full month ahead of the dreaded Christmas, had purchased whiskey, wine and Baileys for his clients. They're stashed in the spare bedroom wardrobe.

Ah, fair play to you, Jesus. I see you performed another miracle. Water to wine and all that, eh? Cheers!

Taking a swig of the lukewarm glass of white wine straight from the bottle, I feel steadier in an instant. Thank the Lord the bottles are all screw cap!

Sixteen

So far, Tuesday in Bangkok is the worst day on record. Day three of the conference has been gruelling and last night Barry had only managed to squeeze in five hours of sleep between backslapping over late-night brandies and economics chitchat over croissants at breakfast. The cigar smoke had given him an ice pick headache.

His mind has been firmly on Rebecca. He can't bring himself to call her. What would he say? A couple of vague texts are all he could manage. Until he clears things up with Shelley, he can't face her sweet voice on the phone. The guilt would be too much. He has switched his phone off for now. He excuses himself in between the spicy main course and the rich dessert in order to send an email to her.

At ten o'clock, Barry manages to escape to his room and lock the door behind him. He loosens his tie. In a funny way, he's grateful that today's pace was cruel. It meant that he managed to avoid Shelley all day. The bed is gloriously empty. He doesn't have to listen to Shelley ask 'What are you thinking?' He doesn't have to endure her asking probing questions about Rebecca and then criticising her. He won't have to listen as she starts every sentence with 'Hey'. What the hell is that about? That's teenager lingo, and he hates that about her now with a passion. Ditto the laughing at everything that he says. Surely, he is not *that* funny!

For the last couple of days, Barry has managed to avoid Shelley by pretending to be engrossed in conversation with the clients. For the last couple of nights, he has managed to slip back to his hotel room before Shelley can corner him.

Barry's stomach churns. It might be the excessive foreign food or it might be the guilt, or a sickening mixture of both. The rich spicy food is not in agreement with his delicate Celtic digestive system. He can't pronounce the names half of the dishes. Most of them are served with noodles and there is not a chip to be found.

Despite his best efforts, Barry has become accustomed to Rebecca's home cooking – if you can call it cooking, that is. Rebecca tends to burn the food to an almost unrecognisable degree, but it's amazing how you get to enjoy the taste of charcoal after a while. Her cuisine features still-frozen-in-the-middle chips and burnt battered cod. Ketchup accompanies every meal, and chicken nuggets feature heavily on the dinner menu. On special occasions, she does cremated potato wedges and cement-thick beans. Not exactly cordon bleu. Often, she rings the local Indian takeaway. This, she claims, is in order to take a break from 'slaving over a hot deep fat flyer'. It's a diet better suited to a picky three year old, but Barry smiles as he thinks about it.

Barry rubs his stomach and reaches for an antacid from his suitcase. That last curry was literally made of hell fire and chillies. He could swear that there was something fishy winking at him underneath the noodles, he just wasn't brave enough to investigate it further and simply pushed it around his plate a lot with his chopstick. He knows it will go right through him. What he wouldn't give right now for a scorched pizza and waffles, heavy on the ketchup, curled up with Rebecca watching another episode of *Pet Rescue*.

The constant coffee throughout the day is strong and bitter, but necessary to keep him awake. The booze in the evenings helps him slip into a deep dreamless sleep. Barry discards his suit on the floor and sinks into the deep soft mattress. So far, he has barely had a minute to think about his fight with Rebecca or how to fix things. All he knows is that they will iron things out when he's back on Irish soil. He has to. He can't imagine a future without her in it. He'll sort this whole mess with Shelley out tomorrow. Exhaustion takes over.

A light knocking on the door grows more impatient, and Barry stirs.

'Rebecca?' he calls out. 'Is that you?'

Barry rubs his eyes and squints at the digital alarm clock. It's only eleven o'clock. He must have just closed his eyes for a few minutes, but he feels as though he is coming out of a deep coma.

The knocking persists. 'Hey! Barry! It's Shelley.'

'Damn.' Barry is snapped back to reality.

If he stays quiet, maybe she'll go away. Shelley knocks again and calls his name. Barry is fully awake now, and doesn't want Nigel to stumble upon Shelley in the hall and connect the dots. He snatches the door open and motions her in quickly. He's tired and irritable. This is not going to just go away, so he had better get this over with quickly – like a Band-Aid on an open wound.

'Hey. You keep rushing off. I haven't seen you properly in days!'

'Yeah, sorry. Been hectic.'

'Sooooo…' Shelley smiles.

Barry notices that she has a bottle of champagne in one hand and a plate of chocolate-dipped strawberries in the other. 'I thought you could use some company.'

Barry is more in the mood for a root canal, but decides to get this over with. He tries to use what shred of tact he can find.

'Listen, Shelley…' Barry trips over his words.

This is worse than root canal. At least you get an anaesthetic for that. At least you get sympathy afterwards. Here, he's just the bad guy.

'This trip. It's been… intense.'

'Hey. Absolutely.'

Shelley is still grinning, completely oblivious to what is coming next. Barry's words will be like a gloved punch to the face, knocking her off her fluffy little hotel slippers and into the lobby.

'And you and I are friends, right?'

'Right. Good friends,' she winks.

'Yeah, but, we need to talk.'

Shelley has spotted the boxing gloves.

'I don't remember what happened the other night, but things got out of hand. I think it's best that we remain friends. Just friends.'

She can hear the bell and the crowd screaming. The bikini-clad model holds up the board. Round one to Barry, ding ding!

'So, you just have your fun and then, what… that's it? Back to Rebecca? Back to that …' Shelley is standing very close to Barry now '… that…Bridezilla!'

Barry shakes his head at the insult to Rebecca. 'Ouch,' shouts the referee. 'That was below the belt.'

'Look. The other night, after the club? It was a mistake. I was drunk. Really drunk. I can't even remember much. I was wrong, and I'm sorry. I'm going to try and make it work with Rebecca.'

'Hey, that's fine. Good luck to you on that one. You deserve each other!'

Shelley stalks out of the room, taking the champagne and chocolate strawberries with her.

Barry exhales in relief. At least now he can finally think straight. At least now he can try and sort out the mess at home. Finally at midnight, he wearily climbs back into the king-sized bed and falls into a deep sleep. He dreams about the scent of Rebecca's perfumed hair as she snuggles next to him on his leather La-Z-Boy recliner back home. He dreams about tripping up over the cat, and black-and-still-frozen-in-the-middle chips and beans that taste faintly of charcoal. But most of all, he dreams about Rebecca. Sweet, funny, caring, infuriating Rebecca.

Seventeen

I've managed to avoid the shower, my hairbrush and any reflective surfaces for two days now. It's best to avoid answering the door to anyone other than Mum, due to my shocking appearance.

Even Jess is getting sick of me, and that's rich coming from someone who licks themselves clean with a kitty cat smelly tongue. He snubs me as I try to rub him, and his rejection stings.

Barry is still silent, and my mobile phone has been glued to my hand at every waking moment. I'm swinging between hating and loving him all over again. I've started to nurse a fantasy that perhaps he couldn't concentrate in the conference, and decided to come home to me, but something bad happened to him. It goes a little something like this:

Barry has landed in Dublin airport and is making his way towards the long-term car park. He holds a bunch of lilies, my favourite flowers, and a jumbo box of Ferrero Rocher in one hand, a magnum of Cristal and a begging love letter in the other: this impairs his driving skills as he veers onto the M50 and heads towards home, desperate to patch things up. But then *bang*! An articulated truck smashes into his car, glass from headlights and hubcaps scattering all over South County Dublin. My darling Barry bangs his head off the steering wheel. The concussion means that he has forgotten those crazy things I said and did, but remembers my face. He has also forgotten who he is, and has been parked in the amnesia wing of a hospital, complete with a gown that flaps open at the back. He's shuffling about and calling himself 'Edward'. Something similar happened in an episode of *Dallas* once and the lovers reunited as if nothing had happened.

This is the obvious explanation. The alternative is that he doesn't love me any more, and that's far too painful to deal with.

A paranoid thought surfaces. For all I know, Barry might never have gone to a conference. He might be lying in the arms of some floozy in Costa del Bray for all I know. Maybe he's at his desk in Ballsbridge, trying to figure out where this relationship is going. I need answers, so I drag myself towards the bedroom, lose a slipper on the stairs without noticing, throw a trench coat over my pyjamas, and head out the door. It's stakeout time.

I'm sitting in my parked car across from Hodges Myrtell and O'Brien solicitors, staring at the reception area. Like any self-respecting investigator, I've got a pair of binoculars for a proper peep. I'm wearing a dramatic black headscarf and a pair of designer dark glasses. It has to be said, this is a good look for me. When I catch a glimpse of myself in the rear view mirror, I smile. I'm like some money-grabbing grief-stricken widow out of *Knots Landing*. My fantasy is then crushed as I realise that I've just one pink slipper on, which explains my difficulty operating the pedals when driving. Well, you can't expect me to be fashion conscious at a time like this!

Barry might be somewhere inside that building. Maybe he's as distraught and dishevelled as I am, unable to pull himself together to attend the conference. Maybe he's unable to concentrate on his work and is slumped across a desk somewhere, calling my name in distress, a single tear rolling down his plump little unshaven face. Perhaps he's like Peter Andre on the Piers Morgan interview after his split with Katie Price, a shadow of a man spilling his guts and sobbing manly sobs.

After about twenty minutes there's still no sight of Barry. 80s FM plays Cliff Richard's classic hit 'We Don't Talk Anymore', and

I turn it up. I mean, I'm way too cool to be a Cliff Richard fan, I like him *ironically*. A couple of teenagers across the road at a nearby bus stop spot me and giggle, so I hurriedly roll up the windows and start the engine. I'm bored now, and desperate for the loo. Also, I'm starting to think that this is what people mean when they use the word stalking.

It's time to face the music. Two days of calling in sick to work are enough for any boss to tolerate. Harry has his limits, and my cards have definitely been marked over the last few months. After last month's alleged tummy bug, my P45 will arrive in the post if I don't get my act together, and that will be devastating. Although I don't have any financially draining kids to support, I've an expensive shoe habit and that kind of addiction seriously needs regular cash injections. Just think, there are sad and lonely shoes out there waiting for me to adopt them and take them back to a loving home. There, they'll reunite with their brothers and sisters whom they have not seen since their creation in the Dolce & Gabbana workshop in Taiwan.

If I'm to build a new life without Barry, I know I'll need something to get up for in the morning. Although the job isn't the career I'd dreamt of, it pays the bills. Climbing out of a hot shower, I wrap myself in a fluffy white towel and wipe the steamy mirror. A sad expression stares back. There are wrinkles there that I've never noticed before. Red rings circle my puffy eyes, my skin is pale and I've spotted a new grey hair. Days of crying have taken their toll on my complexion, and my recent diet of Chinese takeaways has wreaked havoc with my midriff. I was lucky to have Barry and I've messed it up.

Being unable to fit into my skinny jeans is nearly enough to push me over the edge. They go as far as my thighs and refuse the rest of the journey. In fairness, they're usually a snug fit, since I bought them in a size ten in order to motivate myself skinny. They normally come as far as my ever growing bottom and I battle them the rest of the way, but not today. I've tried on six outfits, and they all make me look plump, so I settle on a pair of Marks & Spencer's trousers. They have become my work uniform, and are black to match my mood. The trousers are usually forgiving around the belly area, in a sucky-in-knickers kind of way, but today, they do little to hide the flabby bulge. They simply displace the fat so that it hangs over the trouser-line in an unflattering muffin-top.

I team the trousers with an orange top that Barry had thought-fully bought me last Christmas. It looks hideous on me, now. I'm like a six months' pregnant Oompa-Loompa that even Mr Willy Wonka himself would cold-heartedly fire for eating too many Wonka Bars on the job.

God, you are really pushing my buttons. Not only am I destined to fly solo for the rest of my life, I'll be doing it with wrinkles, grey hair and saddle bags. Help! Honestly, if I bump into the neighbours, I'll never talk to you again.

Amen.

PS, did you really have to add PMS to the mix right now? I'm not responsible if I break a few commandments, especially the one about 'Thou shalt not punch someone in the face'.

PPS, please let Harry take one look at poor sad little old me and become shocked by my deathly pallor. Let him insist that I return to my sick bed without delay. He could explain to the HR department that I'm medically unfit for work, and instruct them not to annoy me by looking for medical certs.

My Volkswagen Golf tears off, and I round the corner at alarming speed. It's already ten o'clock, so I'm dead late. It's raining and my windscreen wipers are still broken. Trying to see where I'm going is like Stevie Wonder trying to operate a dumper truck through rush-hour traffic.

I step on the accelerator and turn the volume on my car stereo up full blast. The sound of Alanis Morissette screeching at deaf-ening levels about some rat that screwed her over makes me feel just a little better. At least my life isn't that bad! That woman needs serious therapy.

It's half past ten as I throw my coat over my chair. With a wave of his hand, Harry summons me into his office.

'Rebecca, come in, please. You look…'

Harry searches for the word and finishes a glazed Danish pastry, wiping the crumbs off his ample chest and eyeballing me suspiciously. The buttons on his shirt are struggling to win the fight to stay closed around the stomach zone. It doesn't help that his tie stops short at this very area, drawing further attention to this unflattering region.

'Thanks,' I deadpan. At least I'm dressed and showered today. He should have seen me yesterday; even my cat couldn't stand the smell. He has coughed up hairballs that have more sex appeal than me.

Harry gives a tight smile and shuffles some papers. The sick leave policy lingers menacingly on his desk. He says that we need to discuss something, but that a coffee would be good before we start.

'Thanks, that would be *fab*!'

Harry has never offered to make me coffee before. Maybe he's not such a demon, after all. Relaxing in the chair opposite, I empty the contents of my handbag onto his polished mahogany desk in search of a headache pill. After a brief hesitation, Harry rises from his chair, mumbling.

'So…' Harry plonks a black coffee in front of me and clears his throat. 'These sick days.'

He looks to me for an explanation. I feel myself cringe deep inside, my stomach clenching.

'And the late arrivals. And the finishing early. This is not some… part-time job, Rebecca. I need you on board, here.'

I'm breathing deeply to stop my breakfast from making a repeat visit there and then on the mahogany desk, and clutch my throbbing forehead. Wednesday hangovers are the worst kind of hangover. Harry is really persecuting me. Next thing I know, he'll be demanding photocopying or other mundane tasks, oblivious to my heartache. Men can be so clueless!

You see, normally I'm well able for Harry. My usual tactic is to talk in circles, and at high speed, until he's so exasperated that the issue is dropped. But I'm just sitting in silence, unable to speak, staring at the columns and figures strewn across his desk. My eyes are stinging and the pages are blurred. I scramble for a defence. I've got about a dozen pre-prepared in a McDonald's drive-through kind of way. But nothing comes.

'So, let's start by talking about the sick days,' Harry's eyebrows are raised.

I'm crying, the absolute shame of it. We're talking proper shuddering plops of tears landing in a puddle on his paperwork. My pitiful face is stained with mascara. Poor Harry doesn't know where to look.

'Goodness,' he blusters, searching frantically through drawers with no success for a Kleenex.

'There, there,' he attempts clumsily.

'Sorry,' I retrieve a tissue from my handbag to dab at my dripping nose. 'Personal crisis.'

Although unintentional, the tears are working a treat. I've never seen Harry so flustered. It has been far more effective than any period cramps/granny on death bed/dental episode/emergency blood transfusion/gastric bug/exotic virus. Why had I not thought of it before? Harry opens his office door, my cue to leave. He says we can talk about it another time.

I leave my coffee untouched, and walk back towards my desk. Judy is engrossed in a phone call and doesn't see me at first. When she glances up, she rushes through her call, and waves frantically for me to join her in her cubicle.

'How are *you*?'

Judy's face is scrunched up in a mixture of concern and pity.

'OK,' I wobble, rubbing a finger under my eyes to remove the mascara stains. We both exchange knowing glances. Now is not the time to talk, we're being watched.

'Head down,' Judy motions towards Harry's office. 'Jesus is coming, look busy.'

Judy's slim legs are crossed underneath her desk, and she pretends to type as Harry approaches. She's dressed in a skimpy black skirt, white shirt and heels. The white shirt only exaggerates her tanorexia and reveals a highly bronzed chest. She's definitely a shade darker than the last time I saw her.

Harry walks towards my desk, but instead of depositing files and folders, he deposits another coffee.

'Er, thanks,' I call over my shoulder.

Judy and I stifle a snigger. The man looks positively mortified.

'Oh my God!' Judy laughs. 'That's a first. I take it you filled him in on your situation?'

'Kind of. So, what's the latest with you?'

Judy is single and likes to talk a lot about how much fun it is. She says that:

a) She gets invited to the best parties and mixes with glamorous people. Her dates take her to exclusive restaurants and trendy gigs, featuring bands that I'm not cool enough to have heard of.

Couples, according to 'The Book of Judy', stay at home on the couch every evening watching *Friends* repeats, slippers firmly on feet. They dip nachos in cheese sauce. This is completely false. Sometimes I dip into salsa.

She has no nappies to change, snot to wipe or bums to clean. Fair point.

She parties till dawn, lies in bed until noon and does as she pleases. She reports to no-one.

However, the thing she conveniently forgets is:

a) Judy goes for absolute rotters. You should see her current squeeze, Ivan, a total rotter. I call him 'Ivan the Terrible', but not to her face, I'm not brave enough. Soon, I'll have to hear her whine about it when the whole affair crashes and burns. 'Nice and reliable' like my Barry are not exactly the type of chap she usually goes for. She finds those sorts dull.

b) This brute Ivan has a serious grip on her. I'm not just speaking metaphorically – I mean, I've seen the bruise marks on her arm. Not pretty.
c) Once, after one too many champagne cocktails at a work party, she confided in me that she was lonely. Said she just wants someone to hold her. This was *before* she projectile vomited on the stairs, and then slipped in it.
d) She's always available on a Friday evening for a last-minute after-work drink. This contradicts her social butterfly with a chock-o-block diary image. It's all highly suspicious!

'How's Ivan?' I whisper. I shouldn't pick at the scab, but I can't help it.

'Fine.' Judy is being cagey. I poke at the wound some more, this time with a big thorny stick.

'Still married, then?'

'He is *not* married!'

I've hit a nerve, now. Ivan refuses to move in with her and meets her only when it suits him. He throws her a booty call around midnight on a random Thursday, and she jumps. My hypothesis is that he has a wife and kids stashed away in a three-bed semi somewhere. He probably keeps them in a cage and practises satanic worship in his spare time. The psychopath!

'Anyway, we're just having fun. It's not serious.'

I sigh. Some people are addicted to drama!

'It's two euro a drink Wild Wednesday in Leggs tonight…' Judy changes the subject.

'Not a chance, love. My liver is literally about to explode.'

There's no way I'm up to the student-filled time warp tonight. It would make me feel absolutely ancient if I bumped into someone I used to babysit while sipping a watered-down Cosmo.

There is a mini mountain of paperwork on my desk. Some of the paperwork has accumulated in my short absence, while some has been gathering dust over the last few weeks. I don't discriminate:

127

they'll all have to wait. Dozens of emails spill into my inbox, and I hit the delete button. They disappear in a blur like magic: *Urgent invoice… budget information… meeting dates.* These are all far too dull to be dealt with by a woman on the edge.

Amanda Maloney from accounts has discovered me hiding behind my partition and I recoil as she makes a beeline for me. I call her Bony Maloney because she's like a walking skeleton. I'd love to shove a Big Mac and fries down her scrawny neck.

'Hi Rebecca,' Amanda's head is tilted to the side.

She's wearing a black bra under a white shirt, which is such a fashion faux pas. I can practically count her ribs. Why won't she just supersize a nice juicy burger meal?

Everyone knows why I've been absent the last two days. 'Poor sad Rebecca' they'll have said over doughnuts, 'Barry won't marry her. Had a big bust-up, then she called in sick.' They probably went on to chat about the weather and the latest affair from *EastEnders*.

'Hi, Amanda,' I pretend to type so that she'll leave.

'If you want to talk about it? I'm here if you need me?'

Amanda has that awful Australian-style inflection that people in their twenties are prone to. There's a lot of it about, it might be catching. It's where all sentences go up at the end, like a question mark? Do you know the one? It's very annoying? Especially if you've never been to Australia?

Talk about it, indeed. She'd love that! It would give her lots to dissect at the water cooler. She could give me advice, and tell me how her and 'her Graham' got together.

'No, thanks,' I manage a false smile.

I'd rather have a colonic irrigation.

Amanda's face registers disappointment, and she retreats across the room. I move the unopened letters on my desk into a drawer so that they won't keep staring at me. I've absolutely no intention of opening them in the near future. In the kitchenette, I fix a snack to settle my stomach and absorb the wine from the night before, which is now churning unhappily. There really should be a government-issued health warning on mixing leftover Indian food and a full bottle of cheap red wine.

My mind flits as I wait for the toaster to pop. My daydream of Barry being asked to leave the conference because his crying is disturbing the others is interrupted by a loud shrieking noise. Clouds of smoke billow from my burning bagel. Through streaming eyes, I open the kitchenette window and fan frantically with a plastic tray at the smoke detector, pleading that no-one will notice. Soon there are people moving on the stairs outside the door.

'*Damn it!*' I curse.

Why had I dunked the bagel twice? Obviously, I can't be expected to work on an empty stomach, that would violate my human rights or whatever. I like my food toasted to a certain degree. Some might call that burnt, I like to call it lightly charred. I'm jumping up and down, waving a tea towel when Brendan from Human Resources pokes his head around the door.

'Ah no! Not again, Rebecca.'

My forehead is sweating profusely as I try to defend myself.

'Yeah, false alarm. Rebecca again!' he bellows down the stairs.

I'd better send out an urgent smoke signal to the big man upstairs.

Oh dear God,

You may remember me from last year. With the strawberry flavored Pop-Tart and the rather tearful explanation to the hunky fire brigade that were waiting outside the building, sirens flashing? The entire company had gathered at the assembly point, and the fire fighters were serious and ready for action. Please God. Don't let that happen again!

With a broom, I manage to knock the smoke detector off the ceiling. It finally shuts the hell up. I've smeared cream cheese high on top of the scorched bagel and am only halfway through eating it when Harry calls me into his office. I feel sick.

'Again, Rebecca? Are you purposely tampering with the fire equipment?'

'No… I…the toaster must be broken…'

'You really must exercise more care when toasting your buns.'

I snort with laughter. Who knew Harry could be so funny?

'Are you...' Harry is looking at me with a dubious expression '... drunk?'

'No! Of course not! Just, like, you know *really* super hungover.'

That ought to explain that.

'Look, Rebecca...'

Harry's face is crumpled as he fidgets with his tie.

'...Perhaps we should just call it a day?'

'Oh God, would you *mind*?!'

I'm suddenly exhausted and unable to stop yawning. This turmoil is messing with my frail emotional health. I mean, there's no point in being a total slave to my career at the expense of my personal life. I've no intention of ending up like a cat-collecting singleton, chained to my cobweb-covered desk. I grab my bagel and handbag and stand up. It's great that Harry is being so understanding about the whole thing.

'It *has* been a long morning.'

My hand is on the steering wheel before it occurs to me that maybe it isn't just today Harry is thinking about when he talks about calling it a day.

Eighteen

It's nice to be home at lunchtime. Maybe I should apply for part-time hours and be home in time for *Home and Away* every day – it's far more of a work–life balance.

I log on to Hotmail, and plod through the various emails. I've forwarded an online penis enlargement scam to Harry – I bet he'll find that hilarious. Although tempting, I ignore the emails advertising pharmaceuticals for sale. My heart suddenly stops beating: there's an email from Barry marked with today's date. With a quivering hand, I click on the message.

SUBJECT: HI

Hi Becks,

Sorry we haven't spoken since our fight. The time difference is a pain and the conference is exhausting. Promise to call you at home tonight. Home Saturday. We really need to talk.

Love, Barry

No wonder the poor chap has been out of contact – between flights and time zones he's probably desperate to reach me! I'll wait by the phone tonight until he manages to get through to me. He's either going to patch things up or end it for good – either way, we will thrash out the intimate details of our love on the rocks tonight, over a long distance line.

The email is friendly but not gushing. He has called me 'Becks' rather than 'Rebecca'. He signed off 'Love, Barry'. All good indicators! Still, I need to analyse every line over and over again within an inch of its life.

Please, God.

Drop what you're doing and help me out here. I know you might have, like, a tsunami or natural disaster to deal with, but this is super important. Also, thanks for averting the fire brigade, but you still owe me big time. You never came back to me on that request for a Fendi bag. Remember? The one with the little diamantés? I'm still slumming it with last season's. Ask and thou shall receive, eh? Anyway! Whatever you do, please let Barry come running back to me. Oh, and would it be too much to ask to have a word with him about the hoovering? Ta.

I'm about to give up when Emer finally answers.

'Oh my God oh my God!' I rant down the line, gasping for air.

'What's up, lovey?'

Emer's standing by and ready to dissect all new information.

'Barry emailed!'

I'm shouting now, arms flapping.

'Great!'

'But he said we need to talk. He's in Hong Kong …or Bangkok or …someplace hot and dusty. He's going to call tonight.'

There's a muffled sound as Emer moves away from her mobile for a minute.

'Cancel my afternoon appointments, Sinead,' Emer barks at her assistant.

Emer is such an angel. In her infinite wisdom, she knows that this dilemma is a real 'Code Red'. No wonder she's my nearest and dearest gal pal. Within minutes, I can breathe normally, and the chances of going into cardiac arrest are slim. A plan of action is emerging.

Firstly, we need to draft a cool reply to Barry. Emer has cunningly devised that our reply must strike the balance between coming across as desperate (which I am, let's call a spade a spade) and blasé. I'm not sure exactly what the latter word actually means, or indeed how to spell it, but I think Emer is trying to tell me to play it cool. With much help from Emer, I hastily type my reply.

SUBJECT: RE: HI

Hi Barry,
I look forward to hearing from you this evening.
  Love, Becks

I hit the send button before I can change my mind.

'Brilliant!' congratulates Emer.

'God, we're a great team, Emer. World domination may be next. We should sign up to Greenpeace or Amnesty International and solve the world's problems. Sure, if we can untangle my love life, what's a little dolphin caught in a net or an Israel–Palestine conflict?'

Emer and I decide that we don't have time to wave placards at evil oil tankers on behalf of Greenpeace, since our hair is too much of a flyaway nature for that kind of thing. Also, the war-torn Middle East is not a top destination these days. We'll stick to Marbella for leisure time, far better cocktails there. Instead, we arrange to meet for an immediate counselling session over a low-fat high-foam vanilla mocha cappuccino, at our nearest café. Emer will coach me through the impending make or break phone call.

As I settle into a booth at Café Boulevard, I feel hopeful. Emer has to abandon an important meeting in order to join me in our urgent consultation, so I have a few minutes to kill. I scan the newspaper, skipping the wearisome news and politics section and go straight to the horoscopes. Apparently, the Moon is in Saturn. By all accounts, that's a good thing. The horoscope reads:

Scorpio: if you have been acting scattered these past few days,
it's time to pull in your energy and concentrate on exactly what
you need to do. You may be able to get a lot done by eliminating

extraneous distractions, and make your dreams come true.
Thankfully, a more positive perspective will emerge in the next
few days.

My jaw drops. *Talk about divine guidance!* Clearly, the spirits are telling me plainly that everything is going to work out. The 'positive perspective' is definitely a sign that everything with Barry will come out smelling of roses. The 'extraneous distractions' is an obvious message that I shouldn't let my silly job distract me from what truly matters. Who am I to argue with the supernatural? It'd be wise to stay at home for the rest of week until this is all sorted out. Over the years, I've learned that it is best not to mess with Mystic Melanie from the paper, she knows her stuff!

To keep me company while I wait, I take pity on a lonely-looking brownie and devour it with a cafe latte and some whipped cream on the side. It's sinful, but I have to keep my strength up. Besides, I'm the type that will likely faint or go into a hypoglycaemic coma if I skip a meal. I'm certainly not one of those annoying skinny types who exclaim 'Oh! I was so busy I forgot to eat lunch!' Don't you just laugh at people like that?

Finally Emer arrives, a gust of cold wind blowing in behind her. She has a brand new Chloé handbag dangling over her thin arm; apparently she got it in New York. She gets all of her clothes there. Although it has been raining lightly, her hair remains smooth and untouched, not a frizz in sight. She unbuttons her beige mac, revealing an expensive-looking charcoal trouser suit and staggeringly high heels, and sits across from me.

Emer has an important phone call coming through, and mouths her apology as she answers it. I'm waiting as patiently as I can, eyeing up the lush pastries in their glass prison. They're begging for early release on account of good behaviour and are highly distracting. I try not to feel annoyed with Emer – she has ditched her high powered job at short notice, leaving her minions without their master, in order to come to my aid.

'No, Andrew,' she instructs. 'No, we have a deadline on this.'

Listening, while pretending not to, is harder than it looks. I've always harboured a little of the green-eyed monster when it comes to Emer. She's successful, elegant and slim. Looking at my reflection in the window, my suspicions are confirmed: I'm in desperate need of a makeover!

Snapping her mobile shut and setting it on the table, she turns and hugs me hello.

'Now listen, darling.'

Emer is all business. I'm a new project for her to manage: one that will drain all of her time, energy and resources.

'This is serious.'

'Well, yeah!' I pout. 'I can't decide between a goat's cheese and sundried panini or the Niçoise salad.'

Emer cuts me off.

'Right. I'm here to help. We'd better get things between you and Barry sorted, or you're looking at the single life in your…' her voice drops to a whisper '…*thirties.*'

She shudders at the thought.

'Now that's all right for Pam, honey, but you want more out of life.'

Ten minutes later, a goat's cheese and sundried tomato panini arrives with a large Coke and an order of fries on the side. Those paninis are never filling, and need a lot of padding in my opinion. I confide in Emer that I'm feeling guilty. I've been nagging Barry and pushing him away until he has finally snapped. The whole ugly mess spills out: the wedding pressure, the arguments, the honeymoon deposit. I even confess about the engagement ring newspaper clipping in his lunchbox.

Over a mixed leaf salad (with a smidge of light dressing and a still water on the side), Emer listens patiently. She lets me get the whole sordid truth off my chest. She never once lifts an eyebrow in judgement, bless her. However, now that I think about it, I don't think she is in fact capable of lifting an eyebrow. The large amounts of Botox injected over the years (even when it was still an experimental practice), prevent such a wrinkle-creating action.

'There's no point,' Emer advises, 'in telling you what you want to hear. If you're going to fix this, you need to face up to reality.'

I gulp. Emer is direct. She doesn't tell me everything is grand and not to worry about it.

Men, in Emer's opinion, scare easily. According to Emer, I've committed cardinal sin number one: I pushed for marriage. Now, the poor guy has run a mile and is having doubts about us over in Asia somewhere, in a different time zone. In a nutshell, it's up to me to convince him that I am in fact not crazy, just crazy about him. I need to give him more time. I need to back off.

'Men want to feel in control, Rebecca. They don't want to be pushed or shoved.'

I hang on her every word. Emer knows men, and she always had the knack for bagging the most eligible guy. She married a successful stockbroker in a bloody recession, for goodness' sake, which was genius. Perhaps her and Dr Phil could team up and do some super show about fixing no-hope relationships!

'You want him to commit, but not have you committed!'

'Steady on!' I bristle but then shut up. It's best not to interrupt Emer when she's in full swing.

'You want to let him think that marriage is all his idea in the first place.'

That sounds tricky.

'Pressuring the guy into marriage is not the answer.'

'OK.'

'He needs space,' she continues. 'He's not going to propose with you talking about it every bloody five minutes.'

'He has lots of space,' I joke. 'He has that whole attic conversion as a man cave. He even has Sky Sports up there!'

'Space from *you*, darling!'

This must be what people mean when they talk about tough love. A two-step plan of action is emerging.

Step one: I have to convince Barry that I'll be an absolute angel from now on. I'll be on my best behaviour, and there will be no more wedding talk.

Step two: I'll greet him on his return from the Far East on Saturday, looking absolutely hot. We're talking Nicole-Kidman-on-Oscars-night-hot. Emer is going to arrange everything.

With the plan firmly in place, we order coffee and a cake. Now, when I say *we*, I mean *me*: Emer doesn't do desserts. Skinny lattes or fruit salads without any cream don't count as desserts in my opinion. I've conveniently forgotten about the brownie I recently scoffed, and consume a pear and almond tart in record-breaking time.

Emer presses a couple of business cards into my hand for the top beauty and hair salons that she frequents in the city. She has a tab, and I've been instructed to charge it all to her. We air kiss goodbye. Emer pays the waitress on her corporate credit card, and I thank her profusely for her help.

'Oh I nearly *forgot*!'

Emer takes a small Brown Thomas bag from her handbag and smiles her perfect Hollywood white-toothed smile.

'What's this?'

'Have a peep.'

I reach into the bag and giggle. A brand new red silk bodice and matching French knickers are folded neatly within pink tissue paper. The tag from the exclusive Agent Provocateur is still attached, along with an eye-watering price tag. I'm unusually speechless.

'For you!' Emer smirks. 'And for fabulous cleavage!'

Nineteen

Since I have yet to encounter my wretched next-door neighbour, I'm still feeling rather cagey following our unfortunate run-in down the supermarket aisles. I scurry up the driveway.

Back home, my head is spinning with thoughts of the upcoming phone call. I rustle up a strong coffee and a cream éclair from the fridge that Mum had dropped off. Don't start, it is a Weight Watchers éclair, and I get shaky in the afternoons if my blood pressure dips!

I've so many versions of how tonight's phone call will play out. The scenarios range from the one where I get dumped over the phone, to the one where he drops everything, boards the next flight to Dublin and then sweeps me up in his arms.

The afternoon passes in a haze of gal-pal texting and visits to the DrPhil.com website for relationship gems – for a bald middle-aged guy, he has a lot of insight. I also take the opportunity to reconnect with news of the celebrity world. There's a fascinating piece in *OK!* about when celebrities go too far with plastic surgery, and some rather juicy snaps of a botched trout-pout from some unfortunate 80s singer who has tried to revive her limp career with fillers and a single re-release. So sad.

I've just enough vigour left in me to reach for the remote control and Pringles and prepare a new herbal tea from my local hippy health shop. According to the hippy behind the counter, this tea revives and replenishes your *chi*. Whatever that is! She insisted that it 'also harmonises your chakras during times of emotional distress', so I was sold. It turns out that cat urine would in fact be a more enjoyable brew. A quick read of the back of the box reveals that the ingredients contain nettles, ginger and chamomile. Yuk! The situation calls for something a little stronger. To steady my nerves, I pour a little Cabernet Sauvignon. Just a wee one.

After flicking through endless channels of day-time drivel and exhausting my selection of oestrogen-fuelled programmes from my digital recorder, I've finally settled on a weight-loss programme with Lorraine Kelly. Those poor fat souls, I empathise, as I lick the icing off a slice of carrot cake. They simply don't stand a chance! However, enthralling as the programme is (and as svelte as it makes me feel in comparison), I just can't concentrate.

I'm unable to shake off the fact that any minute now the phone will ring. I keep checking to make sure that the phone is in its cradle thing. In fact, seconds later when the landline does actually spring into action, it makes me jump out of my skin, and I slosh wine on myself. It's only bloody Mum inviting me to bloody yoga at the bloody church hall.

'I can't talk now, Mum. I'm in the middle of a total calamity! My relationship is hanging by a thread!'

'Alright, darling.'

'Look, I'll have to call you back. Barry is phoning soon. To talk it out and he…'

She hangs up. I feel a red mist of rage descend over me.

By six o'clock, I'm climbing the walls. Every minute feels like an hour. I check my watch relentlessly. Having topped up my glass a couple of times, I decide to cut myself off. Barry should find me relaxed but not sloshed.

My mind wanders into dangerous territory. Perhaps Barry is stuck in some shabby third world type hotel, with only a coin box in the hall that is now broken. Perhaps he has been attacked by thugs and is in a bath of ice, minus his right kidney. Perhaps he has been framed as a drugs mule and is rotting in some Bangkok prison, drugs hidden in private places. I've seen documentaries about Asia and the slums and what not. I know about these things!

Facebook, although highly annoying, distracts me for a few minutes. It should be called Bragbook, as all of the updates are from nauseatingly loved-up child-obsessed friends of mine. They drone on about how clever their children are, or how they are being whisked off for the weekend to somewhere fancy to celebrate an engagement. With my own relationship hanging in the balance, it's hard to stomach. A friend from school has posted a 'hilarious' picture of her jam-smeared tots, smiling their gummy grins. Another harps on about potty training her gifted toddler. She has posted pictures of the baby's every developmental milestone from a first smile (which is probably wind) to a first day at nursery (big whoop). An old classmate boasts about how her little Abigail has won a medal for Irish dancing. Teachers are so politically correct these days, the whole class probably got one.

Don't they know that I might never get married? Don't they get that I might never flounce down the aisle in a cream lace overlay gown with Swarovski crystals? Don't they realise that I might never churn out little mini Barrys? Plump, funny, clever little mini Barrys?

I swallow the desire to slap these proud parents with a flip-flop in their smug face upon our next encounter. The phone is ringing! Sweet Jesus, it's him! Not wanting to appear too keen and reveal that I'm stuck at home willing the phone to ring, I let it ring a few agonising times until I can no longer stand the suspense.

'Hello?'

My heart is hammering in my chest, causing a whooshing in my ears.

'Hi, baby.'

God, we're off to a good start. He called me baby! Barry's voice sounds deep and sexy, and I long for him.

'How are you?' we both blurt at the same time.

'I'm fine, Barry. Really missing you, though.'

'Mmm.'

Right. Here's my chance to fix what I have so foolishly broken. I've pushed Barry away with my stupid obsession, and have come so close to wrecking everything. Who could blame him for wanting to run a mile? Well, I'm not going to let that happen. I'm not letting him get away without a fight.

'Look, Barry. I am so sorry. I don't know what you must be thinking right now. I've been a total pain. Honestly, I don't know how you stick me.'

I remember the script that Emer drilled into me, and deliver it verbatim. Barry is the love of my life, and I'll be damned if I'm going to let him slip away from me.

'Hmm, you could say that.' Barry is smiling, I can hear it in his voice. 'Listen, Becky. I'm just so tired from fighting with you all the time, you know? Things used to be so much fun with you, and now you're so… I don't know, serious. You've just pushed me and pushed me…'

'I know, I realise that now. I've been thinking about nothing else.'

'Becky, the last few days have been rough. I can't wait to get home. We'll sit down and try to sort it all out.'

I feel my smile broaden. Things are going to be alright. I exhale in relief.

'OK.'

'Anyway, there's something I've got to tell you.'

'Oh?'

'Yeah but… look, we'll talk when I get back, alright?'

'OK.'

'I love you, Rebecca. You drive me nuts, but I love you.'

'I love you too, Barry.' A tear rolls down my face. 'See you Saturday.'

After I've hung up, I hold the phone handset close to my chest. People search their whole lives for someone as fantastic as Barry, and I nearly pushed him away. I'm never making that mistake again. The tears gather, climbing up my throat higher and higher until the dam bursts.

'From now on,' I sniff to an unconscious Jess, 'I'm going to treat that man like a king. I'm going to stop nagging him about getting married, putting the bins out, unloading the dishwasher…well, let's start with the nagging about getting married part first. I don't want to overcommit.'

I text Mum with the news, and open a bottle of Grey Goose vodka in merriment. It's a bottle that Barry has put away for Christmas, but I'm sure that he'll understand. The ice clinks in my glass and an episode of *TOWIE* is about to start. Things are looking up.

Twenty

When I wake up, I'm groggy. It's as if there is sandpaper in my mouth. That last glass of vodka and cranberry mustn't have agreed with me. The volume on my phone seems to have increased by a few decibels, and it's ringing persistently. Could it be Barry? I scramble under the covers and try to answer it before it rings out. With a wave of disappointment, I see that it's Mum. Who else would call at such an ungodly hour?

'Hello, Mum.'

I'm annoyed now. It's only a minute past dawn, surely. Not even the birds are up at a time like this. I've already given her strict advice not to wake me up or call before a reasonable hour. You know, like lunchtime. She knows to only call my mobile phone early if:

a) Her house is burning down and the fire brigade are not available to assist. Even at that, I'm not sure I'd be much help to her. The smoke affects my sensitive eyes, and my fire training cert from work is way out of date.

b) She has won the European lottery (Irish Lotto is also acceptable) and wishes to share at least half with me.

Apart from these two rare incidents, I don't tolerate such early bird twittering.

'Good morning, darling.'

Mum is acting far too cheery for my liking. Something must be done to stop her.

'Mum. It's very early.'

'Not at all, sure your dad and I have been up for hours. Haven't we, Gerry?'

'Hours,' Dad replies in an equally chirpy tone. I have no idea what this pair are on. It must be a strong dose of geriatric flipping happy pills or something.

'Great news about the phone call last night. You two will be back on track in no time.'

Mum is still banging on, as is my head. I reach into my bedside locker, fumble until my fingertips find the familiar plastic packaging, fish out two painkillers and swallow them down with something sweet in a glass tumbler on my locker that has been sitting there for some time.

'Sure, it was just storm in a teacup…' Mum exhausts even more clichés.

I'm desperately trying to think of an excuse to get her off the phone and enjoy my weekend lie-on.

'But sure, listen, I won't keep you.'

'Huh?'

That isn't like Mum not to prattle on for hours on the phone while I have better things to do.

'Look, I know you must be on your way to the office, so I don't want to get you in trouble.'

Oh, dear. The woman has clearly lost her marbles. I rub my temples and try to make the throbbing and the queasiness go far, far away. I'll have to look up homes for the elderly, or have her sectioned. This will eat into my soap opera time. First, she calls me at dawn, and then she doesn't even know what bloody day of the week it is.

A wave of sickness sweeps over me as I realise that it's Thursday. What's more, it's already nine thirty, and so I'm officially late for work. Again!

'Oh God, Mum! I'm flipping late now, I can't talk.'

144

'OK, darling. But look, before I hang up…'

'Mum, I can't…'

'You know Nuala?'

'Mum!'

'Nuala? Nuala Cleary?'

Silence crackles on the line.

'Nuala? John's wife Nuala? Nuala and John?'

'Yes,' I sigh.

'Well, Nuala and I had an appointment with this psychic Michael for Friday afternoon. Booked it months ago.'

'OK, Mum. That's great. I have to…'

'But Nuala can't go. Going in for a hip replacement. Poor woman can hardly walk these days and the doctor says that…'

'That's fantastic!' I interrupt, having already put two and two together. A trip to a fortune teller is just what I need. This way, I'll know for sure what lies in store for Barry and I.

'So you'll come with me, then? It'll be just a bit of fun, you know?'

'Definitely.'

'Great, love. Talk later.'

Mum hangs up. She has stopped using the word 'bye' at the end of her phone calls. It's all quite unnerving, all of this daytime TV since her retirement is having a bad influence on her. I check my watch again. With Barry's impending arrival back to our love nest in forty-eight hours, I need to ensure that I'm looking ravishing for our reunion. What could be more important than that? I can't achieve all of the above whilst stuck at my desk. There's no getting around it, I'll have to call in sick. Again.

A grin spreads across my face as I remember that the golden rule of sickies states that one must always call in sick for at least two days. It looks far more genuine than one day. Anyone can have one day off, a real ailment takes at least two days to recover from. This will block the rest of the week off nicely.

Unluckily for me, Barry is away and Mum is not answering her phone when I try to call her back, so I have to make the dreaded phone call by myself. Life is so unfair! Trust Harry to be at his desk and accepting telephone calls at the unreasonable hour of nine thirty-three. What a slave driver! I'd hoped that I'd be connected to his answering machine, and that I'd be able to cough my way in a frail manner into his voicemail.

I announce my (life-threatening for all he knows) vomiting bug.

'Again?' the insufferable man replies.

'Yes. Another one. I'd never forgive myself if I passed it on to anyone at the office.'

I cough into the receiver.

'Right. I'll have to inform the HR department. I assume that you'll furnish me with a sick certificate from your GP?'

'Of course,' I deadpan.

The monster will probably ask me to provide blood test results, next. This is employer bullying! Where has this man's venom come from? Have I not been a loyal servant? Have I not given him five years as a dedicated employee, the best years of my life? This is a direct violation of my employee rights. I'll have to contact the Trade Union and ask them to investigate; there may be a tribunal and everything.

Amid violent fictitious coughing, and what I can only describe as highly convincing retching sounds to complete the ugly effect, I hang up. For all Harry knows, I'm at death's door, and could pass out at the drop of a hat. I'll text him later to say that I've been hospitalised and am on a drip for dehydration. That will keep him quiet!

Those speech and drama lessons that Dad had reluctantly agreed to pay for during my school days (thanks to my highly persistent and unrelenting daily requests) have really paid off. Dad had been reluctant about sending me, since I'd grown bored of every other class he had paid for. I had declared boredom and quit just as soon as he had shelled out for the uniform and/or musical instrument, much to his irritation. The list of discarded hobbies during my school years includes: ballet, Irish dancing, hockey, juggling, piano and recorder. If he could hear my convincing efforts moments earlier, he'd be so proud.

The truth is, I'm a natural actress. The drama teacher had described me as 'spirited', and she always raised her eyebrows when she said this, probably to emphasise my extraordinary flair and hide her obvious jealousy towards my God-given talents. Perhaps I was an Oscar-winning Hollywood actress in a former life, living it up in some Malibu mansion until I took a champagne and sleeping pill accidental tragic overdose in the bath. You never know.

In order to secure a sick cert for today and tomorrow, I dial Dr Logan's number. The secretary patches me through.

'Ah, Rebecca. Yes. How are we?'

'Yes, hi Dr Logan. OK, thanks.'

My voice is small: I'm aiming for 'upbeat-even-though-I'm-critically-ill'. It's a pretty good attempt.

'Recovered from that bout of anxiety, then?'

'What? Oh, em yes, Doctor.'

I'd forgotten about that one. A notebook would come in handy, it's hard to remember all of my previous ailments. I was feeling anxious last month about Harry harassing me for the missing petty cash, and needed a sickie. Anxiety is easy enough to fake, you just need a packet of tissues and a list of symptoms copied and pasted from Google.

'So, what can I do for you, Rebecca?'

'Well…' I adopt a weak voice. 'I seem to have a vomiting bug.'

My voice is frail, now, almost a whisper. It's probably because all of the imaginary puking has really taken it out of me. 'It's coming out all ends, you know? Just awful. Bleugh!'

I fart loud enough for him to hear on the other end. It's the kind of emission I normally keep for when I'm in Harry's office and want a grilling to end. There are no windows in his office, you see.

'Blasted rotten dose, Doctor. I can't keep anything down.' I retch, and let his imagination do the rest.

'Oh dear!'

'Yes, it's awful. In fact, I'd come down the surgery myself except I wouldn't want to pass it on, you know? Highly contagious and all that…'

'OK… yeah, absolutely. Don't want to pass the thing on. Plenty of fluids, of course. It should pass in a day or two. Will I write a cert for work, then?'

'Gosh, OK.' It's as if the thought has only just occurred to me at this point. 'I mean, if you think that would be best…' My voice is like a sleepy kitten now. I have just enough strength left to cough.

Wow, I'm good. The cert will keep Harry satisfied for today and tomorrow. Forget him, anyway. Sure, today is what I like to call Facebook Friday and Judy and I have Candy Crush tournaments on a Thursday. I can easily catch up.

Hopefully, my award-winning performance on the phone to Harry will leave him in no doubt regarding the validity of my alleged illness. The cert is just to cover my ass. In fact, Harry is probably doing a whip-round the office at this very moment, in order to send me flowers and thank me for my selfless consideration regarding my refusal to spread my highly contagious viral illness further amongst my cherished colleagues.

I've had a number of mysterious fictitious illnesses this year. When calling in sick, I have gone through the alphabet of diseases, ranging from Arthritis to Zellweger syndrome. The latter has nothing to do with Renée Zellweger, it's some rare metabolic thing that gives you an enlarged head. Clever, huh? It involved a lot of wearing of hats upon my return to the office. Thankfully, hats suit me.

Last August, when I had reached the letter M for migraine, Harry had quizzed me.

'Don't migraine headaches usually involve an aversion to strong light?' he had cruelly quizzed me in the office upon my return. It was at that point that I realised that a sleeveless shirt revealing sunburnt arms was not the best wardrobe choice that day. I had made a half-hearted attempt to convince him of the link between vitamin D and headache prevention, but he remained unconvinced. Because of the sneaky Irish sun, many a pasty soul, such as myself, have been caught out this way when they take a couple of harmless sick days in the back garden instead of sitting in a dim cubicle. In employment terms, presenting sunburn upon your return to work is a big no-no.

Harry seems to be harbouring some (ridiculous, I know) grudge regarding my September absence. It was a humongous hangover that I had cunningly disguised as vertigo. It was almost true, as I was very unsteady on my feet. And believe me, V was a tough one to think up! I'd to really think hard to pull that one out of the bag. The whole thing was blown way out of proportion. There had been no need for Human Resources to get involved.

I don't want to think about work any more. I've only forty-eight hours before Barry's return. What I really need are the three Rs – Rest, Relaxation and Retail therapy. After a short lie-on until eleven, a hot power shower and a strong coffee leaves me wide awake and wired. It has been literally days since I bought myself anything nice. As part of Emer's two-step plan, a little shopping is in order.

My shopping uniform is as follows:

a) Jeggings – half jeans and half leggings, these are the best invention ever. The elasticised waistband allows me to slip easily from one designer frock to another.
b) Ugg boots – super comfy, and allow for hours of walking (and calorie burning, hurray!) as I pace the department stores.
c) Tunic top – hides the bulge so I can hold my head up high amongst highly trendy, skinny sales assistant types.

After a quick slap of make-up and a hearty breakfast of Sugar Puffs, I break out the expensive filter coffee (strength 5) that Barry keeps for perking up before breakfast meetings. Today is going to be a marathon, and I need a full tank.

As I stir my coffee, I daydream about our inevitable reunion. When Barry returns home, I'll be dressed in something tight and black. We'll be just like Tom Cruise and Katie Holmes (back in the good old days, before Scientology and divorce ruined such a cute couple) smiling into each other's faces. Barry will be jumping on Oprah's couch, thrilled to be back in my glorious bosoms and will whisk me away to an exclusive ski resort where he'll indulge my every whim. We shall be rubbing shoulders with the royals in matching ski goggles. Wills and Kate will sip hot chocolate in the hot tub with us and swap stories while their regal babies gurgle in the arms of the nanny.

I grab my keys and take the M50 exit for Dundrum. Now, I must explain. Dundrum is not simply a shopping centre, it's my local Mecca. For me, a trip to the centre is on a par with a religious experience. Seriously, where else can you find BT2, House of Fraser and Harvey Nichols, otherwise known as 'The Holy Trinity', all located under the same roof? This, my dears, is my place of worship.

The problem is that the shopping centre is located dangerously close to my home. Don't laugh! When you have a shopping addiction, this is pure temptation. Sometimes, the urge for me to spend is overwhelming. The tempting lovelies displayed in shop windows are just too much for me to resist, especially during a mid season sale. They call to me in the night.

Some people turn to drugs or alcohol for solace. For me, shopping is my vice. There are days when Harry is demanding files left right and centre, and I invent some excuse to go there after work to get my fix. Some evenings, I fawn Barry off with the excuse of working late, then hide the paper bags and dispose of the tags: classic and shameful spendaholic traits. Barry chastises me like a child for hitting my overdraft just a week after payday. On the rare occasion that he notices I'm wearing something new, I say 'What, this old thing?' and laugh it off, claiming that he's inattentive to detail and clearly afflicted with colour blindness.

When I step through the glorious front doors, my shoulders drop and my blood pressure falls. My credit cards, maxed as they are, will be taking a rest today; I have Barry's card at the ready. I'm itching for the first purchase, the first high. Why should I not have the latest Coach handbag that I saw Posh drape over her skeleton-thin elbow in *Xposé* last week? Or the Jimmy Choos that Carrie in

Sex and the City raved about? Am I, like the ladies in the L'Oréal advert, not worth it? Why should I limit myself to buying a skirt in black when it comes in every colour you can think of? Don't I deserve the best? We aren't living in Amish-ville Pennsylvania, churning butter and wearing the same old plain black frock, last time I checked! I'm an emotional person, and need to express myself through clothing and accessories!

In House of Fraser, I search for something to knock Barry off his size ten loafers and into my arms. I'm like the proverbial kid in a candy shop, except instead of buying toffees and lollipops with pocket money pittance, there's a high limit on Barry's credit card and I know the pin number. *I know the pin number!*

In the cosmetics hall, I reach for an overpriced Crème de la Mer moisturiser. To hell with it. 'Do you believe in miracles?' the label reads. Well, that's good enough for me, I'm sold! And since my skin has taken a beating this last week (what with all of the crying and sleep deprivation playing havoc with my complexion), I decide to give it a shot. What good are clothes and make-up when your skin is in tatters? I'll never win back Barry's affection with worry lines and blotches, I need to glow!

The first high is reached as I thrust my Visa card at the assistant. I then trawl the racks for something to blow Barry away, but nothing inspires me. Past Ralph Lauren and Lacoste I traipse, and through Coast and Warehouse I wade. In the changing rooms, I half-heartedly try a few selections on for size. Everything I try on makes me feel like an absolute ogre, and not even Princess Fiona, but Shrek himself. It feels like I'll burst out of these shoddily constructed skimpy frocks.

'Sizes these days have definitely shrunk,' I tell a sales assistant. She's too busy texting to consider my dilemma seriously.

'Perhaps you can try on a size fourteen?' she mumbles without looking up from her screen.

The absolute wench has the body of a teenager and cannot possibly understand my predicament.

'The whole thing is a conspiracy,' I shout at her from behind the curtain. It's as if the recession has forced designers to use cheap material that rips easily when you try to force yourself into a size ten in the changing room and then hear a shredding sound as the zip gives way and you feel like the Incredible Hulk. I toy with the idea of writing to the *Irish Times* to encourage further discussion on this hot topic and blow the whole thing wide open. Erin Brockovich has nothing on me, I may even receive a journalistic award for my brave efforts. But before I can start my letter to the editor, I need to be rescued. My armpits are trapped, and I'll have to be wedged out. We've all been there.

'Help! It happened again!'

The sixteen year old is updating her Facebook status, and pretending not to hear me.

Dejected, I put the ripped garments back on a hanger and run away in the direction of BT2. Finally, I settle on a darling little two piece by Karl Lagerfeld that does wonders for my bulging Ned Kelly. I team it with a pair of Stella McCartney's, a stunning Frank McQueen scarf and a cute Mulberry satchel with studded detail – which I am bound to get endless use out of for work/nights out with the girls. It's therefore highly economical in the long term and a sound investment. I can't believe I failed economics in school, I'm such a genius. If the teacher had only used fashion metaphors, I'd have aced it.

I also choose a pair of Miu Miu sunglasses. Seeing as how it's November and not exactly tropical outside they're on sale and therefore a *bargain*. Quite frankly, I don't see how I can live without them. As the cashier scans the items, I visualise myself looking demure and stylish, welcoming a jet lagged Barry with open arms back into the bosom of our loving home once again. He'll forget his fatigue and fall in love all over again. The cash register pulls me back from orbit and into the real world. I hadn't realised quite how pricey the handbag was, but I swiftly push the party-pooping thought to one side and present Barry's credit card to the pretentious cashier with excitement.

The bags are getting heavy and I am suffering from a serious affliction, shopper's elbow. I cross the courtyard and wander into Harvey Nichols' café. Shopping is a real skill set that I possess, I reflect over the seared scallops to start followed by the Confit of Goosnargh duck leg. I could even switch careers to become a personal shopper. On second thoughts, I don't think I could help poor sad hopeless people devoid of fashion sense to spend their money all day, even if it is a charitable career choice.

Fully restored, I leave a generous tip. A little bit of 'me-time' was definitely what the doctor ordered. I'd better go home, I'm jumpy in case anyone from work spots me. My vomiting bug alibi wouldn't stand up what with all of these pretty paper bags tied with designed ribbons dangling from my wrist. I'm just feeling far too fabulous to pull it off. Instead of the deathly pallor one might expect, I have a lovely clear and luminescent complexion – I call it a post-shopping glow.

Twenty-One

Upon my arrival home, I scuttle to the front door, still trying to avoid Bernie from next door or anyone in her housewife posse. Thankfully, she must have so much gossiping to catch up on, following our recent clash in Tesco's, that her social diary is full. Perhaps she will be asked to be keynote speaker at the Bored Housewife Club AGM, I think caustically.

Usually, she's twitching net curtains or carrying out some imaginary gardening. (This involves looking at the plants without actually tackling them. I also partake in such a hobby, it's rapidly catching on.) I thank the Lord for small blessings and carry my shopping trophies through the front door with a sigh of relief. Even Barry is not around to challenge the new shopping bags and exhausted credit card, so I don't even have to check if the coast is clear before parading them into the lounge and plonking them onto the leather couch.

'Good God, have we been burgled? Jess? Jess?' I check that my beloved feline is here, and not snatched in some cat-napping drama. Thankfully, he's curled up in one of my grubby jumpers on the hall carpet.

The smell that hits my nostrils is the first thing to offend the senses. It's a mixture of body odour, stale beer and sour cream and onion flavoured Pringles. It smells like a frat party has taken place.

I'm like a parent coming home from a relaxing weekend away, like in that hilarious TV advert where the kid has completely trashed the free gaff. I expect to see a half-dressed cheerleader come out of the bathroom with the captain of the football team, tripping over a can of beer.

The sad truth is that I have not in fact been burgled. The lack of forced entry or any shards of broken glass is a dead giveaway. It's a shame really, then I could have blamed the mess on being the victim of a crime.

The pong is simply the smell of self-loathing and partying that I've been carrying on by my sad self over the last few days. I'm starting to understand why Mum keeps banging on about it every time she arrives over with care packages and rubber gloves. She has tried in a futile way to clear some of the rubble. She should have told me to 'cop the flip on' as the kids these days say.

Perhaps this is Mum's fault for not hosting an intervention. She let me rot for days. I should report her for neglect! I step over empty crisp packets, Pringles tins, chocolate wrappers, snotty tissues, takeaway trays and beer cans. Honestly, if Debbie from the Slimmers' Club could see me now, she would be shaking her little fat head in judgement.

The diet has fallen spectacularly off the wagon. In fact, the wagon is not even in sight any more, only the dust is visible down the trail. I've consumed enough calories in these last few days between takeaways and gargle to keep even the most loutish lad in XXL underpants.

The living room curtains are askew – it's as if I've been too half assed to open them fully. The TV is still blaring. The clock from *Countdown* ticks as the Carol Vorderman replacement (who is great but will never be as sexy or smart as the original) sashays across the screen in a tight-fitting hot pink jersey dress. The Richard Whitely replacement (who will never be as handsome and witty as the original) is looking bemused and has clearly failed to solve the conundrum in time, but tries to retain his dignity as the candidates press their buzzers. I reach for the remote control to mute it.

The shocking splash of burgundy on the cream wool carpet is the most disturbing vision in the room, and there are many to choose from. The wine bottle lies lifeless on its side with its contents drained. I ought to draw a chalk outline to complete the crime scene investigation look. Even the large bottle of carpet cleaner (*industrial strength*: I have experienced this kind of trouble before) and a sponge will struggle with this particular stain.

Upstairs, I know the house of horrors gets worse: un-made beds, wet towels and clothes lying on the floor. In the kitchen, I stifle a scream at the ghastly mess. If sweet Barry could see our love nest now, he'd be horrified, and this is a man that I have to nag to scrape his plate and put his socks into the laundry basket!

I have not cooked in days (Pop-Tarts, I'm assuming, don't count as cooking?) and the takeaway menus are in disarray on the counter top. This is the very least of my problems. A half eaten 'Mr Wong's 3-in-1 delight' is smeared across a plate, flies circling in anticipation. Foil takeaway packaging is piled high on the counter top.

I imagine Barry, travelling thousands of miles back from Ho Chi Minh City or wherever, weary and hungry. He opens the door and his plump jaw falls. I explain that I've turned into Waynetta Slob in his absence, fag hanging out of the side of my mouth. Our hot make-up sex is impinged by the rancid stink emanating from the rubble pile.

Now is not the time to panic. I've forty-eight hours and a rock-solid alibi to excuse me from work. Kim and Aggie will be proud of me, I'll write to them announcing my triumph against filth. The *How Clean Is Your House* duo may even feel moved by my sorry tale and start a whole new series devoted to people who have been so self-obsessed and wretched that their boyfriends refuse to marry them and then go away on a business trip after a huge fight and the house falls apart. They could call it *Dumped and Living in a Dump.* Catchy, eh? I'll send an urgent email to Channel 4 to suggest same.

Tempting as it is to sit down (post-shopping swollen ankles are now reaching critical point and I'm in desperate need of a G&T), I know I can put the cleaning off no longer. The dishes are piled high in the sink, and the dishwasher is full. The bins are overflowing. Since this is Barry's job, I had simply refused to tackle this over the last few days whilst also nursing a broken heart slash hangover. Next to the overflowing bins, there are empty beer bottles lined up like soldiers on the kitchen tiles. As the whiff is overwhelming, I decide to tackle this first. It's either that, or the Health Department might get a call from Bernie from next door complaining about the pong. She'd say that she's worried that a murder victim is rotting beneath my floorboards; I wouldn't put it past her.

After much jostling, the bin bag splits. Again, my laziness is to blame: rather than change the bin, I've crammed it beyond reasonable capacity until the lid sits wide mouthed and gaping. I had made it clear to Barry when we moved in together that I won't carry out this horrid chore. Barry has strict instructions regarding bins, because I've a genuine reaction to nasty niffs, and it's therefore not my fault that I can't do whiffy jobs. I scoop up the gunge and attempt not to gag, holding the offending bag at arm's length and placing it into the wheelie bin.

Like a criminal removing all fingerprints, it's starting to look like the crime never happened. After I open every window in the house, I let the fresh air pour in and don a pair of pink marigolds.

It is eight o'clock in the evening, and I can hardly move. When I'm brave enough to move an inch or two, I'm in such muscular agony that I quickly retreat to the comfort of the freshly scrubbed couch. I dare not move a cushion out of place for fear that I'll have to go through the cleaning marathon once again. The sudden burst of intense housework preceded by a legendary shopping trip is enough to give anyone a cramp in their calf muscle. As soon as either shopping or cleaning becomes an Olympic sport, I shall be proud to carry the torch for this fine nation.

I sip a G&T that can definitely now be described as for medicinal purposes, and munch a six-pack of Skips. The house smells lemony fresh, and I relax into the soft leather upholstery with relief. I even use a coaster for my wine glass. When I devour a microwave Marks & Spencer's meal for one and a generous helping of garlic bread, my tummy starts to churn. Perhaps my body has gone into shock after such excessive cleaning. Like a triathlon competitor, I should have warmed up and stretched before the event. Now my system is probably having a gastric meltdown.

I distract myself with an especially gripping episode of *Antiques Roadshow*. Although I don't like to publicly admit that I watch it (*please* don't tell anyone), I always particularly enjoy the bit where some old dear brings in a chipped tea pot. You can tell that she's blatantly hoping it's some priceless family heirloom only to be told that it's completely and utterly worthless. She probably picked it up for a pound in her local Oxfam, dusted it off and tried to pawn it off as an antique discovered lurking at the back of her auntie's attic. The look of sheer devastation as her face crumples is the bit I particularly relish.

Sometimes, you can tell that the old fart is trying not to cry (there goes the new hip replacement that she had been saving up for). Then her bottom lip wobbles. Usually, much to my utter disappointment, they are infuriatingly composed and say 'Ah well'. But you know that they are really crushed inside emotionally, you know? Mum got me hooked on it once when I was off school, as I was sick with scarlet fever (it was the real deal on that particular occasion, but the illness mysteriously surfaced again years later when I couldn't face the office during an audit by the finance team).

Anyway, *Embarrassing Bodies* follows swiftly afterwards on Channel 4 and the sight of an elderly gentleman with a highly contagious and angry-looking rash on his inner thigh makes me clutch my stomach even more. It would be just my luck (and highly ironic) if the make-believe vomiting bug fairytale that I have spun is actually coming into effect. Is this what you call

Karma? I pray that my weekend reunion with Barry will not be spent uttering sweet nothings from the bathroom floor and talking to God on the toilet.

Being sick after you call in sick is a little bit like the boy who cried wolf. It's worse than a wet fortnight in Lanzarote when all you have packed are bikinis and a toothbrush. I should know, this happened to me once. I don't want to talk about it.

Then I recognise the sensation – there's no mistaking it. Guilt! I felt this once before, when I had scratched Dad's car. (By accident, of course. As if you need to ask! The fact that he had refused to buy me my own wheels that summer was entirely coincidental.) It is like a mixture of dread and nagging, with a vigorous washing machine stomach.

You see, I've been visualising Barry's credit card statement arriving through the post any day now. It terrifies me. What had I been thinking spending such an extortionate amount? As the rain beats down on the double-glazed windows, I curse myself for buying a pair of sunglasses, that I'll have to wait months (or until the next colossal hangover) to wear!

Now, Barry isn't the type to throw an absolute hissy fit (bless him) but he will not be best pleased. I'll have to make sure that he's so loved up with the new, improved me that he will forgive my spending splurge. Perhaps I'll have to make him my love slave and tie him to the bed posts for days to prevent him from checking the post!

I'm missing Barry so much that I spend the rest of the evening consuming calorie-laden comfort food. Nachos loaded with sour cream and chive dip, real butter on top of butter-flavored microwave popcorn – they help me to forget my worries. I'm glued to *You've Been Framed*. I must confess that I thoroughly enjoy watching elderly and slightly inebriated people fall over on the dancefloor at weddings. Barry doesn't get the show, he labels it as facile.

'It's just stupid people falling over,' he once said.

'Exactly. That's the entire point. I watch it to give my brain a rest!' He didn't buy it.

I'm deliberating between a packet of Hobnobs and a packet of Toffee Pops (I know, it is a no brainer: both) when Mum calls.

'I've been so awful to poor Barry, Mum. Let me fill you in on "Operation Win Back Barry" and my plans to look ravishing.' I lick the chocolate off my Hobnob.

'That's great, darling. Get yourself some new underwear. Always works a treat.'

'Mum!' I choke on the crumbs.

'I'm just saying, darling. Anyway, if you're going to be off tomorrow, why don't you come with us to the parish hall? There's Zumba at ten.'

'Us' refers to the retirement club. I hesitate. Jumping about with a pack of geriatrics isn't exactly how I planned to spend my sickie.

Then again, I push away an empty bottle of wine and a family pack of cheese nachos which have made me queasy, some exercise might be good.

'Hmm,' I deliberate.

'Zumba,' my mother reads from the parish newsletter, 'is the new high energy dance craze sweeping the exercise world!'

I snigger and picture her in a pair of hot pink Lycra shorts. I'm tempted to give it a go, the flyer on my fridge has been leering at me for weeks now. The skinny twenty-somethings are dancing themselves thin. They think they're better than me with their gravity defying breasts and their pert bottoms. They scream at me like exercise-addicted drill sergeants.

'Hey, butterball!' Tiffany the instructor shouts at me from the flyer. It's not very professional of her to call me a butterball, I should complain to her supervisor. 'Zumba is a rocking party for a rock-hard body! Join us!'

'I would have, Tiffany,' I reply. 'But I've been busy. I have a full-time job. I have a new soap opera to catch up on. I have a boyfriend who I've been awful to and need to make up with.'

She sneers. Telling all of your friends that you'll sign up to a class and hanging the flyer on your fridge does not burn calories.

Emer has been banging on about Zumba for months now. She fits in a Zumba session before her sunrise spin at the local gym and still manages to be at her desk for eight. Show off! Says she burns, like, a thousand calories or something outrageous at each session. The last time I burned a thousand calories was when I forgot about a pizza in the oven.

'OK, Mum. Count me in.'

I tip half a bag of bath salts into a bubble bath and strip off. An hour and a half later, scrubbed and buffed, I emerge. My fingers and toes resemble prunes. In a white fluffy hotel robe (*stolen*, much to Barry's shock horror during a recent stay at Monart spa) I collapse onto the plump divan king-sized sleigh bed. Moments later, in a pool of my own drool, I fall into a deep sleep.

Twenty-Two

The dregs of a memory linger when I wake.

I was back in the Trinners sports hall. Sorca (must be pronounced Soooor-Cawh *as if marbles are in your mouth or else she will correct* you) *and I were in yoga class, trying to lie on mats and think transcending deep thoughts. You know, hippy shit. However, the instructor had a speech impediment. 'Picture a bootiful wed wose,' she instructed as I cackled. 'A foo moon.' Sorca's shoulders jiggled beside me. I tried my best, honestly, I did, but it was all too much. I convulsed in hysterics, and was politely asked to leave. I humbly dragged the mat behind me.*

Perhaps my subconscious was telling me not to make a total ass of myself at Zumba this morning.

'Morning, Jess.' I pad downstairs for a caffeine fix.

Second thoughts niggle.

a) I'll have to shave my legs.
b) I'll probably be the only one in attendance under the age of sixty.
c) My muscles are still screaming at me from the clean-a-thon yesterday.
d) Last night's drinks contained far more gin than tonic.

I reach for the milk inside the fridge. Tiffany the Zumba instructor winks. I haven't got the heart to let her down. Also, Barry will be so proud of me. He has been encouraging me to find a hobby for months now (as if juggling a conflicting soap opera schedule *and* planning a wedding haven't been exhausting enough). As always, though, Barry was right.

Upstairs, I catch a glimpse of my flabby self in the mirror. Barry says I'm perfect just the way I am, and that I shouldn't change a thing, but all I can see is excess fat and cellulite. I've added an extra large bottle of tanning cream and some press-on nails to my shopping list so that I can really Essex it up before my sweet lover comes home. I shall be glorious for him! After much rifling through my bomb site of a wardrobe, I discover a hidden gem lurking at the back.

'Yes! I'd forgotten about that!'

I remove the tags from a new workout outfit that Barry had kindly bought me last year in the sales in order to support my New Year's resolution to get fit. It's electric blue and stretchy – quite the trendy little number when teamed with a new pair of trainers that have also been hiding at the back.

The Lycra top stretches at the belly, exaggerating my newly acquired paunch. I should have gone for the large size. Who am I fooling with the unforgiving 'medium'? These Lycra sizes are built for stick insects with exercise addiction, anyway – everybody knows that! Before leaving, I try on another three outfits, but revert back to the stretchy number and slap on some leftover fake tan and a truck load of make-up. Mum has already arrived when I pull up at the church car park.

'Darling, hi! This will be great fun!'

Mum hugs me as I scope out the rest of the class, and try to adjust the knickers line of my granny pants through the shorts.

'Welcome,' Alfonso bounces into the hall.

Dark chest hair protrudes from his black Lycra top and let's just say that his matching Lycra shorts are tight. Very tight, in fact. He lifts a muscular arm to slick back his wavy jet black curly hair.

'Are ju ready to *Zumba*?'

I suspect that his South American accent is highly exaggerated for the ladies. What a cliché.

163

Alfonso bends over to load up the music. He hits the disco lights and pumps up the volume. Just as well – the attendees could definitely be described as mature, and some are probably hard of hearing. Some of them look like they might drop dead mid rumble.

He jumps onto a makeshift stage and wiggles to the Latin beats. The retirement club shuffles about in an attempt to copy his actions. Like an uncoordinated elephant, I move two steps behind. When the horde moves left, I move right. When they move up, I move down. My clapping misses the beat.

All in all, it's pretty do-able. I mean, I used to dance on a few tables in my time, I'll have you know. I was no stranger to dancing for vodka shots with Adam behind the bar in Club 92 back in the day.

'Ju did a great warm-up! Now let's Zooombah!'

Alfonso gyrates his hips as the smug smile slides from my face. The old dears at the front cheer and whoop as they wave their bingo wings. Alfonso is bumping and grinding like no-one's business, his pelvis going into over-drive. I can't divert my eyes from his jiggling shorts, it's hypnotising.

The Golden Girls in the front row are giving it some serious wellie. Perhaps they are one hip thrust and bosom shake away from a cardiac arrest, but at least they'll die happy! It's a shame that I didn't bring my glasses along. I'm too vain to wear them outside of the house, despite my shockingly poor long-distance vision and horrible typing skills at the office. I struggle to keep up with Alfonso's moves and am forced to do a combination of:

a) Copying the old dear in front of me. However, this is like the blonde leading the blonde.

b) Freestyling it. Luckily, I'm very resourceful this way. See Adam behind the bar in Club 92 for references. He even does my job application references, too. He describes me to potential employers as 'flexible, eager to please and an awesome grinder', which amuses me no end.

The rhythm is contagious. Alfonso winks at me, and I'm scarlet like a twelve year old at a One Direction concert. Wait till Barry sees me tomorrow, I'll be skinny and toned with new killer moves. He will want to whisk me off for a bit of dirty dancing Patrick-Swayze style, and then on to some swish hotel afterwards to have his wicked way with me.

Thirty minutes in, I feel the burn. Boy, do I feel the burn. It burns from my ass to my thighs to my lungs and everywhere in between. When I breathe, I pull in ragged, hot air. During a quick break, it's obvious why Mum had reminded me twice about the towel and water bottle. We resume our gruelling party. Another thirty exhilarating minutes later we emerge, purple in the face and perspiring furiously.

'See ju next time, sexy ladies!' Alfonso mops his brow.

The session has come and gone in a calorie-smashing blast. We bid farewell to all of Mum's gang. They have a bridge game lined up for the afternoon, and a trip to Cavan planned for the following week, bless their pension-drawing hearts. This retirement thing looks like a lark.

My legs are like jelly and my thighs are all of a quiver as I try to navigate the church hall steps with a wobble. Squinting at the sunlight, I see a familiar face beyond the church gates. She is waving frantically in my direction and has three children: two toddlers in a double buggy, and another strapped securely to a material pouch around her chest. Judging by the enormous pregnant belly and elasticised waistband trousers, she has another one imminently on the way.

'Rebecca!' she calls breathlessly, pushing the double buggy along the gravel path.

For the life of me I can't remember her name. 'Hi!'

The search for her name continues. I filter through school and college, but yield zip.

'This is my mum, Joan.'

Freakishly, my mother is back to normal complexion, and offers her hand in greeting.

'Hi, I'm Angie,' the woman simpers. 'An old school pal of Rebecca. God, it's been *years*!'

'Ah yes! Great to see you, Angie. How are you, Angie? Wow, you've been busy, Angie.'

She motions to her little ones. 'This is River, Blossom and Sky. We're just off to mother and baby yoga.'

Angie reaches up to brush some wild hair from her face and reveals an unshaven armpit under a smock (probably woven from hemp or something eco friendly). Her gaggle of children look unnaturally happy – not a tantrum in sight. She is probably still breast feeding all three of them. Perhaps she has drugged them with junior Valium pills (or something of a herbal, alternative nature).

In school, she was a bit of a teacher's pet. We were friends when I needed homework copied or before the cool kids arrived.

'So tell me about you! How have you been?' she quizzes.

'Well, nothing to tell really…' I panic '…I'm still working in PR.'

I hold back on the wee fact that I'm a meagre assistant in a dead-end job (which isn't even technically PR), fetching coffee and internet surfing all day, and that I'm currently out on sick leave and have received a verbal warning for same.

'Great.'

'Yeah. Barry and I are doing just great. Never been better!'

I'm in full porky pie mode and unable to stop myself. Pinocchio would be shocked. I fail to mention that:

a) The last time I saw my beloved, he was furious following a blazing row.
b) I threw a cushion at his head.
c) I have a wedding planned, honeymoon booked and a wedding dress selected, but Barry has *not* proposed to me. Yet.

I'm keen to change the subject before she spots that:

a) I have, in fact, no wedding ring or even an engagement ring on my finger.

166

b) I have piled on the weight since she last saw me. Even if I was a teenager when we last met, that is no excuse.

c) I'm looking pretty rough after the class. Purple and sweaty is not a good look for me, especially when you add stretchy Lycra to the already delicate mix.

d) My mascara has run and my hair is dishevelled.

e) In the cold light of day, I see that the hastily applied false tan is looking streakier than a bacon butty.

'And you have another one on the way!' I motion to the giant stomach protruding from her cardigan.

'Yes,' she thrills. 'Little Forest is due this Christmas!'

I'm lost for words at her hideous taste in baby naming, but manage to hold back my guffaws. Mum and I continue to smile and nod like toy dogs on the back window of a Nissan Micra. Her patterned trousers hang on her otherwise slim frame and fall to her Crocs. I find myself staring at a single chin hair, unable to pull away from its mesmerising stare.

I'm not listening when she talks, I'm daydreaming about what make-up I'd apply to her if I had my merry way. *She will weep with joy at the transformation. I'll de-frizz and crop her mousy hair and dye it a deep plum. Or maybe a light caramel. I will ceremoniously burn her wardrobe and introduce her to the world of couture, producing the tweezers and waxing strips with glee. Her husband will be so thrilled with the makeover that he will knock her up again and take her away for a night of passion and a steak dinner. Or a Quorn bake; I think she's a vegan.*

Rubbing the sleeping baby's head, she continues. 'I'll have four under four soon.'

Does she want a flipping Blue Peter badge or something? As if this is a world record achievement or something. Snore!

'No point in waiting once you hit thirty, eh?' she smiles in my direction. 'And you'll be next! How far along are you? Is this your first?'

Before I've a chance to reply, I catch a sideways glance of myself (and in particular my Lycra-clad belly) in the reflection of the parish windows. I'm aghast. My mouth falls open like a goldfish. How have I let myself go to the extent that an old school chum thinks that I have a bun in the oven? I'm going to bin those Lycra shorts the minute I'm home. Unless someone is literally about to give birth at any moment, it's best to keep one's mouth shut. I learned that lesson the hard way at the office Christmas party last year when making small talk to the boss' wife.

All I can do is stare. She's starting to ruin my day off entirely! I can feel fresh sweat beading on my forehead.

'And you're great to keep the exercise classes up while you're expecting,' she attempts, puzzled and desperately trying to fill the deafening void between us.

'No kiddies for Rebecca just yet, Angie,' Mum rescues me. 'Ah, sure what's the rush?'

She smiles sweetly, and utters a classic line that I'll never forget. Perhaps I will one day regale people at her funeral with it when I give a heart-warming eulogy.

'Sure, there's plenty of time for dirty nappies and cracked nipples.'

Once I get over the fact that my mum has used the words '*cracked*' and '*nipples*' in the same sentence, I feel a triumphant grin spread across my face. My opinion of Mum has now shot through the roof. She is now officially my new idol.

'Anyway, must dash,' Mum continues as I stare mutely at my trainers. 'Rebecca is due back to the board room shortly.'

The dig is genius. Clearly Eco Mother does not work or pay taxes. We screech off in our fuel-guzzling-ozone-layer-destroying cars, leaving a stunned Angie in a plume of toxic emissions. Her children smile obliviously.

Twenty-Three

The short taxi journey to Suvarnabhumi airport is filled with a most uneasy silence but Barry is grateful. Shelley has avoided him since their painful exchange the other night but now they must face the journey back together. Without her thick make-up, she is looking pale.

As the taxi veers through the city, he closes his eyes and pictures Rebecca waiting for him at home. The perspiration runs down his back, and he imagines lying next to her under the cool cotton sheets of their bed. The city lights are pretty beautiful. It's the only tour of the country that Barry has had. He takes in the aromas of the Thai night markets filled with people. He gazes at the hustle and bustle of the red light district which passes in a blur.

Barry's jaws are aching from the non-stop smiling and small talk marathon over the last week. Thank God it's all over now and he can just go home to Rebecca. According to his itinerary, the flight from Bangkok to Amsterdam will take nine hours, followed by a short flight to Dublin. With some luck, he will be seated as far away from Shelley as possible and can catch up on some much needed sleep.

Nigel's hangover is now in full swing, and Barry is sure that the sick bag on the aeroplane will be definitely called upon during their long journey home. Almost a week spent in the company of the boss has helped Barry to come to a conclusion – the man is a complete ass. He had suspected it for years, but had only ever had to endure him in small doses. Now, there's no doubt.

Barry's mind repeats the image of him waking up with Shelley next to him in the bed, reminding him of his unforgivable actions. It was the biggest mistake of his life, the most idiotic, drunken, cruel act. He's grateful that he can't remember the sex, because it's one less slide in his mind's never ending slideshow of horror. He will probably feel sick and regret it forever. Anyway, the thing with Shelley, whatever it was, is well and truly over now. He will just have to confess everything. If Rebecca will forgive him, he'll make it up to her. He'll do whatever it takes to win her back.

Nigel leans forward in the taxi as if he might be sick and Shelley inches away from him. There are beads of sweat on his brow and he's looking decidedly grey. The taxi bounces over a pothole in the city streets and Barry rolls down a window. It isn't surprising that Nigel is in a delicate state. The man had consumed enough Tiger beer, saki and brandy to knock out a sailor. The man's liver must be pickled by now, and he has probably contracted every STD going, thinks Barry. He wonders how far past sixty Nigel is. He wonders who would get a promotion if the old git keels over.

The conference is finally over, and what's more the Nagasaki account has been clinched. It has taken Barry's last drop of patience and energy, but it's in the bag. The old fart had even made reference to making Barry partner. However, it was well past midnight and his words were slurred and his breath was hot and stale. The git had consumed enough alcohol to sedate a horse. He could barely hold his own head, never mind hold a pen. Barry realised that he should have made him sign something.

Barry smiles as the taxi approaches the airport. He's a fraction closer to home, closer to Rebecca, and closer to getting his life back on track. The three passengers scramble with seatbelts. The taxi driver retrieves luggage and they approach the check-in desk.

Nearly there, thinks Barry. *Hold on baby, I am coming home.*

Twenty-Four

'You do know that I don't meet in any board rooms, Mum, don't you?'

Mum passes me a fresh cream éclair and a steaming hot cup of tea laden with three spoons of sugar. You know, for the shock of my earlier encounter.

'Yes, darling.'

'Unless I'm bringing the tea in,' I put my chin in my hands as my lip wobbles.

The hemp-clad tree hugger has really left me reeling. I'm on a major downer. It's not the mistaken pregnancy comment (unsurprising when you look at the additional pounds that I have stored up like a bear hibernating for the long winter ahead) that bothers me. After all, a few more Zumba sessions with Mum will sort me out, and I have my stretchy knickers to hide a multitude of sins.

What bothers me is anyone knowing that I am unmarried with a rubbish career. It makes me feel like a loser. I mean, it's bad enough for my ego being mates with the super successful Emer (but not so much Pam, my ego is safe with her). Other friends like Karen, who used to know how to party like a pro before the babies came along, have moved on with their lives and are living in domestic bliss. They're leaving me behind. Meeting them is a hurtful reminder that, although I have a man who loves me despite my annoying ways, I've got no glittering rock or snot-nosed dependents relying on me.

'I just wish I hadn't pushed Barry so hard to propose,' I sulk to Mum.

'But you can't rush these things, darling.'

'I know. And yet we fight constantly about it. I nag and drive him crazy. He says he loves me, but he's not ready to get married.'

Mum smoothes my hair. I can't stop the tears from coming, they spill hot down my face.

'The truth is, Mum, I just want Barry back. Proposal or not, it doesn't matter any more. I just want him back.'

With that I collapse into her arms and the sobs take over. Mum reassures me, as only mums can do. She says it will all work out. She tells me to hang in there. There is no mention of firing out a grandchild. She holds back on discussing my biological clock. This is her idea of cutting me some slack.

'And I haven't stopped eating all week.'

'Listen, you and Barry are meant for each other, darling.'

I sniff. 'Really?'

'Definitely! Sure, who else would put up with you?'

'Huh, ain't that the truth! Anyway, we will see what this psychic has to say about the whole thing this afternoon.'

'Very exciting.'

'Hi Fairy!' Dad arrives into the kitchen and rifles through the *RTE Guide*. We discuss the *Corrie* plot line at length, paying great attention to what a total witch that Sally Webster is turning out to be. He still denies watching the programme. It's highly suspicious given his in-depth knowledge of the plot line.

'See you at six, Mum.'

I pop home to change before the psychic appointment – I want to look my best when my destiny is being revealed.

On my way, I stop off at my local supermarket to stock up. I decide against going to Tesco, for obvious reasons. Instead of booze and junk food, I pick up a selection of fruit juices, lettuce, brown rice, lentils and stir fry vegetables. It's like Gillian McKeith's wet dream. I'm in full detox mode now. My body is a temple, after all. I

172

also buy slimline tonic to go with the gin that I desperately deserve after all my hard work, and get stuck in as soon as the key is in the door. The clinking of the ice in the cool glass and the fizzing of the tonic are like angels singing.

In the sitting room, there's an ice pack on my thighs (at this point, they are never going to speak to me again and never want to hear the word 'Zumba' in the foreseeable future). I catch up on *The Only Way Is Essex* repeats. That Marc is being a real creep to Lauren. She tells him to 'shu-uuup'.

The brown rice, stir fry vegetables and lentils taste like cat litter wrapped in cardboard. Gillian McKeith had failed to mention this when she promoted the dish on her recent *You Are What You Eat* show. Instead, she brazenly rummaged with a disapproving tut-tut through the snack cabinet of a portly man with a penchant for pickled onion flavoured snacks. I persevere due to my ravenous hunger.

Gillian would surely like to know that when I try to make the drink from her recipe book, it turns grey, frothy and lumpy. Also, it has so much pulp that I think I'll be sick. There is vegetable and fruit juice splashed over the kitchen tiles. It smells faintly of socks. A fresh G&T takes away the taste.

I text Emer.

Off to top psychic shortly. Hope to Christ he tells me something good. XoXo

Immediately, my phone beeps in response.

Fab babes. Good luck!

I can hear Mum's car pulling into the driveway as I throw on a semi-clean pair of jeans and a shirt. I slap on some fresh lippie and pouf my hair. The search for two shoes that match is quite the challenge as they all come spilling out of my wardrobe. FYI – I have regularly been known in the past to wear mis-matched shoes to the office as I race off both late and with a hangover in progress. Both shoes might be black, with one left and one right, but definitely not a pair.

You see, I'm the type of person who likes to create the illusion of clean and tidy. I can give you a quick master class if you like. Basically, the technique involves the following:

a) Shove bits and pieces that you have no home for into a designated random drawer (this includes car keys, miscellaneous keys that you have absolutely no idea what they unlock, dead batteries, a torch with no batteries, old currency such as the Franc that has absolutely no monetary or sentimental value whatsoever, obsolete mobile phone chargers, takeaway menus – preferably out of date – telephone bills in need of payment that you are hiding from your loved ones, sewing kits, various buttons and miscellaneous). Repeat action until said drawer is at critical bursting point and difficult to open.

b) Pile clothes, shoes, coats, scarves and handbags into your bedroom wardrobe. No need to sort winter from summer and avoid confusion in the mornings while you are desperately late for work. No need to filter out ill-fitting clothes, such as those skinny jeans which you swear you'll fit into one day, and the loose baggy ones. Why make life easy on yourself? Continue until it is stuffed, but yet the bedroom floor is bare, hence creating the false impression of tidy.

c) The next step is of utmost importance. Are you listening, now? There may be a pop quiz at the end of this, so pay attention. Do not, under any circumstances, allow anyone (especially your mother-in-law, for goodness' sake) to open said drawers or wardrobes, even if they tell you they are cold and in need of a cardigan. They will discover your secret shame.

The result of such a wonderful household method is that your house looks clutter free and super tidy, just like you see in those minimalist magazines I keep on my coffee table. Unfortunately, however, the inevitable downside is that you cannot find anything that you are looking for. This is especially true at nine o'clock on a Monday morning, while you frantically search for socks.

Also, I'm obliged for legal reasons to warn you that you may suffer from a mild concussion when you open a press door and have a random object fall on your noggin. Examples of falling items include an 'Ab Trimmer Pro' that your brother bought you one birthday (which although you hinted heavily that you wanted, were highly insulted that he bought you since this basically translated as 'you are fat').

In my opinion, the system is worth it for the spick 'n' span illusion it creates. There is nothing cluttering up my window sills or cabinet tops. It soothes my easily upset OCD. My friends often comment on how organised the house looks. They say that they didn't realise that I was such a neat freak. I then thank them profusely but wrestle with them if they take it upon themselves to open a drawer in search of cutlery. Of course, there's another school of thought that basically promotes actually tidying out your drawers and wardrobes, but who has the time for that?

'Crap!' I can hear Mum in the driveway as I struggle into my now matching black boots. I pile the unwanted clothing back into the wardrobe, closing the door with difficulty.

'She's absolutely fine, Bernie.'

I strain to hear Mum's conversation with the wagon next door, peeking through the curtains.

'She's had a dreadful flu this week, poor love.'

I snigger. That will put Bernie back in her box. The absolute cheek of that cow pretending to ask after me, as if she is concerned!

'Yes, probably run-down from her important job, Bernie. You know how it is. Are you working yourself, Bernie? No? Ah. That's a shame. The recession is tough on everyone, eh? Anyway!'

Mum waves her hand in a breezy gesture before Bernie can attempt to explain that she is not in fact unemployed but a housewife.

'Must dash, Bernie. We have an important appointment to attend.'

Mum has her key in the hall door, just as Bernie closes her front door with a thud.

'All set, darling?'

'All set,' I reply, grabbing my make-up bag, handbag and a Pop-Tart to have as a snack en route.

Mum's ancient Nissan Micra reverses ever so slowly out of the driveway. The indicator is flashing as soon as the key turns in the ignition. The decrepit vehicle beeps as it reverses, like a truck.

On the M50, the car putt-putts along while we chat. Mum is driving well below the speed limit, which drives me nuts. My right foot is pressing on an imaginary accelerator to will her on. She doesn't seem to know what fourth gear is for.

'So, have you been to see this fortune teller guy Michael before?' I quiz Mum as we make our way towards the city centre at the speed of a tortoise in pain. Cars are overtaking and beeping at us. Mum does not notice.

'No, darling.'

Mum's indicators are still on from a couple of miles back when she exited a roundabout.

'But Nuala goes every few months. John has had very poor health, and they have a lot of worries.'

'Uh-huh.'

I fumble with the car radio and tune out Radio Granny FM that she likes so much. I tune in some '90s music. Who needs constant weather updates and people calling up to complain about water taxes when, somewhere out there, there may be a radio station playing 'Rhythm Is A Dancer'?

'Well, anyway…the last time Nuala went,' Mum whispers.

She is overtaken by an elderly man in a 1996 white Ford Fiesta that is in a more shameful state than her rust bucket. At least her car has working windscreen wipers.

'Michael told her that she was going on a long journey.'

She pauses for dramatic effect as I raise my eyebrows.

'The very next week,' she utters in hushed tones, 'she won top prize at the bingo.'

I wait in anticipation.

'A cruise!' Mum exclaims, unable to contain her excitement.

'Spooky,' I deadpan.

'I know!'

Witty sarcasm is wasted on Mum, it goes right over her head. This fortune teller had better be good. Perhaps he might predict a cruise for Barry and I. Perhaps it will be a honeymoon cruise! Or a fiftieth wedding anniversary cruise!

'And,' Mum interrupts my fantasy of a candlelit supper at the captain's table, Barry dressed in a tuxedo. 'He told her that her daughter Mandy has a boy and a girl!'

'Doesn't she have two girls?'

I'm poking holes in Mum's story now. My dream is deflated, like a burst dinghy. The cruise ship has set sail, without us on board.

'Well, yes,' she blusters, 'but Nuala admitted to me once that the little one is very boyish. I mean, she could turn out to be a…' Mum covers her mouth with her hand '…lesbian.'

I stifle a laugh. Mum thinks that everyone is a lesbian. Even me at one point, but like I told her, Karen and I were just really good friends, and everyone experiments in college.

'Then Michael said that he was definitely detecting a real masculine energy and that must have been where he got confused.'

'Amazing,' I smirk. The cruise ship has struck an iceberg and has sent out a distress flare. Barry and I are wearing matching life jackets.

'Oh, I almost forgot. Here's the really incredible bit.'

Mum is highly excitable now. Her speed temporarily reaches fifty kilometres per hour as we approach Donnybrook junction. She soon realises her error and takes her foot off the accelerator again, much to my disappointment.

'Michael said that John is sick, which of course he is. Isn't that uncanny?'

Her question hangs in the air, unanswered. I search for a diplomatic reply.

'Not really. Nuala is ancient. So chances are that her husband is either long gone or equally decrepit. She's probably closer to the angels than Michael is.'

Mum shoots me a disbelieving look.

'Rebecca! Anyway, then he got this message from the spirits!'

Mum's hands are off the steering wheel now in a giant gesture. Her head is turned to face me, looking for my reaction.

'Wow,' I fake, motioning frantically towards the windscreen so that she will return her full attention back to the road before we met the angels ourselves for real.

'Yes. It was beautiful, Nuala told me. He closed his eyes and said that John would have trouble with his heart.'

'Oh?'

That is a teeny bit spooky, I must admit.

'OK, it turned out to be his lungs that gave him the trouble, but that's the organ right next to the heart, so he was in the right region.'

We park the car on George's Street and make our way to meet the fortune teller on Exchequer Street. Michael meets us at the door. At a guess, I reckon that he is in his late fifties. He is wearing a white collarless shirt with jeans and flip-flops.

Mum enters first, practically curtsying when she greets him. I sit in the corridor outside and catch up on my celebrity gossip on my iPhone and tweet to my loyal followers. I'm a smidge nervous. I mean, Barry and I are at a crossroads. I need divine intervention.

'Listen,' I give myself a pep talk. 'Relax. This guy talks to dead people for a living. What's the worst that could happen?'

Twenty minutes later, Mum flits out. It is my turn.

Inside the cramped room, there are two comfortable chairs and a mini side table where he has laid out some angel cards. A tea light candle flickers, and a wind chime tinkles by the window. We sit down opposite each other and I smile nervously.

'You're very welcome,' Michael reaches for the cards.

As instructed, I close my eyes. Michael tells me to breathe deeply. I am focussing on a burning question. He shuffles the well worn cards. After holding my outstretched hand over the face down Tarot cards, I select nine. Michael arranges them face up on the table in a Celtic cross spread.

The first thing I notice to my absolute horror is the death card. The grim reaper is glaring at me. I raise my hands to my face.

'Not to worry,' he smiles. 'Death simply means a new start. It is the end of an old era and the start of a new one.'

Maybe this is the end of living in sin and the start of wedded bliss. He flips over the second card and his forehead creases.

'You have been deeply troubled.'

'Oh my *God*!' I exclaim. 'That is absolutely freaky.'

I rant at racehorse announcer speed. In fairness, he charges by the half hour and I want my money's worth.

'Honestly, I have had an absolute mare of a week.'

My chin wobbles, and I can feel tears prick my eyes. My voice wavers and Michael hands me a tissue without interruption.

'I've been so terribly awful to my boyfriend and we had a total blazer. Then he stormed off and went away on a business trip, and then I didn't hear from him and I was all, like…' I search for the words frantically and flap my hands.

'Messed up!'

My incoherent babbling sounds like a teenage cast member of *Beverly Hills 90210*.

'And then! I had to call in sick from work and the woman next door was mean to me in Tesco!'

Michael remains unfazed. His hands are clasped in a Zen-like fashion. He's probably used to irrational emotional women spilling their guts to him on a daily basis. I have to put my hands over my mouth to stop myself revealing any more. Everybody knows that when you visit a psychic/angel-healing/fortune-telling/spirit-medium-type person you are supposed to sit there innocently and say nothing. You're meant to let them do all the talking! It's impossible for me to shut up for long enough to achieve this.

'Yes, I'm sensing a difficult time recently,' he murmurs vaguely.

This is worse than going into the doctor's surgery and telling him you have a blinding headache and fifty flipping euro later, you are diagnosed with having a blinding headache. My irritation grows as Michael flips over the next cards.

'I can see you are very in tune spiritually,' Michael speaks softly.

Finally! That is one undeniable truth. If I wasn't a movie star in a past life, I was a Buddhist monk. Michael must have astonishing, mind-blowing, spoon-bending powers.

The next card to be revealed is a queen on a throne, and the following one looks like a court jester.

'Even though he doesn't always say it, he loves you very, very much indeed,' continues Michael.

'Yeeeeees…' I fish. 'Go on.'

The next card looks like a goblet thing and I'm pretty sure I see a few gold coins on another.

'This card tells me that you must learn to be more selfless and mature. You must respect those who love you most.'

My cheeks blaze; he's obviously thinking about what a wench I've been to poor Barry.

'The angels are warning you about your spending.'

Well, that's complete rubbish. I have only really had one shopping splurge in the last week, and that was for therapeutic reasons. Perhaps the angels are concerned about me spending good money to see this phoney.

'Look,' I level with Michael as he turns over a card revealing the sun, moon and stars. 'Do you see Barry and I working things out? Is there a diamond engagement ring in the cards, or what?'

My voice is bordering on trembling at this point, and has risen a couple of octaves. Deep breathing is out the window. My angelic smile has faded and in its place is a blotchy face that is being dabbed by a snotty Kleenex. It's time to lay the cards on the table, if you'll pardon the pun. Michael looks slightly confused. Perhaps he is not used to such direct questioning, tears and general hand flapping. Well tough. At fifty shagging euro a pop, I need answers!

'Can you tell how many carats?' I persist. 'Diamonds or sapphires? Are you getting a precise date?'

I press the man for more exact details. He slowly shakes his head, not sure how to reply.

'The angels are telling you to be patient. All will happen in good time,' he speaks gently.

Huh! What kind of a wishy washy mumbo jumbo is this? I need black and white facts, here. Be patient? Is this guy for real? That's easy for the angels to say! They haven't got a scrapbook of ingenious and elegant wedding plans and no ring on their angel fingers. They are living it up on cloud nine or wherever they are residing, and I'm facing the harsh reality back on earth! I need to know if Barry and I are going to have a fairytale ending. Will there be a coffee and cream theme? Will I have those little mini cupcakes at the reception? Will I ever get rid of this cellulite? All of the essential questions burn in my mind.

I think of Barry, weary and laden down with files, making his way back to me in Dublin. None of those things seem to matter any more.

'Will Barry…' I whisper, 'forgive me?'

'Your dream,' Michael looks straight into my bloodshot eyes and passes me a box of tissues, 'will come true.'

Relief washes over me in an instant. I sit bolt upright in the chair.

'This dark haired man of yours,' he continues as I remember the salt and pepper streaks through Barry's hair, 'loves you very much. And you'll be parents within a year or so, I see.'

'Woah! Back up,' I say. 'Me? A parent? No, I don't think so… not yet, surely?'

'I see you cradling a baby girl,' he speaks mysteriously, 'while a young toddler…a boy… runs behind you.'

He rubs his temples, trying to tune in the image like that of an old television set.

'Ehhh … Sorry, Michael, but I don't think … not for a few years, surely.' It's all I can manage.

Two children? Unlikely! 'I see you stepping away from your career…'

I lean in closer to catch every word. This is more like it. Perhaps he can picture Tammie and I at the shelter while Barry slaves away at the office all day?

'…to become a full-time mother.'

No! Surely not. Imagine me, standing next to Bernie, a fully paid-up member of the bored Housewives Club. A stay at home mummy? I think not! I mean, kids are great, and I hate my job, but still! My face falls with sheer horror.

'Have you had a brush with the law?' Michael's face is serious.

'I beg your pardon?'

'Yes, I see a speeding fine arriving in the post?'

'I don't know *what* you're talking about,' a hot flush creeps up my face.

On the way home, I fill Mum in on the whole happy ever after and babies prediction. She's thrilled with the idea of grandbabies. It's just starting to get dark out, but Mum insists on putting her full beam lights on, blinding oncoming traffic. She prattles on about how Michael predicted that she will be taking up golf in the near future and how the angels are watching over her. Dad will need to watch out for falling branches or something ridiculous.

'Yes, yes,' I say impatiently, trying to push her towards the good stuff. 'But what did he say about *me and Barry*?'

Mum has been so wrapped up in getting a reading for herself that she had failed to pummel him for further essential info regarding myself and Barry. Our future is hanging by a thread and she is talking about unlikely forestry injuries!

'Sorry, darling,' apologises Mum as we pass Foxrock church at a sluggish pace. She puts her hazard lights on for a reason best known to herself.

'In fact… he didn't mention you at all!'

'Thanks a bunch, Mum.'

The angels have snubbed me! Everyone apart from me featured in her brief reading – Dad, herself and someone who name starts with the letter 'N' who should be careful of a conman. Mum is planning on calling Nuala as soon as she is home to warn her. Even Ian got a look in. Apparently he and his on-again-off-again girlfriend are heading for splits ville. Well, that is more predictable than a *Hollyoaks* storyline.

Back home, I pour a stiff drink. This time tomorrow, Barry will be back on Irish soil and – all going well – back in my arms. The phone rings. It's Joyce. We haven't spoken in absolutely ages (apart from via Facebook, which doesn't count as direct human contact, really). Joyce used to be great for a laugh, and during our years in college we had some pretty wild times. However, since her daughter was born she has become positively dull. Perhaps when the kid is older she will resume having a life once again.

Joyce is delighted to have caught me. Hearing about me and my glamorous life will brighten up her day tremendously. It will give her something to talk about, other than how adorable her kid is. I tell her how great things are with me:

a) I'm just back from 'my Zumba' (I allude that I attend regularly, and there is some confusion which I fail to clear up regarding my status as teacher rather than sweaty pupil).

b) Earlier, I rustled up a gourmet low-carbohydrate, low-fat, high-in-fibre supper (personally endorsed by Gillian McKeith) and a fruit smoothie. I'm a culinary genius.

c) Barry and I are doing great and so loved up. I hint at the idea that while on a business trip, he is scouring the Orient for a diamond whopper. I have a stunning dress picked out at Vera Wang's. It's very exclusive. A psychic has practically promised me that we may be in fact inches away from getting engaged. He is winging his way home, business class, tomorrow. I mention 'business class' three times to make sure it lands. I have the perfect little slinky number waiting in my wardrobe to wow him with.

I think I have an addiction to lies. I can't stop. I think Dr Phil covered it on his show once. Must dig it up on the digital recorder and see what my prognosis is. Probably incurable.

'Wow, Rebecca. Sounds great.'

Joyce falls for it hook, line and sinker. She complains that herself and Liam don't get out much these days. Little Katie-Jane (isn't that just a dreadful name to call your child? I mean, pick a name. Is it Katie or is it Jane?!) is three years old. The little minx is still not sleeping through the night, and all of their money is being drained by the mortgage and crèche fees. I yawn through most of it. She describes in great detail the hilarious things little Katie-Jane said last week, but I'm drifting far, far away.

The phone call is just the medicine I need. It's proof that the grass is not in fact greener on the married-with-kids side of the fence. On that side of the fence there are crèche fees and sleepless nights. On that side of the fence, there are few nights out and little disposable income. Joyce probably wishes she could hop back over to the Zumba-teaching, healthy-cooking, no-nappy, free-and-easy side of the fence.

'Anyway, I'm so glad I caught you,' Joyce goes on.

I smell a rat.

'I have some *amazing* news to tell you.'

It is a freakishly large, toxic waste-chugging, weight-lifting rat that dwells in the sewers and beats up other rats for fun. She didn't call to hear my glamorous news, after all. My jaw drops to the ground as she explains that she is expecting not one but two babies in six months time. She has been violently ill for weeks now. Puking non-stop, apparently. Sounds heinous.

'Twins! Can you believe it, Rebecca?'

First Karen with twins, and now Joyce. There must be something in the water.

'*Jesus!*'

I can't think of anything else to say. Barry and I might never wed and have babies, and she's contemplating aloud whether they will be boys or girls or one of each. She is toying with the name Parker – goes for a boy or a girl. Ditto Taylor. Don't you just *hate* it when people go on and on about themselves like that?

Luckily, her lasagne is burning and has set off the smoke alarm. She has to go.

'What a shame. I'll call you tomorrow,' I promise.

See? I can't stop lying. It's a genuine medical affliction, now. I'll have to ask Dr Logan about it. There might be a pill for it. Or a cream.

I take a stiff G&T to bed for an early night. It is mixed with the slimline tonic and I didn't even have any Doritos this evening. The weight is virtually lifting off me. I am out like a light.

Twenty-Five

It's ten o'clock when I wake on Saturday morning. Because of my prudent ways, I'm hangover free and feeling super fab. Life is great. Today is the day when Barry returns to me. According to the psychic who advised me spiritually, all will go swimmingly.

I text Emer.

> *Barry home 2day, yay! Psychic yesterday predicted happy-ever-after bliss. New frock @the ready. Beauty & hair appointments a go-go.*

She texts back within seconds.

> *OMG Babes, Totes meant 2b! I will be buying a hat soon! U will b so super hot! XoXo*

After my treatments, I'll nip home to change, plump a few cushions and then welcome Barry home with open arms. He'll find me relaxed, with smooth tanned legs and looking foxy in my new clothes and boosted cleavage. He will be drooling for me. Later, we will talk all our problems far, far away and I will allow him to woo me. What could possibly go wrong?

The nerves are starting to kick in over breakfast. My mind flashes back to the last time I saw Barry and I cringe at how thoughtless

I was. I catch my reflection in the metallic toaster. There's a new line on my forehead, and it's making me look crumpled and old. This is going to be a tall order for the makeover fairies. I grab my keys and head out.

Uncharacteristically punctual, I arrive just in time for the one o'clock appointment at Select Beauty Salon in Foxrock that Emer had booked. It's going to cost her an absolute fortune, as she has booked me in for the works as an extra birthday present. What a pal.

When I draw near the front door, I consider how quiet the place looks. The door is locked and the blinds are down. Over the window a short handwritten note reads:

'*Dear customers, due to a sudden bereavement in the family, we have had to close at short notice. We apologise for any inconvenience this may cause.*'

Closed? Sudden bereavement in the family? I just can't catch a break! I howl, startling an elderly lady as she passes laden down with shopping bags. How can this be happening to me? The bloody cheek of them to close, leaving me high and dry. Trust my luck to have someone bloody die at a time like this. Frankly, it is so inconsiderate! This is such a tragedy for me, personally. Surely on a Saturday afternoon all other salons will be booked out. I have a mind to leave a snotty note of my own.

As I start to hyperventilate, drastic thoughts race through my frantic mind.

'Agh!' I try to steady myself.

They say that absence makes the heart grow fonder. There is some truth in that, I'm sure. Barry says he doesn't know what I'm talking about when I complain about my figure and my crow's feet. However, if Barry sees me like this, I'm sure that I will be the exception to that rule. Don't get me wrong, he loves me dearly. He says he loves me unconditionally, and that he still fancies me first thing in the morning in my fleece penguin pyjamas and with no make-up. He's like a smitten kitten. But let's be honest – everyone has their limits.

'Crap, crap crap!'

My reflection in the salon window is hideous. My nails have been chewed beyond recognition. My hair has more splits than an *Emmerdale* story line. It's greasy and the dark roots are in desperate need of a touch-up. I worry that someone may start to suspect that I am not, in fact, a natural blonde. Imagine! My make-up needs to be set rock solid, for an evening of either passionate make-up sex or crying into a bottle of Pinot Grigio.

My body is also a disaster zone. The cellulite plastering my bottom means that any kind of nookie will definitely have to be with the lights off. Also, you know how you have to let your leg hairs grow to a certain length before you can wax them? Yes, well let's just say that my hairs are, ahem, definitely of an acceptable length. And you know that bearded lady Conchita Wurst from Eurovision? I've a chin hair that would shock her. And as for my underarm and bikini line, it is a jungle down there. Take my word for it. Envision the abominable snowman and you will be in the right ball park.

I call Emer. She will know what to do.

'Hi, Becks, are you looking glam already?!'

'Code red! Code red!'

'OK. Breathe.'

'Fecking closed, Emer. Closed!'

'What?'

'Someone died, or whatever.'

'Right. Plan B. Don't panic!'

Within minutes, Emer has calmed me. I no longer require a paper bag in which to breathe, which is always a bonus. A plan is beginning to form. I'll race to another venue in Ballsbridge, while Emer makes an urgent phone call and pulls some serious strings. She will settle the bill over the phone.

Minutes later, and with clear disregard for the speed limit, I screech the Volkswagen Golf into a parking space on Baggot Street. I feed the parking meter with all of the spare change I can find, since this is sure to take quite some time. I'm feeling pretty confident. If any speed cameras have caught me bombing along, I'll be able to explain the heart-wrenching scenario to the judge in court. Surely, the police are sympathetic to real-life emergencies.

'Your honour,' I debate in my vivid daydream, tear rolling down my law-abiding, God-fearing face. 'If a man can speed for something silly like his wife having a baby, then a lady should be able to speed for urgent beauty treatments. My relationship was hanging in the balance!' I am in the courthouse, dressed demurely in a pale pink Chanel skirt suit with a small pillbox hat with netting worn on the side of my head. It's quite a good look on me. My blonde hair is pouffed like Jackie O's. All charges are dropped. The judge commends me on taking such brave action in raising awareness of the scandal of split ends. She asks me where I got my outfit. Sorted.

I totter in high heels to the front door of Mishka's Beauty Salon. I'm out of breath and dishevelled.

'Hi. My friend Emer called ahead for me. Rebecca Browne?'

The receptionist looks at me doubtfully, shaking her head. Apparently, there's absolutely no possible way that she can squeeze me in without an appointment. She says she has a cancellation on Tuesday.

'But…'

I can feel the coffee and Pop-Tart breakfast churning in my otherwise empty stomach. I hold on to the reception desk to steady myself.

'But this is an emergency!' I protest. My lower lip quivers for good effect. Told you I can act. 'Didn't you get a call from Emer to explain? Don't you recognise an emergency when you see one?'

There is nothing else left to do but cry. I peek sideways to see if it is working. My chest is tight and I can't catch my breath. Perhaps this is the onset of a cardiac episode. Perhaps I will die looking like this! I try to undo my bra so that I don't pass out, while I plead with Tracey at the desk. The salon is one of my regular haunts, I explain. As it is close to work, I have been a loyal customer for many years. In fact, if you add up all of the lunchtime (slash entire afternoon) appointments at this very establishment, I probably have put the owner's children through college. Eyebrow tints, waxing and full body massages, although essential, do not come cheap. Tracey remains unfazed. I decide to pull out the big guns.

'Right. Get Mishka. Tell her I'm desperate. Tell her it's urgent.'

The receptionist stares back blankly. She looks all of about eighteen, ridiculously thin with red streaks through blonde hair.

'Go on!'

A moment later Mishka appears, scowling. Emer, it seems, has come through for me after all. She got straight through to Mishka on her mobile and has earned herself a big hug and a champers cocktail on me next time we meet. The large Ukrainian woman runs a manicured finger down the appointments book. I hold my breath in case she changes her mind. She bulges in a grey pinafore with her black hair pinned into a severe bun, studying me with a serious expression. I plead my case.

'Mishka, can you fit me in? I'm sure Emer explained. It's been hell. I had a fight with Barry and now he's coming home...' my voice trails off humbly.

Mishka is transfixed on my nails. Her eyes then move up my body and fall on my face. She turns to her assistant.

'File! Paint! Scrub! Wax!' she roars.

I interpret this outburst to mean that I'm being granted The Full Works. I relax into the velvet purple sofa as the latest copy of *Vogue* is thrust into my hands. All around me, staff scurry.

'Thanks again for fitting me in...' I mumble meekly.

Mishka is a hidden gem. Although I've been attending her salon for four years now, the most personal information I have clawed out of her is that she is from the Ukraine. She isn't much for small talk, and is not the least bit interested in the tedious details of my love life. She won't be enquiring 'Where are you going on your holidays, love?'

I brace myself for a leg and bikini line wax. Tears spring to my eyes as Mishka's muscular arms whip strips up my legs. I force myself to concentrate on Barry and how nice it will be for him to stroke legs that don't resemble porcupines. I cringe as the towel moves a fraction – it reveals a bush in need of some serious pruning! In fact, I wouldn't be surprised if Jane Goodall was found in there, studying gorillas or whatever. I lie back and think of Barry. This will all be worth it for him! When I meet him tonight, I will eat humble pie – and a large portion at that. I am, in the immortal words of and Cheryl Cole, going to 'Fight for this Love'.

Wrapped in a white fluffy robe, I lie back on the salon leather chair. I presume that I'm as smooth as a baby's bottom by now, although I'm in too much agony to check. Mishka's thin lips are curled into a grimace, as she observes my toes with the chipped red nail polish that covers the black nail polish underneath. She reaches for the pumice and mutters to herself, in what I can only imagine is Ukrainian. She always makes me feel like one of the ugly sisters when I arrive, and Cinderella when I leave.

Mishka soaks my feet while I recline in the pedicure chair and check out the latest celebrity wedding in *Hello!* magazine. Her assistant has worked her magic and stripped my abhorrent toenails down to their original colour. My tattered fingernails are next. The staff are not miracle workers, but they do their best. Mishka rolls her eyes as she observes the chewed wrecks. She is judging me. She is thinking what a lazy uncaring slob I must be.

As my nails dry, a petite Asian woman slowly massages my face. I recline further into the soft leather chair and close my eyes. The music is soft and soothing and a blanket has been placed over my legs. A beautiful image forms in my mind.

A warm breeze blows. Barry presents me with a bunch of red roses and a magnum of Moët, as he disembarks a private jet from Hong Kong looking dapper. (What? It is my fantasy, I can imagine whatever the hell I want to.) Suddenly, Barry is on bended knee and begging me to become his wife! *Yes*, I say. *Yes, yes, oh yes!* It's best to play it cool.

A loud chainsaw-like noise interrupts my beautiful dream. I turn to see what imbecile is disturbing me, and realise with total mortification that it is in fact my snoring. The warm breeze is the nail dryer. Wiping the drool from my mouth, I cough self consciously.

I'm clear about what I need to do tonight. We are talking drastic action, here. If I want Barry back, I'm going to have to do some serious grovelling and apologising. No amount of promising is too much. I don't know whether it is the sting of eyebrow tweezers or the stress of the last few days, but my eyes start to water, and I swallow hard.

Twenty-Six

Barry has two hours to kill at Schiphol airport, Amsterdam. There's only so much duty-free buying, window shopping and coffee drinking that a man can take.

The first leg of the journey was surprising pleasant. Shelley was upgraded to business class with Nigel, which left Barry gratefully alone. He didn't care that there wasn't much leg room for a man of his frame. He didn't care that nine hours like a caged tiger in a metal box was enough to bring out the claustrophobia in anybody. He was just delighted to be alone. The passenger beside him didn't try to talk about the weather.

Thankfully, exhaustion took over and he had slept. He was sure that he had snored like a freight train, but he was past caring. Even the food was edible. Although distinctively cardboard-like, the lasagne was bland and salty. It had reminded him of Rebecca's home cooking, and was a welcome change from the spicy stuff he had endured over the last few days. Not a curried noodle in sight!

Across the departure area, Shelley and Nigel enter the executive lounge. Barry spots Shelley's arm linked around Nigel's. She is laughing. It seems she has moved on already. At the boarding gate, he finds a comfortable bench and completes a pretty tough crossword. He feels quite smug. Later, he reads the newspapers from cover to cover.

For the fifth time, he checks the electronic flight display. His jaw drops as the word 'DELAYED' appears next to the KLM flight from Amsterdam to Dublin.

'Ah, no. This trip just keeps getting better!'

This mistake, or whatever it was with Shelley, is in the past now. He is sure of it. He can't stand the idea of working with her from now on. It is so uncomfortable that he entertains the idea of looking for a position elsewhere.

It has been almost a week since he has seen Rebecca. He knows how close he came to screwing everything up. But he won't let that happen again. He will tell her everything. He is clear now on what he wants. He is ready to put all of the fighting behind him. He wants to make it work.

Barry switches on his mobile. Although the red battery light is flashing urgently at him, there is just enough juice left in the tank to text Rebecca to say that he is on his way home. He rummages through his jeans pockets until he finds enough coins to make a couple of Dublin calls at the payphone to put his plan into action. He glances across the departure gates and spots 'Bubbles Seafood and Wine Bar'. He finds a bar stool and orders a Scotch. A bit of Dutch courage is what he needs. The warm liquid hits his stomach and a satisfied smile spreads across his face.

Twenty-Seven

At last, my unmentionables are mentionable. My eyebrows no longer have the look of a homeless person. My make-up is applied expertly and powder keeps it rock hard. My legs are smoother than a pick-up line at a late licence wine bar. My nails are just like elegant little petite shells. I reach into my coat pocket and check my iPhone. There is a text from Barry.

Landed in Amsterdam OK but next flight 2 Dublin delayed.
See you at home, baby.

The next stop on my makeover itinerary is only across the busy street. Dermot is a top hair styling professional, and an absolute pet. And you know, a hairdresser is for life, not just for Christmas. Important note: Dermot must be pronounced DerMOSH in a camp lisp. Take it from me.

Luckily, I had called ahead yesterday and was slotted into a three o'clock cancellation. None of the staff at the hair salon have ruined my day by dying and cancelling my appointment like the last place.

'Rebecca! Good to see you, lovey!'

Dermot sashays across the salon and air kisses me.

'Been a while.'

He leans over my scalp and raises a sculpted eyebrow, silently judging me for my inch-long black roots in desperate need of bleaching, no doubt.

Dermot's assistant offers me tea and passes a few more celebrity magazines my way. One of them is *Image Bridal,* and at the sight of it I turn pale. Following a short wait, I'm escorted to the leather swivel chair by a maudlin Goth teenager. Newsflash: eyebrow piercings and black lipstick are not flattering. Someone should have a word with her mother. She drapes a black robe over my clothes.

Enjoying a hot tea and some biscuits, I catch up on the latest antics of Kim Kardashian and her crazy family. I would literally kill for her sleek brunette locks, and momentarily flirt with the idea of requesting a chestnut brown 'do' with glossy extensions, but then thankfully regain my senses. Impulsive hair decisions are always regretted.

'What's it to be then, lovey? The usual?' Dermot asks as he smoothes one eyebrow.

'Yes. But blonder and choppier!'

Upon examination of my limp two-toned hair, he pouts dramatically.

'Darling, those splits,' the flamboyant stylist exclaims. 'And the roots, lovey. You came to me just in time.'

Dermot eyes up his own highlights in the mirror.

'Yeah,' I murmur, mortified at the state of myself.

Dermot mixes his hair colour in a plastic bowl. He is great for a girlie natter.

'So. Trouble in paradise?' Dermot cuts straight to the chase. 'Tell me everything.'

Like all good stylists, Dermot is enthralled to hear all about my entangled love affair. Either that or he is just plain nosy. Either way, I have an audience, so I launch into it and leave out no details. Before I know it, he has finished pasting in the colour to my hair. He nods and makes compassionate noises in all the right places. His shock horror hand-to-mouth and tut-tuts encourage me on, as he applies the tin foil pieces to my roots.

After a long stretch to 'let me cook' he returns. The colour is declared a total success and the metallic strands are removed. He leads me to the sink for a rinse out. As the unenthusiastic apprentice lathers my hair, I picture myself running to Barry's open arms. I will be a vision in platinum blonde.

'Conditioner, lovey?'

The teenager snaps me back to reality.

'Sure.'

Back in the leather swivel chair, Dermot and I continue our counselling session. I spill my guts. It's great to get a man's perspective – even if he is the type of man who would fancy Barry more than me. And what's more, he gives good advice. The man has had his share of heartache, so he knows a thing or two.

'Sounds like you were well on your way to becoming a Bridezilla, lovey! Sure, it was only two years ago,' Dermot insists on reminding me every time we meet. 'I was dumped for a…' he hushes his voice '… woman.'

'Sure, you were too good for him, Dermosh.'

Dermot winks at me in the mirror and starts to cut. He's going for gold with the scissors, snipping and hacking with gusto. Strands of hair fall to the floor around my ankles. I keep my mouth shut: the man is a thoroughbred professional, who am I to question his creative talent?

'Don't be afraid to whip out the industrial strength hairspray, Dermosh. The hair has to be perfect for the evening. Imagine cardboard.'

'Got ya, lovey. I have just the thing.'

I smile at the reflection of a younger, blonder, and altogether trendier me. The hairspray and blow-dry finish the job. Damn it, he costs a fortune, but he's worth every cent.

'And now,' coos Dermot with a lisp, 'you're a fairy princess.'

'Thanks.'

I kiss him on the cheek and put the extortionate sum on Barry's Visa card. Thank goodness for the high spending limit.

'Conditioner,' Dermot calls after me as I bounce out the door. 'For God's sake, lovey. Use conditioner!'

Every reflective surface smiles back. Barry is bound to scoop me up in his manly arms only hours from now. I'm looking good, and I know it. My stomach flutters all the way home. I ditch the car in the driveway, flattening a struggling few rose bushes in my haste, and then head straight up the stairs towards the bathroom cabinet like a woman on a mission.

I've stripped down to my pants and have thrown my clothes into the laundry basket. Following my successful makeover, the only thing that's standing between me and bodily perfection now is false tan, and plenty of it.

I reach for a tin of 'Tan-in-a-Can'. It's the latest tanning cream to be endorsed by *Celebrity Goss* magazine. Apparently that slapper from *EastEnders* swears by the stuff, she wears it by the bucket load. I hesitate. Perhaps I shouldn't be taking beauty tips from someone so tacky and orange who wears neon plastic hoop earrings. Still, I'll give it a whirl. What's the worst that can happen?

There is only one thing worse than being slightly on the over-weight side – that is being overweight and pale. As if the sight of my generously proportioned thighs (think chicken drumsticks) rubbing together is not enough to put you off your family-sized KFC bucket, imagine said thighs wobbling in glowing white. Yes, now you have the appropriate mental image. Well, everyone knows that a tan makes you look seriously slimmer. It instantly trans-forms glow-in-the-dark jelly belly into toned and tanned. It's like an optical illusion or something.

I pour myself a stiff drink and bring a selection of crisps upstairs, before generously slapping the tan on. I must stand crab-like for a while in order for the tan to dry. The last thing I want is for the tan to rub off on my new clothes and leave an unsightly orange rim. I'm far too classy for that kind of carry on, and favour the more natural beauty look, as you may have guessed.

The nerves are flipping shot. Shot, I tell you. I'm inches away from a nervous bloody breakdown. Mum will have to sign the commitment papers when the GP recommends that I be carted away. A hunky male nurse will be injecting me with a sedative in no time as I slide into sweet delicious unconsciousness and into a straight jacket.

The vodka is warm in my stomach, and I steady myself. A mental collapse would be rather inconvenient at present. I mean, I'd miss Barry's homecoming dinner this evening and would never find out if we were meant for each other. It would be like investing years in *Lost* and then missing the last episode (crap as it was, I'll grant you). It's best to keep the head and push on, I am a trooper. After twenty minutes of texting, crisp-munching and crab-walking in skimpy pants, it seems that the tan is now dry. I check myself out in the mirror.

Correction. There *is* something worse than being overweight and pale, after all. That something is being overweight and orange! Shuddering, I realise that I've been perhaps a little heavy handed with the tan. You can't blame me, I'm desperate for the instant slimming effects. The brown marks on my wrists and ankles are beyond dodgy, and my hands look like I've taken up a new career as a potato farmer. The *TOWIE* cast would ditch me with a bitchy remark. Even in dim lighting, and even if Barry were to take his thick glasses off, there's no missing the streaky rasher effect. It's as obvious as Leslie Ash's trout pout.

This is a flipping crisis, and I've come over all wobbly. The psychiatric nurse is looming again, brandishing the threatening needle as the liquid overflows from the sharp tip.

With elbow grease and a wet face cloth I get scrubbing, making a special effort around the wrists and ankles. I try again, and the end result is more 'beach babe' than 'beached whale'. The psychiatric nurse backs off – he has more pressing patients to deal with, like that mad old one from *Loose Women*.

I tackle some false lashes with extreme difficulty – poor hand–eye coordination teamed with stiff drinkies on a near empty stomach is a tricky combination for someone applying glue! At least now if I check in to the rest home for the very, very nervous, I'll look pretty.

'Goodbye pasty and hello tasty!'

With hand on hip, I admire myself in the mirror. Not bad. Not bad at all. Time is marching on, and the tanning has taken longer than planned. All I need to do now is to change into my drop-dead gorgeous outfit and prepare some top nosh for Barry. He should be landing soon.

In the bedroom, I hide all messy discarded clothes under the bed. Removing the tags, I slip into my recently acquired two piece outfit with saucy red bodice underneath and stand in front of the full-length mirror. The bodice is literally a miracle worker in the tummy flattening department. It should be canonised for sainthood, there's not even a whiff of Chinese takeaway-and-cheese-puff overindulgence. The silky French knickers look fab under the new clothes. I finish the look with killer heels, it's a knock out. I've chosen a simple silver chain that Barry had bought me last Christmas and the diamond tennis bracelet. The makeover is complete.

The stairs must be navigated gingerly due to the high heels. Hunger gnaws at my stomach. No wonder – I've skipped lunch. In my thirty years on this planet I have literally never ever done this before. I rummage downstairs for a quick fix. FYI: Dutch courage on an empty stomach will not end well. I learned that lesson in my teens, when I'd consumed considerable amounts of cider at the Rugby Club under-sixteens disco with very little dinner. Let's just say that there was puke in Mandy Byrne's hair and that she was no longer my BFF and that she never spoke to me again. Another vodka Diet Coke and a Pop-Tart later, I'm ready to rock.

I have promised Barry a dinner, and I'm sure that he must be starved after his flight, poor chap. A home-cooked meal is the least I can do for the love of my life. They say that the way to a man's heart is through his stomach and Barry has always appreciated my efforts in the kitchen. I decide to pull out all the stops and do his favourite for tea. Chips and beans it is, then.

The deep fat fryer is bubbling away nicely, as are the beans in the pot. I've laid the table with Newbridge silverware and John

Rocha table napkins. A red rose ornates the table to finish the look. Ah, only the best for my Barry!

I'm peeping out the curtains, giving Bernie from next door a run for her money. Any minute now Barry's Jag will appear in the driveway and Operation Win Back Barry will be in full swing. The red bodice is starting to cut off the circulation to my ribs slightly, and the French knickers are completely wedged up my bum giving me an almighty wedgie. Hopefully they won't be on for long, if you catch my drift. The balls of my feet are burning from standing and cooking in high heels. I check myself in the mirror. The discomfort will have to be tolerated. I'm only gorgeous!

Another quick peek out the curtains confirms that there is no sign of him yet. I top up my glass. It's best to just knock the rest of the vodka back straight and hide the empty bottle at the bottom of the rubbish bin. Otherwise it looks like I'm a total lush. Which of course, I'm not! The rain is pouring down and bouncing off the granite slabs that snake their way up my driveway.

I've a sudden and unmerciful urge to use the loo. It won't take a minute and, sure, best to go now while he is still on his way. I don't want to interrupt our passionate make-up sex with pesky peeing.

Mid flow, with French knickers around my ankles, the smoke alarm starts shrieking. I jump up to silence the fecking yoke but somehow my heels get caught in the silky material. Next thing you know I'm stumbling out of the downstairs loo and landing splat in the hallway. Smoke is billowing from the deep fat fryer and the beans smell like they have reached more than 'well done'. It's just as well Barry likes his food crunchy.

The key is in the door. No! Not yet! Not like this! It's too late. He's standing there in the hallway. There is a grin on his handsome face.

'Everything OK?'

He's laughing, breaking his absolute heart laughing at me. The wretch. Come to think of it, I'm laughing too. Thankfully the vodka has provided my body with a cushion and I didn't feel a thing.

Barry helps me up and then races into the kitchen to switch off the deep fat fryer. He waves a tea towel at the smoke alarm after he has opened the French doors to let the smoke out. Living with me meant a crash course in fire safety over the years. While he is busy, I scramble in the hallway to compose myself. I kick the shoes off, smear on yet another coat of bright red daring lipstick and smooth my hair for the umpteenth time. My cleavage is hoisted into the stiff boned bodice, and my boobs are almost touching my chin. Gravity has no power here.

I enter the kitchen like nothing has happened and take a deep breath. Believe me, if you were the one in a restrictive corset like this you would know – that's easier said than done. This is it: make or break time.

'Welcome home, baby!'

'Thanks. I see you've been busy in the kitchen?'

'Kind of.'

'Ah, Becky. And you set the table and everything.'

'Let's have a look at this dinner. Not too bad.'

I'm stirring the beans. Well, when I say stirring, I mean it's in a cement-mixing kind of way. I scrape the stuck ones off the bottom of the pot but they are black. Experience tells me that the whole pot will taste of burnt now. Even brown sauce mixed in won't hide it. I tried that the last time.

'The chips are grand. Not too bad at all.'

I examine the contents of the deep fat fryer. I wouldn't say they are black – more of a dark, dark, dark brown colour. Quite dark, if I'm honest. Totally edible, though. You just need to avoid any loose fillings.

'Well, I stopped off on the way home.'

Barry is brandishing a large brown paper bag. My eyes are streaming. Once the smoke clears, I get the heavenly whiff.

'Is that a…?'

'Yup.'

'Indian Palace?'

'The one and only!'

'With an extra portion of…'

202

'Peshwari nan? Yup.'

'And a side dish of…'

'Aloo ghobi? Naturally.'

'And did you get the…'

'Poppadums? Of course!'

'Onion bhajis? Samosas?'

He raises an eyebrow and smiles. He knows me so well. Barry rips the paper bag open on the counter and I get a proper look at him. He removes his heavy overcoat.

'Great. Welcome home, Barry. Can I get you a drink?'

'Thanks. I also picked up a bottle of red.'

Barry and I have dished up the giant Indian feast and are sitting opposite each other at the table. My chest is whooshed up to glorious proportions.

'Barry,' I struggle.

There's a crack in my voice. I sound like fifteen-year-old Rebecca crossing the Rugby Club under-sixteens disco towards Ray Healy. Boys are on one side and girls are on the other. Except this time, I'm not vomiting halfway through the speech that I had been preparing for weeks in front of my sparkly pink mirror. This time, I'm not standing there asking a boy to dance. I'm standing there, asking the man I love with all my heart if somehow, he loves me too. If somehow, he will stay with me, dodgy tan and all.

Barry looks up, smiling nervously. Has he always looked so well in a suit? He looks slimmer. His glasses rest on the table and he rubs his eyes. They are a deep crystal blue. There's a fleck of hazel there that I have never seen before.

'Listen,' Barry and I speak at the same time. We laugh at the clumsiness.

'I'm sorry,' I manage to blurt out in a rush.

I am sorry for talking over him. I am sorry for being a giant pain in the arse. I am sorry I laced this bodice up too tight and now I am about to faint into my red wine.

'Look, Becks…'

Barry speaks quietly. I dread his words. I wish that he would stop. I shrink away from what is coming next.

'This whole wedding thing is driving us apart. I can't … take it any more. We argue about it non-stop. We can't go on like this.'

It's all my fault. It's too late. I've ruined the best thing that has ever happened to me. There is nothing I can say to convince him. My eyes fill up. The tears are close to brimming over, and I curse myself for ruining my make-up job. Waterproof mascara is never tear-proof, I don't care what the adverts say.

'I know.'

My voice is meek. I cannot control the tears rolling down my cheeks now, and sloshing onto my fab new top. The cleavage provides a glorious platform for the tears to pool and then roll.

'It's just…' Barry pulls his collar away from his neck like it is too tight. He is fidgeting with his napkin. 'You know I love you, right? Of course I do.' He is struggling, visibly uncomfortable in his skin.

'No, it's alright.' I interrupt him.

Spare me. Don't say it out loud. There is no need to try to soft soap me.

'I'll be out by the end of the week,' I sniff.

I am bluffing, of course I am. I have absolutely no bloody intention of me (or my impressive shoe collection) going anywhere. However, the water has to be tested.

Dear Jesus,

This is not going well. Please tell the angels to tell that psychic that I want my money back. Let Barry be a gentleman and:

a) Insist that I will stay in the comfort of our leather sleigh bed with Egyptian cotton sheets, while he slums it in some Holiday Inn or other den of disease.

OR (preferably)

b) Take me back. I promise to be good. Well, good-ish.

Amen

'I'll go to Mum's.' I am pathetic. I droop my head but peek at him from the side to see if he's taking the bait.

'And why would you go and do that?'

Barry looks at me, perplexed. A lopsided smile has broken out across his full lips, revealing his white teeth. For a second, I dare to think that perhaps there is still hope for a fool like me. I hold my breath.

'Rebecca, it's not like we are going to have to break up, just because we've had a … a fight,' he stammers and takes my hands. 'Well…it was a whopper fight. A few of them, really,' he smirks.

He stops. His face now has become quite serious.

'But anyway. Look, I've been a fucking idiot. I want to tell you something. I'm sorry too, you see—'

'No. No, don't,' I squeeze his hand. Whatever it is, I don't want to ruin the moment.

'But there's something I need to tell—'

'No. Just tell me that you love me and that we'll put all this behind us.'

'OK… I love you, Becks. Flipping drama queen,' he smiles. 'Don't you know I'm stuck with you forever?'

'Oh shut up, Barry! I love you too. Ya big silly man.'

My mascara-stained face turns towards Barry.

'Pour us a large one, will you?'

We have made a sterling effort with the grub. We laugh about Barry's slave driver of a boss and I tell him about what a nasty man Harry has been to me when I called in sick, filling him in on his request for sick certs and other inhuman demands. His bright eyes crease in amusement as I describe how much pain I am in after Zumba with Mum. We pick from each other's plates, connected again.

'But listen…' Barry leans closer.

He is clearly very uncomfortable with all of this talk of emotions and feelings and what not. This is not his usual territory, but he's trying to clear up this God-awful mess.

'It will happen for us… the whole… you know… wedding thing. Because, you know…' Barry clears his throat. 'I love you, and all that. We'll get married, we just need to give it more time. Right?'

'Right.'

I give him a watery smile.

'You flipping mad thing,' Barry laughs. 'Honeymoons and wedding venues, eh? Honestly!'

It's all the reassurance I need. I promise dutifully to lay off with the weekend wedding fairs and ordering of bridal magazines.

'Anyway,' he continues, attempting to move the conversation on to a more testosterone-fuelled topic. 'You're looking hot. I want to rip that top off you later.'

We both erupt in laughter and open another bottle.

'Is it new?' he waves a finger up and down as he eyes my designer two piece suspiciously.

He knows better than to question the shoes. I've collected so many pairs during the course of our relationship and have devoted more wardrobe space to the beauties than I would like to admit. Besides, according to Barry (like all men if you ask me), all shoes look the same.

'This old thing?' I smirk. 'Don't be silly.'

By ten o'clock we're both yawning. Our stomachs bulge as we try desperately to digest the inordinate amount of grub packed away. Luckily, the lacing has loosened (under enormous strain) on the corset, and I no longer feel dizzy. Barry divides the last few drops of red wine from the second bottle and we drain our glasses.

'To us,' I venture, raising a glass to Barry.

'Come on,' winks Barry, 'I'm fecking wrecked. Let's get those tits out of that top before you explode.'

We leave the tikka-masala-sauce-smeared plates, cutlery and lipstick-stained glass on the kitchen counter and turn off the lights. It can wait until tomorrow. There are more important things to attend to right now.

Twenty-Eight

When I open my eyes, I'm keen to check that Barry is still there. Our time apart has been rough, and I want to know that last night was not just a beautiful dream. He is lying on his side, mouth agape and snoring heavily. His large frame is taking up the lion's share of the duvet. I poke him in the ribs and tell him so. Surprisingly, he's a bit miffed about being woken up, and rolls over.

There's a familiar throb in my left temple. The red wine might be to blame. I look lovingly at Barry and watch the rise and fall of his chest. There's a guttural snore coming from the back of his throat. His toenails are sharp and the hair on his feet tickles me. Thank God all the ugliness is behind us, now!

I dial Emer's number. She's always up early on a Sunday for exercise classes.

'Dying to know,' she answers the call.

'It was dreamy,' I whisper into the phone. 'We talked it all out. It was just like Carrie and Mr Big getting back together.'

'Ah, great,' Emer cheers.

'Listen, I bloody mauled him like a tigress.'

I recall throwing myself on top of him as he tried to get his suitcase in from the boot of the car. Hopefully Bernie next door was occupied with putting her brats to bed and was away from the window.

'Emer, we never even made it up the stairs and onto the bed! Let's just say, we are well and truly made up after our little falling-out this week … if you catch my drift.'

'You dirty feckers!' This is as close as Emer ever gets to cursing.

'I know, it's great. Anyway, call you later.'

I hang up and reach for some heavy duty hangover pills from my bedside locker, knock back two and relax. It's really odd – the medicine bottle is nearly empty. Thank God Barry and I are all patched up. The way I have been behaving, I deserve to have lost him forever. Well, never again. I'm going to stop being pushy. I'm going to stop nagging him. Starting from now. Well, as soon as I've gently reminded him about the bins. They won't empty themselves, you know.

Lowering my head back down onto the pillow is tricky and the room spins. Soon, my breathing is rhythmic and matches Barry's. We are like two spoons in the cutlery drawer. Naturally, he's the large clumsy serving spoon and I'm the petite solid silver tea spoon.

'Good morning, sweetheart,' Barry croons three hours later. 'And how are we?'

His voice is sleepy and hoarse.

'We,' I smile, 'were asleep!'

'Sore head?'

'No! Well, maybe a smidge.'

It's now midday and therefore officially the afternoon. Barry can therefore no longer claim jet lag or whatever shoddy excuse he has brewing in that crafty mind of his. I insist that he go whip up a deluxe breakfast for the two of us, pronto.

I also emphasise the fact that I'm monstrously hungover and can't possibly make it down the stairs. I'm far too fragile and hence must be served in bed. Don't you start, now, you hear? The hangover is definitely his fault for bringing the wine. Everyone knows that you drink more when you're nervous, which is also his fault. He should know better than to keep topping up my glass in my delicate state. He made the same mistake on our first

208

date, when he bought me several vodka Red Bulls and I was violently ill the next day. How irresponsible of him! Some people never learn.

I slink back under the warm duvet. Barry serves me hot sugary tea and croissants with a heavy lashing of butter and raspberry jam. In fairness to Barry, he makes a great cuppa. However, I deduct brownie points, since the eggs are not dippy, and I had to wait a whole ten minutes for him to get back from Supervalu with the pastries. He's so slow in the mornings!

The thumping in my head is starting to fade. I relish the feel of his hot skin against mine.

'So, what do you want to do today?' I ask.

'Nothing,' he smirks with a cheeky glint in his eye.

He pulls me closer and gets pastry crumbs all over the bedspread. I'm in a good mood, so I don't make him clean up straight away.

By lunchtime, I drag myself from the bed and into the shower. The hot water jet hits my back. Barry pulls back the shower curtain dramatically and joins me. We carry on like hormone-raging teenagers who meet behind the bike sheds instead of going to class.

I swear to God, we never usually act like this. Our hands and mouths are all over each other's naked bodies in full-on soapy glory. I'm getting fifty shades of Barry and loving it. Honestly, it's like something raunchy out of *Desperate Housewives* or the like.

With a white fluffy towel wrapped around his waist, Barry kisses my neck. I'm wearing the white fluffy robe that I had accidentally-on-purpose stolen from Monart. It's like we have found a worm hole that has taken us back in time four years to the dingy flat in Ranelagh. I watch us in the steamed-up mirror. Barry's arms are wrapped around me.

'I love you,' he whispers into my hair.

I smile at our reflection.

We dress in our lounging clothes – deliciously matching his'n'hers tracksuits which I had snapped up at 50 percent off at The Gap last spring. Don't you just love a bargain?

'Fancy a takeaway and something on Netflix tonight, then?' I suggest as we flop on the couch. 'I never feel up to cooking after mucking out the dogs at the shelter, haha.'

We tuck into a beans on toast lunch, which is balanced on our laps. I'm too tired to cook, despite my earlier promise of a gourmet luncheon, but he doesn't seem to mind.

Barry drops his fork heavily on his plate and stares at me for a second.

'You've forgotten, haven't you?' A smile spreads across his lips. 'Typical.'

I strain to recall, but the silence gives me away.

'Fiona's dinner party? We said we'd go? I told you about it!'

My face is blank for a moment and I scramble until the penny finally drops.

'Oh God, not Fiona!' I roll my eyes.

With the stress of the week, I had completely put Fiona and Tom's dinner party out of my mind. I must have agreed to go in order to shut Barry up at some stage in the recent past. A couple's dinner party is hardly top of one's priority list when one's relationship has gone to the dogs.

'Who throws a bleeding dinner party on a *Sunday night*, anyway?' I whine. 'Christ. Do we *have* to?'

Barry knows full well my feelings on Fiona and Tom. They are a nice enough couple. You know, if you like the tiresome married kind. They all studied law at Trinity College together, where boring Fiona met boring Tom, then had a boring wedding and went on to have boring children.

I often remind Barry that I, too, went to Trinners, the old 'alma matter' as he likes to call it. He's not impressed with my feeble arts degree, however, which took up ten hours of lectures a week (most of which I missed). He reminds me that I didn't mix with the law students except to crash their stuffy parties, steal their drinks and stagger off in the direction of the Pavilion Bar. Happy memories.

I reel in the whinging. I've got to be on my best behaviour.

'It's just that I want you all to myself.'

'Look,' debates Barry. 'We won't stay long…'

I feel myself caving, clearly beaten. It's best to let this one go, in case it starts to rock the boat and causes another row of Titanic proportions. The moral of the story is to never date a solicitor. They will argue their way through absolutely anything and use their superior intellect at every convenience, much to your annoyance. Loving someone so clever and brilliant has its downside!

After lunch, I clear the plates. Barry promptly announces that he has to head out to the office. On a Sunday! This leaves me gobsmacked.

'What?!' I can't stop myself. I try to shut up, to keep the lovey-dovey atmosphere going. The verbal diarrhoea ejects and I can't mop it up fast enough. 'But you're only back from Hong flipping Kong!'

'Bangkok.'

'Oh. Whatever. And now you've got to go to work?! On a Sunday?!'

I realise that I'm shouting, but I'm unable to stick a cork in it. I am watching myself from above, as if I am having an out-of-body experience and telling myself to shut the hell up. But the shouting me cannot hear the floating me. The slave-driving office has ruined our carefree fun and the mood is now sour.

If we split up, it'll be his boss' fault. One day, I might have to battle the heartless company in the courtroom when I sue them for ruining my relationship and therefore my life! It will be a tough battle, but I have watched *Legally Blonde* so many times (plus I've been to the musical in London) that I have picked up a few tips. Some of the script is in my head, verbatim. You'd be surprised how much you can learn from Reese Witherspoon!

'It's only for an hour,' Barry attempts to placate me when he sees my face like a slapped bottom.

He doesn't realise that I am picturing myself in a pink two piece, swearing on the bible, glistening tear rolling down my face, that Hodges Myrtell O'Brien stole my man.

'Fine.'

I have learned from previous experience that this 'only an hour' business translates as 'see you when the office closes'. He's bursting my bubble!

With workaholic Barry offside, I meet Tammie at the shelter. Marmalade's kittens have grown so much since last week, you wouldn't believe it. We have christened them as follows: Buttons, Muffin, Champers (that was me) and Cosmo (guilty of that one, too). When I drive home, I'm smiling as I remember how Major used to sniff my pockets, knowing I'd sneak in a bacon flavoured dog biscuit just for him. His treacle-coloured eyes would stare at mine until I handed over goodies.

Back home, I get cosy on the couch and catch up on my soaps. I stretch out full length, with the remote control firmly glued to my hand, and a blanket snugly over my knees. It's bliss!

I know that I've let my soap opera commitment slide while Barry was away, and I'm in desperate need of a catch-up. I follow most of the soaps, but dropped *Fair City*. Even though I was hooked on Nicola and Paul's affair, I decided not to watch any more, as I was worried that I might start talking with a skanger accent. Between juggling a full-time job and keeping things steamy in the relationship department, it's no wonder there are not enough hours in the day. After a soap opera marathon, I send an email I'd been meaning to send for ages.

Dear CNN TV executives,

How do you sleep at night? I'm writing to tell you that the harsh cancellation of *The Young And The Restless* is unacceptable. Perhaps it was suggested by some clueless boardroom type with no sense of real women's needs. Ricky was about to go on trial for Eden's murder, and now I might never know the outcome. It was simply unjust to leave loyal fans *hanging* like that without any consideration for their feelings!

I now have been left with no choice but to fill the void with *The Bold and the Beautiful*. Now, don't get me wrong, it's addictive stuff. However, I have to invest in a whole new relationship. It has taken quite some time to figure out who's sleeping with whom and who's back is being stabbed by whom, and who has woken up from a coma. Please do not further alter the viewing schedule as, frankly, my nerves are shot.

YOURS IN TOTAL AND UTTER DISGUST,

Rebecca Browne

The memory on the digital recorder is full, which I can't explain. I'll have to delete all of Barry's *Top Gear* to make room for *Holby City*. I feel a fleeting stab of guilt, as it is his only real television joy in life, and the *Holby City* episodes are repeats (but classic episodes nonetheless, one might argue). If Barry notices, I can blame it on a power surge and say thank goodness that my soaps are unaffected.

I dial Emer's number to discuss at length an article about Holly Willoughby without make-up. She looks forward to my frequent phone calls.

'Sorry, chicks,' she answers.

'Wait till you see how shocking Holly looks without the slap. She is still a stunner, though. She'd be in my "if-I-were-a-lesbo" top ten *at least*!'

'Sorry, chicks,' she repeats.

'Not even foundation on her face.'

'Can't talk. I'm furniture shopping with Dave.'

'So?' I picture her in some overpriced designer store in Donnybrook, Dave's unlimited supply of cash at the ready.

'The interior designer has messed up on fabrics. Just sorting it all out now.'

'Sounds dull.'

I hang up with a heavy hand. I didn't even get to tell her about our nudey rudey antics in the shower that morning.

I dial Mum, eager to spill the beans on how loved up Barry and I are.

'Hi, Fairy,' Dad answers Mum's mobile.

'Oh, hi. Get Mum,' I insist.

'Sorry, Fairy, she has gone out with the Bridge Club. Should be back at—'

Click, I hang up.

I dial Pam. She's a last resort, but she will do. The phone rings out, but I don't leave a message. A text comes through immediately.

Hiya BECKS! Just here with Dougy! Having a dirty night away! He's so fab! Catch ya laters! XOXO Pams

Dougy? Pams? Already, they have pet names for each other. And what's all this about a night away? They only just bloody met! Also, there are far too many exclamation marks for my liking, and distinct bragging. I delete the text so I never have to see it again. She needs to just put on her big panties and be a good friend.

Dearest Jesus,

Ta for making Barry forgive me. Perhaps you could see to it that he pops the question this side of Christmas? I mean, it's just a matter of time now, and he can't keep his paws off me! Also, if he lost a stone or two, that'd be a bonus.

Now! Regarding Pam. Look, you know I don't like to meddle. Not my style. But this new chap is completely unsuitable. I mean, his name is Dougy, for Christ's sake. Sorry for taking your name in vain, but this is important. Please ensure that the doomed relationship crashes and burns sooner rather than later so that we can all focus our attention on relationships that truly do stand an ice cube's chance in hell, like me and Barry.

Also, if you could see to it that Mum's Bridge Club reject her and Emer's re-modelling goes horribly wrong, I'd be grateful. Didn't the bible say 'Thou shalt not ignore a friend in need?' Well, obviously I'm paraphrasing. This is the twenty-first century. Get with it.

Over and Out,

Rebecca

'Flip sake!' I direct my disappointment at Jess. He's busy licking parts of his body that I'm not comfortable discussing. 'Oh, Jess, you filthy thing!'

With nothing better to do, I reluctantly start some housework. As I change the sheets and throw some laundry into the washing machine, I think about the dinner party scheduled for tonight. If there's one thing even more annoying than smug engaged people, it's smug married people. You know the type. Always banging on about their kitchen extension plans or what their darling baby did next, when you really couldn't give a toss. They launch into stories about their family camping holiday in France and about how little Jake is top of his class.

You see, the inevitable thing about engaged and married people is that they never fail to ask you 'The Dreaded Question'. It usually catches you by surprise. The married person manages to launch it upon you when there is a hush in conversation, or when you are choking on your starter and spluttering onto someone's hand-embroidered lace tablecloth.

'So,' they will no doubt eyeball me this evening, 'when are you two getting married?'

I beg that tonight will be different. The scab on that particular wound is only just setting, and doesn't need picking again.

The '*Big M*' seems to overshadow everything we do. Suddenly, all of our friends are married. We are the odd ones out, destined to be Paddy last in the race to the top of the altar. We're the only ones not in the club. Some of our friends even have children. Our social calendars are a brutal reminder of our single status.

At least it's only a dinner party and not a christening. I've never liked christenings, as I object to being in close proximity to a snot-nosed screaming baby all day long, who is dressed in a nauseatingly cutsie pie white doily, and is inevitably moments away from throwing up all over it. I try to make fake coochy-coo noises. Otherwise, people think I'm being rude, Barry once pointed out. There's always a tot screaming in the church, unrestrained by their negligent parents. Also, there's rarely much free gargle at these events (not that this ever stops me from wetting the little darling's head, mind you) and grub is always of the finger food variety.

Weddings used to be fun before people starting asking 'When will it be your turn?' In the good old days, weddings were about the champers, the free bar and the slap-up four-course meal. It was such fun making catty remarks about the bridesmaids' dresses and guessing how many months pregnant you thought the bride might be. I used to dance to AC/DC and the Bee Gees and look fabulous, having spent an entire morning at the hair salon being pouffed and blow-dried.

Now, these events are ruined. I spend every social event trying to avoid The Dreaded Question. It makes me cringe and squirm and sweat profusely. I then end up starting a drunken row with Barry in the car on the way home. But I'm not going to be knocked off my perch by The Dreaded Question tonight. Not a chance.

Twenty-Nine

Barry returns at six o'clock and loosens his tie as he steps through the front door.

'Jesus,' he unbuttons his jacket. 'That idiot had me tied up for hours. Thought I'd never get away.'

'Never mind, baby,' I soothe.

Trying to recapture the puppy love atmosphere, I rub his back. I'll be damned if I'm going to let that bald-headed slave driver ruin our high. Barry climbs the stairs and discards his shoes and socks on the landing floor, making his way towards the shower. Next to be strewn in a haphazard manner are his trousers. He leaves the toilet seat up and the toothpaste lid on the counter. His suitcase remains on the spare bed, probably full to the brim with dirty laundry. I swallow my annoyance.

I'm squeezing myself into a grey jersey wrap dress and wrestling into a pair of black leather boots. The dress usually works wonders by hiding the midriff bulge, but today it's failing miserably.

'Miss Piggy!' I say to the mirror.

Barry is whistling on the toilet. Even the sucky-in pants, which I seem to be relying on these days, are not doing their job. I scold myself. Just because we had enjoyed a slap-up takeaway last night, there was no need to finish off Barry's bhajis as well.

'Hi sexy buns,' Barry squeezes my bum as he passes in his underwear in search of fresh socks. 'You look gorgeous.'

Turning to the side in front of the mirror, I look at my reflection. The booze is bloating me something wicked. I suck in my tummy and vow to hold it in for the rest of the night (or the rest of my life if necessary). Passing out is not a concern at this critical time.

'I need to look good tonight,' I tell Barry who is already dressed and dithering over aftershave.

'You do!'

No doubt someone will ask The Dreaded Question, and I need to hold my head up high. Also, despite the fact that our hostess has two young kids (aged about four and five if I remember correctly – I tend to switch to autopilot when people mention their charming children), this doesn't mean she has let herself go. Au contraire! Far from frumpy, she manages to fit in gym sessions, kickboxing classes and a sixty-hour week at the office. Her children, although boisterous, are always well turned out, and she dresses to impress. It makes me sick.

Barry looks handsome in a striped shirt tucked neatly into a pair of dark jeans. After some deliberation, he commits to Davidoff Cool Water and splashes it on his neck. He hums to himself. Out of the suit, he's relaxed. I smirk. He is no Denzel Washington, but he is mine, all mine.

Much to my delight, Barry agrees to drive. Unlike me, he takes work seriously and doesn't want to over-do it. He says there is some stake-holder meeting or other in the boardroom over breakfast tomorrow.

I've stolen a bottle of expensive plonk from Barry's clients' Christmas stash, and stuck it into a sparkly gift bag. We pull up outside the detached gated residence in Blackrock and Barry buzzes the intercom. At the top of the paved driveway, two perfectly rounded bay trees with red bows decorate the heavy oak front door.

'Well! How are the love birds?' beams Fiona.

She is standing at the doorstep with a flute of wine in one hand and a bottle opener in the other. How does someone with two high energy children and a full-time job in advertising manage to look so immaculate?

Fiona takes our coats and we kiss on the cheek. Tom shakes Barry's hand and we are led into the living room. Justin and Jason (whom we refer to as 'The Terrible Two' behind closed doors) charge through the living room without as much as a hello. They proceed to bounce loudly up the stairs in matching Spider-Man pyjamas. Cue WWF-style-wrestling noises, much thrashing and death threats on the wrap-around landing above us in full view.

'I'm going to get you,' screeches one boy to the next. I can't tell them apart, they are equally naughty.

'Aren't they a handful?' I laugh my phoney chuckle with my eyebrows raised.

Tom thrusts a glass of wine nearly full to the brim into my hand and I sip immediately. I like that about Tom – he always gets the booze flowing as soon as you poke your nose into the hallway.

I feel myself relax as the warming liquid slides down my throat.

'I thought you said the Terrible Two would be in bed!' I whisper to Barry.

He pretends not to hear and goes into 'man mode' with Tom. They compare notes on how their respective sports teams are doing, leaving myself and Fiona to make small talk. We smile and admire the other's outfit.

'Malou is putting the boys to bed,' Fiona explains. 'The woman really is a *saint*. She has prepared a lovely meal for us tonight.'

Life must be sweet with a Filipino nanny.

I hand Tom the bottle of red wine. Fiona leads us both into the sitting room and I admire the plush furnishings, candlelit coffee tables and sparkling chandelier. It makes our three-bed semi look like a poky student den. It's probably best if I never ever invite them to ours again.

Tom introduces us to the other couple, Fionnuala and Oisin. Fionnuala is a stay at home mum, is groomed to perfection and has more diamonds on her left ring finger than I can count. At a guess, she's in her later thirties and gets a lot of expensive facials. Her blonde hair is coiffed and she has a flawless tan, which I guess is from spending the entire school holidays in Marbella. This out-trumps my 'Tan in a Can', so I instantly dislike her.

'Oisin,' Fiona continues with the introductions, 'is a financial controller.'

Soft spoken and dressed in grey slacks and a pullover, he sure looks like one. There is a downtrodden air about him. As the night goes on, I realise that it's probably due to the fact that he can't get a word in edgeways with his wife who talks enough for both of them.

Little Justin comes bounding into the room, coughing a phlegmy cough and wiping his snotty nose on his sleeve.

'Sorry, Miss Fiona,' Malou follows sheepishly behind, looking deflated. 'They still no in bed.'

Justin holds a balloon from Burger King. For a five year old, he's plump. The last thing I would do with a rotund child like that would be to feed him fast food. His pyjama top rides up on his round belly.

'Poor Justin,' coos Fiona for our benefit, 'has had a nasty cold, haven't you, chicken? Been off school.'

She furrows her forehead in sympathy and we all return the gesture like sheep. I hope she keeps the kid away from me. The little chap is a veritable Petri dish, and I'm due back at work tomorrow.

The child does not reply. Instead, he gawps at the assorted crudités Fiona has spread out on the coffee table. However, as they are of the carrot and dip variety, he turns away in disgust. He faces Barry and hands him the balloon.

'Is that a present for me, Justin? Good man!'

Barry confidently takes the child by his pudgy hand. The child nods and smiles shyly.

'He's absolutely great, Tom,' beams Barry as he ruffles the boy's spiky hair.

I am curious to know:

a) if I have some antibacterial hand wash in my purse, and
b) how the others will react if I spray the child with some Dettol. I'm thinking that might not be wise.

'Not long now till we have our own little rascals, eh Becks?'

Barry bounces the balloon off my head, and I wonder whether there is a sharp pin in my purse. I assume that Barry's comment must be some kind of a joke, so I laugh hysterically and slap my thigh. Barry will get a good grilling later to find out what *exactly* he meant by that. An uncomfortable silence follows and someone finally changes the subject.

Almost an hour passes. I'm about to chew my own arm off with the hunger. I'm knocking back the white wine like goodo and trying to endure some idle chitchat about Fionnuala's 'adorable' baby Aoife. The artificial smile I have plastered on my face will crack at any moment, as I'm not sure how much more of this kiddie chat I can take. Honestly, how anyone could find a baby's daily antics of eating, sleeping, burping, crying and throwing up on your shoulder in the slightest bit amusing is beyond me. Anyway, because I am such a nice person and all, I grin through it.

'And Malachy's toilet training is going so well!' continues Fionnuala. 'He is so clever!'

I resist the urge to point out that:

a) he is in fact three years old for flip's sake, and
b) it is poop, and therefore not a big whoop.

I've even managed to nod and add in the occasional 'ahh' and 'really?' It seems to do the trick. Perhaps I am too convincing. Fionnuala continues her monologue and even reaches into her purse to produce an entire professional album of the urchins featuring various snapshots of them in the bath and lying bottom up on a furry rug. I'm about to give up hope.

When Tom isn't looking, I reach for the wine and top myself up, a desperate attempt to stay sane and tolerate the baby talk. How much more can one say about a child's ingenious use of the potty?

'Honestly, I think Malachy is gifted. His Montessori teacher told me he is the best in his group at Play-Doh.'

I wonder what one must do in order to gain the prestigious title of 'Best at Play-Doh'. Does one's snake have to be curlier than the other children's? Do you get extra credit for consuming less of the stuff or shoving less up one's nose?

'Wow. You should get in touch with Junior Mensa.'

I am dripping with sarcasm, but it's all I can do to entertain myself.

'Gosh, yes. Will do.' Fionnuala makes a note in her pocketbook and then launches into another rendition of 'what baby Aoife did next'. My mind is miles away. I'm fantasising about what Barry meant last night over dinner when he said 'It will happen for us… the whole … wedding thing.'

I glance across the table at him. He's fully absorbed in conversation with Tom. The candles on the table flicker, reflecting a gentle light on his handsome face. Did he mean this year? This side of Christmas? The old me would have pressed him for an exact date! The old me would have prepared a refresher course PowerPoint presentation detailing exactly what style of ring I like in case he's forgotten! But the old me is wearing duct tape over her big fat relentless gob, and is locked in a basement somewhere, and the new, improved Becky is on her best behaviour.

Fiona excuses herself and disappears from the table. My eyes blaze into hers, but she fails to notice. *Please don't leave me with Momzilla!* Fiona climbs the stairs to help her exasperated nanny put the two mini monsters to bed. She returns shortly afterwards, although I can still distinctly hear some thumping and crashing upstairs, possibly along with soft sobbing from the help.

Fiona then saves the day by calling us all in to sit at the dining table. As we enter the room, we are wowed by the perfectly set table with elegant place sets and fine silver cutlery. She has even sprinkled rose petals on the table.

She serves up a 'home-made' potato and leek soup with crusty bread which is delicious. It was probably prepared by the exhausted nanny as she wrestled with the Chuckle Twins. Fiona is suspiciously wearing a spotlessly clean frilly half apron over her skirt, which is presumably for show.

'Enjoy,' Fiona invites us to start, but I have already slurped my way through most of it. With shame, I think of my cupboard filled with tins, my freezer filled with ready meals and my drawer filled with takeaway menus. The last dinner party I threw involved dialling the Chinese takeaway and cracking open a bottle of wine. We ate it off our laps.

'Mmm,' Barry praises Fiona. You'd swear he's never fed at home, he's acting like a starving kitten! He's making a show of me.

I'll talk to Barry about getting one of those Filipino nannies. They would come in handy about the house, and might do a turn-down service with chocolates on the pillow. Tom and Barry are both solicitors, so their conversation inevitably leads to the Bangkok trip and the Nagasaki account. What a snore fest! With no other option, I lean back into the girls' talk.

Fiona serves the next course, chicken à la king.

'We're just thrilled with Justin's acceptance at school,' she thrills.

I gulp back the vino and pray that the two of them shut the hell up. I'm rather hoping that one of them will take a breath, so that I can somehow wangle into the conversation how Barry had surprised me last night with an intimate candlelit supper and how we are so loved up right now. I want to subtly mention that we are child free and care free.

'Naturally, we registered him with the academy as soon as we conceived him,' continues Fiona.

'Naturally,' I deadpan. She probably punched in the telephone number as soon as Tom rolled off of her.

I'm dipping in and out of consciousness, with only the wine for company. Before I slip into a coma, I hear Fiona say 'special school'. Aha! Now it makes sense. No wonder he needs a special school, what with the hyperactivity and the snot wiping. Perhaps they will also send him to boot camp to help him work off his spare tyre. I picture the attention-seeking fatty trying to get over a high jump and snigger.

223

Sadly, Fiona and I differ in the definition of 'special'. Fiona, of course, is referring to a school for the gifted child, which probably has a name like 'St Rumpelstiltskin's' and costs like a squillion euro per term or something, plus your first-born as down payment.

'Little Jason,' Fiona reveals with pride, 'is really excelling in his pre-school. They teach Japanese and Tai Chi.'

Again, the child has been enrolled since he was a foetus.

'Wow. Fantastic,' Fionnuala looks impressed.

If it wasn't for the Botox, I feel that Fionnuala's eyebrows would be raised. It's just a shame that the Japanese will be wasted when the boy is working in McDonald's sixteen years from now. I snort into my napkin. A boy who uses his Action Men figures to pick his nose is probably not a future university candidate. I'm smiling sweetly as I polish off the last of my wine, and Tom immediately refills my glass like a dutiful host. Fiona has become rather animated.

'I mean, it's an absolute necessity to enrol your little ones into a good school before they are born.'

Oisin is nodding politely, and Fionnuala is shifting uncomfortably in her chair.

'Fionnuala, what school have you enrolled Aoife and Malachy in?'

'Well…' attempts a flustered Fionnuala. She looks to Oisin for help, but his face is blank.

'Malachy is three, and Aoife is only sixteen months, so…'

It's fun watching Fionnuala squirm. Spoilsport Fiona ruins my fun by dashing into the kitchen to arrange the next course. Tom clears the plates, and I make a half-assed offer to help and am relieved when my offer is declined.

Fiona returns promptly.

'Just something simple,' she utters modestly as she presents the profiterole mountain.

Melted chocolate sauce and cream tantalisingly slide from the tip of the masterpiece, and strawberries cascade down the sides. Barry oohs and ahhs in appreciation. I am torn between:

wanting to push the others aside and get stuck in with a pitch-fork, and

secretly wishing the culinary creation will fall flat on its face so I can smugly say 'Never mind.'

Barry looks like a sweet little boy on Christmas morning. It's not surprising, really. The only dessert he usually gets at home is a Viennetta from the freezer. Sometimes, I buy him a '99 if I'm feeling particularly amorous and/or in need of some cash. I'll have to try harder.

As if the profiteroles weren't enough to blow your socks off, Tom follows in with a chocolate fondue, and the creamy gooey oozing chocolate spills out over the top of the fountain and trickles down the sides. Show offs! My mouth is agape. Surrounding this, Fiona has arranged a selection of delicately cut fruits and marshmallow pieces. We gather around and chomp on chocolate-coated bananas, melon and kiwi. Naturally, I try both desserts. It seems rude not to.

'We should buy one of these gismos,' chirps Barry excitedly, admiring the chocolate fondue set. I'll get him one for Christmas. He digs in with gusto. All manners are now forgotten and we clamour for another helping. The Rat Pack CD plays in the back-ground and Barry squeezes my knee under the table. He gives me a wink and an adorable chocolate-toothed smile.

'Delish!' The wine and Irish coffees are making Fionnuala slur her words. 'It's been a nightmare getting out lately. Our third nanny has been off with flu. Honestly, I think we might need to let her go.'

'Sorry, third nanny?' I know I shouldn't, but I can't resist.

'Well, yes. There are twenty-four hours in a day, and they work eight-hour shifts…'

She looks at me as if to say 'Isn't it obvious? Doesn't everyone have three nannies?' I catch Barry's eye and see that he is suppressing a smile. I knew it! No wonder Fionnuala is so happy and slim. No wonder her baby is such a source of delight – she hardly sees the kid!

'You should get yourself a live-in Filipino, Fionnuala. Excellent workers. Oh, I'll have a job working all this food off!' Fiona rubs her perfectly flat belly.

'Oh, Barry is just back from a business trip to the Philippines, aren't you, Barry? Anyway, don't worry, Fiona! Just get yourself a pair of these sucky-in knickers,' I flash the waistband of mine. At this point in the evening, the undergarment is under massive stress and is digging into my ribs. It's cutting off the circulation and has left a red mark. The booze and chocolate churns happily in my now bloated stomach. Fionnuala looks slightly horrified and gives an embarrassed titter.

Fiona retreats to the kitchen to make a strong black coffee for a giggling Fionnuala.

'So, when are you going to make an honest man of him, Rebecca?' Tom laughs.

Uh-oh. There it is. The Dreaded Question. How could he? I decide I no longer like Tom. I can't think of anything sharp or cutting, so I just gulp back the wine and concentrate on stopping my face from turning beetroot red.

'Ah, you'll have to watch this space, Tom.' Barry grins at me.

Thankfully, the conversation veers to baby Aoife's vaccinations and Justin's violin lessons. I down a large brandy, and it helps things along nicely.

'Slow down on the booze, Becks,' whispers Barry, glancing sideways at my once again empty glass.

'I should give the nanny a call,' says Oisin. He meekly passes his grinning wife a strong coffee. 'Let her know we are on our way home.'

'Nonsense,' Fionnuala shoos the idea and her husband away, knocking over the candlestick. 'We're only getting started.'

Ten minutes later, Oisin is hoisting a protesting Fionnuala into a taxi and I'm kissing Tom and Fiona, thanking them for a great night.

'Our place next time,' promises Barry. 'Becks does a wicked macaroni and cheese.'

'Yes,' I agree. 'It's not from a packet or anything!'

That ought to show them!

'It was a good night,' Barry turns to me as we are stopped at the traffic lights.

'Yeah.'

'You know everything's going to work out for us, baby, don't you?'

And in this moment, I do.

Thirty

I send another text to Emer, Pam and Mum. For some reason, the three of them seem to have fallen off the face of the earth tonight. It's highly annoying, as I am yet to share my exciting news about my rekindling with Barry. How inconsiderate of them!

Barry and I sit outside the house for ten minutes. The stars are out and there's a cool breeze. Barry puts his coat over my shoulders, even though I'm wearing a coat of my own. It's only eight degrees out and he must be feeling like a frozen pea. I smile. I've fallen in love with Barry all over again tonight. I'd watched the clumsy way he ate his soup and dipped his sleeve in the chocolate fondue. He's endearing and smart and funny. And most of all, he's mine. I lean across and kiss him.

'Nice. What was that for?'

'Just because.'

'I don't deserve you,' Barry looks at his lap.

'I know,' I smirk. 'But here I am.'

Barry turns the key in the front door. I've one foot on the bottom step of the stairs and am heading in the direction of bed.

'Come into the sitting room for a sec, Becks,' he says.

Before I can protest, he takes my hand, opens the door and switches on the light. My first thought is 'What is Mum doing here?' She stands in the middle of the living room dressed in pearls and her best frock. Her hair has been set. Dad stands proudly beside her with his hand on her shoulder.

Come to think of it, there are lots of people in the sitting room. Ian, Emer and David, Pam, Doug, Barry's mum and dad. They're all standing there, smiling at me. There are tea light candles lit, and red roses scattered about the room in various vases that I don't recognise.

I turn around in confusion. My second thought is 'Why is Barry on bended knee?' There is a small black velvet box in his hands.

Sweet Jesus. This is really happening! Somebody press pause, I want to save this moment forever. A tear rolls down my cheek. All faces are focussed on mine, their breath is held in unison. Mum is clutching Dad's hand. In Barry's right hand, a glittering ring sparkles, free from its plush box.

'So. Rebecca. Will you marry me?'

Emer has her hand over Pam's mouth to stop the squealing. Judy is knocking back a large G&T. I put my hands on Barry's handsome face.

'This is all so unexpected!'

Barry slips the ring onto my left hand and it fits perfectly. It is the ring of my dreams, exactly as per my instructions!

'Were you in on this, Dad?' I've regained the power of speech.

Barry pops a bottle of bubbly and Mum fusses about in cupboards looking for champagne flutes and dusting them with a tea towel.

''Fraid so, Fairy,' replies Dad. 'Barry called me from the airport on Saturday. To Rebecca and Barry,' he toasts as we raise our glasses.

'Thank God!' Mum hugs me. 'What a relief.'

'Here's to my three accomplices,' Barry cheers. 'We've been out all day, haven't we? Flowers, champagne, collecting the ring…'

Pam, Emer and Mum nod their heads frantically, confirming their involvement. They huddle close by, examining the ring and letting out little screams of excitement.

Barry's mum Margaret and dad Patrick are next in line to congratulate us both.

'Well done,' Patrick shakes my hand awkwardly and slaps Barry on the back.

'I finally have a daughter,' slurs Margaret as she kisses me on the cheek. Margaret doesn't usually drink, but is nursing a rather large glass of wine. 'Barry is an only child, and I always longed for a girl,' she confides to Mum.

'I think there's been some pre-engagement celebrating going on while we were at dinner,' I smirk at Barry. The future mother of the groom and the future mother of the bride are sozzled and emotional.

The doorbell rings and in burst Tom and Fiona.

'Congratulations!' Tom thrusts a bottle of expensive champagne into my hands.

'You guys were in on this too?'

'Well, we had to get you out of the house,' teases Barry.

The party continues into the early hours. We have run out of champers, but not to worry, I've found a bottle of peach schnapps at the back of the press.

'Technically speaking,' Barry pulls me to one side and holds on to my elbow, 'you never actually answered my question.'

'Yes!' I shout.

I have a pain in my face from smiling.

'I wanted it to be …' he searches. 'Special. A surprise.'

'Well, you succeeded.'

My head is swimming. Between the wine and brandy at dinner and now copious amounts of champagne and schnapps, the room is spinning. Barry bundles me into bed and the hall door closes with the last of our guests departing. I fall asleep with a grin on my smug face, clutching the diamond ring.

When I open my eyes again, I reach for my left ring finger. There it is. The beauty! The rock sits proudly, in all its glittering glory. Barry snores heavily beside me. Although I'd only gone to bed at three o'clock, I can't sleep for long. It's like being a child on Christmas morning, waiting for the sun to creep up over the horizon before bounding out of bed and down the stairs to open presents. In my excitement the night before, I hadn't opened the engagement gifts. What a bonus – on top of the best moment of your life you also get presents!

At seven o'clock, I can take the anticipation no more and creep downstairs in my fleece pyjamas and fluffy pink slippers. It's great that I can curl up on the couch, bridal magazines at my feet, no longer hidden in crafty places.

There's so much to do, and thankfully I've been clever enough to get a head start, I congratulate myself as I stroke the bulging wedding scrapbook tenderly. Where to start? On the laptop, I look up www.mrs2be.ie (the official wedding inspiration website for the engaged community), and blatantly steal ingenious wedding ideas from future brides left right and centre. The ringtone on my mobile is now set to Billy Idol's 'White Wedding'.

There are certain tasks for Barry to tackle. It's his big day too, after all. He can handle the paperwork side of things. You know, the state requirements thingy and giving the Catholic church three months' notice and the full sleep-inducing shebang. Besides, he's far better at that kind of thing than I am. He'll really enjoy that. My creative talents are best used elsewhere and not quashed by such dull tasks.

Dad doesn't answer when I call. Probably still asleep. Well, he'd better wake up, I want to make sure that he offers to pay for the wedding. Naturally, he'll want to please his only precious daughter on the most important day of her life. I'm the light of the man's life, in fairness. Surely Dad has put aside a decent lump sum and isn't blowing my entire wedding fund on frivolous things like health insurance and cholesterol medicines? Just because he's retired now doesn't give him the excuse to fritter away what I'm entitled to! Perhaps he'll pass out when he sees the price of the honeymoon!

I'm mindlessly shoving stale cheese puffs into my mouth. The room is littered with lipstick-stained wine glasses, empty champagne bottles and half-eaten nibbles from last night. But that will have to wait.

Before we passed out, we'd drunkenly decided that we'd get married the following June. This is only seven short months away! I'm ever so slightly torn. On one hand, I'm peeved that I can't drag the drama and excitement out for as long as possible. On the other hand, I can't wait to marry the love of my life.

Thirty-One

That was some party last night!

Barry rubs his eyes and checks the alarm clock on the bedside locker. It's only seven o'clock, but Rebecca is already up. She's probably wasting no time with the wedding arrangements, in her absolute element! Well, she deserves it. He decides to leave her to it and rolls over.

Calling the jewellers from Amsterdam, followed by a call to Rebecca's dad, had been the right thing to do. He knows, deep in the marrow of his bones, that he wants nothing more than to marry Rebecca. The engagement ring had been weighing heavily in his jeans pocket yesterday. He had developed a slight tremor since collecting the extortionately priced item. It had been a thrill, Barry thinks, to sneak the big surprise past Rebecca. She didn't suspect a thing! It had been worth the sweat, effort and minor coronary he had suffered before popping the big question.

Rebecca, for once, had not orchestrated the proposal – it's one thing in his life that he can claim fully. God knows she'll take over with the wedding. She'll micro manage it to death. But sure, whatever she wants is fine. She can have the best, and Barry knows that he is going to spend the rest of his life feeling guilty about Bangkok and trying to make amends. A text interrupts his train of thought.

Hey Barry. If you change your mind, you know where I am. Shelley.

He swallows hard and deletes it. Then he deletes Shelley's number from his phone.

Thirty-Two

All I want is to shout our joyous news from the rooftops of every building in Dublin city. Oh, and a formal press announcement in all of the national and regional newspapers. Scratch that, anyone can have that. We should have a full photo spread in the *Irish Times*, featuring Barry and I gazing lovingly into each other's eyes. I'll have to update my Facebook status to 'engaged' and add a photo album with dozens of shots showing the ring glistening at every imaginable angle. Then I want to climb the tallest building in the world and let off one million silver balloons. I'll then tweet every single detail of the proposal and tell the story over and over to strangers I meet on the street. Maybe I could hire a blimp with a banner blazing across South County Dublin declaring our intended nuptials. But first things first, I'll throw a party!

'Top of the to-do list is the engagement party, Jess.'

The cat doesn't seem in the least bit impressed with my staggeringly fabulous ring, and has no suggestions regarding the party. What sour grapes.

The engagement party has to be perfect, and I mustn't crumble under the intense pressure of it all. I'm a sheltered child, after all. And what better way to celebrate our love affair than to flash the diamonds and flaunt our everlasting love in the faces of all and sundry? The spotlight will be firmly on me, and I will enjoy every last glistening moment of it.

Being the centre of attention will require me to look my best, so I dial Emer for some advice. As head bridesmaid, it's in her job description to discuss the wedding at length and offer a twenty-four-hour consulting service.

'It's only seven o'clock,' Emer yawns. 'We just got to bed four hours ago!'

'Now. The engagement party. I'm thinking next Friday. Strike while the iron is hot, and all that. Being pretty is not going to cut it. I need to be ravishing!'

Emer dutifully scans her phonebook for beauty salon numbers.

'I want people at the engagement party to say how *stunning* I am, Emer. With the engagement party so close, I'll tell Barry I need some cash for essential beauty things. You know, like Botox. I mean, I need to be perfect. The engagement photos are going to be something I will one day show our grandchildren for God's sake! Oh, just think! Grandchildren!'

That morning over a late breakfast, Barry catches me on the phone to Harrods in London discussing wedding cakes.

'Yes, the Kim Kardashian five tier. Uh huh.' I hush my voice.

As Barry appears over my shoulder, I jump, then shoo him away.

'Take it easy,' he jokes. 'You'll have nothing left to organise by lunchtime!'

But his teasing is futile. He knows I'm already swept far, far away to a land that is no longer fantasy but reality. It's a world of fairytale weddings and after dinner speeches. There is no reeling me in, now. I even gave Marianna the green light on the Vera Wang dress. I'm loving every minute of being a full-time bride, and have time for nothing else. Every waking moment is consumed with wedding thoughts.

'It's a total bummer to have to go to work today. It's like asking Cinderella to resume her floor-sweeping duties after the ball.'

I yawn and wonder if I could tell Harry that I'm still ill. Surely he won't have seen my drunken engagement pictures on Facebook.

'Does that make me Prince Charming, then?'

'Of course.' I smile.

I'll go to work, because today is different. *I am engaged!* Before leaving the house, I pause briefly at the hall table and begin practising my future married name with a pen and paper in my best handwriting.

Mrs Rebecca J Costello

Mrs Rebecca Costello nee Browne

Mrs Barry Costello

Mrs Rebecca Costello–Browne

Such decisions! I've settled on the latter – posh people are always double barrelled these days.

During my drive to work, I'm so mesmerised by my new engagement ring that I nearly crash the car. Luckily, I'm able to pull myself away from the ring's dazzling glare in time to see the oncoming truck and swerve back on to my side of the road. See how it glistens in the late November sunshine? It's quite the blinder! Barry has truly been listening to my blatant hints all along, and it must have cost him an absolute fortune! I want to show it to every living soul and then watch it sparkle at every angle, taking in every tiny yet magnificent detail. It's so comfortable and fits perfectly, like it has always been on my finger. It's truly meant to be.

I arrive into the office two hours late, beaming from ear to ear. Harry asks me to step into his office and discuss my recent absence, and I swan past his glass-cased office with my head held high. The previous week seems like a lifetime ago. It's as if life before I became engaged never happened. I was dead before last night, and now I have come to life. The past was in dreary black and white, and now I'm living in glorious Technicolor!

Judy arrives half an hour after me, wearing dark sunglasses.

'Fab night!' I squeal at her. 'Wasn't it just amazing? Oh my God! I think I'm still drunk! What was your favourite bit? Wasn't it the most romantic thing you've ever seen? Did you know in advance? Oh, does Barry remind you of Richard Gere? Oh, tell me again what you think of the ring!'

When I pause momentarily to take a breath, Judy rubs her temples and eases herself onto her chair.

'Uh-huh.'

Her hangover is obviously in full swing.

At lunchtime, I stumble upon a wedding stationery shop and find the most adorable 'save the date' cards in cream-embossed card. Since they are on sale, I snap them up faster than a Drew Barrymore marriage, letting out a little yelp as I hurry over to the counter. The snooty sales assistant is not quite as enthusiastic about my thoughts on colour themes for my wedding as I am.

Thirty-Three

Emer, Pam and I have planned a last-minute PEPP – that's Pre-Engagement-Party Party to you. There's much to discuss. We need a full night of pampering in luxurious five-star surroundings in order to thrash out the wedding plans. Emer has booked it all and insists on paying the bill. She really was an excellent choice of head bridesmaid!

As it's Friday morning, I just have to get through one gruelling day, then leave straight from the office and check straight into heaven. My beauty essentials are stuffed into an overnight bag in the boot of my car. I'd better tiptoe past the reception desk – once again, I'm dead late.

There's a small crowd huddled around the reception desk, and they do not see me slink past. They're whispering something about Harry. Judy is flapping her arms at the desk next to mine.

'Amazing news!' she squeals.

'Oh?'

'Just heard. It's Harry's mother. Something about a coma? They're not sure she will pull through. The old bird had a fall down the stairs last night at the nursing home, bashed her head quite badly. Quite nasty, apparently.'

'No way!'

'Way!'

238

This is unbelievable. With any luck, Harry will be out for absolutely ages! *Dear Jesus,*

Nice one! This could be just like when Marlena was in a plane crash in Days of Our Lives, *remember? That coma went on for, like, four years! Can you please see to it that the geriatric codger lingers indecisively for a long time? I'm not saying let the incontinent old dear, like, suffer, or anything. Don't touch a blue-rinsed hair on her bashed head unless absolutely necessary. But you know, perhaps the sweet old thing could just dip a toe in and out between the spirit world and this for a while. It would keep Harry occupied until the wedding is over. We all need to make sacrifices, and I hear the old dear is ancient, so she wouldn't even notice. She probably doesn't even know what day of the week it is, anyway. That would be fab. After a few months, you could say 'Step into the light, Carol Anne' like that little lady in the* Poltergeist *movie, and she could pop her proverbial clogs and float over to the old pearly gates or whatever. Then Harry would be tied up with the funeral arrangements. Then he will be heartbroken and decide to take some compassionate leave. Or, you know, have a nervous breakdown. You choose!*

Sympathetically yours,

Rebecca

'Fantastic,' I relax.

Judy and I exchange smirks. Life is so great. An ingenious thought strikes me. Harry is highly unlikely to call me from his mother's hospital bed in pursuit of invoices. I am free for the day!

'Actually, Judy…' my evil plotting goes into overdrive. 'I just realised. I've got to slip out. Office supplies. Staples and… stuff. You know. Anyway, probably won't be back for quite a bit.'

'Sure. Absolutely! In fact, I myself… think I left the oven on at home… and the iron. Best dash back and check on things. Could be an inferno otherwise…'

We snigger. Judy is such a dosser. Luckily, I have yet to remove my coat, so like a flash I make my way towards the door. Suzie on reception has started a whip round for 'Mabel'. There is talk of sending flowers. Such a waste – the elderly one can't see or smell them. In fact, they should be sending me flowers. I am engaged!

I reverse the car into some heavy oncoming traffic and ignore the honking horns, desperate to get away. When I reach Merrion Square, I park with one wheel on the footpath and another on double yellow lines. Who cares? Emer's assistant buzzes me in.

'Stroke of luck,' I am breathless with excitement. 'My boss' elderly mother is in a coma. He won't be in for the foreseeable future!'

'Fab!'

'I know. Score!'

Emer invites me to help myself to a cappuccino from the coffee machine. She has a mahogany desk littered with expensive gadgets and important-looking files. The windows are floor to ceiling, and there is a view of Merrion Park.

After much magazine reading and a liquid lunch on the company account, I have convinced Emer to cancel her afternoon meeting. It was only some boring old finance meeting, anyway. We decide that she should leave work early so that we can get a head start on the trip to the spa. After all, we are only going for one night. Pam is available at the drop of a hat. By three o'clock, we are all in Emer's convertible Mercedes cruising down the N11. The soft top is down, despite the fact that it's a grey November day, and my hairdo will be ruined. 'She's like the wind,' we croon, 'through my tree. She rides the night, next to me.' The *Dirty Dancing* soundtrack is blaring on Emer's powerful car stereo. The girls and I have an awful lot in common, but it's our love of Patrick Swayze that especially bonds us.

In our deluxe triple room at the Marriott Druids Glen hotel, we ditch our heels for slippers and our work clothes for white robes. We shuffle down the corridor in time for our spa appointments. Our jacuzzi and spa treatments are followed by a bottle of bubbly and some Belgian chocolates in the relaxation room.

'Here's to the bride!' Emer raises a glass of champagne at the dinner table. We're on our third bottle already, thank God she's paying the bill.

'And here's to the bridesmaids!' I cheer.

We tuck into fois gras and fillet steak.

'So, tell us!'

Pam thinks that she is speaking in a normal tone. The truth is that the elderly couple at the table next to us have asked to be seated elsewhere, as our screeching and whooping has disturbed them. I'm not bothered. I am engaged!

'What's it like being engaged to Barry?'

'Girls, it's amazing. We are just, like, so in love. We're, like, sympatico, you know? Soul mates. Honestly, all that drama is behind us now.'

I tilt my head back to get the last drop of champagne from my crystal goblet. Emer gets the attention of the waiter to arrange another bottle.

It's true, what I said. Barry and I have rebuilt the crumbling rubble of our relationship, brick by brick. We are reunited and fully committed to working on our relationship, just like Wayne and Colleen Rooney. Well, apart from the seedy infidelity with shady prostitutes and the endless wealth part. I mean, I don't mean to brag but as a couple, we rock!

'The only trouble is that Barry says we need to establish a budget for the wedding.'

Emer wrinkles her nose at the word 'budget'. It's such a yuk word, isn't it?

'I mean, I told him that the bridesmaids' dresses should be Diane von Furstenberg creations, right?'

'Obviously.'

It's a no brainer. Emer and Pam get it.

'Yeah, well, he says they are way too expensive. Says we are in a recession.'

I roll my eyes. This recession is such a downer. Surely it's all over by now?

'And what did you say to that?' Pam asks. She is picturing the alternative, some hideous article from Penneys.

'Don't worry about it, girls. What he doesn't know won't hurt him!'

I raise my glass heroically. Emer shrieks and claps in delight as we clink our glasses. 'This calls for more champagne! What's

keeping the waiter?' Pam clicks her fingers at the head waiter. He has just finished laying a new table at the opposite side of the dining room for the elderly party poopers who are now shaking their heads in our direction.

Pam is not one to be ignored. She re-enacts a rather convincing version of that scene from *When Harry Met Sally*. You know the one. She does that sometimes. You know, just for fun. The restaurant seems a lot emptier than it did earlier. Oh, well. That just means better service for us.

'Boo to Barry and his budgets,' I say. 'Bloody pain.'

'I don't really get the whole … *recession thingy*,' admits Emer.

Pam and I exchange looks. Pam is an office temp, and earns enough to cover rent and fund a boozy weekend. I have a measly wage at a dead-end, boring job. Also, I'm on a verbal warning from Harry. However, that's more about my punctuality than the economy. Emer, however, is in another league. Her credit, it seems, has certainly not been crunched. She is oblivious to negative equity and pay cuts. She doesn't notice the worrying increase of grimy charity shops in well-to-do neighbourhoods. These things are not on her radar. I suspect that she is rather enjoying the fact that the essentials (such as shoes and accessories) are cheaper nowadays.

'Right, girls!'

I'm keen to press on and cover important topics, so I steer the chat to the most important topic this century – the Browne/Costello wedding. I've taken the liberty of drawing up an agenda. If only I could be so focussed at work. If only I could pour some of my creative juices into the business world, and make a success of my career. It's just that I can't be bothered. The agenda is typed and everything, take a look.

Bridesmaids meeting, November 20th

In attendance:

1 Ms Rebecca Browne (soon to be Costello), aka the Bride to Be,

2 Mrs Emer Smith, Chief Bridesmaid,
3 Miss Pam O'Leary, Bridesmaid
Venue: Marriott Hotel, Druids Glen
Chair of meeting: Rebecca
Minute taker: Pam

Agenda

1 Examine the following question: what kind of knickers should Rebecca wear during the engagement party next weekend? The sucky-in-kind would ensure that everyone says how skinny she is, but are not going to light Barry's fire.
2 Discuss what kind of knickers Rebecca should wear on the wedding day. Please note that a white lace thong would keep it super classy, whilst minimising the visible panty line, which is a thorny issue.
3 Consider what kind of knickers Rebecca should wear on honeymoon. Pink polka dots are very in this season and say 'fun in the sun'.
4 How many times should Rebecca cry at the engagement party next week? It is imperative to agree on a number that best conveys the love and devotion of the happy couple, whilst also demonstrating that Rebecca is not emotionally unstable.
5 How much should Rebecca drink at the wedding? Not so much as to be paralytic, and not too little that she won't be bendy enough to partake in 'Rock the Boat'. It is a delicate balance that must be adhered to.
6 Any other business (relating to the most important wedding of our lifetime).

Thirty-Four

I can hardly concentrate in work this week at all. It is no surprise, what with the high from the night away and now the pressure of an engagement party to plan all at once. I log on to my computer, unable to pull myself away from wedding websites and party venue websites. This is in full view of Harry, whose patience by now is clearly wearing thin. Turns out his mother pulled through. Bummer.

I've never been so productive at a desk in my whole life. Instead of chasing invoices, I chase hotels for available wedding dates. Instead of calling creditors, I call function rooms for the engagement party. I request quotes for individually iced cupcakes with the letters R and B artistically intertwined – I had seen this in *Confetti* magazine and it had taken pride of place in my wedding planner scrapbook.

During my lunchbreak I slog away, ticking item after item off my 'party to-do list'. I delegate the making of appointments for hair, nail and miscellaneous (ahem, Botox) to Pam and Emer. I'll tolerate no slacking in the bridesmaid department. It's all coming together rather nicely. Naturally, I can't manage all of this party planning in my own time. God forbid! Therefore, I must accomplish my bridal tasks during working hours. I need my rest once I get home after a tough day slaving away at the office.

At two o'clock I call everyone in my phone book (OK, also Barry's and Mum's phone book) to personally tell them the news and invite them along to the engagement party. I start each phone call with 'OhmyGod hiiiiiiiiii! Did you hear the news?! You'll never guess who's engaged!' I then stop for breath. 'Me! Yes! On a scale of one to ten, how excited are you?!'

It proves a great opportunity to rehash the proposal story over and over. On each re-telling of the story, the diamond becomes more glistening, Barry becomes more handsome and the flowers become more extravagant. Some phone calls take up to an hour each, especially the ones to old college buddies with whom I had lost touch over the years. There is a lot to fill them in on, and my throat is dry and sore for some reason. Also, Barry has been grumbling about the 'bloody mobile phone bill' of late, so it's good to use the work line. This way, everyone is happy.

'Emer. Me again. Listen, I need to know your thoughts on what kind of champers I should serve at my engagement party.'

Harry appears over my shoulder and hovers, so I shoo him away. He drums his fingers on my desk in a most annoying way.

'Yes, Emer, I know you're at work. I am too!'

Jesus, she is being so selfish and unavailable. Harry is breathing very loudly.

'Tell them to wait for you in the boardroom, Emer, I've loads of things I need you to do… Hello?'

Emer has been cut off. Perhaps her phone network is under repair. I ring again and her assistant tells me she is in a meeting. We will have to have words later. If she is to take her bridesmaid duties seriously, this performance is seriously under par. She may wish to apply for leave of absence if work is getting in the way.

'Rebecca!'

Harry is clearing his throat. Thankfully my chair swivels easily, so I turn to face the wall and dial Mum again. He finally gets the hint and shuffles off. Some people are so clueless! I christen him 'Harry the Horrible' under my breath. He is blatantly expecting me to work like normal at a time like this! I mean, you only get married once or twice in this life. With my Barry, it'll only be the once for me. You know, unless we renew our vows in Hawaii. I'm not Elizabeth Taylor after all. It all has to be done just right.

Perhaps Harry will offer me a day off. I'm not sure if there is such a thing as 'engagement leave' in the Human Resources policy. If not, I'll campaign for its very introduction. But right now, I've far bigger fish to fry and no time for Harry's petty demands. His emails requesting that I send him creditor reports and demands for some stationery are ignored. Letters remain un-typed and post remains unopened and stacked untidily. He makes his own damn coffee.

At four o'clock, I am called to take minutes at a meeting. I gaze out the window and imagine my entrance at the engagement party, sparkling left hand on hip. I picture myself sweeping down the aisle.

'Rebecca, read that back, would you?'

The chair of the board meeting is speaking to me. I stare blankly at him and blink.

'What?'

'Read that last bit back, please.'

'Did you hear I got engaged? Hah, isn't the ring just fab?'

My mind has well and truly checked out. I look down at my foolscap pad and it is blank – unless of course you count the five-tier cake doodle and a cartoon of Barry in a top hat with a six-pack. If my brain were an email, it would be officially 'out of office'. I'm excused from the meeting. Nice one!

I don't care if the entire office has to hear the proposal story multiple times. I flash the ring in every available face, including the delivery man when he asks me to sign for a package. I've absolutely no shame. He is a bit rude, though. I'm only halfway through my story and getting to the good bit where Barry is on bended knee when he looks at me sheepishly.

'Sorry, Missus, but I have to go. More deliveries to make.'

The cheek!

Although Katarina the Russian cleaning lady has very limited English, I spare no detail.

'I mean, he just chose the ring himself. Excellent taste.'

Katarina nods 'Da!' in all the right places and makes little Russian noises as she takes in the extravagance of my ring.

I join Amanda at the water cooler.

'A June wedding. So much to do!' I greet her.

She shuffles uneasily and attempts to change the subject, but I am talking too quickly for that.

'Goodness, Rebecca. Five o'clock already. Must dash.'

Look, I know that she has heard the enchanting story already, but she is so obviously jealous that 'her Graham' hasn't popped the question yet. She is blatantly trying to sabotage my bliss. I cross her off the party invitation list.

I confirm the party for Friday night with the receptionist in the swish city centre location hotel (as featured in TV3's *Xposé*, don't you know). I send out email engagement party invitations. By six o'clock, I am yawning. The adrenaline is wearing off. Even Harry is gone and only Katarina and her bleachy whiffy mop remain. I've a headache starting.

Once I leave the office, I find myself sharing the big news with absolute strangers on the street. Every opportunity to tell all and sundry about the forthcoming wedding of the century is grasped with both hands.

'I have absolutely no idea when the next bus is due,' I beam at one old lady hunched over a shopping bag outside of the local Tesco. 'I do, however, know that I shall be a bride in just seven months! Couldn't you just *die*?!'

I flash my ring finger in her general direction and brace myself for her overwhelming admiration. She doesn't seem to hear me, however. The poor old dear is ancient and may have a hearing and/or visual impediment or something. Bless her. I'm sure if she was in possession of all of her faculties she'd be bowled over. Also, she doesn't seem to be free to attend the engagement party. It is probably for the best.

Whilst inside the supermarket buying bread and milk, I strike up a conversation with the young man stacking the shelves.

'Ah yes,' I interrupt his concentration and general tin straightening duties. This appears to be the extent of his job. Pathetic, really.

'It's all go-go-go when you're planning a wedding!'

He glances at me and then behind him, unsure of whom exactly I'm addressing.

'Anyway, I mustn't stay and chat all day,' I continue. I brush away an imaginary stray piece of hair from my face (my hair does not stray) and linger my rock at his eye level. 'I have a vintage-style elegant wedding to organise!'

The chap returns to his work, shaking his head. He is probably, like all men, crushed that I am now officially off the market. Poor sad creature. Next I'm off, bread and milk under one arm, to start another witty conversation with the check-out girl. I've decided that we can be friends, now. She probably won't recognise me from the wreck I was last week. I have put the unfortunate event behind me. That was back when I was single. I have changed, now. I am engaged.

When I hand her my Laser card for payment (using my left hand, naturally) I linger. She stares blankly at me until I motion (subtly, of course) to my ring finger. I grin a toothy grin. Oddly, however, she is also unavailable for the engagement party. This is perhaps due to a work schedule clash. Perhaps it is too painful to celebrate other people's love when you yourself are sadly without any hope of ever being loved. I wouldn't know. As I mentioned, I am engaged.

When I arrive home, I curl up on the couch. I tell Barry to get up off his bum, get the takeaway menus out and get the wine uncorked. I've been working hard all day. Once again, I reach for the phone.

'The usual,' I croak into the receiver. Blast this throat.

'So, how's this little party coming together?' Barry enquires.

We are sitting on the couch eating a Rebecca and Barry special: chicken balls and chips, sweet 'n' sour chicken, curry chips, rice, spare ribs, prawn crackers and a large bottle of Coke. You should try it. Add some vodka to the Coke and you have yourself a little party for two. *Antiques Roadshow* is on the telly and we are glued. I am unusually quiet, having reached talking saturation point from a full day of chatting. This has never happened before.

This little party? I repeat Barry's words in my mind. *Little?*

'Oh, just great,' I gush, delighted that he is taking an interest. 'You know. No big deal. I will just be inviting a small group for an intimate and exclusive gathering.'

His eyebrows rise but he does not break his gaze from the television screen. Mistrust is sweeping across his face.

'How many is a small group, Becky?' his voice is pitched slightly higher. Not a full octave, just a note.

The antique dealer looks older than the article being inspected. Although the vase was made in China, it is not from the Ming dynasty. My money is on the pound shop. The woman looks crushed.

I roll my eyes.

'*God!* Relax Barry, it's nothing lavish. Just about two hundred of our closest friends!'

I manage to hold in the smirk that is threatening to break out across my face. My self control is tested to its limit. 'Sure, TomKat had five hundred at theirs!'

His jaw drops and he turns to look at me. He is unable to speak.

'Sure, I've even extended the olive branch and invited my dreary work colleagues. Oh, and your stuffy solicitor crew. Spoke to some Shelley somebody. Probably your secretary, is she? Bit of a dozy thing, is she? She didn't even know we were engaged. Anyway, the hotel is offering a great rate for the room and DJ.'

I reach for the prawn crackers. Finally, Barry regains the power of speech.

'DJ? Jesus, Becks. Sure didn't we have a party when we got engaged Sunday night? This isn't the bloody wedding. You told me you'd like a small party!'

'That doesn't sound like something I'd say, now does it? Anyway, it *is* small, Barry. And Sunday was the proposal. That so doesn't count, silly,' I retort.

Honestly, he is such a wet blanket sometimes. I refuse to let him quash my party-planning pride. I think it best not to mention my enquiries about marquees, floral arrangements and signature cocktails. Best to let the dust settle.

This evening, he catches me in a hushed phone call in the downstairs loo. I am speaking to the hotel and firming up the canapés order. He has become suspicious after my revelations over dinner. All he has caught are the words 'goat's cheese', 'duck' and 'champagne toast'. I swear to you, I think he is going to hit the roof. What is his problem?

'What's wrong with a small gathering in the house?' Barry debates as I reach for the Chardonnay. 'A couple of cocktail sausages and a few bottles of plonk.'

I set my face to shock-horror mode.

'Eh, pardon? What the actual hell?'

Barry knows now that he has crossed the line. He looks away pronto.

'Have we met? This is not a frat party!'

The credits are rolling for the *Antiques Roadshow*, so I select an episode of *Bridezillas*. This will show Barry how lucky he is to have a dignified and elegant bride, unlike those dreadful trashy types one sees so much of on the box lately. Latisha swings for her fiancé Jamal in front of the reverend. The entire family is brawling in the aisles. Classic!

I decide to ignore any future party suggestions from Barry. He genuinely has no imagination. I've got the skills to coordinate this whole operation, otherwise it is becoming clear that if left to El Cheapo here, we would end up with something *simple*. I recoil at the thought.

'Let's just try and reel it in a little,' Barry attempts a compromise in vain.

'But I want to celebrate our undying love,' my bottom lip wobbles. Gets him every time.

I retreat to bed before he can tackle me further on the issue. Besides, the wine has run out and all of that grub is making me sleepy.

It's six o'clock on Thursday, and I'm waiting for Barry in Starbucks. We have so much to talk about, and if I don't meet him outside of our home he will have his feet up on the recliner, with one ear on the telly and the other ear on the toaster waiting for his dinner to pop. Like a honey trap, the array of pastries lure him in, and I have his undivided attention. At the top of my agenda is a hotel venue for the wedding. Now, hotels are booked up in advance like you wouldn't believe, so it's essential that we book something quick as lightning. The truth is that I really have my heart set on Odescalchi Castle, Italy. I know what you're thinking – isn't that where Tom Cruise and Katie Holmes got hitched? The heart wants what the heart wants!

I slip the castle idea into conversation casually when Barry takes his seat. He splutters into his frappuccino dramatically. I consider myself an evil genius. You see, the word cappuccino is Italian and Odescalchi Castle is in Italy and Tom Cruise got married there. Clever, eh? I'm sneaky that way.

'Sure, they spent a fortune on that wedding. What a waste!' Barry scoffs.

I sit open mouthed. I'm flabbergasted at his cheap ways.

'It was three point five million dollars, *actually*,' I correct him.

He has already changed the subject to cake. No, no, not to wedding cake. Instead, he is talking about the chocolate chip muffins behind the counter and deliberates whether he should have one. I blast his sugar addiction; he is really far too easily distracted.

'Look. I'm not, like, totally disillusioned or anything. I know we can't spend, like, *squillions* of euros on a wedding, and I know that the Cruise castle must have cost a bomb.'

Barry slurps his drink. It's most unflattering.

'And, I know that Andrea Bocelli as the wedding singer is a *tad* out of the wedding budget. *Obviously!*'

He looks at me like I have two heads.

'But, listen. I can haggle a deal. I've sent an email to the castle booking office explaining that the Cruise–Holmes marriage is well and truly over, so perhaps they will give me a discount!'

Barry looks unconvinced.

251

'Maybe they are translating the email as we sit here! Maybe they are putting together a hasty reply! I will check my emails when we are home.'

'What about the local hotel?' Barry has finally committed to a chocolate éclair and I have pointed to the largest slice of carrot cake I've ever seen. If only he could be so decisive when it comes to the wedding.

'What…White's Hotel?'

I lick the cream off his éclair for his own good. His cholesterol is probably sky high and I don't want him to die before we are married. That would kind of ruin the day. Also, the insurance policy won't pay out until we're wed. Just kidding!

'Yeah, Becks. I hear they got the function room repainted after the fire.'

'No,' I laugh.

This is a joke, right? I don't have time for jokes, and no-one would seriously make a suggestion like that to my actual face. His expression remains blank.

'Eh, you can't be serious. I don't recall anyone important getting married there, Barry.'

This should end this ludicrous idea. There! On to more sensible suggestions.

'Rebecca, my parents got married there.'

'Yeah. Exactly. So, no-one important, then. Barry, I can't name one celebrity that got married there. It only has four stars for God's sake. Think bigger! Think five star! Brian and Amy.'

'Who? Are they college mates of yours?'

It's useless. It's like trying to teach advanced *Jane Eyre* to a dyslexic worm.

'Seriously. I'm talking about the O'Driscoll–Huberman wedding? Lough Rynn Castle?'

Barry's eyes glaze over. I have lost him again. He is gazing into the distance. His eyes linger on the muffins. I guess it's up to little old me to pull off a star-studded elegant wedding with celebrity inspiration.

Back home, I wheel the wheelie bin to the end of the driveway. I am shocked to see the extent of my wicked ways. It's only eight o'clock on Thursday, but I have managed to get through an obscene amount of white wine this week alone. It's for stress relief purposes, you understand. I refuse to let you judge me. If Gillian McKeith ever replies to one of my letters (or faxes, emails or voice messages) and decides to dedicate a bridal-boot-camp-type makeover TV show to me, I will be in for a right ass kicking. Just look at the takeaway packaging and wine bottles!

I add another empty wine bottle to the glass recycling bin, just as Bernie from next door appears. I hadn't seen her skulking about, she kind of just crept up on me. She is in her dressing gown. I wonder whether she is having an early night or whether the lazy wretch didn't get dressed today.

Although I try to close the lid in a hurry, she catches a full view of the contents of my bin. Truly mortifying.

'Bernie, hi! Have you heard the news? Guess who's engaged! Me! On a scale of one to ten, how excited are you? Let me show you the ring…'

She just walks off. Cow!

I've been so busy this week organising the engagement party that I have been ordering takeaways like they are going out of fashion. I vow to throw away the menus and remove the Chinese takeaway numbers from my speed dial once the party is over. Barry says I'm being silly, but I'm telling you, it's going to take a miracle not to look dumpy on the wedding day.

Thirty-Five

It's six o'clock on Friday morning, and I am camped out on Grafton Street. No, I'm not trying to secure One Direction tickets. It is even better than that. Let me explain.

Last night, Emer called me in a flap. Emer doesn't usually do panic. It is beneath her. However, there was a pretty good reason for it, so I forgave her. She'd had a tip-off from the powers that be in Brown Thomas that a once-off invitation-only flash sale will be held in the morning. Now, Emer spends a considerable sum in the store – probably more than I earn – and doesn't get excited by sales. She prefers the full-priced shopping because there are less bargain-hunting riff raff about the place. However, she knew that I would be interested, since my wallet has a bottom, and therefore tipped me off. She couriered the ticket straight into my greedy, outstretched paws.

I sweetly ask Barry to accompany me.

'Ah, no. No way! I'm still tired from the conference and all that. Not a chance, Becky. Can you not wait until the Stephen's Day sale?'

Barry is referring to the annual sale event which forms an important part of my yearly calendar. I am one of those ladies who queue up for the sale on St Stephen's Day at six in the morning: a barbaric hour to be awake, I grant you. While most are still digesting the turkey and clearing up the wrapping paper that has been strewn across the living room floor, I am planning my attack.

'Barry,' I try to remain calm. 'How can I explain this? Friday night is our engagement do. In case you have forgotten!'

Barry rubs his eyes. He knows I am not about to back down. He seems very keen to please me these days.

'I need something amazing to wear. Something amazing and half price!'

I try to appeal to his miserly nature. It's like poor Tiny Tim asking Ebenezer Scrooge for more coal for the fire or something.

'Can you not go without me? I'm rubbish at fashion.'

'True. You are totally appalling at fashion. Which is why, once I have chosen something utterly radiant for my good self, I will buy you something less...' I point to his sad little wardrobe '... less ... stripy. Honestly, Barry. We both need something new. It's bad luck otherwise. Superstition, I believe. Also, I need you to drive me. You know how I hate the BT car park. It's too squashy.'

'Feck sake!'

'Ah. Thanks. Love you! What a great team we are!'

The crowd shuffles uneasily, exclusive invitation grasped in their claws. When it comes to shopping, this is the big leagues. I am thirsting for something new and shiny. Normally, I am the sort of lady who views anything marked as 'bargain', 'reduced', or 'on sale' suspiciously. I naturally assume that it must be faulty or deformed in some way or that there must be something horribly wrong with it. I feel comforted when things are reassuringly expensive. The Brown Thomas sale is the only exception.

I eye up the others. I am pretty high up in the queue, invitation in hand. I know that if I want to get in quickly and get out unharmed and laden down with glorious purchases, then like a military operation I must use precision planning. I don't need a blueprint of the store; I've got the floor plan burned into my brain.

The lady next to me looks petite and innocent with flawless make-up and a designer trouser suit. She is fooling no-one. I know that, like the rest of the sharks, she is ruthless in her merciless pursuit of luxurious items at knockdown prices. She knows how to run in impossibly high heels. There is a smell of desperation in the air. Personally, I blame the recession.

As usual, a remarkably grumpy Barry holds my purse. It is his job to ensure that I am not trampled upon. However, once the doors open, I find myself being pushed further and further to the back by these brazen broads. I give the evils to anyone trying to muscle in ahead of me. These designer-clad divas can be cold blooded!

Pam has let me in on her little secret to success when it comes to this kind of thing. The trick is to use your elbows. When used at the right angle and with enough force, you can deter even the most determined of competitive shopping sisters. Pam had shamelessly revealed this little nugget of advice to me one afternoon while Emer and I were admiring her new Yves Saint Laurent clutch over afternoon tea at The Westbury. Emer thought the whole thing to be *savage*, but I was picking up priceless tips and noting them mentally. *We don't all earn six figures, darling*, I almost quipped. I bit my tongue as she was footing the bill as usual.

I rush towards the coveted handbag section, which is the most crowded of all the departments. Having already dreamt of the leather-bound beauty that shall be mine for 50 percent off, I go in for the kill. Marc Jacobs, DKNY, Calvin Klein – they are all there for the taking at a fraction of the cost.

I reach for my prize – the Louis Vuitton. It's a classic in any language. A long-nailed Asian hand snatches the trophy from under my nose. The snooty cow turns on her Pied a Terre heels in the direction of the nearest till. I'm momentarily stunned and then snap back into action.

I need to step it up a gear.

'Quick. Fetch me another purse, please,' I direct Barry sharply. Shopping here is like a competitive sport!

I make my way towards a Diane von Furstenberg frock. I snap it up ahead of a barrage of onlookers for a mere €350. What a deal! Barry nearly chokes when I tell him the price.

'Don't you want me to look amazing at the party?'

He really doesn't understand the value. Not everyone gets it. I mean, she uses pure silk in her once-off creations for goodness' sake. It would be a sin to allow that one to slip through my fingers and into the manicured hand of one less deserving than myself. It is, truly, the Holy Grail of bargains.

Barry follows most impatiently two steps behind me. He sighs and makes no effort to keep up whilst carrying my purchases. It's only eight o'clock and already we have trawled the handbag, cosmetic and clothing section. Barry reports directly to the till and dutifully produces his wallet to make payment. He grumbles about how I have crossed the spending limit.

'As if,' I reply, 'there should be a limit on essential items!'

Barry treats me to a full slap-up breakfast in the top-floor Domini & Peaches café. I revel in my new purchases and imagine myself looking very glamorous at the engagement party.

'I'm going to be late for work!' Barry complains.

'Don't be silly. Here, have another coffee.'

On a full stomach and fully restored, we descend to the men's section. An unenthusiastic Barry reminds me of a twelve-year-old Ian being led by Mum to get his school uniform.

Please don't feel sorry for Barry. He is only looking for attention. His services as a clothes mule and cash machine are well rewarded. I choose an Armani suit for him. It is tailored to perfection, and does wonders to hide his bulges around the middle section. He looks very dashing, I must admit. And at half price, I have saved him a *bundle*, which leaves more cash to be spent on the woman in his life!

Barry drops me to the office and gives me a kiss on the lips. I call Emer when I reach my desk.

'Perhaps I will only wear white until I am wed. They will call me "The girl who wears white". What do you think?'

Emer thinks this is a genius idea.

It feels like Friday afternoon will never arrive. At three o'clock, I stand up from my cubicle. My shoulders and neck are strained

257

from all of the frantic phone calls and last-minute arrangements.

'Keep calm and party on!' I repeat the well known mantra used in war times to myself. This engagement soirée is simply a drill, I remind myself. It is on a far smaller scale than the Big Day. It is a costume rehearsal, if you will, for the wedding itself. Yes, there is pressure – it will set the entire theme for the wedding. Yes, all eyes will be on me. But I can handle it. I have been dreaming about this since I was five years old!

Before I leave the office, I text Mum, Emer, Pam and all of my gal pals to make sure they are all set. My mobile battery is flashing red from excessive texting and I've a pain in my thumb.

I dial the hotel. By now, I have the number stored in my memory banks forever.

'Hello? Yes. The future Mrs Costello calling. Uh huh. Pass me through to Sinead, the events planner. What is it regarding? It is regarding me making sure that she has secured every detail. Everything needs to be perfect for our magical celebration.'

There is a stifled snigger on the line. I am not impressed. She is not grasping the scale of this event. Amateur!

The snooty cow on hotel reception has deliberately put me through to Sinead's voicemail.

'Sinead. Rebecca again. Just another quick check in to make sure that everything is in place for the event tonight. Disappointed to get your voicemail again. I've ruled the hotel out of the wedding venue shortlist. Anyway, call me.'

I hang up. I am starting to wonder whether this Sinead has my event at the top of her priority list. She has been 'in a meeting' every time I called this week. I will be charitable. I will assume that she is, as we speak, instructing her colleagues on the flawless roll out of the VIP – Very Important Party, rather than avoiding my calls.

I sneak past Harry. Luckily, he is absorbed in a heavy duty phone call and doesn't notice me leave.

It has been two hours in the hair and beauty salon, and I am looking seriously lush if I do say so myself! My blonde highlights are extra blonde for the occasion, thanks to a highly excitable Dermot who is due to be in attendance at the big bash. My nails are a deep vixen red and my eyelashes are of gravity defying proportions, thanks to Mishka and her highly dedicated crew. Sadly, Mishka is otherwise engaged for the evening.

Thirty-Six

I drive home at warp speed and in a dreadful panic. My nerves are jangling, and I'm flicking nervously from one radio station to the next with no satisfaction.

I pray.

Jesus, give me a sign. Tell me if tonight's party will be a massive success or a giant car crash.

Ta, Becks.

The next song is by S Club 7, so this is definitely a divine sign that the night will go swimmingly. After all, there ain't no party like an S Club party. Everyone knows that. However, the song after that is Wham's 'Careless Whisper'. Jesus, what does this mean? I'm never gonna dance again?! Guilty feet ain't got no rhythm?! That could be a bad omen.

I call Mum to ask her opinion. She is quite spiritual, so she will understand. Her number is engaged, so I drive on and flick the radio until I hear a song that bodes better for tonight's outcome. By now, I am in danger of chewing my own arm off. I realise with a sudden jolt that I have skipped lunch due to the blurred last-minute arrangements. This is a first. On the plus side, this probably means that I am practically fading away like Posh Spice. We have so much in common, her and I. The downside is that I could pass out later during my engagement photo shoot, and unconscious is not a good look. Just ask Lindsey Lohan.

My body is probably going into deep shock. I am not used to such extreme starvation! Secondly, the magnum of champagne that I am planning to drown myself in later on will probably go down better in a lined stomach. I am so wise.

I reach into my glove compartment for an emergency supply of sugar, and consume a king-sized Mars Bar in just two gulps. It sticks in my throat like a rat in a python. The sugar surges through my body, and the gnawing at my stomach fades.

I feel that the Mars Bar may be feeling lonely, so I wolf an entire family-sized bag of peanut M&Ms. Gillian McKeith is always banging on about how good nuts are for you. Consuming these while breaking the speed limit around a busy roundabout is a testament to my excellent driving skills. Once I am home, I park the car sloppily. The windows are still rolled down.

I have never known party planning to be so stressful – the 'Real Housewives of Orange County' make it look easy! Although listed as a key skill on my CV, the closest I have come to meticulous event organisation is inviting Barry's family over for a Sunday roast last year to celebrate his birthday. It ended in a flushed apology, as I produced a cremated chicken with accompanying chargrilled vegetables and fanned the smoke detector with a tea towel. Tears flowed from the smoke-stung eyes of our hungry guests. Barry rang in a pizza.

If this engagement party is getting my knickers into such a twist, imagine what the flipping wedding will be like. I will have to watch myself for signs of stress and general overdoing it. I can't spare another wrinkle or worry line. Perhaps I will ask Dr Logan for a sick cert from work between now and the wedding. Just to be safe.

Pam told me once that a woman called Annie (her friend from the office's neighbours' cousin's best friend, apparently) once got so worked up about table plans for her wedding that her hair fell out. I am not making that up. Just ask Annie. Or rather, 'Alopecia Annie', as she is now known.

261

I scuttle up the driveway with great haste. Barry is already home. I realise with a jolt that it is now six o'clock, and our party is due to start in just one short hour. That is just a measly sixty minutes… or three thousand six hundred seconds! I slam the door shut and screech up the stairs.

'Barry! Barraaaaaay!'

To my dismay, I discover him in the sitting room. He is relaxing on the couch reading the *Financial Times* newspaper. He is still dressed in his day suit without a care in the world.

'Hi, Becks,' he yawns. 'You look sexy.'

I resist the urge to throttle him. Finger marks around his throat would ruin the photos. He then produces a cool drink in a crystal glass.

'A stiff G and T,' he offers. 'Thought you could use it.'

The man is a saint! I down the lot in one go. It is for my nerves, so don't judge me! Placing the glass back on the mantelpiece, I bark at him to get a shagging move on and practically push him up the stairs. I turn the telly off and hide the remote.

'Relax, we have *loads* of time,' he protests.

This statement merely demonstrates Barry's distinct lack of understanding with regards to my need to look absolutely *perfect* and make a big entrance. It is a red flag to a bull.

'All *you* flipping have to do is change clothes and splash on the expensive celebrity aftershave that I bought you last Christmas and you are ready to rock. I even bought you a new shirt and then went to the trouble of laying it out this morning so as to avoid the very possible embarrassment of you choosing something garish that might clash with me and/or upset our beloved photos. I have to think of everything!'

Barry does not reply. Quite wise of him, really.

I grapple with getting into:

a) An industrial strength pair of miracle underwear, which promises to boost me where I need boosting and flatten me where I need flattening.

b) Tan tights in a 'small'. My pride wouldn't allow me to buy a medium.

c) My new dress, which must have shrunk a size or two since purchasing it or else may have been incorrectly sized by some teenage trainee shop assistant. There is no time to write a strongly worded email. I think size 14 is the new size 10, anyway. Something funny is definitely going on.

'Help me with the zip,' I beg Barry.

The tag removal is a delicate operation. Barry fumbles with the nail clippers. I slip into some darling white kitten heels. Next, my make-up and hair do are analysed in the close-up mirror. This mirror usually shows every blackhead, facial hair in need of tweezing and eye bag. We all have one like it. The slap was expertly applied an hour earlier and hasn't moved a millimetre. The hair remains flawless and stiff like cardboard. More lip-gloss is applied and more hairspray is sprayed. Perhaps a full can is overdoing it, but I am taking no chances. Also, in the very words of Cheryl Cole, it's 'because I'm worth it'.

As I smooth my dress down in the mirror, I like what I see. Barry is a real gentleman, and I'm sure he would tell me I am like an angel from heaven, but he is having some sort of spluttering choking attack from the hairspray. He says he's feeling light headed.

'Cop the fudge on and get the shagging car started, will you?'

My foul language demonstrates my shredded nerves. The adrenaline is kicking in big time as Barry drives off towards the hotel in the city centre. He is still coughing, the attention seeker. My pulse is fast and my stomach churns in a sickening swirl with a mixture of anticipation and excitement. Honestly, the chocolate and gin combo has nothing to do with it.

Soon, all our friends, family, co-workers, acquaintances and neighbours (well, those who are not the spawn of Satan) will be enjoying our elegant soirée and basking in the fabulousness of the undeniable love we have for each other. I'll be flashing the rock about something rotten, and all eyes will be on us: The Happy Couple.

'What are you doing?'

Barry is eyeing me suspiciously.

'I told you, Barry. I've been practising my smile in the mirror all week – it's a cross between ecstatically happy, being serenely in love and being at peace with the world. I think I have nailed it.'

Barry laughs. Does he even realise that the engagement album will be looked at for generations to come? Does he even care about making a show of me? I hope he will shape up in time for the wedding just seven months away. He has been highly uncooperative. He refuses to practise smiling or take practice photos.

'Just relax, will you? I'll be smiling… normal.'

I roll my eyes. He hasn't got a clue.

'Stop over-analysing things, Becky. Just enjoy the night.'

'Fine. Stick with your geeky, unprepared toothy grin, haha. I have been using whitening strips all week and have just the right pose prepared. It is a Hollywood glam/red carpet at the Oscars fusion. It can't fail.'

I ask Barry to park as close as he can to the hotel.

'Becks, I have pulled up to the front door. I can't get any closer!'

'Yeah, but even five metres in delicate kitten heels is too much. These shoes are not designed for walking in.'

Mum and Dad arrive. I switch from Queen Bee to Princess Sweetie-pie, and my annoyance evaporates. Barry and Dad shake hands and Mum and I hug hello. We walk through the hotel reception together and make our way to the function room.

The moment of ecstasy is now upon us! As I open the main doors of the function room, I see that the hotel staff have done an amazing job decorating the room. Tea light candles light every table and soft music is playing. The ice sculpture is breathtaking. A barman tends the bar and others take coats. It is exactly as per my orders.

Mum and Dad greet a neighbour who is first to arrive. Mum is in her element. She talks excitedly and her arms flap even more than usual. Dad is getting the drinks in and looks smart leaning at the bar in a pair of beige slacks and a sports jacket.

Karen arrives next. Getting away from her kids for the evening is rare, and she is already lashing into the white wine. She links arms with her husband Frank.

I flash my left ring finger into her face with a squawk.

'Can you believe it?'

Although we have spoken several times during the week, I go straight into the proposal story again. In case she missed any detail the first few times.

'I told you it would all work out! Sure, you'll be married with kids just like us in no time.'

We rehash our hilarious night out at the karaoke Chinese, and Frank tells me what a state Karen was in when she arrived home.

'Seriously though, Becks,' she cringes. 'Babies and hangovers do not mix. Never again.'

'Never!' I agree. 'Well, apart from tonight. Obviously!'

'Obviously!'

Karen and I clink glasses.

Dad arrives over with a G&T for me, and joins Barry who is greeting some work colleagues with a firm handshake at the door.

'Oh, and of course then there's the hen night, Karen! It's going to be legendary. Emer will be in touch about that. She is in charge, so it's all going to be *super classy*.'

I direct this last comment at Frank. Karen and I exchange sniggers.

'God, Rebecca. Please tell me we'll be going away somewhere for the weekend. The kids are doing my head in. No fecking nappies or bottles for forty-eight hours would be bliss… well, apart from bottles of vodka!'

Karen guffaws. Frank looks horrified at the prospect of keeping three under three alive and well for such a duration.

'Absolutely,' I continue. 'Emer was thinking New York?'

The blood drains from Frank's face.

Our conversation is cut short. There is a commotion at the entrance. Pam arrives with a deafening squeal. The whole room turns to look as she throws her arms around me. Her new MOTM

(Man of the Moment) is also in attendance, and introduces himself shyly as Doug. I shake his hand as Pam circulates, spotting college buddies. Doug is too polite to interrupt me, as I launch into our happy news.

'Oh, Doug! Barry's proposal was all so unexpected!'

I clutch at Doug's shirt as if we are old friends. My throat is raw and I'm growing giddier. He smiles uneasily at me, and glances sideways as I explain our wedding plans. I think the poor chap is in awe of me. Can you blame him? I suppose God, in all of his wisdom, knew that we can't all be fabulous.

Emer and hubby David follow closely behind. Much air kissing, hugs and insistence that the other is thinner ensues. The ring is inspected once again by Emer. She gasps dramatically at the sheer magnitude of it. Her voice raises quite a few decibels.

'Ah, Rebecca. It's such a stunner. Like you.'

'I know!'

Emer's diamond ring is truly staggering and probably has more carats. She usually celebrates at the Ritz Carlton, but says that the party is exquisite. We talk a mile a minute. David looks lost, unable to get a word in.

Barry welcomes his parents at the main entrance, along with some more suits from the firm. There is much raucous laughter and back slapping. There is a woman in the group hovering around Barry. When the crowd dissipates a little, she takes Barry's elbow and leans in closely. She flicks back her long brown hair. They whisper like this for some time, but Barry looks agitated. He glances behind him constantly. He shakes his head. I catch him mouth the word 'no'. He makes a gesture towards the door and she leaves.

The penny drops. How did I not see this before? I bet he is organising a wedding singer for me!

The room is filling up nicely. Staff wearing white gloves circulate the room with lovely little nibbles on silver trays. At every table, someone has bought me a white wine or a cocktail. I circulate and knock the drinks back as fast as I can while recounting the joyous proposal story over and over again.

The brunette is back. She is heading in my direction. Barry's face registers alarm. He excuses himself from his conversation with Nigel and moves in her direction. Once he sees that the woman has reached me he backs off.

The woman stands in front of me. She is pretty and slim, and dressed in a navy knee-length dress and has stylish glasses. She looks a bit red and blotchy around the eyes, but a bit of concealer could fix that. This is important if she is going to stand at the top of the church and sing me up the aisle. I mean, it doesn't matter if she has a singing voice sent from heaven itself. If she were hideous looking it would throw off the whole wedding.

'Rebecca, I just wanted to say…'

'Yes?'

'…You're a very lucky lady.'

'Eh. Thanks. So, do you do any Wham numbers? Or Lionel Ritchie? Mariah Carey? Or is it more 'Ave Maria' at the church kind of stuff?'

She walks off. How odd! Barry follows her out. They are probably discussing her thoughts on Michael Bolton as a choice for our first dance. So thoughtful!

As the night goes on, the pain in my face from smiling is growing. My cheeks are absolutely aching. My ridiculous grin is like the Cheshire cat from *Alice in Wonderland* on LSD. I am drunk on the attention, although the wine may have a small role to play. I am quaffing champagne and clinking glasses like nobody's business. The canapés are divine and everyone seems suitably dazzled.

As nine o'clock approaches, more and more guests arrive by the bucket load. Aunties, uncles, long-lost cousins, college friends, class mates, old work colleagues, current co-workers, Slimmers' Club members, hairdressers past and present and ex-boyfriends. The drink is flowing and waiters circle faithfully with the yummies.

At ten o'clock, Judy arrives. She says that she had another party on earlier and couldn't possibly have arrived any earlier. It was something very glamorous and exclusive, no doubt. She is wearing a short black revealing dress and high boots. The tan is completely overdone and bordering on orange.

'Ivan…' I cough the word *terrible* '…not with you tonight, then?'

'He was. He had to dash off. He has another commitment.'

'Eh, yeah! His wife and three kids!'

Shit. I didn't mean to say this out loud. Personally, I blame the booze. I laugh uncontrollably. Judy does not.

'Anyway,' Judy continues. 'I hear Harry is buying a round of drinks, which is rare. I'm off to get a vodka.'

'Oooh. Get one for me too. Tight bastard owes me one. Make it a large.'

'Will do.'

We kiss on the cheek and she joins our colleagues at a nearby table.

A large mountain of presents has accumulated on a nearby table. I am really hoping there is a chocolate fondue set in there somewhere. Or a karaoke machine. That is something that we can both enjoy. Barry and I could bond over Patsy Cline hits, and I could teach him a thing or two about Vanilla Ice lyrics while he pours me drinks to loosen my vocal chords. Barry is remarkably tone deaf and claims not to like karaoke, but I think if he gave it a try he would learn to love it. Marriage is all about compromise, after all. If there is no karaoke machine I'm sure I could swap a lame toaster for one. There is a mini mountain of cards. There had better be cash in them. Or vouchers. But cash is best.

Looking around the room, I do a rough headcount and realise that we have far exceeded the rough two hundred guest list estimate. The more the merrier, I cheer. This is my moment in the sun. Soon it will be someone else's turn to get engaged or get a promotion. I'll be like yesterday's newspaper wrapping on soggy fish 'n' chips. Why shouldn't I make the most of it? Why shouldn't I squeeze every last drop of happiness? I will get as much mileage out of this as possible.

'You see, it's all a government conspiracy,' I strike up an in-depth discussion with Amanda from the office. 'Bridal gowns are purposely made at least two sizes smaller to make you feel absolutely pants about yourself. There's a whole thing online about it. You can look it up.'

'Fascinating.'

Amanda and 'her Graham' have suddenly got to leave at short notice and excuse themselves. It's so obviously sour grapes.

From the corner of my eye, I see Barry. He is clinking politely on a glass to get everyone's attention. His feeble shushing attempts are in vain, the laughter and banter are drowning him out. He persists, unnoticed.

'What on earth,' I cringe, 'is he up to?'

This is definitely not part of The Plan. He has been given *strict* coaching for the evening:

a) Wear the outfit I have selected.
b) Buy me copious amounts of alcohol .
c) Tell everyone how *desperately in love* we are, and finally (but most importantly).
d) *Don't make a show of me.*

This suspicious glass clinking is a deliberate stray from the modus operandi. I have warned him there will be severe consequences (i.e. permanent removal of the remote control) if he does not follow the action plan.

'Quiet!' roars Pam. She flaps her arms.

'*Shut up, you're ruining it!*' I send Pam a telepathic message. She doesn't receive it, as she is not as spiritually tuned-in as I am. She persists in hollering.

Before my eyes, the scene unfolds. I'm unable to stop it. Slowly, people turn their heads. Finally a hush descends upon the room and all eyes are on my beloved, hanging on his impending words. I hold my breath. The false smile I have plastered on has far too many teeth on show to look genuine.

'*No,*' I think. '*This has not been scripted. You will mess it up entirely!*'

'Speech!' cheers Pam. 'Speech!'

A hot fluster creeps up my neck. The bodice of my underwear is making it hard for me to breathe.

'Eh. Sorry…' mumbles a flustered Barry, pulling at his shirt collar. 'I just wanted to say a few words.'

'*What are you playing at?*' I panic.

'I just want to say a few words,' Barry repeats, stronger now.

His voice is more commanding. He sounds just like he is protesting someone's innocence in the courtroom. I giggle.

'Thank you all for coming,' Barry clears his throat and takes my hand.

Here it comes. He is going to blow everyone away with some gushing declaration of love. It's possible that I might literally burst. I scramble up all of my self-control. Under the influence of so much champers, this is a major challenge.

I manage to keep a lid on it. In my mind I am screaming 'He's mine. All mine. And he wants to marry me. We're in love!'

'As you all know, Rebecca and I have been together for four happy years. I look forward to many more years together.'

There is a round of applause.

The man is a God, I am so very lucky to have him. Thank the Lord he forgave my intolerable dramatics.

'I will be very proud to make her my wife in June.'

Dear Lord,

Please let Barry marry me before he changes his mind. Also, if you can see to it that I get that Vera Wang original, I will be most grateful.

Amen.

Yours angelically,

Rebecca

PS, sorry I haven't been to, you know, like, church or anything in a squinchy bit, but as you can imagine I've been very busy. Very! You organised the last supper and all of that so you know the pressure it will be to cater for a couple of hundred guests. Loaves and fishes and all that jazz.

PPS, if you could swing me that Rat Pack band that Gary Barlow had at his wedding, I'd be eternally grateful.

Barry looks directly into my eyes and raises his glass. 'Here's to you.'

My eyes are welling up. Although tears are usually on tap for dramatic purposes, these are the real deal. I want to press pause. My entire life has been leading up to this one magical moment. It is likely to never reach such nirvana again. Everyone is watching. Cameras are flashing. I just hope that I am not so squiffy that I won't remember this tomorrow.

There is a smattering of applause and I take in every last drop. I look around the room at all the smiling faces and ponder. *Perhaps we will be giving you all marital advice. We are such good role models.*

The surprise speech has racked up a few brownie points, and in my inebriated state, I promise to return the favour that very night. I believe my exact words are 'I'm gonna rock your world tonight, baby!' Unfortunately, I am within earshot of his mortified mother Margaret (aka my future mother-in-law). She smiles graciously, clapping for Barry and pretends not to notice.

A champagne bottle pops inches from my left ear and in unison the crowd raise their glasses.

'To Barry and Rebecca,' the party cheers.

I pan the room to take in all of the smiling familiar faces. I see Mum and Dad, grinning and draining the last of their drinks. Ian and Cindi are clearly 'on again' based on their entangled body language. They stand beside Dad who is feeding them full of free drinks all evening. Ian has even worn a *tie*, I notice. He looks *respectable*. This is totally unheard of in the history of Ian. Perhaps he has scrubbed up in order to really congratulate us. What a turn-up for the books! Or perhaps he has come straight from a job interview? Nah, I correct myself cynically, that is a less likely scenario.

Pam, Doug, Emer and David are clapping. Karen has her head cocked to the side with a sentimental smile. I memorise the looks on their faces. It is priceless.

'Thanks everyone,' I mutter.

I realise then that there is absolutely no way on this earth that I will be one of those brides who gets up at the after dinner speeches and says a few words because:

a) I am useless at public speaking, and avoid it at all costs as if my life depends on it – just like babysitting.

b) I will probably be in floods of mascara-staining tears and the lipstick will have been rubbed off and I'd have a red-wine-toothed grin.

c) I will probably be slurring my words.

The chatter resumes and people rejoin their conversations. A waiter circulates with glasses of Moët on a tray for all of our guests.

The brown-haired church singer is back. Her glasses are off, and her eyes are even blotchier. I'll have to reconsider her for the prestigious position if her skin condition doesn't clear up. These things can be contagious. She is coming towards me again.

'Right. I just want to say one more thing to you.'

'Yes?'

I notice that she has a glass of wine in her hand, it's all very unprofessional. I don't want some wino alco-type person on the job. She might muddle the lyrics to Michael Bolton. That would be simply unforgivable.

'You don't even appreciate Barry.'

'Pardon?'

'Ask your precious fiancé what he's been up to.'

This is all very oddball behaviour. I mean, Barry only kept the secret from me because he wanted to surprise me with booking a singer. It's hardly criminal activity! I open my mouth like a fish to respond, but she turns and walks away. I look around. No-one has noticed our exchange as they are all caught up in conversations of their own.

Well, I'm sorry, but Barry will have to be more selective when choosing staff. I will have to tell him to pull the plug on her gig. I couldn't have her and her volatile ways on the big day. God knows what she is capable of.

Thirty-Seven

'What the hell are you playing at?!'

Barry has a firm grip of Shelley's scrawny arm, and they are huddled outside the function room in the hotel corridor. She says that her arm is starting to hurt, but he doesn't let go. She needs to get the message. She needs to leave them alone. Shelley pulls away.

'I thought I told you to go home, Shelley. No-one wants you here. I told you not to come tonight. This is my engagement party. For fuck's sake! I told you to stay away from Rebecca.'

'Hey, yeah. Whatever. Nice fiancée, Barry. She treats you like dirt.'

Barry rubs his temples. The function room door opens as some neighbours spill out into the lobby in search of a spot for a sneaky cigarette. Barry smiles at them. When they leave, he turns to Shelley with a glare.

'Never,' Barry hisses, 'mention Rebecca again, got it?'

Shelley sneers. 'Whatever.'

'Listen, Shelley. I'm sorry. OK? It was one stupid, drunken night. I don't even remember most of it. But it's over. I know you're upset.'

'Upset?' Shelley laughs. 'Hey, don't flatter yourself, Barry,' she is biting her lower lip. 'You didn't tell her, did you Barry?'

'No,' Barry puffs out his cheeks. 'I tried. Couldn't do it, it would break her heart. But I will. In my own time. And Shelley?'

Barry's eyes are like icebergs – cold and clear.

'She's not going to find out from you. Got it?'

'Coward.'

'Have you got that, Shelley? I'll tell her. Me. I'll do it. OK? Anyway, looks like you and Nigel are getting along nicely,' Barry smiles caustically.

There is a silence between them now, a terrible awkwardness.

'Look, Barry. I've applied to another firm. They're looking for someone in family law. Hey, probably for the best.'

'Probably.'

Barry looks over his shoulder.

'Right. I've got to go.'

Thirty-Eight

Barry says that the clock has struck four in the morning, and I am to stop regaling our nearest and dearest with amusing tales of how we met. Some try to escape from my tight grasp in order to grab taxis and relieve babysitters of their duties. The hotel bar has closed and the bar staff refuse me another sniff of champers, even if I *am* a beautiful bride to be.

Before being assisted out into the fresh air, I insist on thanking each and every staff member personally for creating such an 'enchanting shindig'. This proves quite tricky to pronounce.

'It was a team effort,' I repeat to Maria from Lisbon.

I'm anxious that she didn't catch the message the first four times. I am a very gracious person and I always remember the little people. Some staff are Portuguese and work in the housekeeping section, with a very loose grasp of the English language. I shake Maria's hand firmly and tell her yet again that her family back in Portu-Land should be very proud.

It's silly o'clock when poor Barry manages to manhandle me like a dead weight into his parked car outside of the hotel. He struggles to get me up the driveway, up the stairs and remove my shoes. That is as far as he gets before I proceed to pass out and drool all over the Egyptian cotton duvet, face down with my head pointing towards the foot of the bed. No-one rocks anyone's world.

I don't remember the getting home bit. There is a gap here which refuses to be filled. I know that is a tad disgraceful to admit this over the age of thirty. However, in my defence, it is my first (and quite possibly last) time to get engaged, which calls for a little bit of the old 'Eat, Drink and be Merry' routine. I have certainly taken that saying to heart.

I wake up at the crack of 1 PM on Saturday.

'I feel absolutely fine!' I declare. 'I've such a high tolerance for drink.'

Barry rolls over.

'There is no trace of any hangover at all. Nothing!' I insist. 'I am not a lightweight like other people, unable to handle their liquor. I could drink anyone under the table. Anyone! Even a sailor. The fact that the room is spinning is merely because I haven't eaten breakfast yet. Anyway, why hasn't the breakfast been served?'

Barry shuffles downstairs. Just because I was unconscious doesn't mean I shouldn't have been offered some eggs and pain pills! Just because I have agreed to marry Barry doesn't mean he can now slack off on his breakfast duties!

When said boiled eggs and pain pills are finally presented to me in bed, the whiff of the blasted things upsets my delicate stomach. I am doubled over with a veritable volcano of vomit splashing on our cream porcelain (celebrity inspired) toilet bowl and ruining our cream marble tiles. The banging in my left temple grows to deafening proportions.

'Oh, God, Barry. I am never drinking again,' I clutch the loo seat and moan.

Barry rubs my back. I am stretched over the toilet bowl in the absolute horrors.

'I think I'm going to die.'

My cries for help are interrupted by violent retching. Thankfully, Barry manages to carry me back (like my puke-splashed knight in shining armour) to the bed, where I resume the foetal position and clutch the sheets.

I pray for mercy.

Sweet Jesus. Why must I suffer like you on the cross? Have I not been a Christian role model to all? I stuck a fiver into the dog pound collection box last year. I forgave Mum for burning my Sunday dinner last week. If I die I should become a martyr!

Terminally yours, Rebecca.

Barry places the plastic pudding bowl on the bedside locker and dons a pair of pink rubber gloves for the bathroom crime scene. He will have quite the job to get it clean again, I can tell you. Also, he misses a few spots. I decide that I will have to have words with him about his shoddy, slapdash attitude to cleanliness. But not now. Now, I need a nurse. Or a cyanide pill.

On the plus side, surely I have cleared my stomach contents enough times to have dropped a dress size – it is like the stomach flu of 2009 all over again. All of the goat's cheese and sundried tomato puffs and mini quiche delights that I had loaded into my mouth in between drinks last night have come back in reverse. It seems there were a lot of carrots in the dishes. The mini spring rolls follow shortly, making their speedy exit into the pudding bowl. Their no doubt astronomical calories are now null and void. Every cloud has a silver lining.

According to Barry, I was absolutely locked last night. Barry seems to have a clearer memory than me for some strange reason. I suspect he may be exaggerating. All I can hold down is hot sugary tea, so I instruct Barry to serve me this every few hours. However, he has started to ignore my feeble beckoning. He seems strangely unable to hear the tinkling of my little bell. I am starting to think that he is doing it on purpose.

Saturday evening and Sunday morning pass in a hungover haze, as I come in and out of consciousness. By Sunday lunchtime, I am feeling just strong enough to make it down the stairs to watch back-to-back episodes of *The X Factor*. I have grown tired of the telly upstairs. It doesn't have HD or 3D, which is so third world.

'How are you feeling, baby?' enquires Barry after I have descended the stairs gingerly. I am careful not to move too quickly.

'Huh,' I reply. 'I have survived. No thanks to you. I think you'd better think long and hard about this whole "in sickness and in health/for better or for worse" vow. Not even a drop of chicken noodle soup to be had from you.'

I suspect that Barry is enjoying having the telly remote to himself all weekend.

'Perhaps…' I snatch the remote from his grip and become absorbed with the judges' houses on *The X Factor* '… I got food poisoning at the hotel.'

I explain my cunning theory on the crab claws, adding in my strong thoughts on legal action. I've described the liquid nature of my bowels in great detail. He doesn't think, however, that legal action would be wise. He says this slowly, like I am insane and he has to explain things very clearly.

'No-one else has reported food poisoning from the canapés. Perhaps the mixture of white wine, champagne, gin and tonic followed by tequila shots and several Alabama Slammers was too much in your system.'

He has his 'trying-to-be-helpful-while-butter-wouldn't-melt' face on. What is with his attitude? He forgot to list the Sambuca.

'So, what… were you keeping track, then?' I retort and stomp back to bed.

Blast Barry and his superior 'I'm the designated driver, I can walk in a straight line' attitude. He can be so holier than thou! Just because he is not hungover till kingdom come doesn't mean he can act like he is *better than me*. I am a victim of inadequate food hygiene standards here. Where is his sympathy? Where is his declaration that he will battle the courts for justice?

Barry follows me upstairs.

'Becks.' He nudges me lightly. 'Rebecca.'

'What?'

Must he annoy me while I am in recovery?

'There's something I need to tell you. I should have told you ages ago. I've been keeping something from you for a week or so.'

I squint at him from under the covers.

'It's OK. I know.'

Barry looks confused.

'OK. Are you … what do you know?'

'About the woman. At the party.'

I can't believe Barry is in a chatty mood right now. I could kill him. Maybe he will leave me alone now.

'Yeah. Listen. Her name is Shelley. We work together.'

'It's alright, Barry. The game is up. I know you booked her to sing at the wedding. But she's… weird. Totally unsuitable. Sorry I ruined the surprise.'

'Wedding singer? No, Becks. She's… we work together.'

I sit up, even though my brain has grown too large for my skull and is clawing to ooze out through my eardrums. I lie back on the headboard so that the throbbing and whooshing lessens.

'We were on the trip together. I was upset. You know, after our fight? I was confused. About us.'

I stare blankly at Barry.

'No, Barry…no.'

'Things got out of hand. I …'

'You what, Barry?'

'I cheated on you.'

Slap! My face burns with the news.

'No.'

'One of the nights I was away. I was fucking hammered. Totally out of it. I can hardly remember what happened, but I woke up next to her. I'm so, so sorry.'

'But… I don't understand. What?'

I'm remarkably calm. This is not how I thought I'd react at hearing news like this. I thought I'd smash a few dinner plates or throw a knicker fit at the very least. The blood flow in my ears has grown louder.

'I made a mistake, Becky. It will … *never* … happen again. I love you so much.'

Barry's face is wet and it takes me a minute to realise that he is crying. I remain mute and lie back down. I stare straight ahead as Barry leaves the room. I hear his footsteps on the landing and the sound of wardrobes opening and closing in the spare bedroom. *Is he packing?* There is shuffling in bathroom cabinets.

Ten minutes later, Barry returns to the bedroom and sits on the side of the bed.

'Listen, I'll go to Mum's for a few days. Let you think this over. I know you don't want to even look at me right now. I can hardly look at myself. If you want to talk, just call me at Mum's. I'll tell her why I'm there, you shouldn't have to pretend. I've fucked everything up. Rebecca, if you can forgive me, I swear…'

'You swear what, Barry?'

'I will never do anything so bloody stupid again. I want to marry you, you know? Start a family.'

Barry stands and reaches for his sports bag.

'I love you.'

I don't answer. I don't question. I don't argue. I just can't.

Thirty-Nine

By Monday morning, I am groggy. Lying in bed all weekend and staring at the ceiling while slowly slipping into insanity can do that to you. I can't bring myself to get up. If I get out of bed and face the world, then that means that what Barry told me really happened. It means that it wasn't just some nightmare I invented. It means that this engagement ring on my finger is a total sham, and that my life is shattered into a million pieces. In a nutshell, it's all total shite.

I send a text to Judy.

Tell Harry I'm still hungover from the party.

I don't care what Harry thinks any more. Sue me.

You know that post-alcohol stage that requires carbohydrates? Yeah, well, I'm there. I force myself into the shower with the promise of a grease-dripping fried breakfast. As I look around our bedroom, I notice that the pudding bowls have been cleared. The bathroom is gleaming. In the spare bedroom, I see that Barry has washed and ironed the clothes and sheets that got puke-splashed.

Turning up at Barry's office today was not a conscious decision. I didn't hop out of the shower, see my shabby reflection in the steamed-up glass and think 'You know what I fancy doing today?

281

I fancy spying on the woman who slept with my fiancé.' I'm not a total head case. I just have slight head case tendencies.

Anyway, stop judging me. I'm the innocent, injured party here. I've got nothing to apologise for. I just wanted to see her, if you can understand that. I just wanted to answer the burning questions in my frazzled mind.

OK, before you brand me as completely insane, you need to bear in mind that:

a) I haven't slept since Barry's bombshell of a confession. Thinking clearly and making rational decisions is not top of my priority list right now.
b) I vaguely remember what Shelley looks like from the party, but I wasn't exactly taking notes back then. The champagne goggles were on, and I was more concerned about her potential singing voice than whether she was attractive. In a nutshell, I need to see if she is hotter than me. I won't rest until I find out. Period.

Sitting in a parked car from noon starts to get old about one o'clock. For starters, I'm desperate for the loo. I've put a fried breakfast and a gallon of coffee on top of a very delicate stomach, so do the maths. Secondly, I'm worried that someone will spot me.

No sign of Barry, and it's two o'clock, which means he is probably working through lunch. I know he's in there, because I can see his Jag parked across the street. I've got Oldies FM on the radio to keep me company. 'Torn Between Two Lovers' comes on. The irony! The sweet fucking irony of it all!

Good Lord, there she is. *Shelley.* I notice her legs first. They are slim and never ending and lead up to an A-line skirt that is a couple of inches above the knee. Her high heels click on the pavement. Although she has got nice pins (I'll grudgingly give her that), she's not a stunner. Her face is a bit pointy, if you catch my drift. She has brown hair. Now, there is nothing wrong with that. I'm not, like discriminatory against brunettes. It's just that Barry always said he loved my blonde hair. I exhale with a huge sense of relief.

There is a man with her. An elderly man! She is linking arms with the old codger. Surely it's not her grandfather? But wait! I recognise him. It's Barry's boss, Nigel. I remember him from the office Christmas parties over the years. How could you forget someone who accidentally on purpose brushes past your boobs while pretending to reach for the white wine in the middle of the table? How could you not remember someone who stares at your cleavage all night as you talk, even if you were wearing a push-up corset and a scoop-neck gown which left nothing to the imagination? On the night itself, it didn't bother me. I mean, I was looking foxy and the man was positively decrepit. I thought maybe I was giving a dying man a bit of joy.

And you know what? The following Christmas party, he was leering at someone else – the legal intern, I think she was. Then the letch put his hand out and flitted past her pert bottom as he was passing through the crowd. That's when I realised that he is just a perv, plain and simple. I remember putting him into a box marked 'dirty old man' and sealing it.

Shelley is smiling. She hasn't spotted me slumped in the driver's seat, parked across the street. They are definitely an item, her and Nigel. I can see them through the window of Café Java, a couple of doors up from the office. I have a sudden image of the two of them in bed together – her all leggy, and him all wrinkled in a pair of Y-fronts. It's enough to make me shudder.

Shelley's foot is rubbing his ankle under the table. How sick! I mean, I saw on *Rikki Lake* once where an old man hooked up with this model in her twenties, but I mean that was different. He was some LA record producer and had a tan. Nigel is all old and just…yuk! The only common denominator between the seedy love affair in front of me and the one on the telly is that the older man in both cases has a tonne of cash. Draw your own conclusions, people!

Shelley is laughing – her teeth are straight and white. Before I realise it, I'm out of the car for a closer look at her. What the actual fuck is so funny? She took my dream of marrying Barry and stamped on it in those silly little clickety clack high heels. The stupid bitch!

In the Café Java window, I catch my reflection. I'm wearing a well washed tracksuit, my hair is greasy and is scraped into a bun. The dark circles under my eyes are like a neon sign that reads 'Look at me! I haven't slept in days! I can't stop repeating Barry's confession in my head!'

Shelley and Nigel turn their heads in my direction. Perhaps they are wondering why there is a bedraggled woman pressed up against the glass, staring at them. Although I can't make out their conversation, I can see Nigel mouth the word 'Rebecca?' Shelley's eyes widen and her jaw drops.

It's weird. I don't remember travelling from the pavement outside the café to three inches from Shelley's face, but here I am. I don't recall screaming 'What the hell do you have to say for yourself?', but the words hang in the air and the staff and diners are staring. I don't recollect slamming my fist on the table, but my knuckles are white and her sparkling water has been knocked over. There is an unflattering wet patch on the crotch of Nigel's trousers from the spillage. The drip dripping on the floor, and the whooshing in my ears is all I can hear.

Shelley raises a shaking hand.

'Rebecca, I tried to tell you.'

'What's all this about?' Nigel is on his feet, but Shelley puts a firm hand on his shoulder and he slumps back in the booth.

'Stay…' I discover I can speak without actually parting my teeth.

'…the hell…' I lock eyes with her. Mine are bloodshot, hers are clear and sparkling.

'…away from Barry!'

Shelley does not blink.

'Look, Rebecca, it's over. We had a bit of fun on the trip. Well, it would have been fun if he wasn't so… uptight.'

'Barry might be uptight. But he's *mine*.'

'Whatever. Anyway, nothing happened,' Shelley stares at her shoes. She is no longer able to meet my eyes.

'What are you talking about?'

'He passed out drunk, OK? I slept beside him but he… He didn't want me. He loves you for some strange reason. Can't think why.'

Nigel is blinking a lot, looking from me to Shelley and back again. It occurs to me that he has absolutely no idea what is going on. Now, let's be clear on this next bit. You know, in case I end up on trial for assault or something, right? Grievous bodily harm, I think that's what it's called. You can be a witness, OK? I didn't actually *plan* on slapping Shelley. I swear. There was nothing premeditated about it. It just happened. In my defence, I believe that years of watching bust-ups in the Rovers Return had slipped secret subconscious training into my naïve psyche, and it turns out that I was well able to do a 'Bette Lynch' on it. The burning in my palm, I was not expecting. Then again, I'd never walloped someone across the face in a café before, this is new territory. I don't usually go around doing things like this, you understand. It's probably because I'm so classy.

'You let him think that he slept with you,' I called behind me as I stalked out.

Forty

When I reach the car, the trembling takes over. It takes half an hour for my heart to reach a normal rate and my fingernails have made an indentation on the leather steering wheel. Because of all the fumbling, it takes a few attempts to dial Emer's number. My fingers keep hitting off the wrong keys, but I finally get through to her. She's at work, but says I can pop in to see her.

I'm barely though the door of her office when it all spills out.

'Oh, Emer. Barry told me that he cheated on me with some floozy from his office when he was away on that business trip to India.'

I use the sleeve of my top to wipe at my nose.

'What? Ah, no. Rebecca, you must be mistaken.'

'Nope. Confessed the whole thing over the weekend. He cried and everything.'

'What, Barry? No! What did he tell you?'

Emer twists the office blinds to give us some privacy. Perhaps she is worried that her colleagues might think she is bullying some hysterical blonde secretary in her office. I mean, I'm not even on the payroll here, but Emer goes through at least one assistant every quarter. You could understand a mix-up.

'OK, so we'd had that huge fight, remember? I'd wrecked his head over getting married and he went off on the trip all confused.

Then he got really plastered one of the nights. I think he went to a nightclub. Anyway, he told me that he thinks he shagged this Shelley one on the trip.'

'He thinks?'

'Yeah, he was plastered. Just once he says. Oh, and get this! It turns out I met her…'

'What? When?'

'At the engagement party. With all the work gang. I thought she was some wedding singer Barry had booked. I'm such an idiot!'

'Will you stop, Rebecca. He's the idiot.'

'I know.'

I reach for a tissue on Emer's desk and blow hard. We sit in silence for a full thirty seconds. I mean, for us that's like a lifetime. Emer breaks the trance.

'Hang on, pet, where's Barry now?'

'He went to stay at his mum's for a few nights. Said it would give me a bit of headspace. He's called a few times, but I just let it ring. He sent flowers, too. I binned them.'

'Oh my God, Rebecca.'

'Emer, I know. I need you to tell me what to do!'

Emer rubs my hand.

'And, so…is it over between them do you think?'

'Yeah, defo. Barry said he's sick with guilt. Says it was a whopper mistake and that it will never happen again. But get this, your one Shelley got the flick from Barry and then went running to the nearest moneybags… their boss Nigel! Honestly, Emer, he's ancient. He's in his, like, seventies, at least. Jesus.'

'Gross! Hang on. You said you met her at the engagement party. What does she look like?'

I roll my eyes.

'Skinny, brunette, wears glasses… might have a nice little shiner in progress…'

I'm trying to suppress a smile, but it flits across my face.

'Oh my God, Rebecca. What did you do?'

'OK, promise you won't tell anyone? I went to see her today. Look, I didn't even mean to talk to her. I just wanted to… you know, get a better look at her. Stalk her a bit, know what I mean?'

'Sure.'

'Jesus, Emer. I saw her and Nigel all loved up in a café. Next thing I know, I'm like screaming in her face in public like some fishwife out of *TOWIE*.'

'Oh sweet Jesus.'

'Yeah. There's more.'

Emer puts her head in her hands. 'Go on.'

'She said that nothing happened. Said she tried it on but that Barry said no and then passed out drunk. She let him think that he's slept with her, Emer.'

'Oh my God. Do you believe her?'

'You know what? Yes, I do. I slapped her. Hard. Across the face. My hand is killing me.'

Emer is speechless.

'I mean, you know I've never done anything like that before in my whole life! God, I gave her a right wallop.'

The corners of Emer's mouth twitch. She is trying to keep a straight face.

'Oh, Rebecca.'

'I know.'

I can't help it. I'm smiling too.

'You absolute nut job. Bet it felt good though, yeah?'

'Yeah.'

Emer looks into the distance.

'I wish I were brave like you, Rebecca.'

'What are you flipping talking about? Sure, you're brave. I bet you put the fear of God into them in that boardroom. They're probably terrified of you. I would be!'

'Yeah, but…'

'But what? Honestly, don't for a second wish you were like me, Emer. I'm a screw-up. You and David have the perfect life together. Perfect!'

'Rebecca…'

'I mean, I'm just going to come out and say it. I'm jealous of you guys, OK? There, I've said it. I feel a bit better, now.'

I'm grinning, but Emer's face is still.

'Rebecca, we're not perfect. Far from it, actually.'

I shoo the idea away with my hand. David having a golf handicap, or not being able to complete some triathlon for charity due to a tennis injury is probably the only flaw she will be able to come up with for that man. He's like something you would order from a catalogue. He even has catalogue hair, for goodness' sake.

'No, really. David cheated on me last year. It was just after we married.'

I'm stunned. This cannot be correct.

'No! But… you never told me. I'm your best friend!'

'I didn't want to tell you. I was so…'

'Angry? Hurt?'

'Ashamed,' tears roll down Emer's face.

'I'm so sorry, love. What happened?'

'It was his brother's stag night in Latvia. Some Latvian stripper in a nightclub. She stole his wallet afterwards. They took some E, apparently. I mean, David doesn't even do drugs! So tacky. He told me as soon as they came home.'

The pedestal upon which Emer and David once perched is toppling. It's so high up I have to strain my neck to see it. It's a place of dinner parties and matching Mercedes, a place where nagging and arguing doesn't exist. But here comes that pedestal now, and it is hurtling to the ground at top speed.

'So you forgave him? Just like that?'

'No, it wasn't "just like that". We went through couples counselling and everything. Took some time to trust him again, you know?'

'Oh my God, Emer.'

The pedestal was made from a heavy glass, and has smashed into so many tiny pieces that even if you had a large tube of superglue, it could never be rebuilt.

'But, listen, Rebecca. About Barry? He made a mistake. A terrible, stupid mistake, by getting close to that woman. But he managed to resist her, Rebecca. And he still wants to marry you, yes? And start a family? We put it behind us. You can too.'

'I don't know, Emer. I just don't know.'

Forty-One

It's been a full week since Barry went to stay at his mum's. In that week:

a) I've called in sick every day. I don't even care enough to get a sick cert. Let them sack me. Harry called to check on me, and I just let the phone ring out.

b) Barry has called every day. Not in, like, a pushy way. Just in an 'I'm such an idiot, please take me back' kind of way. I text him to tell him what Shelley said, and that I believe her, but I'm feeling very confused. I let the calls go to voicemail. He says he misses me terribly. I'm pretty sure he is desperate to have me back.

c) Barry's mum Margaret called. She said that Barry was devastated and that he didn't know that she was calling. She said that he was a good man. I know that she is right.

d) My mum called over to help me with the wedding plans. I had planned on keeping all the drama to myself, but after about five minutes, I sang like a canary. For future reference, you should know that there is absolutely no point in asking me to keep a secret. It's best that you are aware of this now before you declare me your new BFF. Anyway, I thought Mum would be horrified with Barry's drunken flirtations. Turns out that she and Margaret have been talking, and now she is in 'Team Barry' too, telling me to forgive him and move on.

e) Emer called to make sure I'm OK and called over last night. As always, she's being a rock. She gave me a list of celebrities who have had their relationships tested. She also cited the lyrics to Tammy Wynette's 'Stand by Your Man'.

f) Pam texted. It was just to ask me do I want to join her for 'Two-for-One Martinis' at Murphy's bar.

g) Oh, yeah. Just to add salt to the wounds, Marianna in Vera Wang bridal store called to say that she has received my non-refundable deposit and has put the order through for my gown. This reduced me to tears. Marianna took these as tears of joy, and I didn't correct her. God damn it, the dress will be fit for a princess, even if I only get to wear it around the house to watch TV in. It is costing a bomb, so we wouldn't want it to go to waste, now would we?

All in all, it's been a busy week. Eircom's shares have probably risen a few points, what with all the additional traffic on my landline. They might thank me personally in their annual financial report. I've also consumed enough beer to put Barney Gumble from *The Simpsons* to shame. I'm hoping that the bin men who look after the recycling collection on Thursdays don't spot that my green bin is full of crisp wrappers and Heineken tins and organise an intervention. Frankly, I wouldn't be surprised.

Anyway, it feels like the entire world has given their two cents on the matter. They have all cast their vote. It turns out that the only voice I haven't heard from is my own. My head is too mashed to decide. All of the other cities have video-phoned the Eurovision Song Contest HQ to place their vote, but there is still no word from The Democratic Republic of Rebecca. They have all granted Barry 'douze points', and the Botoxed, sequined hostess Svetlana is standing by, waiting on my call. They can't tally up the final vote until I call in, and the lines are about to close!

Well, I'm sorry, Svetlana, but I still don't know. I haven't got a clue what I'm going to say to Barry when he comes over later to talk things out. The best thing is to just look into his sweet face and wait for divine inspiration to hit.

The doorbell rings. Svetlana says that the time is up and if I don't call her now, my vote won't count but I may be charged for the call. She is so forceful, this one! I tell her to back off, or I will kick her Eastern European butt so far across the continent, she won't know which end is up.

Barry is standing at the front door, I can see him through the curtains as I linger in the sitting room. Even though it's lashing rain, he doesn't want to use his key to let himself in, as he is still in the dog house. He is hunching, the collar of his jacket raised to his ears, and the rainwater rolling off his chin. I decide to keep him waiting another minute. It's the only amusement I've had all day.

'Hi,' a dripping Barry is waiting to be invited in. He looks absolutely exhausted.

'Right. I suppose you should come in then.'

I fold my arms and quickly look away. I'm trying to be all frosty, like I'm Anne Robinson on a bad day, and Barry is some acne-ridden-sweat-patch-afflicted teenage dumbo out of *The Weakest Link* that forgot to bank the dosh and then got the answer wrong to something simple like, 'What is the capital of China?' I mean, everyone knows it's Taiwan. I suppose not everyone has a degree in geography like me, though. We can't all be clever, I guess.

Once I've subjected Barry to a sufficient dose of the cold shoulder, I stand aside and hurry him through the front door. I don't want Bernie to get a whiff of the trouble. She'd be pedalling that piece of hot gossip faster than Lance Armstrong on steroids. That's all we shagging well need!

'How have you been?' Barry stands in the living room and removes his damp jacket.

'Fine.'

This Anne Robinson stuff feels wrong. If I don't stop, I'll be purchasing a pair of specs so that I can sneer down my nose at him, and tell him to stop dripping on the rug. Sneering without glasses is just not the same. I saw a cute pair in Claire's Accessories that were just darling. They had these cute little diamantés on the sides, and were like something from the fifties, you know? Anyway! Stop distracting me will you? I'm trying to get this sorted out.

'Why don't you sit down,' I nod at the couch.

For once, Barry is putty in my hands. He is no longer a solicitor with an impressive legal degree from a top university, and I am no longer just a silly little executive assistant with a measly arts degree. I'm the prison guard with the heavy keys in my hand, and he's the jailbird offender with an empty begging dish in his hands. I have the upper hand. For once, he's not going to debate. He's not going to defend or excuse. He's not going to argue. He's not going to outsmart me. He's not going to bamboozle me with science, like a member of his jury until I'm so exasperated that I give in.

'Rebecca, I'm so very sorry. If Shelley says nothing happened, then I'm relieved. I only love you. Please believe me.'

There is more than a hint of desperation in his cracked voice. There is more than a flicker of pleading in his eyes. He knows he has royally messed up. He is responsible for the rolling waves that tipped our little boat over. He is trying to figure out if we can navigate this storm.

Barry is drowning in guilt, and I am standing at the shore with a life ring in my hands. I have a choice:

1 I can walk away from Barry, from our life together, from everything I've even wanted.

2 I can throw that life ring, and I can throw it hard. I can pull with all of my strength when he grabs hold, until the man I love is safely back in my arms. He will spend the rest of his life remembering how I pulled him out of the water. Maybe, just maybe, we can make it.

Over the last two weeks, I've had a taste of life without him. I didn't like it. Engagement ring or not, I want him back.

'Yeah, listen Becks. We can get past this. Oh, and I was thinking! We could check out some wedding venues this week. Sample some nice wedding cake? Flick through the honeymoon brochures? Whatever you like, baby. *Anything*.'

The word 'anything' hangs in the air for a minute.

'A wedding fair, you say?'

'Yeah, Fitzpatrick's Castle have one on today. It starts at three.'

'I thought you said that hotel was too pricey. You said it was beyond our budget.'

'I know. I was an idiot.'

'Well… that's true,' I grin.

I notice the creases in his handsome face when he smiles. He is like a scolded Labrador puppy that wants to come back in from the back garden and into the nice warm house. He didn't mean to chew your new Italian loafers. His eyes are deep blue wells pleading for forgiveness.

'Yeah, we could have some afternoon tea in the lobby afterwards. They do those teeny cakes that you like so much,' he ventures with caution. 'What do you say?'

He is drifting out to sea and waving his arms. In the distance, a giant wave is building.

'I suppose…'

A smile sweeps across his tired face.

'Really?'

'Maybe…'

All successful grovelling attempts should be accompanied by food, I don't care what you say. This one is no different. Barry peels open a soggy brown paper bag to reveal some pastries. I hope that his spell in the rain while waiting at the front door hasn't ruined the contents. He knows I can't resist anything from the bakery department in Butler's Pantry. There is more chance of me turning down an opportunity to go on *The X Factor* and make an absolute show of myself, and anyone who has ever met me, than to turn down pastries.

Barry slices the croissants with a sharp knife and layers cream on top of jam on top of butter. Just how I like it. He spoons a generous dollop of sugar into my tea and passes it in my direction. I feel his stubble as he kisses me on the cheek. He is hesitant, unsure of how I will react.

'So,' he looks deep into my bloodshot eyes. 'Do you still want to marry me?'

I throw the life ring out to sea and he grabs hold. It's the right thing to do and it feels good. The little boat that had capsized has been turned over and we climb back in, ready to resume the journey. The wooden slats on the boat that were hammered by the waves can be repaired, in time. I smile. Paddling that boat all by myself would be lonely and my arms would get tired. Besides, I would never navigate the seas without my partner. I'm rubbish at map reading.

'I do.'

Acknowledgments

Without the tireless efforts of my literary agent, Frank Fahy, this book would not have come to life. Thanks for taking a chance on me!

A big cheers to my editor, Caroline Kirkpatrick, for her encouragement and advice.